CRITICS CHEER FOR
RITA HERRON
AND *MARRY ME, MADDIE!*

"Rita Herron's lovable, laughable style . . .
will keep the reader in stitches."
—*WordWeaving*

"Rita Herron's style sparkles in
Marry Me, Maddie. Without a doubt Rita Herron's
rising star boldly shines in this book."
—Amazon.com

"*Marry Me, Maddie* is a charming,
humorous and flat out fun read. Rita
Herron is an author to watch."
—*Romantic Times*

"Get set for an entertaining
read with a lively set of characters."
—*Scribes World Reviews*

A HOT SURPRISE

"It seems Dr. Jensen has a surprise for us today."

"I do?" Abby cut a questioning look toward the talk show host.

"Yes." Segoda stood and gestured toward the side of the stage. "She's brought her husband here to meet us, folks."

"I have?" Abby squeaked.

A man suddenly bounded onto the stage, broad shoulders thrown back in a light blue designer shirt, Italian loafers clicking as he paraded toward her.

Abby found herself immobilized by shock.

"I'm sure our viewers want to know if you practice at home what you preach in your books," Segoda prodded.

"Yeah, we want to see this hunk in action!" a woman in the audience shouted.

Before Abby could open her mouth to protest, the man pulled her up to stand beside him. "I'm Abby's husband, Lenny," he announced with a devilish grin. Then he swooped her in his arms, lowered his head and captured her mouth in a deep kiss that sent her senses reeling.

Abby clung to him, her legs bowing like dandelions in the wind. She had talked about hot lips in her book, yet she'd never tasted lips that held as much fire as this man's. Or been pressed against a body that could make her forget a crowd was watching.

And that the man kissing her was a complete stranger.

Other *Love Spell* books by Rita Herron:

MARRY ME, MADDIE

RITA HERRON

UNDER THE COVERS

LOVE SPELL

NEW YORK CITY

To Kate:
A great editor and friend;
thanks for everything....

LOVE SPELL®

June 2002

Published by

Dorchester Publishing Co., Inc.
276 Fifth Avenue
New York, NY 10001

ISBN 0-505-52488-0

The name "Love Spell" and its logo are trademarks of Dorchester Publishing Co., Inc.

Printed in the United States of America.

Visit us on the web at www.dorchesterpub.com.

UNDER THE COVERS

Chapter One

The Faker

"No more faking orgasms, ladies and gentlemen," the newscaster's voice boomed from the television. "Not if you and your partner take advice from leading sex therapist Dr. Abigail Jensen in her new sex manual, *Under the Covers*. Just let me read you a short excerpt."

"It's not a sex guide and I'm not a sex therapist!" Abby waved a hand toward the announcer. "The book is for marriage therapy!"

Abby's twenty-one-year-old sister Chelsea rubbed her hands together in gleeful anticipation and plopped down on the sofa. "I can't wait to hear this."

"Dr. Jensen gives this advice in her chapter on erotic foreplay: 'Slowly massage his inner thigh with your finger. Trace a long, sensual path from the curve of his toe up his calf, then circle around to tease the thick muscle—"

Abby pressed her hands over her ears, her face burning as the reporter quoted several more passages out of context.

"With chapter titles like 'The Orgasmic Kiss,' 'Fantastic

1

Fantasies.' 'Most Passionate Positions,' and 'Naughty Seduction Games,' it's no wonder this book is flying off the shelves," the young newscaster continued. "In addition, this commercial has been running during daytime soap operas."

The picture changed to show a scantily clad, voluptuous redhead reclining on a bed of satin sheets with a copy of Abby's book resting between her parted knees. A brawny man with jet-black hair dressed in red silk boxers kissed his way from the woman's toes up to her knees, where he knocked the book aside with his head before engulfing the woman in a steamy kiss. Dubbed-in oohs and aahs floated around the rocking couple.

"Oh, my God," Abby whispered.

Chelsea flicked up the volume on the remote, her charm bracelet jingling. "Cool, Mom's new boyfriend really came through for you with that ad, sis."

Yeah, it was a little over the top, just like her mother.

"With each purchase of *Under the Covers*, customers receive a free set of satin pillowcases to stimulate their own sensual pillow talk," the announcer explained. "And it certainly looks like Dr. Jensen's suggestions are working for this couple. They're hotter than the record temperatures outside."

"Man, I have to find out how to do that orgasmic kiss thing, Ab. Can I take a copy of the book home tonight?"

Abby rolled her eyes, grabbed a miniature Reese's peanut butter cup from the bag, and popped it into her mouth. The last thing her little sister needed was advice on sex; words of wisdom regarding a lasting relationship would be more pertinent.

Under the Covers had been out only two days, and Abby was grateful that it was selling. She hoped that couples would benefit from her years of experience as a marriage counselor, and the extra money she would earn from book sales couldn't hurt. She seemed to have an inordinate number of needy relatives who often turned to her for "loans."

But she hated the media attention. Reporters were always looking for the most scandalous, juiciest story, and they would exaggerate, embellish, even lie in their quest for sensational headlines. She'd learned that painful reality as a child. She grabbed another candy and devoured it—the chocolate treat was both her nemesis and her salvation. "You don't need to read my work. You're not married."

"You mean it's only for *married* couples?"

"Well, no, not exactly. It's supposed to help all couples improve intimacy in their relationships." Abby paced in front of the bay window, feeling exposed after the latest spotlight on her book, and even more so when she realized anyone on the street could see through her front window. She added curtains to the list of items she had to pick up for her new house.

"Then give me a copy, Abby. I have a new boyfriend."

Abby groaned in disbelief. "*Boyfriend?* You never see a guy more than twice."

Chelsea scratched her blond head in thought. "I went out with that carpenter three times."

"Great."

"Nah, he was kind of boring. But he did have a big tool—"

"Chelsea," Abby warned.

". . . belt." Chelsea's green eyes twinkled. "Especially his hammer."

Abby threw up her hands. "You are incorrigible!"

Chelsea reached for the blender. "And you're awfully uptight for someone who wrote a sex guide."

"It is not a sex guide." Abby stopped abruptly, nearly tripping over the cluster of boxes in the corner. What in the world was she going to do with her baby sister?

Even worse, what if the press discovered the truth: that she'd been following her own advice and it hadn't been working? That she had faked a few orgasms herself?

And a lot of other things . . .

* * *

Rita Herron

Hunter Stone situated himself in a metal chair in his boss's office and glared at the junior reporter, Addleton, the ass kisser, leaning against their boss's cluttered desk. Files, unedited copy, layouts, dirty coffee cups, and Twinkie wrappers covered the once shiny black-lacquered surface. Shelves overflowed with old copies of the *AJC—Atlanta Journal and Constitution*—and the faded white walls held framed evidence of Emerson's writing credentials. Ralph Emerson, the chief editor of the *Journal and Constitution*, had nothing in common with the legendary Ralph Waldo Emerson, except that they both had male genes and two legs.

This Ralph Emerson scratched his protruding stomach, a copy of the morning edition in his hand, smoke stains yellowing his teeth. "Great story, Addleton. That piece on the bombing near the Fox Theater came in just in time for the front page."

Hunter frowned. So far Addleton, number one kiss-up reporter, had outscooped him on everything. But only because Hunter had a black streak on his file from his previous job, and Ralph hadn't unleashed him from the repercussions of it yet.

He'd been at the *Chicago Tribune* before the *AJC*, and one lousy error of judgment had flagged him as a man who would do *anything* for a story, including the unethical. Just because he had hidden in the senator's private bathroom and overheard confidential details about his affairs . . . Well, when he'd moved to Atlanta his reputation had preceded him, and though he had managed to get a job at the *AJC*, he'd been given only piddly stories to cover. After a month, he was damned tired of covering crappy pieces like the recent Maltese pageant and the pancake-eating contest at the local elementary school. Not that he hadn't enjoyed the pancakes . . .

"Hey, great piece on the hog-hollering contest in Gwinnett County," Addleton said as he loped past him, a cocky grin pasted on his conceited face.

4

Hunter glared at him, but ignored the barb. After all, the boss was watching.

As soon as Addleton cleared the door awning, Emerson handed him a list of assignments. Hunter thumbed through them in disgust. The local soup kitchen, the daisy festival . . . He'd missed his dinner with Lizzie twice last week covering some of the same kinds of stuff.

"Look, Ralph, you know I can handle bigger pieces than this. Why don't you give me a chance?"

Emerson opened a peppermint and popped it in his mouth, his concession to a nonsmoking office. "You dig up something on your own time, I'll take a look."

Hunter nearly fell off the chair with relief.

But Emerson jabbed a stubby finger toward him. "Only I don't want any trouble, you hear me?"

Hunter nodded, thanked him, and strode back to his cubicle. He'd knock out these easy stories, then look for something bigger. Not a criminal piece yet, but something timely that would draw a lot of attention. Anxious for a lead or at least a topic, he dropped into his chair, logged on to the Internet, and searched various bulletin boards, looking for anything that might make big news.

An ad for a new sex-talk book, one of those self-help things, called *Under the Covers* drew his eye. The author was none other than Dr. Abigail Jensen, who'd made landmark sales with her new release.

Holy hell. Abigail Jensen—the psychologist who'd toured the country offering seminars on marriage. The woman who'd planted seeds of doubt in his ex-wife's head about their marriage.

Oh, yeah, Abby Jensen had wreaked havoc in his personal life with her theories.

He ran a hand through his hair, reading further. So far the woman had avoided interviews, refusing requests.

Why?

Did she have some secrets she didn't want to share?

He shut down his computer, snatched up his cell phone,

and strode from the noisy den of reporters hacking away at their computers, his adrenaline pumping. Somehow he would get an interview with Abby Jensen. After all, she owed him one after the way she had interfered in his life.

She was not the know-all, do-good counselor she portrayed herself as. He knew firsthand. And he would take great pleasure in writing all about her.

And if he dug up some dirt on her, the story might convince Ralph to let him do some criminal investigative reporting, and make his career.

Of course, it might ruin hers, but that would simply be the icing on the cake.

"Oh, my gosh. Look!" Chelsea pointed to the TV, where the camera zoomed to the bedding section in a nearby shopping mall holding several cardboard boxes of Abby's book, along with the free sets of gift-wrapped pillowcases.

Abby gaped.

People literally grabbed the books from the boxes and rushed to the counter to pay for them. Another camera focused on a bookstore where a long line of people wound outside the door, anxiously waiting for their copy. The report quickly switched to a mob of customers in a local discount store who were actually pushing and shoving to get the last few copies remaining on the store's shelf. An elderly woman in an orange jogging suit wrestled with an overweight bald man for the last book.

"Well, I never." Abby sat in shock while her sister poured margarita mix into a blender, added tequila and crushed ice, and punched the button. The sound of grinding ice filled the silence.

"You hit on something big, sis. I wish I could come up with a get-rich-quick scheme."

"*Under the Covers* was not meant as a get-rich-quick scheme," Abby said. "I hate the downward spiral in marriage statistics today and want couples to realize the sacred

6

value of their union. Once they've committed, they should give marriage their best shot."

"You're such an idealist, Abby. Marriage is archaic. It doesn't fit with contemporary couples; you know, *Sex and the City*—"

"Sex in the suburbs is not exactly dead, you know."

Chelsea harrumphed.

"Family and marriage should be appreciated more, treasured and coveted, not just the sex part but the love and commitment."

"Hey, I'm committed"—Chelsea raised her eyebrows—"to staying single."

Abby shook her head and laughed in spite of her difference of opinion. Everything about her and Chelsea was different from their homes to their hairstyles. Chelsea, with her long blond hair and big boobs, rented a loft above the arts theater where she worked; her apartment was completely art deco, her wardrobe trendy.

Abby, with her mousy brown bob, on the other hand, had bought a nice little cottage house, furnished it in a homey country style, and wore a middle-class wardrobe that screamed not to be noticed.

"Face it, sis, most marriages are doomed from the start," Chelsea continued. "Just ask our oldest sister."

"Victoria is a divorce attorney. Of course her views are skewed." Abby sighed; she worried so about Victoria. Whereas Chelsea jumped from man to man, Victoria never dated or paused from her busy work schedule to give a man a chance at being decent. Her apartment in Buckhead, an eclectic mix of styles, her wardrobe, Anne Klein, her sophisticated raven chignon shouting "Hands off."

"Victoria's dealing with reality." Chelsea dipped the rims of the glasses in salt, waving a bejeweled finger as she spoke. "But don't get me wrong; I think it's great you're such an optimist, especially in light of our parents' history. And I'm envious you're making money doing something you really want to do."

Abby shook her head. She could use the money; not a month went by that Chelsea or her mom or another relative didn't turn to her for a loan. And it didn't escape her that Chelsea had sided with Victoria—the only thing her sisters agreed on was their doom and gloom view of marriage. Growing up, Abby had often played referee between her sisters and also between her parents, who'd never actually tied the knot into respectable parenthood.

No wonder she'd turned out to be a marriage therapist. "Don't you like your job, Chels?"

"Sure, the theater's fun, but the money's sporadic, and then there's the inconsistency of jobs." She wiggled her eyebrows. "The guys are pretty hot though."

Abby laughed.

Chelsea poured the drinks into two tall, frosted glasses and handed one to Abby. "Did Lenny help you research your book?"

Grateful for the quick buzz of alcohol, Abby sipped her drink. "What?" Her husband, the man she'd fallen for and married within three months of meeting him, the man who hadn't had the least bit of interest in sex lately. Or in her.

Chelsea licked salt from the rim of her glass, eyes glowing. "Well, did he?"

Abby's stomach twisted. As an advocate for marriage, how could she confess that her own had been void of titillating touches lately? "You know I don't talk about my personal sex life, sis."

"Oh, rats. I wanted some juicy stuff. Victoria acts like a nun, and you're so secretive it's pathetic." Chelsea winked. "Guess I'll have to read the danged book."

Abby's gaze raced back to the TV. She'd kept a journal of the various exercises she'd had couples try over the last three years. One of her associates had persuaded her to submit the journal entries as a book, and she'd done so on a whim, sincerely wanting to help her patients and share her expertise with other therapists.

She'd never dreamed the book would be advertised as a sex guide.

Or that people might associate the contents with her own personal life. What if people began asking questions . . . ?

Hunter was going to get a copy of that book or die trying.

He braced himself for a fall as the crowd lunged forward, dozens of hands groping for the last copy of Dr. Abigail Jensen's new release, *Under the Covers*. A white-haired lady wearing three-inch-wide clunky heels plowed her foot on top of his, but he wedged himself into the second row. He was six-three, his arms a foot longer than hers, so he reached above her head and snagged the binding with the tips of his fingers. Someone poked him in the side and he fought the urge to push back. The heat wave was making everyone crazy these days; that was the only logical explanation. Otherwise, why would normally sane people be fighting over a book?

Dammit. At least he had an excuse. He needed the copy today because of work. If not, he wouldn't be buying it at all.

His hand tightened around the spine, but a female hand swatted at him. "No, it's mine."

"I was here first but I had to go to the bathroom," a pregnant woman said.

"Your small bladder is not my problem," a thin man snapped.

"Good grief," Hunter muttered.

A middle-aged woman glared at him, then patted the pregnant woman's hand. "It'll get better once you have the baby, hon."

"My husband has a bladder problem," an elderly woman announced.

The gray-haired man beside her coughed, and Hunter offered him a sympathetic look. "Verna, you don't have to tell everything."

"It's nothing to be ashamed of, Henry. Lots of people have bladder-control problems, especially when they cough or sneeze. My aunt Wilma worked for a urologist. . . ." She launched into a litany of surgery techniques to repair bladder disorders, which sent a combination of embarrassed giggles and irritated looks through the crowd.

Hunter ignored them and tugged at the book, feeling sweet success at his fingertips.

But a set of red acrylic nails pierced Hunter's skin, clawing at his hand. Someone slammed a purse into his head, and the old lady with the three-inch shoes kicked his shin. He yelped and released the book to ward off another blow when two more sets of hands grappled for the copy. The cardboard box collapsed, the paperback hit the floor with a thump, and people dropped to their knees scrambling to retrieve it. A sweaty man nearly fell on him. Hunter dodged him and dropped to the floor too, feeling like a fool.

Seconds later, someone shrieked, "Look, she got it!"

Everyone turned on hands and knees to see a teenager with a nose ring, trotting toward the counter with the book tucked firmly beneath her arm, her dozens of colorful bracelets jangling. "I'm buying it for my mother," she yelled. "It's her birthday."

Several people huffed and grumbled.

Hunter stood, dusting off his jeans. For her mother? *Right*. He'd bet a hundred dollars the girl had snatched it for herself. She'd probably take it to a sleepover, and all the teenagers would hover in the basement with flashlights and highlighters getting the education of their lives. Or worse, she and her boyfriend might study the book *together*, taking tips and learning various sexual positions from the now famous Dr. Jensen. Add child corruption to Abby Jensen's list of sins.

His own five-year-old daughter's innocent face flashed into his mind. In a few years she'd be a teenager. He couldn't stand the thought. He wanted to keep her innocent forever.

He certainly didn't want her views tainted by some know-it-all sex writer who paraded as a therapist. Why, the marriage counselor he and his wife had visited when their wedded bliss hit the rocks counseled them into divorce, then counseled his way right into Hunter's ex-wife's bed. Hunter had not only paid the man's fees, but now was paying his ex-wife child support and having to share his little girl with the slimy shrink.

Dr. Abigail Jensen had been the catalyst for all his problems. His ex-wife had attended a lecture the cunning therapist had given in Chicago, where they'd lived at the time. After Shelly had heard the woman speak, she'd complained he wasn't romantic enough, criticized everything he said and did, including the way he made love. He couldn't help it if he'd been tired a lot and their relationship had suffered. He'd been trying to build a career, put food on the table; then Lizzie had come along and Shelly had been hormonal and obsessed with her extra pounds . . . Dr. Jensen's lecture had started the wheels of discontent turning in Shelly's head, and their marriage had gone for a rollercoaster ride straight to hell. Yep, Abby Jensen was a marriage *wrecker* in his book, not a therapist who helped couples stay together.

The very reason he wanted to ruin the woman.

Shaken by all the publicity, Abby switched TV channels, but a faintly familiar face flashed onto the screen—the preacher who had married her and Lenny.

For a brief second the past year flitted through her mind. The good parts.

And bad.

A year ago, Lenny had convinced her to elope at a resort in the north Georgia mountains. The special honeymoon getaway came at a steal for only five hundred ninety-nine dollars and included the reverend, marriage certificate, witnesses, organ music, champagne, and a weekend at the resort called the Velvet Cloak Inn. Smitten with the man and not wanting to grapple over wedding plans with her unorthodox parents, who would have squabbled over every detail, she'd agreed.

"Ladies and gentlemen, we have another late-breaking story," the reporter announced. "Rev. Tony Milano, who has been marrying couples at the famous Velvet Cloak Inn in north Georgia, was arrested today for fraud."

Chelsea refilled their glasses with fresh margaritas. "Isn't that where you got married, Abby?"

Abby nodded and turned up the volume.

"Apparently Mr. Milano is not a real man of the cloth, as he professed, and is not legally qualified to perform marriage ceremonies. Therefore"—the announcer paused, letting the tension build—"if you and your spouse were married by Mr. Milano, your marriage is not legitimate."

Abby gasped.

Chelsea slapped her hand on her thigh. "Oh, my gosh."

"I have to find Lenny," Abby whispered in a weak voice. "Where is he?"

"I don't know. He left on a business trip three weeks ago and I haven't heard from him since."

Chelsea raised an eyebrow as the announcer gained speed. "Mr. Milano has also been accused of conning couples out of their retirement money by offering them vacation packages at another resort in Tennessee, a resort that sources have proven doesn't exist. Milano was released earlier on bail, but law-enforcement officials report that he has disappeared and may be headed out of the country. If you have any idea of his whereabouts, please contact your local police."

"I can't believe it," Abby whispered in shock. "Lenny and I are—"

"Living in sin," Chelsea chirped, twisting her crystal necklace between blue fingernails.

Abby's chest constricted. "We're not married."

The doorbell rang and Abby shot off the sofa, sloshing the cold drink all over her bare thigh.

Chelsea dropped her fingers from the clear crystal. "You want me to get it?"

Tears threatening, Abby grabbed a napkin and swiped at her leg. "I . . . you don't suppose reporters have already found out that I was one of Milano's . . . his fakes?"

Chelsea shrugged. "So what if they did? You and Lenny can get married by a real preacher. Plus, it'll make great publicity."

Abby groaned in horror. "The last thing I want is more publicity about my personal life." Lenny's face dashed into her mind—had he heard the news? And if he had, what would he say?

Would he want to get remarried?

The doorbell rang again, the sound pealing through the room like fingernails on a chalkboard. Chelsea's gaze locked with hers.

"See who it is," Abby whispered.

She huddled behind her sister as they inched to the door. Chelsea peeked through the peephole. "It's a tall, skinny guy with glasses," Chelsea said as if she were suspicious. "Oh, and he's wearing a mailman's uniform."

"It *is* the mailman." Abby rolled her eyes and waved Chelsea aside, then opened the door.

"I have a certified letter here for Abby Jensen Gulliver." He held out an envelope and a clipboard for her to sign. "Are you the Dr. Abigail Jensen who wrote that book *Under the Covers?*"

Abby nodded. "Gulliver's my married name." *Although Gullible should be.* "Jensen's my maiden name." She'd almost said her *real* name. Which it was, since she wasn't technically married.

The middle-aged postman beamed at her. "Wow, I can't believe it. My wife bought a copy of your book, and, man . . . it's hot."

13

"I hope you two enjoy some of the exercises." Abby signed for the letter.

"Oh, yes, ma'am, it's already doing wonders. My wife never would . . . Well, she didn't like to try different things until she read your advice. She especially liked that chapter on oral—"

"Great." Abby cut off what she thought might have been a long-winded personal confession, which didn't seem appropriate on her front porch. "Have a nice day and tell your wife hello for me."

She thanked the postman, then closed the door, but a bad premonition engulfed her as she walked back to the den. What if the letter was some form of notification from the police about her illegal marriage? Would they question all of the people involved with Tony Milano? Subpoena them to testify against him?

Chelsea sat cross-legged on the sofa with her drink, her gaze fastened on the TV. "They said that preacher married over a hundred couples last year. He made a killing off those phony resort investments."

"And I just happen to be one of the lucky ones who only fell for his romantic honeymoon haven." She narrowed her eyes, surprised there was no return address. "This is odd."

"What?"

"It's from Lenny. Why would he send me a certified letter?"

Chelsea shrugged. "Maybe he found out about the fake marriage and he's proposing again?"

Yeah, right. He hadn't been so formal the first time. Her fingers trembled as she tore open the envelope and removed the plain white sheet of paper.

Dear Abby,
You have probably seen the news by now and know that our marriage was a sham.
When we married, Abby, I thought I needed a wife. I

wasn't ready to admit a lot of things to myself, much less to the world. But time and circumstances have changed things. Since the police have found out about Tony, he has to leave the country.

I can't continue this farce of a marriage, not when I finally have the chance to be with Tony, the love of my life.

Good-bye, Abby.

Abby swayed and sank to the sofa in shock as the words swam in front of her eyes.

"What is it, sis?"

The letter fluttered to the floor. "It's a Dear John letter," she said in a weak voice. "Lenny left me for . . ."

Outrage filled Chelsea's eyes. "He ran off with another woman?"

"No." Her gaze swung to Chelsea, her stomach plummeting. "He ran off with another *man*."

Chapter Two

The Voice of a Vamp

Hunter tried to momentarily forget about the queen of sex, Dr. Jensen, when his five-year-old daughter's innocent voice called his name. She raced toward his SUV, her Angelica doll clutched in one hand, leaped into his arms, and planted a sloppy kiss on his cheek.

"Hey, Daddy."

"Hey, pudding."

"You'll have her back by bedtime, won't you?" Shelly wiped a speck of dust from the door of her silver Mercedes sports car.

Hunter nodded tightly and ruffled Lizzie's blond curls as he buckled her into the front seat of his Explorer. "We're just going to dinner, Shelly."

"Good. Daryl says it's better for children to stick to a schedule."

Hunter circled around to his side of the car, his jaw aching from clenching it. For the past fifteen minutes his ex had lectured him on Daryl's idea of parenting. As if

Hunter intended to take advice from the wife stealer on how to raise his own child.

Besides, a routine schedule was a sore subject between him and his ex. During their marriage he'd encouraged her to put Lizzie on a schedule when she was a baby, but Shelly's version of a schedule meant whatever tickled her fancy at the moment.

Or whatever sale hit the malls.

Maybe she'd changed. After all, she actually seemed concerned about Lizzie's diet. Yet he couldn't help but think Shelly had gone to the extreme the other way.

"Oh, and make sure she eats properly." Shelly pointed to the tofu-and-bean-sprout café beside them. Apparently her new husband was also a health fanatic, or maybe Shelly had taken up an alfalfa-sprout-and-seaweed diet. She'd always jumped from one diet to another. Flitted from one *man* to another, even after they were married . . . only he'd been too foolish to know it. She'd been young and beautiful and charming and had a great pair of legs. . . .

And he'd been a fool for following after those legs and not looking to see if the woman had a brain on top of that body.

Shelly huffed. "Are you listening to me at all, Hunter?"

"I'll make sure she eats," he said, refusing to argue in front of Lizzie.

Shelly briefly touched Lizzie's forehead with a manicured hand. " 'Bye, sweetie. Have fun."

Hunter frowned and watched her climb into her car, adjusting her outfit to smooth out the nonexistent wrinkles in her linen skirt. He wondered if she ever hugged their daughter, ever cuddled or played with Lizzie.

"Daddy, what's this?"

His ex's Mercedes screeched as she peeled from the parking lot.

Hunter swung his gaze toward Lizzie and mentally groaned. "It's a book, honey."

Dr. Jensen's book. He'd finally gotten a copy at the

fourth store he'd visited. Of course, he had a few scratches to show for it.

"What's the name of it?"

He climbed into his seat, took the book from her, then tossed it onto the backseat. "Uh . . . *Under the Covers*."

Lizzie's big brown eyes looked up at him innocently. "Is it a bedtime story?"

"Sort of. For adults, I guess."

"Oh, I've seen it afore." Lizzie patted Angelica's head. "It's that sex book Mommy gots."

"What?"

"That sex book. Mommy readed it to Daryl."

"Really? What did she say about it?"

"She talked about doing the mattress mambo."

Mattress mambo? He made a mental note to warn Shelly that Lizzie's ears were bigger than she might realize.

"What's mattress mambo, Daddy?"

"Uh, it's complicated, honey." Sweat dribbled down Hunter's neck. "Daddy's supposed to interview the author of the book and write a story about her for the paper."

He had to change the subject. "I heard your tummy growl. What do you want for dinner?"

Lizzie licked her lips. "French fries."

He laughed, then steered the car across the street to the nearest fast-food burger place and parked. "All right, but you have to eat some hamburger, too."

Lizzie frowned. "Icky Micky said hamburger comes from dead cows."

"Who's Icky Micky?"

"This boy at school that gots cooties. He throws dead bugs at the girls on the playground." She undid her seatbelt and crawled into his lap. "Do hamburgers really come from dead cows?"

Hunter swung her from the SUV onto the sidewalk. "Afraid so."

"Icky Micky said they grinded up their guts to make 'em."

"Well—"

"Are we're eatin' bloody guts and stomachs, Daddy?"

"Well . . ."

She clapped her hands over her ears. "Angelica and I don't want to eat bloody cow guts and ears, do we, Angelica?" Lizzie wiggled the doll's head back and forth as if it were saying no.

"You don't have to, honey. Let's have chicken fingers instead."

"Icky Micky said they cut-off chicken toes to make chicken fingers."

Hunter wanted to strangle Icky Micky. At this rate they'd be eating nothing but nuts and berries. "We'll just have french fries then."

Lizzie exhaled a big sigh of relief. "Good."

"By the way, where does Icky Micky get all his information?"

"From his number one stepdaddy." Lizzie held up three fingers. "He gots three daddies. And his mama gots the sex lady's book, too."

Hunter gritted his teeth. The book obviously hadn't helped her stay married any more than Dr. Jensen's advice to Shelly had.

Would he wind up as a number in a long string of fill-in fathers to Lizzie someday?

"What do you mean, he left you for a man?" Chelsea snatched the letter from Abby's hands and skimmed the contents. "What a cold and impersonal note. That slimy SOB."

"That slimy *gay* SOB," Abby clarified.

"Bi, not gay," Chelsea corrected. "I mean, you two did have sex . . . um, didn't you?"

Abby clenched her hands, battling tears. "Yes, Chelsea we were married almost a year. Of course we had sex." Not mindboggling sex, but okay sex, Abby thought, remembering Lenny's reluctance to please her in certain ways. In fact, he had been just as cold and impersonal as the letter the last few weeks of their marriage.

She dropped her head in her hands, a dozen memories suffusing her. A million telltale signs . . . God, she'd been such a fool.

Had Lenny known Tony was a fake all along? Had everything been a lie?

She'd thought she was in love with him, especially during those first few months. And even after the initial sizzling attraction had worn off, she'd tried to make things work. Her whole world revolved around family and commitment, and she refused to become another statistic on the dismal divorce charts, so she'd pulled from all her resources to spark their romance back to life.

But Lenny had never wanted her. Had never loved her. He'd been lying to her, pretending he wanted to be married to her when all that time he'd been hiding in the closet, struggling over whether or not to open the door and step out.

She rocked herself back and forth, her insides aching.

"I figured you two were wild in bed," Chelsea said, oblivious to her turmoil. "After all, you are a sex therapist."

"I'm not a sex therapist," Abby said for what felt like the hundredth time. She swiped at her eyes. "I'm a couple's therapist. And obviously not a very good one if I couldn't tell my own husband was gay."

"Bi."

Abby sniffled. "Same difference."

"Not really." Chelsea flipped a strand of her blond hair over her shoulder. "Did you know . . . he swung both ways?"

"No." Abby flopped her head back on the sofa, feeling dumb and hurt. Why *hadn't* she known?

The unpacked boxes scattered across the hall and den glared back at her. She considered the bag of comfort candy, but her stomach protested.

"Had he been acting different lately?" Chelsea asked.

Abby chewed at a hangnail. "I didn't think about it then, but yeah. He was sort of cool and distant before his trip. And I was surprised he was going to be gone for three weeks."

"Hmm. You haven't talked to him since?"

Abby shook her head, hating to admit the truth. "Not even once. And he just left his things in the apartment and told me I could move them. But the rent's paid up through the month, so I left them there so he could sort them when he returned."

"Did he show any interest in the house, talk about the future?"

No. "Not really." But he had let her ramble on and on about fixing it up, making a nursery. "He gave me full rein. Told me to pick the colors I wanted." She paused and looked at her sister, realization dawning, along with all the little signs she had dismissed in her efforts not to become a nag. "He didn't even complain when I chose this striped-print design for the chair."

"A bad sign?"

Her lower lip trembled. "I thought he was just being sweet, trying to compromise." The way she had in bed.

Chelsea gave her a sympathetic look and picked at the hem of her tie-dyed T-shirt with the words, *The truth will set you free* emblazoned on the front in neon pink lettering.

The truth about Lenny jolted through her, fighting with reality the way the kaleidoscope of reds and oranges warred with one another on her sister's shirt. "He . . . he never planned to move in here. He was planning to leave with Tony all along."

"I'm really sorry, Abby." Chelsea squeezed her hand. "I know how you feel about marriage. This must be such a shock."

Abby hugged her arms around her middle, willing herself to hold back the landslide of tears pushing at her eyes. Like a damn bursting, they spilled over.

"I'm an idiot, Chels." The tears gushed out. "I . . . I kept trying to make him happy while he was cheating on me with a m-man."

Three hours later, Hunter dropped Lizzie back with her mother, then hit the computer at home to research Abby Jensen's background before he approached her. This article had to be good.

No, not good. Outstanding.

He wanted to ressurrect his reputation, move up the ladder of success at the AJC, make enough money to give Lizzie everything she wanted. And maybe have more time off to spend with her. These bogus little assignments had him working day and night for nothing. If he missed time with her because of a big story and made a name for himself, at least she would be proud of him.

A half hour later, he leaned back in his desk chair and propped his booted feet on top of the scarred oak. *Interesting.* Dr. Jensen's family wasn't exactly the pinup poster for marriage. In fact, her parents had never married. They'd shacked up together over the years while they raised three girls.

Dr. Jensen's mother had been a real wild child of the seventies. He'd found an article about her staging a riot in college, another of her burning her bra on campus, then small bits about her in various college performances. After college, she'd played a bottle of ketchup for a TV ad and had an affair with the mustard man. She also coasted through men and careers like some women did with hairstyles. Dr. Jensen's father had once been a roving artist who sculpted nudes and liked to gamble. Apparently he'd spent several years in the pokey when his daughters were in school.

An old photo clipping of Abby at age twelve drew his eye. The camera had captured her shattered look of innocence as she was herded from the courtroom. Bright sunlight highlighted her frizzy brown pigtails, freckles, and clunky glasses, as well as the big tears in her luminous dark eyes.

His stomach clenched. The other two girls had hidden behind her, the youngest a cute little blond with two braids, the older one a serious, sad-looking child with straight dark hair and an angry scowl. The picture had been taken the first time the father had been arrested.

Their father had landed himself back in the pen again a couple of years ago and was still incarcerated.

Hunter's stomach twisted again. While he'd attended church with his parents on Sunday mornings, Abby had probably visited her dad in jail. A twinge of sympathy reared its head, but he squashed it. Success came at a price. Both hers . . .

And his.

She'd have to give up some of her privacy for fame, and he would have to be ruthless in his quest to make a name for himself. He read further, details jumping out at him. The oldest sister, Victoria, had earned a reputation as a cutthroat divorce attorney. The youngest, Chelsea, had followed in her mother's footsteps and worked as an actress at a local arts theater. She'd actually starred in a couple of commercials—once as a mop, the other time as a bra model.

Hmm. Both girls were still single.

But Abby Jensen had turned into the rose among the thorns—the proponent of love, marriage, and happily-ever-after endings. A newlywed herself, she should celebrate her first wedding anniversary in a week.

He clawed through his hair, searching for an angle. Was her marriage as ideal as her words of wisdom implied?

A grin laced his mouth as he picked up the phone. He'd called earlier for an interview but she hadn't answered. He'd try again.

And again and again until she gave him one.

* * *

Abby blew her nose, accepted another tissue from Chelsea, and ignored the phone. It had rung a dozen times in the last half hour, but she'd staunchly ignored it.

"Here, throw another dart at Lenny's picture," Chelsea said, smiling snidely at the battered photo. "It'll make you feel better."

Abby wiped her nose and flung the dart at Lenny's face, this time slicing him between the eyes. So far she'd snagged his forehead, the tip of his nose, and both of his ears.

"Shoot for his chin this time," Chelsea said.

Abby slammed another dart toward the wall, blinking through swollen, red eyes. She missed the chin but caught him in the center of his mouth.

"That fat lip should make kissing impossible." Chelsea refilled their drinks. "Too bad we don't have a full-length one. You could nab him right where it would hurt the most."

"But he doesn't have a heart."

Chelsea tapped a finger over her lips, then pointed downward. "I was thinking lower."

A rumble of laughter burst out as Abby envisioned the picture, although she spoiled the tension-released giggle by lapsing into a wail.

Chelsea wrapped her arms around her and patted her back. "I wish I could do something like conjure up a spell. I have one called 'Baby Come Back—' "

"I don't want him back," Abby cried. "Not now I know he's a cheat and a liar."

"Shh, I know. It'll be okay, Ab. I know you're hurting right now, but look on the bright side—"

"My husband just left me for a man; what bright side is there?"

"Well . . ." Chelsea chewed on her lip. "Now you can play the field again."

Another sob lodged in Abby's throat. "But I hate playing the field. That's the reason I got married."

The phone rang again, adding a sharp trill to her pathetic sob.

"Damn. That phone has been ringing off the hook all night." Chelsea planted her hands on her hips. "If you don't answer it, I will."

Abby swiped at her sore eyes, blew her nose, and jerked up the receiver, praying it wasn't someone phoning about Lenny. Or another nosy reporter. "Dr. Jensen speaking."

"Dr. Jensen, Hun . . ." Static crackled over the phone, obliterating his name. ". . . from the AJC—"

Abby cut him off before he could continue. "I'm not giving any interviews. Now please leave me alone."

"But wait, I just want to ask you how you got the inspiration for your book."

Abby silently cursed all men. "I really can't talk now, Mr. . . . ?"

"Stone. Hunter Stone."

The alcohol was making her head fuzzy. "Listen, Mr. Stone, if I wanted an interview I'd call you."

"Just answer that one question. What can it hurt?"

Reporters could twist anything into dirt, Abby thought. "The book is a composite of exercises I conduct with my patients. End of story."

She glanced at Lenny's picture, memories of her honeymoon flooding her.

"And have you tried these exercises yourself?"

Oh, had she! But she was way too smart to answer a question like that. "Listen, Mr. Stone, my private life is my business. Now good night." She dropped the phone in its cradle, praying the man would take a hint. The last thing she needed was a reporter adding to her humiliation by nosing into her personal life and exposing her secrets. . . .

He would expose all of Abby Jensen's secrets, Hunter vowed, his body tingling from the sound of her seductive voice. That low, husky voice had quavered, though, as if full of emotion. For a moment he'd even thought she might be crying. Had she been upset about something?

And if so, what?

He dismissed the possibility, reminding himself she was cold and calculating. She'd simply been playing a seductive little game, the way cunning women did to entice a lover. Using that breathy bedroom voice, low and sexy the way a man craved in the middle of the night with the lights turned off and nothing but the two of them between the sheets.

Shit.

He stood and slammed down the phone. So the woman had a voice that could reduce a man to jelly and give him a hard-on the size of a . . .

His ears were still ringing from when she'd dropped the damn phone to hang up on him. To hell with what she'd said—her private life *was* news now; she'd opened the door to the public when she'd become an instant celebrity.

Yep, he'd find all the little details about her life that had led to her book, to her marriage, to her cockeyed belief that she could tell other people how to run their lives.

The way she had when she'd convinced Shelly he was a sorry husband.

Tomorrow he'd find out the name of Abby Jensen's publicist and see what kind of information he could weasel out of her.

He grabbed *Under the Covers* along with a beer, adjusted the air conditioner, undid the top button of his denim shirt, and stretched out on the sofa to dissect the book. Tonight he'd read; tomorrow he'd research her background in even more detail, see if he discovered any ghosts lurking in her closet. Then he'd figure out a way to finagle an interview. An exclusive maybe.

He lifted the back cover and studied her picture. Slender, small-boned. Serious, soulful eyes. Her lips were too full. Her hair too dark and curly.

Not his type at all.

No, he much preferred busty redheads or voluptuous blondes.

Thank God he didn't have to worry about being physically attracted to her.

She'd probably had that publicity photo retouched, too, so in person she didn't even resemble it. Photographers worked wonders with computers today, smoothing out age lines, covering up flaws.

He chuckled, took a long pull from his beer, and skimmed the introduction to her book—just as he'd expected, a lot of hogwash about wanting to improve your interpersonal skills with your partner. How to communicate. Mars-Venus theory. Making eye contact. Reflective listening. Focusing on wording your needs so they became a request, not a criticism of the other person. *Don't take your problems to the bedroom.*

Some of the same stuff Daryl Jeffries—aka the bastard Shelly had married—had babbled when they'd first met the shrink. Hunter yawned and flipped a few pages. Hmm, exercises to try with your lover. This must be the gritty part that had everyone in such a spin. Skeptical, he took another sip of beer and began to read.

The Seductive Whisper
   There are several stages of seduction, moving from that first moment of contact to the culmination of the sexual act. Men rely heavily on their physical and visual senses for arousal, while women are aroused through all their senses and emotions. . . .

It didn't take a brain surgeon to figure that out. He skipped to the next section.

Exercise one: Getting in the mood. From the moment you walk into the room, or meet your man, offer him a look that will tell him he's special. Attractive. Desired.
   During dinner, a walk together, a ride in the car, whis-

27

per in his ear how much you want him. Lower your voice
to that intimate level you associate with privacy, the one
you save for the dark.
     The intimate voice of a vamp.

Like the voice Abby Jensen had used on the phone.
He skimmed forward some more and found a section on
exercises to set the mood.

For the man: Play soft music in the background. Dance
with her in your arms.

Hell, he'd danced with Shelly. Once or twice. And
they'd watched movies. Lots of James Bond flicks; those
were his favorites. All the *Die Hard* and *Rocky* sequels, too.
And *Star Wars*. God, he loved sci-fi movies. And he had
taken her to that festival celebrating horror in cinema.
Satisfied, he read on.

Gently trace your finger, then your mouth over her fingers,
her knuckles, down to the sensitive skin of her palm. Cradle her hand in yours, press it to your thigh, your chest.
Let her feel the way your heart pounds when she's near.
Whisper in her ear the naughty things you'd like to do to
her. The ways you want to touch her. The ways you want
to make her writhe with pleasure.

This was ridiculous. He swiped at another bead of sweat
and unfastened another button. No real man talked like
that. Did they?

Stroke the side of her cheek with your thumb. Touch her
hair. Wind a strand around your fingertip. Kiss the soft
ends and brush them against your rough jaw. Watch the
hunger grow in her eyes. Feel her desire in her heated
breath.
     Now, close your eyes and imagine her performing a slow

strip tease for you. Murmur what you see, the things you like about her. Not just the physical aspects. The way she smiles. The way her eyes light up when it's raining outside. The way she caresses her own body. The soft, heady sound of her laughter.

He groaned. Did women really want to hear that garbage?

He was burning up, he realized. The damn air conditioner must not be working at all. He'd have to call and report it. He shucked his shirt completely and stared at the next paragraph.

Describe the strip tease. Her removing one item of clothing after another. Dropping them to the floor. Think about what you want to do to her and tell her in that bedroom voice. Whisper how her mouth would feel beneath yours, how her ripe, warm breasts will spill into your hands, how her breath will feel touching your own male hardness, how you will fit inside her, how you will pleasure her, how her voice will sound whispering your name in the throes of ecstasy.

Wet your lips with your tongue. Say her name, letting desire echo in your voice. Tease her neck with your tongue.

Trace a finger over her lips. Gently stroke her mouth with your thumb. Let her take your finger into her mouth and lick the tip, suckle the end. Imagine her doing this to your sex.

Listen for her breath to hitch. Watch her breasts rise and fall, her nipples pucker for your touch. Brush the barest of kisses across her forehead. Her nose. Down her cheek. Into her hair. Her neck. The sensitive skin of her earlobe. Along her shoulder blade. Down her arm. Over her hardened buds. Near her heat. Bring your hand away before you touch her. Slowly move back to her mouth.

Gently. A little more pressure now. Let her feel the urgency building.

Cradle her jaw with your hands. Lower your mouth. Tease her lips apart with your tongue. Nibble at her lower lip. Then close your lips slowly over hers. And taste a slice of heaven.

Hunter shifted restlessly on the sofa, momentarily envisioning Abby Jensen's mouth coming toward him. Her lips touching his. Her tongue . . .

He slammed the book onto the coffee table. He would not let that woman's writing affect him. Hell, he was a journalist—he knew firsthand the power of the written word. He made his own damn living by twisting it and turning it every which way.

Her sentences were written by an expert in manipulation—the words were meant to be titillating. She wasn't saying them to him. And he hadn't been fantasizing about her.

Muttering a loud curse, he headed to the bathroom to take a cold shower and forget the nonsense in the book—and the fact that as he'd read, he'd heard her seductive voice purring out every word.

Anger suddenly churned through Abby. She needed to be angry, she realized. Anger was better than hurt. "How dare Lenny Gulliver use me." Tears blinded her vision, but she blinked them away, fighting the heartache of her lost marriage. All she'd ever wanted was a nice, quiet, happy life: a fulfilling career, a loving marriage, a stable family. The type of stable family she'd never had. The loving marriage . . .

And I thought I had it all, but this past year's been a total lie.

The beautiful room she'd wanted to decorate, to raise her kids in, closed around her, hot, stifling. She pressed the cold glass against her face, willing her heart to mend itself.

"Lenny made a mockery out of our marriage because he was too chicken to admit he was gay. How could I have been so naive?"

Chelsea refilled their drinks. "You want Victoria to sue him?"

Abby shook her head. "For what? Humiliating me?" Tension hummed between them as Abby paced the room. She stared out the big picture window, replaying the last three weeks in her head. When she'd bought the house, she'd thought it would be a new beginning for her and Lenny. The flowers had been blooming, the grass green and lush. But the heat wave and drought this past week had parched the brilliant colors and turned everything brown. Left everything looking desolate.

Just like she felt inside.

Seconds later the phone trilled, sending her nerves into a dozen pieces. Both their gazes swung to the machine.

"I can't deal with anything else today. If it's Victoria, please don't tell her yet. And if it's that reporter again . . ."

"Why won't you give them an interview?" Chelsea asked. "In spite of what Lenny's done, you're a star, Ab."

Abby hesitated. "Because I'm not comfortable with the slant they're giving the book. And you know how I feel about reporters."

Chelsea nodded as if she too was remembering the embarrassing spread the local press had written about their mother's affair years ago. And then their father when he'd been arrested . . .

The phone trilled again, and Chelsea checked the caller ID. "It's a New York number."

Panic slammed into Abby. Rainey, her publicist.

"Relax," Chelsea said. "They can't know about Lenny yet."

Abby nodded, took a deep breath, and reached for the phone. Her sister was right. She had to calm down. Not give Lenny the power to destroy her.

"Abby, hello, it's Rainey," her publicist said in a sharp New York accent. "I have good news."

She could certainly use some of that.

"Do you have any idea how well your book is doing?"

"Pretty well, I think. I know some of the stores around here are selling out."

"They're selling out everywhere! Congratulations! And that satin pillow idea was ingenious."

Thanks to her mother's latest lover. Her mom who used to play two-bit parts in commercials as vegetables. She'd been a stalk of celery once, broccoli, a carrot. . . .

"We've decided to send you on a publicity tour," Rainey continued. "We'll have you visit bookstores, TV stations, a few radio shows. The way things are going *Under the Covers* will hit the *New York Times* list before week's end. We want to be ready to meet the public's demand."

Abby clutched the phone cord, twisting it in her fingers. "Listen, Rainey, a tour's not a good idea right now."

"Why not? Everyone wants to meet the genius behind this fascinating book."

Abby's mind raced for excuses. How could she go out in public and promote a book about marriage therapy when she couldn't hold her own marriage together? And how could she tell this woman and her agent and editor and the whole world her marriage had been a total sham?

Chapter Three

The Lusty Look

"I can't believe I let you talk me into this makeover." Abby stepped into the fitting room of the exclusive dress boutique Egor's where Chelsea insisted they shop, and grimaced. The Paris designs were expensive and the staff wanted to dress her with their own hands. She was thankful it was one of Chelsea's more upscale choices, not the outlandish favorite where Chelsea, a real bellwether, purchased her lime heels and leopard-skin pants.

"Look, Abby," Chelsea said, "you have to do the book signing, so you might as well look good."

"I only agreed to the book signing because Rainey refused to take no for an answer. I still think it's a bad idea."

"You told her about Lenny?"

Abby winced miserably. "Yes. She almost went into heart failure when I suggested admitting the truth and forgetting the interviews."

"So do the interviews and enjoy your fame. You'll be so fabulous no one will care whether or not you have an albatross of a man around your neck when they do find out about loser Lenny."

Like that would really happen.

Chelsea wrapped a gold chain belt around Abby's hips and adjusted it. "There."

Abby gestured toward the revealing neckline of the shell. "This outfit is just not me. . . ."

"I know. Don't be such a prude." Chelsea laughed, hot pink lips pursed. "It's perfect. That neckline accentuates your cleavage."

"I'm not a prude; I'm modest." Abby pivoted in the mirror to study the back of the short blue skirt. She really had to lay off the Reese's cups. "Don't you think it's a little tight in the butt?"

"Honestly. God gave you *assets*, so use them." Chelsea shook her head, crystal earrings dangling. "If I left you on your own, you'd show up in a feed sack."

"I would not." Abby glanced at the flowing dress she'd chosen earlier. So it didn't hug her figure or show the lines of her body. That was what she intended. She'd always favored a more traditional style, especially in her clothing. It matched her conservative approach to life.

Marrying Lenny had been her one impulsive decision.

And the biggest mistake of her life.

She unzipped the skirt and dropped it to the floor. If she wore a feed sack, at least she wouldn't have to worry about her hips being too big. She could eat all the Reese's cups she wanted. "This is too short. I'm wearing the calf-length dress."

"That one with the high collar? Good grief, Abby, you'll look like a nun!"

"I will not; it's perfect, classy. If I wear that short one, every man around will be ogling my legs. Giving me that lusty look—"

"That's exactly the point."

"Well, I don't want to be ogled."

"You're hopeless." Chelsea jerked the long black dress

out of reach. "This is hideous. Now try on that red silk suit with the camisole. It'll look sexy."

Abby dragged it on under duress. "My butt's too big, my ankles are too thick, and my boobs are too small to look sexy."

Abby's cell phone trilled from her purse, and she clicked it on while Chelsea stacked up her clothing finds. "Hello."

"Hi, Dr. Jensen, this is Hunter Stone from the AJC again. I realize you were busy yesterday—"

"I'm busy again today, too. How did you get my cell phone number?"

"Your publicist, Rainey Jackson."

"Rainey gave you my number?"

"Yes, she faxed me a bio and some photos, too."

Good grief, he sounded so pleased with himself. Rainey obviously didn't share Abby's distrust of reporters. "Mr. Stone, I have no interest in talking to journalists. Why, one article I read implied that I acted out my exercises with my patients."

"Maybe if you meet me, I can get the details right this time," Stone said.

Oh, wouldn't he love that? But she didn't intend to be tricked into anything. "I told you no, and I meant it."

"Listen, Dr. Jensen, the press is going to write about you, so it would be easier if you cooperated. Give me an exclusive, and I'll print the truth. I swear."

His voice sounded strong. Sincere. But Abby didn't trust him for a minute.

"We can talk about your ideas," he continued. "People want to know if your own love life inspired you, if any problems in your marriage or past played into this. . . ."

Abby heaved a breath in and out, panic attacking her as his words faded into an echo around her.

"Dr. Jensen?"

He knew the truth. Why else would he mention problems in her marriage?

But he couldn't print the truth because it was too hu-

miliating. Just as it had been when her father had been
arrested and all her mother's lovers had been plastered
across the papers. The pictures of her in the paper at age
twelve flashed back in painful clarity. She imagined the
new ones and the accompanying headline: *Like Mother,
Like Daughter, Both Forgo Traditional Wedding and Live in
Sin.*

Suddenly her lungs tightened, she lost her breath, and
she dropped the phone. The handset banged against her
leg as she heaved in and out, but she couldn't catch her
breath. The room spun, her pulse raced, and her skin grew
clammy. She had never had a panic attack before, but she
recognized the symptoms.

Chelsea took one look at her, shrieked, then pushed her
into a chair and shoved a paper bag into her hand.

He had shaken Dr. Jensen, Hunter realized as he replaced
the phone. So much that she'd hung up on him again. Or
at least she'd dropped the phone and he'd heard some wild
breathing in the background.

Or maybe she had some kind of sex game going on and
he'd interrupted.

He chuckled, envisioning the scenario and a photo of it
on the front page of the paper. The minute that breathy
voice of hers had wavered he'd sensed he was onto something. Something about her past, her personal life . . .
maybe even her marriage.

He had to figure out what she was hiding.

The familiar adrenaline rush of an impending break-
through zigzagged through him, and he contemplated going
incognito to her scheduled book signing. If Abby Jensen
even suspected he was the reporter who'd been hounding
her, she'd run like crazy.

But how could he disguise himself so he wouldn't be
recognized later on when he zeroed in for the kill?

His gaze scanned the room and he spotted the video of
Tootsie he and Lizzie had rented the other night, and a sly

grin curved his mouth. He'd dress like a woman. After all, he'd disguised himself as a bag lady once to investigate a thug in Chicago. Dr. Jensen might warm up to a female at the signing and spill a few tidbits about herself. Things her publicist had been careful not to reveal when he'd questioned her earlier.

He scavenged through Lizzie's dress-up trunk, wincing at his image in the mirror as he yanked on white tights and a humongous, old-fashioned flowery dress that had belonged to her former nanny, a plus-size woman with bad taste. The dress had dragged the floor when Lizzie put it on, swallowing her whole, but it hung midcalf on him, and with a little padding it almost fit. Except for the bust area, of course. A little stuffing helped fill that out nicely. A curly red wig came next, then bright orange sunglasses with rhinestones and a floppy hat that covered most of his face. Perfect.

Finally he stuffed her book beneath his arm, suppressing the fact that Abby's words had aroused him the night before. Luckily she wasn't his type.

Nope, he preferred busty blondes and redheads, not pale-faced, frizzy-haired brunettes who dressed like schoolmarms. Even if they did have sinfully seductive voices.

Besides, who would want to be caught dead in such a getup in front of a woman he wanted to impress? He painted his lips red and blotted powder on his face to cover his beard stubble.

Sheesh. The things he did for his career . . .

Chelsea Jensen would do anything for her sisters.

Oh, she knew she was a screwup. At least according to her oldest sister, Victoria. But Abby had always cut her a break, and now Abby was the one in trouble, and she had to do something.

For God's sake poor Abby, had almost hyperventilated in the dressing room of Egor's, the most expensive and only exclusive shop Chelsea bothered to drop her plastic in.

Now, if *she* were going to hyperventilate it would be over that sexy tie-dyed bikini she'd seen in the window, or a pair of fuck-me shoes with rhinestones and feathers, not a man.

Especially one who was gay.

Damn Lenny Gulliver.

If she found him, she would tie his dick in a knot with her curling iron and pluck his lying tongue right from his mouth with her tweezers.

She teetered on her new hot pink heels, strutting toward the elevator to Victoria's office, smiling and waving her acrylic nails at the stuffy suits and dressed-for-success nine-to-fivers running to and fro. The women had no fashion sense what so ever. Never had Chelsea seen so many plain black pumps in one place. And the men all had navy and red striped ties that screamed conservative and wore their cell phones attached to their leather belts like a second penis. God, no wonder Victoria stayed home and did her laundry on Saturday night; her pickin's weren't just slim; they were practically nonexistent.

The elevator whizzed up eleven floors, the mixture of expensive perfumes and colognes of the inhabitants sending her into a tizzy to name the different fragrances, a little game she'd enjoyed playing since second grade. The elevator jolted to a stop, and a tall dark-headed man with a woodsy smell—Stetson, she guessed—elbowed his way out as if his life depended on a ten-second exit. Moments later she stood in the hall outside Victoria's office, her stomach already flip-flopping back and forth, that little demon of insecurity that dogged her whenever she was in Victoria's presence whispering all kinds of nasty things in her ear. Like the fact that she shouldn't have worn the bumblebee costume. But she'd had little choice. She was on break from her commercial shoot and hadn't had time to change in and out of her costume, and still make it to Victoria's office and back in an hour.

She hugged her jacket around her, hoping to conceal

most of the costume. To heck with what Victoria thought about her outfit anyway; this talk was not about her; it was about Abby. Ignoring the butterflies in her stomach, she tapped on the door to Victoria's office and pasted on her best Reese Witherspoon smile. Victoria had to agree to her plan.

And if not, well, she'd do something on her own—whatever it took to help Abby.

Abby stared through the double glass doors, her hand trembling. Although at least a hundred people stood in line waiting to purchase her book, she had never felt more alone.

She also felt like a fraud.

What if someone had discovered the truth and revealed it any second? Like that nasty reporter Hunter Stone. Maybe in a few days or weeks when the pain wasn't quite so sharp, she could confess.

"It looks like we have a good turnout." The bookseller, a tall, attractive redhead named Katrina Blake, gestured toward the people waiting outside. "We'll probably sell all the books here and take orders for more. Can I get you anything before we start, Dr. Jensen?"

Thank heavens she'd used her maiden name on her book.

"A glass of water would be great." Abby fanned herself. *Although a double scotch would be nice.* The mall air conditioner must be on the blink just like half the units in the town. If she'd worn panty hose, they'd be melted to her legs like plastic wrap.

The bookseller set a cup of water on the table, her heels clicking on the marble floor as she headed to greet the eager customers. As soon as the glass doors slid open, the crowd rushed in, and Katrina ushered them into a line, having roped off the area into lanes in advance.

Excited chatter and laughter mixed with the soft piped-in music from the store. Men and women of all ages, sizes, and nationalities waited eagerly for an autographed copy.

Abby's hand trembled as she signed the first book. *One person at a time*, she told herself. She could do this.

"I'm so excited to meet you, Dr. Jensen," a young woman holding a baby on her hip approached. "I'm Tammy."

"Nice to meet you, Tammy." Abby jiggled the child's chubby hand. "What an adorable little girl. What's her name?"

"Lisa Sue. Her daddy and I think she's pretty cute, too." Tammy nuzzled her daughter's fuzzy head to her own cheek and Abby's heart squeezed. She had wanted a baby, had planned to talk to Lenny about it soon. . . .

"Dr. Jensen, I need to ask you something. Randy and I are doing okay, marriage-wise, but nursing takes a lot out of me, and I've been tired and Randy's a morning person, if you know what I mean, and I'm not. I need my coffee in an IV, especially after being up all night with the baby. I just fall back into bed smelling like sour milk and can't get in the mood. And we never go out anymore. Do you have any advice?"

Abby scribbled a note in the book. As much as she might like to, she couldn't give individual counseling sessions today or they'd never finish. Maybe she should pass out business cards, offer a free session with every book.

No, she was here only to sign enough books to please her publicist. Besides, she had her hands full now with everything else. She couldn't possibly take on more clients.

"You might try a baby-sitter," Abby suggested. "Plan a date night once a week. When the baby gets used to that, take a romantic weekend together—just you and your husband."

The woman brightened and thanked her. A tall, broad-shouldered woman wearing a floppy hat and bright orange sunglasses towered over several people in line, scrutinizing Abby. She shifted, uncomfortable with the woman's pointed stare, and she couldn't help but notice the lady's broad hands. She also had the hairiest arms Abby had ever seen on a female. She squinted to see more clearly—the woman's jaw was broad and covered in stubble.

Good grief, the woman in the flowery dress was a man.

A cross-dresser—or a transvestite?

She bit her lip not to laugh, then ducked her head, blinking to focus on her handwriting, but her right contact lens slipped, irritating her eyelid. Acting on instinct, she rubbed her eye. It was the wrong thing to do. The contact flipped out and the room blurred in front of her. She scanned the table, patting the books and her lap, her legs, her chest, but didn't see the darn thing anywhere.

An elderly woman leaning on a cane grunted as if her legs were about to give way. Abby blinked and tried to focus, hurriedly sweeping her hands over the books one more time, even leaning close to the surface to inspect them for the contact, but the table wobbled, and she realized the woman had clutched it for balance. *Poor thing.*

To make matters worse, a baby in the back started crying, and two people complained that they had appointments to make. Refusing to cause a scene and have everyone search for the lost lens, Abby decided to plow through the signing without it. The idea of holding up the line any longer than necessary was too horrible to contemplate. She'd just have to deal with blinking and squinting through the rest of this publicity nightmare.

After the spindly little lady wobbled off with her copy in hand, a divorced military woman in her sixties enlightened her on the singles club she'd joined and some man with a bulldozer tattooed on his arm who had swept her off her feet. The eighty-year-old man behind her had just gotten married for the sixth time and wanted this marriage to last longer than the others.

A grungy man with a beer belly stepped forward and wagged a finger in her face. "My wife read this and now she says I'm not a good lover—"

Abby drew back, stunned at the man's vehemence.

"She was always satisfied before, lady." The robust man

slammed his fist on the table, rocking the stack of books. "You have to talk to her."

The bookseller approached and spoke in a hushed voice to the man.

"I'm sorry you're having problems, sir," Abby said calmly, although his tone frightened her and added to the headache forming behind her eyes from not being able to see.

"What are you going to do about it?"

"I think you'd better leave, mister."

The cross-dresser stepped forward, took the man's beefy arm, and hauled him away. Abby reminded herself to check the parking lot before she went to her car.

Seconds later, the cross-dresser came back inside, broad shoulders stretching the flowery dress, feet thudding loudly as he/she stalked back to join the line. Abby's right eye twitched as she tried to distinguish his/her face.

Abby Jensen had been flirting with him—rather, with his female counterpart—Hunter realized as he returned from carting off the obnoxious redneck. She'd been winking and blinking and giving him that slit-eyed look she talked about in her book. What did she title it—the lusty look?

Was she a lesbian?

Could that be the secret Abby Jensen was hiding?

Whew-eeee, what a story that would make.

Or maybe she liked to ride both sides of the sexual seesaw. Well, he would not fall for the lusty look.

He had a job to do and he'd do it. Landing bigger assignments might make the difference in his getting more time off to spend with Lizzie. Frustrated memories of their last hasty good-bye pushed to the forefront of his mind.

When he'd dropped Lizzie off after dinner the day before, Shelly had announced that she and Daryl planned to take Lizzie to Bermuda for two weeks in the winter. With his ex-wife's money and the shrink's, they'd be bribing the child with their gifts and trips and he'd never see her.

He couldn't let that happen.

Scattered applause brought him back to the present. The bookseller came over to shake his hand and thank him. Abby Jensen winked at him again, beaming an appreciative smile as bright and warm as the summer sunshine. *Damn*. The last thing he'd needed was to bring more attention to himself while incognito. Besides, if her fans knew he'd come here in disguise to desecrate their female icon, they wouldn't be clapping or thanking him.

The crowd parted, allowing him to move forward to her table. This was his opening.

"Thank you for getting rid of that man," Dr. Jensen said.

Something hot and surprising flamed inside him at the sound of her voice, but he banished the heat and thrust his copy of *Under the Covers* toward her. For the briefest of moments their fingers touched, an electrical charge zipping through Hunter that sent a shudder coursing through him. *What the hell . . . ?*

Fighting the sudden chemistry, he cleared his throat and raised his voice in his best imitation of a feminine pitch. "It's a pleasure to meet you, Dr. Jensen."

"You, too." She winked again and his libido stirred to life, strong and steady.

He forced himself to ignore the traitorous beast. Mousy, brown-haired Abby Jensen was not even his type.

Except she wasn't mousy, brown, or plain. The candy apple–red suit she wore dipped low enough to reveal a hint of cleavage, not the schoolmarm outfit he'd expected, and the color contrasted well with her dark hair and those vibrant dark eyes. . . .

The lady beside him coughed into her hand and glared at him, and he remembered he was supposed to be acting like a woman, not ogling or flirting with the doctor.

Another wink; then she narrowed her eyes. He was thankful the sunglasses hid the heat simmering in his own. "Who do I sign it to, Ms. . . . ?"

He was contemplating a fake name when a commotion erupted behind them. Two men, a woman in a yellow suit, and a young, skinny guy wielding a camera on his shoulder strode in, scanning the crowd and pointing. "There she is, fellows."

Three or four others followed. The press.

"Start rolling," a seedy-looking guy all in black ordered.

Panic flitted onto Abby Jensen's face the moment the camera zoomed in on her.

Protective instincts arose, along with Hunter's curiosity. Just why was Dr. Jensen so nervous?

Victoria Jensen gave her client, Marcus Baldwin, an encouraging smile. Normally she tended to lobby on the side of the female in custody issues, but she wasn't stupid. This man had been unjustifiably hurt and deprived of seeing his children by a vindictive, conniving, spiteful woman who did not have a heart. He should be on *Montel* or *The Oprah Winfrey Show* stating his case. The poor man had been shuffled from one lawyer to the next to no avail and had actually been arrested for knocking on the door to see his children. His story was heart-wrenching, his love for and devotion to his children obvious.

If only her own father had loved her and their sisters half as much.

"I promise I'll do whatever it takes to get your boys back."

He stood, shoulders rigid, his heartache in his eyes.

"Thank you, Ms. Jensen. I appreciate this."

She rose to escort him out, promising to start action immediately, when the door swung open and Chelsea waved.

"Oh, hi, sorry. I didn't realize you had a client."

Her secretary must be at lunch.

Mr. Baldwin smiled gravely and headed to the door, the weight of his pain obvious in his slow gait. As soon as he left the outer office, she turned to her sister.

"What is it, Chelsea?"

Her sister launched forward, her jacket flapping open to

reveal a yellow-and-black bumblebee outfit. Victoria rolled her eyes, wondering what Chelsea had up her sleeve—well, her costume—this time.

Chelsea leaned against Victoria's desk, a mass of bobbing insect. "I'm worried about Abby."

Victoria's heart skipped a beat. "What's wrong with Abby? Is she sick?"

"Not exactly, although I thought she was going to pass out at Egor's today."

"Egor's? Who is Egor, and why did Abby almost pass out?"

"It's a long story."

It usually was with Chelsea. "Maybe I'd better sit down."

"Maybe you could poúr us a drink."

"Chelsea, it's too early for alcohol. Besides, I have to meet another client later."

Chelsea winced and Victoria realized she'd sounded like a prude. "Okay, okay. I was only joking about the drinks."

Victoria frowned at her sister, Marcus Baldwin's case fresh on her mind. "Listen, if you're in trouble and need something—"

"No, no, it's not me. Not this time." Chelsea chewed on her lip. "It's Abby."

"What about Abby?"

"She didn't want you to know. . . ."

"Know what, Chelsea? For heaven's sake, if this is some of your dramatics—"

"It's not." Chelsea swallowed. "Lenny sent her a Dear John letter and left her for a man."

Victoria fell back into her chair as if she'd had the wind knocked out of her. "What?"

Chelsea spent the next ten minutes detailing the letter and the story about the fraudulent marriage.

Victoria pressed her fingers to her head, a migraine beginning to shoot pinpoints of pain behind her eyes. "Dear God, we have to do something."

Chelsea grinned. "My thoughts exactly. For once, sis, we agree on something."

Now, that was a scary thought. "What do you have in mind?" Victoria asked suspiciously.

"You tell me your plan first."

A diversionary tactic if she'd ever heard one. But she'd play along. Only, she had to think for a minute. "Well, I suppose I could see what I could find out about Lenny. I do have a friend on the police force." At least there was one guy who'd been asking her out. Mostly she had avoided his calls.

Normally, her life revolved around work, twenty-four-seven. In fact, nothing but the call of sisterhood could tear her away from her job.

"That's a great idea. I knew you'd help, Victoria."

Victoria folded her arms. "Now, what do you have in mind?"

Chelsea pushed herself away from the desk and practically flew across the room. "Well, first I have to finish my shoot; then I'm going to check out the gay bars."

Abby's hand cramped, her eyes were bleary, and a headache had started pulsing at the base of her neck. Forget vanity—she should have worn her glasses. At least then she would have been able to find the nearest escape without blinking every two seconds.

Her deodorant had probably worn off as well. And now a man dressed like a woman was staring at her as if he/she might be interested in her sexually. But she didn't have time to deal with the cross-dresser—she had to face the nosy reporters rushing toward her. She squinted again, wondering if that obnoxious Hunter Stone lurked in the group.

Keep calm. Don't act suspicious. And for God's sake, don't hyperventilate again.

She braced herself for the onslaught of questions. In a few minutes she'd be home, away from the hoopla, and in a few weeks the publicity would die down and her life would return to normal. A sexy man would never get the best of her again. Of course, first she had to fend off the reporters.

And keep her failed marriage a secret.

Abby clutched the table as if she might jump up and flee the scene any second. Hunter's investigative instincts roared to life. Why would she panic? She was an instant success, her book the talk of the town, her career on a roll. Why *wouldn't* she welcome publicity?

"Just sign it generically," he told her when she winked at him again.

Her fingers trembled as she scribbled her name; the smile she aimed at the camera looked forced.

He grabbed his book, moved into the thick of the group, and watched her sweat.

Suddenly all half dozen or so of the reporters fired questions at her at once. Abby's breath seemed to hitch in her throat as she quickly signed the last of the customers' books.

Avoiding the camera, Hunter ducked into a nearby aisle, grabbed a book off the shelf, and stuck his face in it. He had to devise a plan to get her alone and get an exclusive.

A lanky man in a suit flashed his press badge, indicating he worked for one of Atlanta's local magazines. "Where did you come up with the idea for your book?"

"How do you research all your chapters?" another reporter asked.

"You're a newlywed yourself, aren't you?"

"Does your husband get involved in your research?"

"What is your secret fantasy, Dr. Jensen?"

"I . . ." She squirmed in her seat, dark eyes flitting toward the nearest exit. "I'm not here to discuss my personal life."

A short, dark-haired woman jammed a microphone toward her. "But you have to give us something."

"We're just doing our jobs," another whined.

Rita Herron

"And you are the news, Dr. Jensen."

"All right, let me make a few comments." Composing herself, she folded her hands on the empty table. Hunter leaned against one of the displays and studied her in detail for the first time, deciding to hold off on his own questions until he observed her actions. She wasn't the self-assured, in-control woman who'd refused him so baldly when he'd phoned for an interview.

This woman seemed vulnerable.

Almost like the little girl in the photo he'd found in her file.

And despite the fact that he usually preferred blondes and redheads, he had to admit she was attractive. Definitely not the bitter, wrinkly, middle-aged woman he'd hoped she'd be.

Wavy hair so dark it looked like midnight framed her heart-shaped face. She'd swept it off her shoulders into some fancy twist, but ringlets escaped and spiraled around her high cheekbones. Whereas he'd expected her pale skin to look sickly, the porcelain white gave her an exotic look. Her lips were full and pouty, painted a delicious dark red that matched her suit. Long, slender hands curled around her book cover, reminding him of the chapters he'd read last night. And her voice rippled out, so deep and husky it made his body thrum with desire . . . the seductive whisper of a vamp. She'd probably perfected it.

He shifted, irritated with himself again for succumbing to her female charm.

"I wrote *Under the Covers* because I wanted to help relationships in distress. I've been counseling numerous couples for the past few years and have noticed similar patterns, which are common problem areas, lack of communication being one of the prime ones."

"So you're teaching couples how to communicate?" the magazine reporter asked.

Someone else snickered. "Yeah, between the sheets."

Abby's full lips pursed slightly, but she seemed to realize

her reaction and tried to temper it, dazzling the group with a radiant smile—the kind of sincere smile that probably hypnotized her patients into trusting her with their darkest, innermost secrets. Admiration stirred inside Hunter, but he fought the feeling. He did not want to like any aspect of her, yet professionalism sparkled in her demeanor.

"Both in and outside the bedroom," she said softly. "Improving a couple's love life also helps improve other aspects of the marriage, and vice versa."

A balding man from the *Gwinnett Daily* elbowed Hunter. "I keep telling my wife that, but she don't buy it."

"If you note the chapter headings, each one incorporates the male and female viewpoint as well as ways to enhance the relationship and open communication. There's 'The Art of Seduction,' 'Fun Foreplay,' 'Body Language to Lure Your Lover,' 'His-and-Her Erogenous Zones,' 'Massaging Your Man,' 'Passionate Positions,' 'Fantastic Fantasies.' "

A heavyset woman in a bright orange dress waved her pen. "So are you advocating group sex?"

"Not at all," Abby said smoothly. "My book is designed to help couples improve intimacy in their relationship— their *monogamous* relationship." She suddenly stood and clutched her purse to her side. "Now, if you'll excuse me, I'm tired. And I'm going home."

The bookseller stepped forward, thanked Abby, and took her elbow, guiding her to the door. Customers stared. Cameras flashed again. The man from the Atlanta magazine followed, earning a back-off glare from the bookseller.

Hunter grimaced when he realized he'd hidden his face in a book on impotency.

"My husband had trouble, too, honey," the woman next to him said, giving him a sympathetic look. "Try Viagra. It worked wonders for us."

He grimaced, stuffed the book back on the shelf, then slid from behind the display and watched the doctor walk out into the mall. In spite of his skepticism and dislike for her, Dr. Jensen had sounded intelligent, sincere, confident, and very professional. In fact, once she began speaking, he barely noticed her hesitation in addressing the group.

Could he be wrong about his observations? Was she truly hiding something?

Abby collapsed into a dark corner booth beside Chelsea, accepted the glass of wine Victoria offered, and slowly sipped it. Though Chelsea and Victoria didn't faintly resemble one another in their looks and styles, tonight they'd managed to put their differences aside. *Thank God.* The three sisters had developed a strong bond through the dark stages of their youth—a bond she certainly needed now.

"How'd it go?" Chelsea asked.

"Okay until the press arrived." Abby shivered. "Oh, and there was this one weird woman . . . I mean man in line."

"What do you mean, weird?" Victoria asked.

"A man dressed like a woman; I'm almost sure of it. And he kept watching me as if . . ."

Chelsea licked her lips, her tongue piercing glittering in the light. "Hey, kinky."

Abby rolled her eyes. Chelsea always saw the bright side of everything. "He gave me the willies."

"Did anyone ask about Lenny?" Victoria asked.

Abby cut a frown toward Chelsea. "Can't you keep anything to yourself?"

"Don't be mad at Chelsea. She's worried about you, and so am I." Victoria hesitated, concern lacing her voice. "I'm sorry about Lenny, sis. What a creep."

"I didn't want you to know. It's so humiliating."

"It's not your fault," Victoria said in a stern voice. "So don't apologize—you have nothing to be ashamed of."

"Yeah, but Lenny should be ashamed of himself," Chelsea mumbled. "If I could find that son of a bitch, I'd cut off his balls and make a pouch out of them."

Abby chuckled, grateful her baby sister had dispelled the tension. Her shoulders and neck were one big knot.

Chelsea raised her glass for a toast. "Here's to castrating Lenny."

The sisters laughed and clinked their glasses. Silence fell while the waitress delivered a tray of appetizers and they all dug in.

"Chelsea said you've been trying to reach Lenny," Victoria finally said, after polishing off a buffalo wing.

Abby shrugged. "I need some closure to all this. If I confront him, I can have that."

Chelsea chomped on chips and avocado dip. Victoria snatched a fried oyster. Abby scanned the tray for chocolate. Where were those Reese's cups?

"I think he's in Mexico with Tony Milano," Victoria said.

"How do you know?"

"I have a friend on the force. Someone spotted Milano and a man fitting Lenny's description with him."

"He did say he was going away with Tony," Abby admitted.

Chelsea smiled wickedly. "Maybe they'll arrest both of them and put them in jail."

A classic case for the psychology books—she'd married her own father.

"I hope he stays out of the country until this publicity dies down," Abby said, thumbing a crumb from her chair and wishing she could brush the memory of Lenny's betrayal away as easily. "I'd hate for him to show up at one of my signings. Or at an interview."

Victoria toyed with her spoon, looking uncharacteristically uncomfortable. "There's something else, Abby."

Abby's heart sank. "What?"

"What if Lenny was involved in Milano's scam?"

Abby dropped her head forward in her hands. "Oh, my God. I hadn't even thought of that."

"The police may want to question you."

"I don't know if he was involved or not." Abby grabbed her sister's hand. "I swear, Victoria. He was so quiet those

51

last few weeks, and he was traveling all the time."

Victoria nodded, her voice grave. "I believe you. But once the police make the connection between Lenny and Milano, they may question you. And if you find anything in the house, any evidence about the investment scams or time-shares, you'll need to turn it over to them right away. I don't want you to get caught in the middle on some trumped-up charge of withholding evidence."

Abby searched her memory banks for any mention of the time-share or any papers she might have seen involving Lenny's finances, but came up blank. It pained her to admit how gullible she'd been. "I can't think of anything, Victoria. You know Lenny claimed he was trying to get his photography business off the ground, so he really didn't contribute much financially." Another clue she should have seen.

"Do you want to press charges?" Victoria asked. "We could sue him—"

"But he doesn't have any money." Another foolish thing she'd done—paid his way while he was screwing Milano. Had he helped Milano steal from others, too? "Or if he does, he earned it illegally."

The jukebox kicked on, the old country song, "Your Cheatin' Heart" blaring out.

"There's a classic for you." The women exchanged tense looks.

"Amen." Chelsea bit into another chip, smiling at a young blond waiter who walked by. "One reason I'm sworn to singlehood."

"I know it's not much comfort, but at least you don't have to suffer through a messy divorce," Victoria offered. "And I'm glad no kids are involved. That makes everything even easier."

Yes, except she had wanted children. "I know you're right. Things are complicated enough right now," Abby said. "Today one of those nosy reporters asked about my husband. What in the world will I do if they keep hounding me about him?"

"You could tell them the truth," Chelsea suggested. "They can't blame you if you're honest."

Victoria coughed. "Unfortunately, we all know that's not true. I can cite at least a dozen cases in which innocent people have been wrongfully accused of crimes, and the trial has almost destroyed their lives."

Abby gave her a withering look. "My publicist went ballistic when I mentioned it, too. She definitely doesn't want me to reveal all. I still can't believe Lenny did this to me."

Victoria shrugged. "I hate it, sis, but you can't let that slime ruin your success. Believe me, I've seen too many men do that, just when the woman they love starts making it big—" She cut herself off, obviously realizing her cynicism was coming through.

"Yeah, wait till things settle down," Chelsea advised.

Abby sipped her wine. Her sisters actually agreed—now she knew the world had flipped on its axis. "I wish I'd published this book under a pseudonym. Rainey said they actually have one author who's so shy they hired an actress to pose as her for publicity purposes."

"I wonder who it is?" Chelsea mused.

"I didn't ask," Abby said. "I figured if the woman wanted her privacy that much, she deserved it. And we all know how vicious reporters can be."

"Yeah, we've all been there, done that, got the T-shirt," Victoria noted wryly.

"Rainey even suggested I hire someone to play my husband. Can you believe that?"

A wicked grin lit Chelsea's green eyes. "Hey, that's not a bad idea."

Abby twisted her mouth sideways. "Don't be ridiculous."

"I'm not." Chelsea tapped her fingernails like a drumroll. "Listen, I can hire one of the actors from the arts center to play Lenny. And no one will ever know but the three of us."

Chapter Four

Body Language

Abby Jensen was going to hire someone from her sister's arts center to play her husband?

Hunter's ears perked up. He had taken the table directly behind Abby's with his back to her back so he could hear her conversation, and oh, what a conversation she was having with the other two women. A tall, potted ficus separated the space between them just enough to shield him, although he'd ditched his woman's outfit in the car. He angled his chair so he could see all three women out of the corner of his eye. One was a voluptuous blonde, much more his type than Abby Jensen, the other sophisticated with dark hair pulled so tightly into a bun her cheekbones almost poked through her skin.

Although the three of them looked nothing alike, judging from their close comradeship, they were either best friends or sisters. The blonde and the brunette faintly resembled the girls in the newspaper picture he'd seen of Dr. Jensen at age twelve, but he couldn't be sure.

Judging from Abby's tone, something was wrong.

She sounded stricken. As if she'd just been delivered some very bad news.

He fought the sympathy that welled inside him. And the other part of him that swelled at the sight of those angelic eyes and those luscious lips.

Angelic dark eyes that held secrets and luscious lips that might be telling lies.

Besides, she was a married woman. Attached. Unavailable to his lusting libido.

"I can't deceive everyone like that," Abby Jensen whispered in a strained voice.

"But it's perfect," the blonde argued. "I'm sure I won't have any trouble finding someone. Just leave it all up to me."

"No," Abby said in a hiss. "I'll just have to find another way to address the reporters' questions."

The blonde jiggled her silver hoop earrings. "What about Lenny?"

"I don't know," Abby said, a note of despair in her voice. "But I'm not ready to reveal the sordid details of my private life."

Hunter scooted his chair back farther, fighting ficus leaves that clawed at his head as he jammed himself closer to Abby's table, then leaned backward in the chair, tilting it on two legs. The waitress across the way spied him and frowned, but he merely waved and cocked his head to the side to listen for more.

"I'll check with that friend of mine from the police force and see if I can find out any information on Lenny," the dark-haired woman said.

Hunter's eyebrows arched.

"Shh, keep your voices down," Abby whispered. "The last thing I want is for all of this to get out. Those nosy reporters would ruin me. What if one of them followed me here?" She glanced around the restaurant, and Hunter jerked his head into his hand, then yanked the menu up to cover his eyes.

Suddenly a beefy face appeared on the opposite side of the opening. Hunter froze, trying to formulate an explanation. "What are you doing, sir?"

"I . . . uh, lost my sunglasses."

The man circled the plant to glare at him. "They're on your head, sir."

"Oh, yes." What was wrong with him? Had he lost his investigative skills?

The man eyed him suspiciously.

Not wanting Abby Jensen to spot him or make a scene, he pivoted and stood to leave, but the back of the chair caught the plant and sent it careening. The waiter tried to grab it, but the ficus soared sideways, and its leafy top landed in the middle of Abby Jensen's table.

Abby and her sisters shrieked and jumped up all at once, sodas and water and food crashing to the gray patterned carpet. Victoria cursed and swiped at her silk pantsuit while Chelsea laughed and picked salsa from her black capris. Abby scooped the chips from her lap, snagged one from the cleavage of her shell, and dropped them back onto the white table.

The waiter and bald maître d' ran over, frantic. "Are you all right?"

"I'm sorry, ladies." The maître d' tried to brush scattered chips from Abby's jacket.

"What happened?" Victoria asked.

"Some strange man had wedged his chair back into that plant. He looked as if he was eavesdropping on you ladies," the bald man said. "When I went to question him, he knocked the plant over as he ran off."

Abby dug her nails into the table. "Was he dressed like a woman?"

The waiter narrowed his eyes. "No, why would you think that?"

"Uh, no reason," Abby said.

"I bet it was a reporter." Chelsea craned her neck to see, as did Abby and Victoria, but only a few curious guests stared back. "They've been hounding my sister for an interview. She's famous, you know. She wrote a book on sex."

Abby glared at Chelsea, ready to throttle her.

The bald man's eyes widened. "Really?"

"Yes, she's *the* Dr. Jensen," Chelsea chirped. "She wrote the bestseller *Under the Covers*, hottest sex tips ever."

Suddenly the waiter and maître d' treated them like royalty. "Let us get you to a clean table, ladies." The waiter whipped a fresh napkin from the new table, whisked it out, ushered Chelsea into a seat, and laid it on her lap.

The maître d' coached Abby to the table. "Yes, and how about a round of drinks on the house."

Chelsea beamed and extended her hands as if to say thanks while Victoria eagerly slid into the rearmost seat of the secluded table. "I'll face the doorway so I can see if anyone else comes looking for you."

Abby claimed the chair opposite her, tension knotting her neck as she tried to forget the incident. Was the man a reporter? And if so, had he overheard their conversation?

Hunter grimaced as he entered his boss's office at the *AJC*, still unable to believe he'd knocked a plant right on top of his target and almost gotten caught. But at least he was onto a hot story, and he had an idea how to get closer to Abby Jensen.

The scents of ink and coffee and stale doughnuts wafted up from Ralph's desk. The man grabbed a jelly doughnut, bit a hunk out of it, and stuffed a handful of notes into Hunter's hand without bothering to look up.

"Here, check out this stuff next."

Hunter glanced at the top assignment and bit back a curse—the ongoing battle between the Little League parents in Fulton County. Dads and moms fighting on the fields like kids; it had become a suburban nightmare. One man had even beaten a referee with a baseball bat and sent him to the hospital.

Not that the story wasn't newsworthy, but . . . he had bigger fish to fry.

Only, he'd made a mess of things at the restaurant. Once that plant had gone flying, he had to disappear fast or lose his cover.

"Get those to me as soon as you can," Ralph said.

"Listen, Ralph, I think I may have a lead on that Jensen woman—"

"I'm putting Addleton on that story," Ralph said. "He thinks he can get an in-depth interview."

"Just give me a chance here." Hunter squared his shoulders and stood to his six-three height, hoping his size might add weight to his argument, but once again Ralph crammed the doughnut into his mouth and didn't bother to look up. Instead he mopped jelly from the copy he was editing.

"Listen, I'm already working on the story. I think I have a way to get close to her."

Ralph finally glanced up, his eyes narrowed in his pudgy face. "All right. You've got twenty-four hours to come up with something." He stabbed a finger at him. "But make sure whatever it is, it sticks. I want facts, not a lawsuit on my hands."

"Right. Thanks, Emerson. You won't be sorry."

Ralph poked the pencil behind his ear. "Oh, and get that Little League story, too, while you're at it."

Hunter nodded and headed to the door. He'd knock that little piece out in no time, then check to see what he could dig up on Abby's husband.

But first he'd head toward the arts center and find Abby's sister, Chelsea.

He had a feeling she would lead him to the story of a lifetime.

* * *

Victoria's questions about Lenny had needled Abby all the way home.

She literally tore apart her new house looking for evidence that her husband—no, her faux husband—might have been involved in a conspiracy with Tony Milano. Adding an arrest for impeding an investigation to her growing repertoire of mistakes would only add more madness to the mayhem. She did not want to be caught unaware if the police approached her with accusations or questions. If she found anything, she'd call Victoria.

Two hours later, she stared at the disheveled boxes and her belongings, which lay scattered helter-skelter all over the room. Clothes, books, magazines, shoes, kitchen gadgets, and small household odds and ends littered the floor. Some of the sketches that had accompanied the chapters in her book sat propped against her desk. She blushed slightly at the nude poses, tempted to put the pictures away. But she needed to remember that she was a sexual being, an appealing woman. It wasn't her fault Lenny had stopped wanting to sleep with her.

He was simply gay.

Trying to make herself believe his lack of interest in her wasn't her fault was another story, though. She had to wonder if she'd been deficient in some way. . . .

Haunted by his lies, she riffled through her office files, studying the ones relating to their finances and investments, but found nothing out of the ordinary.

Nada. Not one thing in her house pointed to Lenny as a criminal.

Unless she counted the fraudulent marriage.

Grateful for small favors, she pocketed her keys, headed to her trusty Toyota, and drove toward the old apartment she and Lenny had shared. The rent had been paid through the remainder of the month, and she still had a key. Had Lenny returned to retrieve his things or were they still there? And if they were, would she find evidence of his betrayal?

Rita Herron

* * *

A sliver of guilt had attacked Hunter on the way to the arts center, so he decided to try one last time to get an up-front interview with the good doctor. He climbed the steps to her porch, a summer shower threatening, the heat beating down on him like a sledgehammer. The blue Williamsburg-style cottage looked like something out of the movies. A white picket fence. Bird feeders in the yard. A patch of impatiens in a flower bed along the front with marigolds in pots on the front porch. Nice and homey and old-fashioned. Traditional.

Not at all the type of outlandish, wild place he might have expected from the contemporary sex therapist.

Dismissing the unsettling feeling that she might not be the vixen he believed, he planned a little persuasive argument. He'd hint that he knew she was hiding something, and if she spoke with him, he'd cut her a break and write the story from her viewpoint. He'd even suck up and tell her how much he admired her work.

How could she resist a fair deal like that?

He tucked his white shirt into his khakis, adopted a non-threatening smile, and punched the doorbell. He only hoped his charm worked with Abby Jensen. Several seconds passed while he waited, the drilling sound of a woodpecker hammering at the roof invading the quiet. He punched the bell again, shifting from foot to foot as he waited. Nothing. Three more times he rang, adding a loud knock to the door just in case she didn't hear the bell.

Still nothing.

Was she home, simply ignoring him?

He glanced at the small garage but the windowless room offered no clue as to whether her car was parked inside, so he stepped to the right side of the porch and peered inside her front window.

His curiosity stirred further.

A group of charcoal drawings of nudes engaged in various forms of sexual contact lay propped against a wooden

60

desk. A couple lying side by side, not touching, simply staring into each other's eyes. A man tracing his finger over a woman's soft, pouty lower lip. Another man with his lips pressed to a woman's long, slender thigh.

He jerked at his collar, perspiration trickling down his back as he studied the other poses. A woman poised with her head thrown back, long hair flowing down her back, her bare breasts jutting forward in offering. A man leaning over a woman's voluptuous body, their naked bodies tangled together. This was the Abby Jensen he'd expected.

Her heart-shaped face floated into his mind and replaced the sketches. He imagined her naked body tangling with his own. Her supple curves, the contours of her hips as she arched her back—

No, he was a breast man, not a butt man. Why would he be imagining her hips?

A cat screeched somewhere in the background, jerking him back to reality. Irritated with himself, he dragged his gaze from the artwork and surveyed what little he could see of the rest of the house through the curtainless window. Clothes, shoes, papers, and books littered the floor, a dozen file folders were strewn across a computer desk, and a lamp lay on its side. Gold candy wrappers dotted the mess. It looked as if the house had been ransacked.

His pulse leaped. What if there had been a burglary? Was the intruder still there?

He craned his neck to investigate further but spotted no sign of life or movement—only boxes and more items scattered haphazardly through the front hall.

Hmm. What exactly had happened at the doctor's house? Had she just moved in or was she packing up to move away now? Maybe she was going somewhere in a hurry.

He jangled his keys as he jogged down the steps to his car. Then he sped off and headed toward the arts center.

* * *

Midnight shadows hugged the walls as Abby finally returned to her house.

She had searched the old apartment, but Lenny had obviously taken any financial and business data with him. She had, however, found several pairs of women's panty hose and garters that didn't belong to her.

If he hadn't revealed his sexual preference in his kiss-off letter, she would have thought he'd had a woman on the side. Now she realized he'd probably bought the undergarments for himself or his lover.

What had she become—a magnet for cross-dressers? Gays? Men confused about their sexuality? Not that there was anything wrong with gay men or women, but . . . she must be putting out the wrong vibes.

Exhausted, she pulled into her driveway, hit the automatic garage-door opener, and coasted inside. But as she climbed out, she noticed a dark SUV across the street. She turned for a brief moment and thought she saw someone inside.

Could a reporter be sitting outside? Or could it be the police—had they found a connection between Tony and Lenny?

Chapter Five

Hot Lips

Victoria wet her lips with her tongue, a case of nerves attacking her. She would rather face a ruthless judge or a notorious criminal than go on a date. In fact, she should be home working now.

But Abby needed her, so she would go through with the evening.

Stefan Suarez, a detective with the Atlanta Police Department, stalked toward her, his dark Latino looks even more appealing in the white button-down shirt and gray slacks he'd chosen to wear. Damn, he was what Chelsea would call a hot tamale.

She clutched the edge of the checkered tablecloth, the scents of Mama Mia's famous Italian food fading as Stefan neared. His aftershave or cologne, whatever he wore, smelled like sex and sin and male, deadly combinations that destroyed the salutation she'd been practicing all day.

"I'm glad you finally returned my call." He slid into the

booth across from her, his piercing brown gaze raking over her with appreciation.

"I . . ." *I have no idea what to say.* "I wasn't sure I would call you back."

He studied her for a long moment, his dark eyes serious and unnerving, giving her just enough time to notice that his dark hair was still damp, the long strands feathering down his neck around his collar. And he wore some kind of gold cross around his neck. And he probably needed to shave three times a day.

"Why not, Victoria?" He reached across the table, pried her hands from the edge, and pulled them into his, a slow smile curving his mouth. "You know I've been interested in you for a long time."

She had to look away. This was not going as planned. She'd met with him only to pick his brain for information about Lenny. "I'm afraid I might have misled you."

"Oh?"

"Yes, I wanted to ask you a favor."

His smile faded slightly. "All right. But let's order first." He flicked a hand at the waitress, who glided over and took their order. Before she could refuse a drink, he'd ordered wine, a dark, rich red that soothed her nerves slightly.

"Now, what was that favor?" He tore off a chunk of bread and she averted her gaze, determined to resist his potent charm. She gathered her senses enough to relate her fabricated story and ask about Lenny.

"So a client of yours was jilted by this guy and you want me to see what I can find out about him?"

"That's right."

He took a long sip of his drink, letting his fingers curl around the base of the long-stemmed glass. She imagined him stroking her skin with those nimble fingers. . . .

"I suppose I could do that." He leaned forward, and Victoria's eyes were riveted to his mouth. "Now, will you do something for me?"

She swallowed. "That depends."

A low chuckle escaped him. "What's wrong? You don't trust me, Victoria?"

"I don't trust any man."

His dark brow shot up, although he didn't look surprised. "Care to fill me in?"

She shrugged. "Comes with the job, I guess."

"And the family?"

"What do you know about my family?"

"Nothing." He offered a sad smile. "Just guessing."

Embarrassment heated her cheeks. "I'm sorry, Stefan. I didn't mean to be rude."

He folded his napkin, his gaze meeting hers. "Don't apologize for being who you are, Victoria. Just promise me one thing."

"What?"

"That you'll give me a chance to prove you wrong."

Abby had hardly slept all night for wondering if the police or reporters were onto her. And then her publicist had phoned at five A.M. to spring her own surprise—she'd scheduled Abby for an appearance on a local talk show called *BookTalk*. Abby had balked, but Rainey had finally convinced her that one interview might quiet the hoopla surrounding her, so she'd agreed. She just prayed it worked.

Summer heat bowed the blades of grass and shimmered off the pavement as she parked in the guest space at the TV station and climbed out of her car. The downtown area buzzed with traffic and sirens and blaring horns. Her heart raced as she mentally ticked off the disasters dogging her.

She was a normal, rational, basically good person; she even attended church and gave a regular tithe. But she'd achieved success only to discover the very same day that her marriage was fraudulent, and that her fake husband and possibly a criminal, was gay and now she'd been thrust into a TV interview that she didn't want to do in order to avoid having to do a string of other publicity stunts.

She had never had secrets in her entire life. She'd always been an open book.

Now her life's pages had been smeared with smut, and she needed to superglue them together to keep them from being placed on display for the public to read. She imagined her face plastered on a grocery store tabloid—the headlines: *Lunatic Therapist Professes Love but Leads Double Life*, *Sex Therapist Nothing but a Fake*.

How much more could a sane body take?

Frantic and debating over whether or not she should skip the country like Lenny, she rushed into the studio at eleven-thirty, praying the interview was short and sweet and to the point. With a name like *BookTalk*, surely the show and staff would be professional and serious, none of that ballyhoo about Dr. Abby and the bedroom.

Several minutes later, after she'd been ushered through makeup, had her hair spritzed and woven into a sleek chignon, and her panty hose replaced—thank heavens for female staff, since she'd ripped her stockings when she'd climbed out of the car—she approached the set with trepidation.

Francine, the director, a distinguished woman with ebony skin and glossy hair, escorted her backstage. "We film before a live audience."

Abby froze. "I thought this was a taped interview. Just me and the anchorperson."

"Oh, no. We want audience participation."

Abby teetered sideways. A poster-sized copy of her cover sat in the middle of two wingback chairs. Bright spotlights glared at her. Through the resulting darkness, a sea of people swam before her frightened eyes.

"We have about five minutes; then we'll call you on." Francine left to speak to the cameraman, and Abby watched, trying to calm her nerves, when suddenly Chelsea attacked her from behind.

"I'm so glad I made it in time."

Abby hugged her, her eyes widening at Chelsea's banana

costume: yellow face makeup, yellow tights, yellow everything.

"I'm auditioning for a commercial for a new fruity kids' cereal after this. I thought dressing the part might help me land the job." Chelsea said automatically. "But I couldn't miss your show."

"Thanks, sis, I need all the moral support . . ." Her words died at the sight of the man beside Chelsea. Light blue eyes the color of a summer sky gazed down at her from a broad, tanned face.

He had a body to match. Six-feet-plus of hard planes, muscles, and sinewy strength, dark hair that looked rumpled, as if he'd just jumped out of a mattress mambo himself, a thick mustache that curled up when he smiled, and a powerful presence that exuded the scent of a lover.

Raw and carnal and primitive.

Her own husband had never affected her like this.

On second thought, the man's hair looked fake. And so did the mustache. But his overwhelming size could not be padded. Underneath he was still as dangerously potent as homemade sin.

Something about him seemed familiar. Who did he remind her of?

No, if she'd met this man before she wouldn't have forgotten him. He had charisma, sex appeal, and the most intense hungry look in his eyes.

He must be Chelsea's latest boyfriend. They came and went faster than race cars at the tracks. She was just about to ask for an introduction when the director waved her on-air.

The voice of the anchorman, Eric Segoda, sprang from the microphone. "Dr. Abigail Jensen is here to visit us today and talk about her new book, *Under the Covers*." He paused for emphasis. "Welcome Abigail Jensen onstage, folks! She's the Dear Abby of the bedroom."

Abby staggered backward as if she might bolt. Applause suddenly rang out and people started chanting her name.

"Abby, Abby, Abby . . . ?"

Chelsea shoved her from behind and she tottered forward.

Abby was thankful the first questions were easy: the idea for the book, her professional expertise, her work ethics, and her beliefs about marriage and monogamy.

"Your workshops, Women First . . ." Segoda paused and Abby nodded in confirmation. "They advocate putting a woman's desires and pleasures before a man's?"

Abby frowned. "Not at all. By nature, women are caregivers. I simply encourage them to consider their own needs and try to communicate them to their husbands."

"So you aren't suggesting women assume a dominant role?"

Abby shrugged. "I'm not advocating either sex take a dominant role. Each relationship is different; it depends on the couple."

"But you find women dominating men sexually stimulating?"

Abby fought the urge to squirm. "As I said, it can be or it might not be, depending on the couple involved, their likes and dislikes, their needs, their preferences."

"We're aware you're a newlywed yourself, Dr. Jensen, and that you've been avoiding the press."

"I simply appreciate my privacy," Abby stated. "I didn't write this book to gain attention. I want to help open the doors of communication between couples."

"To keep the divorce rate down?"

"Yes."

"So where is this husband of yours, Dr. Jensen?" Segoda smiled, his eyes crinkling. "All of Atlanta is dying to meet the man."

Abby's gaze flitted across the stage, her heart racing in a panic.

"Oh, wait." Segoda pressed his finger to one ear; then a jaunty smile flashed onto his handsome face. He glanced offstage, where the coproducer gave him a thumbs-up signal, then turned to the audience with a cheeky wink. "It seems Dr. Jensen has a surprise for us today."

I do? Abby cut a questioning look toward Segoda.

"Yes." Segoda rose and gestured toward the side of the stage. "She's brought her husband here to meet us, folks."

"I have?" Abby squeaked.

"She has," Segoda said with a chuckle.

The man who had come with Chelsea suddenly bounded onto the set, broad shoulders thrown back in a light blue designer shirt, Italian loafers clicking as he paraded toward her.

Her shocked gaze turned to Chelsea, who waved her hands in joyful exuberance.

"What's your husband's name?" Segoda asked.

"Len . . . Leonard."

"I'm sure our viewers want to know if you practice at home what you preach in your books," Segoda prodded.

The microphones planted in the audience captured their enthusiasm. "Let's hear it from the husband," a woman shouted.

"Yeah, we want to see this hunk in action."

Before Abby could open her mouth to protest, the man pulled her up to stand beside him. "I'm Abby's husband, Lenny," he announced with a devilish grin. Then he swooped her up in his arms, lowered his head, and captured her mouth in a deep kiss that sent her senses reeling.

Abby clung to him, her legs bowing like dandelions in the wind. She had talked about hot lips in her book, yet she'd never tasted lips that held as much fire as this man's. Or been pressed against a body that could make her forget a crowd was watching.

And that the man kissing her was a complete stranger.

Hunter heard the roar of the crowd and realized he must be acting his part well.

He was *acting* wasn't he?

Tunneling one hand through Abby Jensen's chignon, he

slowly pulled out the pins and felt the long, wild tresses tangle around his fingers. Her hair felt like silk, satiny and soft between his fingers. And it smelled like fresh rain and roses. She sank into the kiss, her tongue dancing with his in erotic love strokes, her hands gripping his arms as if she might collapse with desire if he released her.

He did have to release her.

Yes, he did. Sometime. And he should be attracted to Chelsea, he thought, the woman who'd hired him just this morning to play Abby's husband, not Abby. Chelsea had the bombshell body.

But Abby Jensen did know how to kiss. . . .

What a stroke of luck to find such a great cover. Luckily, Chelsea had agreed he should wear a disguise in case someone recognized him or a photo of the real Lenny surfaced. Unfortunately, he hadn't been able to finagle out of Chelsea the details of Lenny's whereabouts or the reason for his disappearance.

The mystery intrigued him.

He traced Abby's mouth with his tongue, nibbled at her lower lip, then gently broke the kiss and pulled away slightly, just enough so her breath still bathed his face. Her dazed look of passion aroused him to the point of pain, and the low sound of excitement that gurgled from her throat cranked the flame of heat in his belly up a notch.

Cheers and whoops of laughter filled the stage, and the anchorman cleared his throat. "Well, ladies and gentlemen, I guess you have your answer. It looks as if Dr. Jensen follows her own rules."

Abby's look of stark shock rattled Hunter. She was hot and obviously a very passionate woman, but she also seemed stunned at her own reaction. Didn't she and her real hubby have this kind of volatile heat between them?

Of course.

She was simply reacting oddly because he was a stranger and she was in shock, he reasoned. And because she was married.

70

She probably didn't expect an actor to turn her on.

"Mr. Jensen," the talk show host said, obviously assuming Jensen was her married name—come to think of it, Hunter hadn't checked to see for himself—"Why don't you sit down and tell us what it's like to be married to a sex goddess?"

Hunter grinned at the audience like a man well pleased, not a far stretch at the moment. Maybe Abby Jensen did know a few secrets in the bedroom.

He'd definitely have to spend more time with her to find out.

A tough story, but someone had to do it. And it would take a strong man to step up to the plate, play her soul mate, and not be knocked out by the curveballs she tossed at him. Like the seductive whisper of her voice. And the enticing, innocent look she displayed for the public.

Hell, she was as innocent as a street girl, he thought.

Abby coughed beside him, and he wondered again at her reaction. She seemed so shocked to have him appear—hadn't she told her sister to hire him? When Chelsea had sworn him to secrecy, he'd assumed Abby had instigated the charade.

Taking her hand in his, he pulled her back into her seat, surprised to find her palm sweating. "Life couldn't be better," he answered. "My wife is making all my dreams come true." After all, that wasn't exactly a lie. His dream of making a name for himself at the *AJC* would come true.

Just as soon as he nabbed this story. Then Ralph wouldn't care about his unorthodox methods—he'd be grateful to Hunter for being so ingenious.

Chapter Six

The Orgasmic Kiss

Abby was thankful that the man pretending to be her husband chatted with the host for several minutes, giving her a few minutes to recover from the shock of his appearance on the show.

And from that erotic kiss.

Even as the gorgeous stranger spoke, he pulled her hand into his, cradling it between his huge hands, then resting them on his thigh. Coupled with his deep, husky voice, the possessive masculine gesture awakened feminine senses left dormant for a long time. So did the scent of his maleness, the heat of his muscular leg, and the friction of his warm palm against her own.

Abby answered any questions directed her way by rote, her convictions firmly planted in her mind. But her subconscious had drifted to another plane, a higher level where her inner thoughts and her body's reaction had reached a catastrophic epiphany.

The orgasmic kiss really did exist. And so did those titillating touches.

Her lips still tingled from her pretend-husband's hot mouth, and liquid heat pooled in her belly, erupting like a brushfire caught anew each time he squeezed her hand or flexed his thigh. And she felt dizzy from his cologne—what was he wearing? Whatever it was, the fragrance enhanced his masculinity a hundred times over.

She had written about the power of the senses, about the orgasmic kiss and those titillating touches, because she'd believed the seductive play of a man's and a woman's lips together, their tongues mating, their souls seeping one into the other, could actually bring a woman to ecstasy.

Although it had never happened with her.

Before now.

Now her body tingled and shivered, her senses reeled with erotic thoughts of this stranger, and her brain had traveled to that faraway, hazy place where passion overpowered reason.

"So one year after the vows, is the honeymoon over?" Segoda asked.

"Our honeymoon will never end," her pretend-husband said in a gruff voice.

Oh, he was good, Abby thought. A wonderful actor.

But he *was* acting, and she could not fall for his seductive allure.

How long could a fifteen-minute interview last, anyway?

Abby glanced at the clock out of the corner of her eye, praying the director would end this maddening charade so she could go home, burrow into a cave, and hide until she found a way to crawl out of this twilight zone she'd lapsed into.

Oh, well, this one public appearance should quiet all the hoopla about her husband. Then Abby could forget about lusty looks shared with strangers and orgasms of the mind and go back to therapy.

To *giving* therapy.

Oh, hell, she might need it herself after this crazy ordeal ended.

"Dr. Jensen," Segoda asked. "Would you recommend your book to newlyweds?"

"Certainly," Abby replied, thinking of the rocky beginning her own nuptials had had on her real honeymoon. "Learning to communicate is important at any stage of a relationship, but establishing a solid pattern at the beginning paves the way for a smoother marriage." After all, if Lenny had been honest and confessed he was gay, their fake marriage would have been much different; it never would have happened. Then she wouldn't be in this mess. . . .

Segoda waved to his assistant, a petite brunette who roamed the studio audience with a microphone. "I believe we have a few questions from the audience."

Abby forced a smile and stared out into the crowd, trying desperately to ignore the fact that the man next to her had slid their joined hands toward his lap. She could have sworn she felt a slight shudder course through him when her fingers clawed for escape. And if her vision was serving her right, he had a hard-on.

Hunter knew Abby wanted him to release her hand, but he'd be damned if he would let her off the hook. He'd torture her the same way she was torturing him with those doelike eyes. After all, *she* had hired *him*.

She was not an innocent.

She was a married woman living a lie onstage and using him in the process.

But he did not want to embarrass himself, so he shifted and crossed his legs to hide his arousal. She bit down on her lower lip, and he shot her a sideways grin that promised heat and lust and that her sex tips wouldn't be lost on him.

The young assistant took her cue from the director. "Yes, sir, tell us your name and what you want to ask Dr. Abby."

A portly man with three white hairs in a comb-over grinned, his pasty complexion reddening. "I tried those ten steps in 'The Art of Seduction' chapter and they worked." He gestured toward a middle-aged woman with dyed blond hair. "Meet the future Mrs. Javarsky. We just got engaged."

"Congratulations." A smile flooded Abby's face. "I'm glad things worked out for you."

A birdlike woman in a tiger-striped dress shot up. "Is it true that your grandfather had two wives? And that your father was accused of racketeering and has mob connections at the Barely There Club on Cheshire Bridge Road?"

Abby tensed beside him. Hunter squared his shoulders, recognizing the woman as a reporter. "No, my grandfather was not a bigamist, and as far as I know none of my family members have ever been involved in mob-related activities."

"How can you advocate marriage when your parents lived together without nuptials? Do you think people should stay together even if they're miserable with each other?"

Abby shook her head. "It's true my parents never married, and no, sometimes I think couples have irreconcilable differences." She paused and glanced at Hunter, her big eyes pleading.

Silently asking him not to give her away.

He recognized the vulnerability there, and empathy plucked at heartstrings he thought had been broken a long time ago.

Her reaction to the kiss aroused his curiosity even more. She obviously wasn't a lesbian, as he'd wondered when she'd winked at him at the bookstore. Or if she was, she liked men, too. Not that he cared. The lesbian angle would have made a nice story, though. . . .

Several people began to debate the war between the sexes, the assistant jumping back and forth between two rows of guests to give them a chance to speak. "Men don't like to be criticized in bed," one man said.

"And sometimes we like for the woman to take the lead."

"After my wife read that book, she left me," a whiny guy in an outdated leisure suit cried. "She said I didn't pass the bedroom test."

"And my wife told me she wouldn't sleep with me unless I learned how to do this bedroom talk," a trucker with a big belly shouted. "She never complained before."

"If the love is there," Abby continued, "you can both work it out, gentlemen. If the feelings are real and strong, not just lust, people can better their chances of keeping a marriage together by learning to communicate both in and out of the bedroom." Her smile dazzled the crowd.

Hunter frowned. Maybe her sister had coached her in acting lessons. She certainly sounded sincere.

"After all, sex with emotions is much more powerful than sex simply for physical-gratification purposes."

"I can testify to that," Hunter said, shocking himself by speaking up.

Abby grinned, obviously assuming he was playing his part.

The audience chuckled.

Hunter lifted Abby's hand against his mouth and dropped featherlight kisses along her fingers. "Let's face it, guys. We can be better lovers if we *listen* to what our ladies want."

"Ahh, what women want," the host commented with a grin. "The million-dollar question."

The camera jumped back to the audience. "The big mystery, you mean," another man commented.

A brunette in her twenties jumped up. "We want men who care."

"And men who take care of us."

"And men who make us scream with pleasure."

"I pleased my woman." A young black man threw up his hand. "See, I wrote crib notes from the book right here to help me out."

"I did, too," a yuppie-looking guy with wire-rimmed glasses added. "We had sex for twenty-four hours straight."

"What about what we want?" a bodybuilder-type man asked.

"Yeah, what about our needs?"

Abby cut in smoothly. "The book addresses both sexes' needs and the fact that each partner needs to listen to the other."

"That's right." Hunter leaned sideways. "Just let your girl whisper in your ear what she wants. You take care of her"—he pulled their clasped hands to his chest—"she'll take care of you."

"I'm afraid we have to close on that note," Segoda said. "But we'd love to have you come back, Dr. Jensen, and talk with us again."

She stood to shake the host's hand, and Hunter followed suit. But just as she extended her arm, a pair of her panties slid from beneath the cuff of her jacket. Hunter grabbed them just before they fell into Segoda's hands.

Pasting a shit-eating grin on his face, he twirled them around his hand. "See, ladies and gentlemen, how can the honeymoon be over when your wife tosses her panties at you everywhere you go?" He nuzzled her neck for emphasis.

Abby's mouth dropped open, the crowd roared, and he covered her reaction with another kiss. Her mouth felt hot, her small gasp of surprise another kick to his libido as he tasted the inner recesses of her mouth. Reminding himself he was still onstage, he slowly pulled away, laced his fingers with hers, turned and waved the panties in the air, then led her offstage.

"That was great!" Chelsea jumped up and down, her banana suit bobbing.

"Great?" Abby whispered between clenched teeth. "It was horrible."

"Nonsense, you were wonderful. I can't believe you pulled that clever trick with the panties."

"That was an accident," Abby screeched. "They must have gotten stuck to my blouse in the dryer."

"Good show, you two." The producer pumped their hands. "Nice touch with that underwear trick."

Several crew members joined in the congratulations.

Chelsea's cheeks glowed pink beneath her yellow makeup as she embraced the actor. "And you were fabulous. I loved the thong."

Abby blushed to the roots of her hair. The man still had the panties wrapped around his hands!

Staff and more camera crew flocked around them, asking for autographs. Abby spent the next few minutes trying to be gracious, accepting praise for what she considered a fiasco and they considered a stroke of TV brilliance. The actor who'd played her husband stood in the shadows and watched her, his eyes gleaming with emotions she couldn't read. Curiosity. Enjoyment over her discomfort.

Lust.

Out of the corner of her eye, she caught Chelsea's wave good-bye. She gestured toward the banana suit. "Got to run for the commercial. I can't keep the fruity flakes waiting."

Abby glared at her, but Chelsea ignored her and dashed out the back. Desperate to escape the show set as soon as possible, Abby thanked the producer and host and turned to leave. As soon as they got out of earshot, she'd find out this actor's name, pay him whatever salary Chelsea had offered him, and say good-bye to him.

And to her TV days.

"Where do we go from here?" Hunter asked as they stepped outside together. The late-afternoon breeze stirred Abby's perfume toward him like an aphrodisiac, sucking him into its seductive lair. They stood under the awning of the building, the parking lot stretched out before them, traffic moving slowly by in the distance.

Abby's startled gaze swung to him. "*We* don't go anywhere, Mr. . . ." She threw up her hands. "Good grief, I don't even know your name. Or what Chelsea told you about today."

"Harry." Hunter extended his hand, grinning when she simply stared at his offering as if he were a bloodsucking slug that had crawled from beneath a rock and would latch onto her any second. Then again, the handshake formality did seem ludicrous in light of their earlier kiss. "Harry Henderson."

A short bubble of laughter erupted from her. "Stage name, right?"

He nodded. "Definitely."

She rolled her eyes, irking him, and he dropped his hand. It wasn't as if she were being completely honest here herself.

"And your sister hired me to play your husband for a day. What else was there to tell me?"

Abby studied him, her eyes narrowed, her suspicions brewing. "Nothing."

Hunter nodded, deciding not to push just yet. "What other shows or interviews do you need me for?"

That telltale blush stained her cheeks again. "Um . . ." She shifted to her other foot, squinting through the fading afternoon sunshine. Her dainty chin wobbled as she tried to collect her thoughts. "None, thankfully. Today was the beginning and the end of my TV career."

"You don't have other interviews lined up?"

"No." She shrugged. "I hate all this publicity."

"Really?" He cupped her elbow with his hand. "Then you won't be needing a husband—"

"Shh." Her gaze darted around nervously, although the parking area seemed deserted. "Can we go someplace and get a cup of coffee? I'd like to finish our business in private."

His eyebrows arched involuntarily. "Lead the way, honey."

79

She glared at him. "I'll meet you at Third Cup. It's right around the corner."

He nodded and watched her rush to her Toyota. Maybe over coffee Abigail Jensen would let her defenses slip and spill the beans about her marriage.

And he would move in for the kill, rake them right into the palm of his hand, and make himself a double-tall latte with the grounds. Then he could sip the fruits of his labor while he lay back and watched his name climb the ladder of success at the paper.

Abby settled into a corner with her decaf mocha, her nerves on edge as Harry Henderson seated himself across from her. Something about the man seemed familiar, but she couldn't quite put her finger on it. It was almost as if she'd met him before. His eyes . . . they were so blue. Where had she seen eyes like that before?

The cross-dresser who'd rescued her at the book signing that day? She tilted her head, studying him. No, she hadn't seen the woman's eyes because of those funky orange sunglasses. And this man was too masculine, too macho ever to dress as a woman, Even in acting a part. Besides, she hadn't actually seen the woman/man very clearly that day.

She pulled out her checkbook, determined to make this short and sweet. Then again, she'd better play nice and find out just how much he knew about her situation. Had Chelsea opened up a whole can of worms or what? Forcing herself to relax, she offered him a smile. "So, Mr. Henderson, how did you fall into today's part?"

One dark eyebrow rose as he leaned back casually in his chair, his big body oozing masculine testosterone. "I stopped by the arts center to find out if they held general auditions and as luck would have it Chelsea said she might have just the job for me." He raised his coffee, his thick fingers wrapped around the cup. "Apparently they hadn't advertised very well for this part. I was the only male, so I lucked out."

Yes, well, Chelsea hadn't exactly advertised that Abby needed a husband. Had she?

Because if she had, those worms might escape the can. . . .

"Have you done a lot of acting?"

"A little." His big shoulders lifted and fell, drawing attention to the way his blue shirt matched his eyes.

Good heavens, she was not supposed to be looking at his eyes. "Where else have you acted?"

"Oh, small-time jobs. Nothing you would have heard of."

She nodded. Not a man of words, was he? Then again, maybe she sounded as if she were interrogating him. "And Chelsea just said you needed to play my husband for a day?"

He sipped his drink, his dark gaze locking with hers. Heat emanated from his blue eyes, from every cell in his body. "Yes. I have to admit I was curious as to why." He leaned closer, his mouth just a hairbreath away. She remembered his lips, the feel of them on hers, and swallowed. "Where is the real superstud husband?"

Abby squeezed her cup so hard, coffee sloshed out. She grabbed a napkin, wiping the whipped cream from her fingers. "I thought Chelsea probably explained."

His gaze trapped hers. "She said he was out of the country. So unless there's trouble in paradise, why didn't you just tell the director the truth?"

Abby's fingers tightened around her cup again. No trouble in paradise. There was trouble everywhere she turned. "I . . . I was going to, but Chelsea had this wild idea and hired you before I could stop her. In fact, I told her the other day I didn't want to do this."

"I still don't understand." He splayed his hands in a questioning gesture. "Why hire an actor? Why not wait until your real husband comes home?"

Abby grappled for a reply. She'd never been good at lying, but the entire truth was just too painful to share. "Because I'm not sure where Lenny is."

He waited, studying her. Was that sympathy in his eyes?

"He's been detained, and I need some time to figure out

81

why and to help him before the press finds out."

"I see."

He did?

A slow smile curved his mouth. "Chelsea said he's in Brazil?"

Mexico. Brazil. Hell if she knew. "Yes." Desperate, she covered his hand with hers. "Please, Mr. Henderson. I need some time. I don't want to do anything that might endanger him."

She was surprised her nose hadn't grown with that whopper of a lie.

His long fingers curled around hers, enveloping her small hand. The touch set off a siren in her mind, warning her that Harry Henderson, apish though the name sounded, exuded sex in spades. He should come equipped with a warning label that read *Danger*.

She slowly released his hand, well aware his dark gaze tracked her jittery fingers as she reached for her purse. "Well, thank you, Harry. Now, how much do I owe you?"

His dark eyebrow rose. "You don't owe me, Abby."

"But—"

"Your sister hired me; she'll take care of the bill through the arts center."

"Oh, right." She'd forgotten how the center worked. She'd just have to cover it with Chelsea.

"Are you sure you don't need me for other appearances?" A wicked grin teased the corners of his mouth. " 'Cause I'm available if you do."

She squirmed and sipped her mocha. "I don't plan any. Today was humiliating enough."

"I thought it went pretty well. The audience loved you."

"No, they loved you . . . I mean your act."

"They did enjoy that quick save with the panties."

She froze, remembering he'd stuck them in his pocket as they'd left.

"By the way, nice choice," he said in a gruff voice.

Abby avoided his gaze, but his husky tone washed over

her like silk along her skin. "They got caught in the dryer with my blouse."

"Uh-huh."

"Really." Abby fanned her face. "I spilled something on my blouse this morning and had to rinse it and dry it before the show and . . ." His low chuckle forced her to let the sentence trail off. "You're enjoying this, aren't you?"

The devilish look remained. "It's hard to believe a woman who's written a sex guide could blush."

"It's not a sex guide."

"Call it what you want, but it is hot, Abby."

"I only wanted to help couples. The divorce rate is just so high these days—"

"Tell me about it."

She searched his face for the truth, seeing it in the sudden sadness in his eyes. "You're divorced."

"Yes."

Sympathy tugged at her. "I'm sorry."

"It's history." He shrugged again, although his expression seemed strained as his broad shoulders stretched along the back of the chair.

She clutched her purse, a case of nerves attacking her. As if the man's raw sexuality hadn't affected her enough, now she was beginning to like him.

Well, maybe not *like*, but at least see him as a real man, not just an actor.

An impossible situation.

He knew part of her secret, and she could not get tangled up with anyone right now. Besides, she was reacting this way only because Lenny had left her ego desperately in need of feeding. "I have to go." Gathering her courage, she squeezed his hand one more time. That electric touch zinged through her just as it had earlier. "And thanks for today. I hope you'll be discreet."

"Don't worry, Abby." He leaned closer again, this time so close he actually brushed a gentle kiss to her hair as he whispered, "Your secret's safe with me."

She sighed in relief and stood, legs wobbling like rubber bands. "Thank you so much. By the way, good luck with your acting. I'll look for you on the big screen." Then she turned and hurried away.

Thank heavens she would never see the man again.

Chapter Seven

Panty Passions

Shaken from the interview, Abby drove toward home, storm clouds brewing above, the interlude with that actor Harry Henderson playing over and over in her head. Had she said too much? Given away too much? Would he keep her secret or would she get caught in her lies?

She had to extricate that man from her mind.

He had been sexy and powerful and too damn charismatic for her. Just as Lenny had been in the beginning. Only even more so . . .

But she'd remedied what little chemistry she and Lenny might have had, she thought with a rueful shake of her head. She'd been so stunning in bed, he had preferred *men*.

Tears threatening, she flipped on the radio to try to calm herself; then the sky darkened to a fever pitch and rain clouds burst open. She cursed and turned on her wipers, and let the tears fall. Tears for the lies she'd told today. For the fool she'd been.

For ever thinking she'd fallen in love with Lenny.

For feeling an insane attraction to an actor her banana-sister had hired to play the husband who'd deserted her.

Traffic crawled to a stop; an emergency vehicle raced by with its lights flashing. The cars in front of her braked to a dead halt. Obviously there was an accident ahead. Traffic would probably be at a standstill for an hour or two while the police cleared it.

Realizing she was stuck, she decided to pull into the local superdiscount store to pick up some supplies. Tonight she would throw herself the mother of all pity parties and kiss her dreams of happily-ever-after good-bye.

Because once again, it was Saturday night and she was single and alone.

Hunter finished his latte with a grin. He knew exactly what Abby Jensen was thinking as she left the shop: she would never see him again.

A low chuckle rumbled from him as he tugged her thong from his pocket and gazed at the skimpy, silky fabric. But this time the good doctor would not have her way.

He would find out exactly why Chelsea had hired him to play Abby's husband.

He just couldn't let her get to him in the process. And for a minute she had. . . .

Then he'd realized she was simply flirting with him because he was privy to part of her secret and she wanted to make certain he kept it. Which proved his original theory about her being manipulative, not the family-oriented martyr type she portrayed herself to be.

The scent of her delicate perfume lingered on his clothes as he left the coffee shop; he'd have to ditch these clothes so he could vanquish it. Just as he had to banish his memory of that erotic orgasmic kiss.

Dammit. The woman was married.

Even if he wasn't working on a story and detested the marriage therapist, he did not, had not, would not ever mess around with a married woman. Not only did he pride his own life too much to chance being murdered by an irate jealous husband, he did have some scruples.

Hunter peeled off the mustache and wig—okay, maybe not stringent scruples, but he had a bona fide reason for deceiving the woman, and the end justified the means. Cursing, he scrubbed his hands through his hair to spike the matted mess as he cranked his Explorer and wove through the heavy traffic and rain. Still, Abby Jensen remained a puzzle to solve.

One minute she was spouting off suggestions to improve intimacy and talking about passionate positions and orgasmic kisses, and the next she was blushing like a virgin.

And that story she'd invented about her husband—what kind of baloney was that?

She had actually looked vulnerable for a moment, sad, as if she were really concerned about the man. Had he been detained on business somewhere? Was he in trouble with the law?

She'd said she didn't want to endanger him. Could he be the victim of one of those business kidnappings he'd heard so much about in South America?

Hmm. That might explain why she wanted to keep his disappearance quiet. And why she was worried about his safety.

Or had something else caused her sadness? Something more personal . . . ? The obvious answer reared its ugly head.

Had her husband had an affair? Had he left her for another woman?

Rain splashed his windows, thunder rumbling overhead, cars slowing to a dead stop. He flipped on the radio to check the traffic reports.

"Folks, we have a nine-car pileup on Peachtree Street, no fatalities or serious injuries reported, but traffic will remain gridlocked for at least an hour while the police clear the scene. And now for the weather.

"The storm is passing through, folks. Believe it or not,

it's headed south and will be gone in a couple of hours."

Hell. He contemplated another route, but up ahead he spotted Abby's Toyota pulling into the big shopping complex. Maybe he'd follow the doctor, see what she was up to. He could pick up some supplies while he was here, maybe drop by Lizzie's later and see if she wanted to go camping, spend some quality time alone with her. If they headed north, they'd drive out of the bad weather.

A father-daughter camping trip, complete with a sleeping bag on the hard, uncomfortable ground, would be the perfect way to help him forget Abby Jensen and her nonsense about bedroom talk between the sheets.

And the fact that even though she wasn't his type, he wouldn't mind crawling under the covers into a nice, warm bed with her—naked, hot, and willing.

Abby fought with the umbrella, cursing in frustration as the wind sucked it upside down, lifted it from her hands, and flung it into the air. She jogged after it, but a runaway grocery cart full of disposable diapers suddenly flew out of nowhere and whacked into her stomach. Abby yelped, stumbled, fell against a Ford pickup, and broke the heel of one shoe.

A pregnant woman ran after the cart, her big belly leading. "I'm so sorry," the woman screeched over the downpour as she grabbed the cart.

"No problem." Abby pushed the buggy toward her, staggering on her broken shoe, then realized the woman was driving the pickup, so she moved away.

"Thanks." Rain splattered the woman's pale face, and she suddenly clutched her stomach in pain. "Oh, my God."

Abby froze. Was the lady going into labor?

"Get in," Abby said. "I'll put your things in the truck for you."

The woman offered a weak smile. "Thank you. I don't feel so good."

Abby's heart raced. "Can you drive yourself?"

The woman fought with the door against the wind, but eventually climbed inside the cab awkwardly. "I only have a block to go."

And where was her husband when she needed him?

Cursing men in general, Abby stuffed the diapers into the other side of the truck, slammed the passenger door, and waved. But suddenly the woman clutched the steering wheel, doubled over and rested her head on top of it, and let out a loud screech.

Abby shivered and ran around to the driver's side. *Dear heavens.* The woman was having her baby right here in the middle of the Wal-Mart parking lot.

"Help!" The woman turned a panicked look Abby's way, then pointed to her stomach. "It's coming!"

Abby swallowed, momentarily paralyzed. She didn't know anything about delivering a baby, but the woman swung open the truck door, bellowed again, and clawed at Abby's arm, jerking her out of her stupor. She jumped on the lower step of the cab and tried to calm the woman. "Are you sure?"

"My water just broke."

Abby glanced down at the seat and saw the evidence. "I'll get an ambulance."

"Don't leave me!" The young girl flopped backward, grabbed her belly, and howled. "I have to push!"

Sweet Jesus, no. Not yet. Didn't deliveries take time, long hours of waiting at the hospital?

"Just hold on," Abby said. "I'm sure you've got—"

"It hurts!" The woman panted and heaved. "I feel the head!"

Abby grabbed her cell phone, punched in 911, and grimaced when the woman screamed again, scooted backward on the seat, and began shoving at her clothes. Abby told the dispatch officer where to come, then hung up and tried to think.

"I've got to push!"

She couldn't have the baby on the seat of the truck!

Frantic, Abby searched the woman's bags for something sterile to place under her. She certainly couldn't boil water! Toothpaste, cosmetics, a toilet brush, rubber gloves—she tore open the plastic gloves and pulled them onto her hands.

The lady bucked up off the seat with a yowl, grabbed the steering wheel, and hit the horn. It blared along with her howl.

"Hang on, honey; the ambulance is on its way," Abby murmured. She ripped open the diapers and spread them on the seat for a makeshift blanket just as the baby's head made its appearance.

Hunter stared in amazement as an ambulance rolled to a stop in the downpour and the paramedics jumped out and rushed to a pickup truck. Abby Jensen had climbed into the truck only minutes earlier with a very young, very pregnant woman. To do what?

Deliver her baby?

An 11-Alive truck screeched in next and a camera crew jumped out, a newscaster fumbling with her rain hat as they ran to the scene. Seconds later, he gaped as the paramedics loaded a woman and a newborn onto a gurney and transferred them to the ambulance. The woman clung to Abby Jensen's hand. Abby looked shaken but relieved.

The newscaster shoved a microphone toward the good doctor. Hunter couldn't hear, but he suspected the reporter had just gotten the scoop on a Wal-Mart delivery by Abby Jensen.

A hero story if he'd ever heard one.

Hunter gripped the steering wheel. *Dammit.* Here he was sitting on a great story and he couldn't move forward and interview Abby himself or he'd blow his cover. Although her heroic act didn't quite fit the angle he had planned. . . .

Abby hobbled toward the store, her hair plastered to her head, her clothes soaked, her emotions riding a rocky roller coaster. After that delivery, she should just go home, but she was here anyway and the traffic still wasn't moving, so she might as well stock up. Besides, what did she have to go home to? Nothing but an empty house . . . no loving husband waiting for her. No baby to rock or feed or cuddle. Not even a dog or the proverbial single girl's cat.

Of course, Lenny had wanted the cat. Another sign that he wasn't the man for her. She was definitely a dog person.

Her heart squeezed as she grabbed a cart and trudged inside. All the hopes and dreams she'd had when she'd bought the house rose like a tidal wave, clogging her throat with tears. The minute she'd seen the little blue cottage with the white picket fence she'd fallen in love with the property. She'd imagined painting the spare bedroom with rocking horses for a nursery, bringing her own baby home there one day, building a backyard sandbox and swing set, Christmases with Santa Claus and stockings over the fireplace.

Having the perfect stable family for which she'd always longed.

The air conditioner blasted her, sending chill bumps up her drenched body, along with the realization that her dreams had died along with Lenny. *Damn him.*

She used a handiwipe to clean her hands and dabbed at her wet face with a tattered tissue, grimacing at the telltale marks of mascara and makeup. She could just imagine her raccoon eyes. She didn't care what she looked like, she reminded herself as she pushed her cart down an aisle. No one in the store would recognize her anyway. Not unless they'd seen the TV camera crew outside. She'd cut that interview short and sweet by turning the attention to the brave young woman on the gurney.

Geez, for someone who hated publicity, lately she felt a magnet drawing her to the camera's watchful eye.

Thoroughly depressed and well into her pity-party mood, she filled her cart with three tearjerker movies, new tapes for her minirecorder, five bags of miniature Reese's cups, and a twenty-four-pack of toilet paper, then saw the sale sign above the tampons—*Buy one, get one free*—and grabbed four boxes. Next went in salsa, chips, three kinds of cookies, a bag of popcorn, a pair of fluffy bedroom shoes, and a baby blue pajama set with pictures of cows all over them. What else? Underwear.

No more embarrassing thongs.

Comfortable, practical underwear that didn't crawl into nether regions and suggest that she might be having sex.

Still shivering, she rushed toward the clothing section, exhausted and weary from the day's ordeal. The choices seemed endless. Elastic waist. Cotton. Satin. Bikini. Control-top. Colored. White. She debated over the control-top panties or the plain white granny panties, then thought, *What the heck*, and tossed in three packages of each.

Oblivious to her surroundings, she swung her cart around to head toward the cash register when she crashed into a man's back. Tall, with massive shoulders, he turned, narrowing mesmerizing blue eyes at her.

Even without the wig and mustache, she recognized him immediately.

Harry Henderson.

Hunter's hands tightened around his shopping cart. Even wet and bedraggled, with her mascara and makeup smeared, drenched to the bone, and a non-blonde, Abby Jensen still stirred his sex to life.

Shit. Shit. Shit.

M-a-r-r-i-e-d—he purposely spelled out the word silently, giving himself time to recover.

She glanced at his cart, her brows arching in surprise at the camping gear and child-size folding chair inside. His gut tightened, though, when he noticed her raccoon eyes. Had she been crying?

Ignoring the fact that her puffy red eyes disturbed him, he glanced at her cart, a smile gripping him at the sight of the granny panties, junk food, toilet paper, and feminine supplies. At the coffee shop, she had flirted with him so he would keep her secret. He'd use the same tactic on her now to get what he wanted—the real story on Abby Jensen. "I didn't expect to see you again so soon," he murmured.

"I . . . didn't expect to see you either," she stammered, her voice quavering, as if she thought he'd suggested *she'd* followed *him*. "The traffic . . ."

"Was deadlocked," Hunter finished. "Figured I might as well take advantage of it."

"I know. I figured I might as well stock up, too." She closed her eyes and grimaced. "I really need to go."

He couldn't let her run off yet. Especially not when he heard the emotion thickening her voice. "Nice save outside with the baby."

She blushed. "I . . . it just sort of happened."

"Really."

"I couldn't very well leave her." She shrugged. "Anyone would have done the same thing."

"I doubt that, Abby." Still, he remembered the interview and the fact that he'd missed out on an exclusive. He'd been sitting there first and could have gotten the scoop. But he was undercover, searching for a bigger story, he reminded himself, and he had to work Abby to get it. Even if she did look sad and weary, as if she needed holding instead of tearing apart.

Where had that thought come from?

He glanced at her cart again, determined to replace that sadness with a smile. "A big night planned, huh?"

That familiar blush added a much-needed splash of color back to her pale cheeks. "My husband's out of town, remember?" She gestured toward his. "How about you? Planning a getaway?"

He chuckled. "Thought I might take my daughter camping."

Her face softened. "You have a little girl?"

Why would it matter to her? "Yeah. She's five. Name's Lizzie."

"Ahh," she said in a soft voice that sounded almost envious. "I bet she's adorable."

Pride swelled his chest, along with the pain of not being with her enough. "She is. She, uh, she lives with her mother." *Because you gave my wife the idea of leaving me.*

"But you do see her regularly?"

"As much as I can." He had to change the subject. He was trying to find out about her life, not reveal his own private one. And talking about Lizzie brought all his vulnerabilities to the surface. Made him feel raw. Exposed.

Besides, the concern in her voice made him question his motives—something he couldn't afford to do. Resorting back to their earlier teasing, he picked up the package of underwear, unable to imagine this sexy woman wearing something so ludicrous. "For an aging aunt, I suppose."

"No." A soft laugh escaped her as she snatched the pack and stuffed it back in the cart. "Um, they're mine."

"You recommend these in your book?"

She hesitated. "Not exactly."

"There's a section about panty passions, isn't there?"

She gulped. "You've read my book?"

"Parts." *Just the juicy ones.*

Her nervous gaze darted everywhere but to him.

"I like the thong better, Abby." He traced a finger over the package. "Although I suppose if the right woman were wearing these, I could get passionate about her."

A wispy sigh of arousal escaped her, floating toward him and wrapping around his sex like velvety fingers. But on the heels of that sigh, something akin to fear flashed in her eyes.

"I . . . have to go."

"Sure." He grinned, elated that he'd rattled her, then lowered his voice to a sexy timbre. "Just call me if you need me, Abby."

She flitted a nervous smile his way, then turned and

hurried away. He forced his gaze away from the sway of her shapely hips as she disappeared around the corner beside the full-figured bras. His gaze flickered over the double-D cups, and he reminded himself he was a boob man. And Abby Jensen did not meet his requirements.

Even if she did have a nice ass and beautiful eyes.

And she had softened when he'd mentioned his little girl. . . .

Four hours and too much junk food later, Abby had cried her eyes out. Her house echoed with the sound of lost love and silence. Not the pitter-patter of little feet, as she'd imagined when she'd moved in. The phone trilled, and she settled her wire-rims on her nose, having ditched the contacts hours ago.

Both her sisters piped in on speakerphone. "Congratulations, Abby," Chelsea said. "Everyone's talking about the show. And you delivered a baby at Wal-Mart!"

"You're amazing, Abby," Victoria said.

She opened her mouth to chastise Chelsea about hiring the actor, but her sister didn't give her a chance.

"I heard on the six-o'clock news that the lady named the baby after you," Chelsea said. "And Wal-Mart is giving you a shopping spree, and the girl a free year's supply of diapers!"

"I . . . I didn't watch the news," Abby said. "In fact, I've been avoiding it." But now she could buy all the granny panties and Reese's cups she wanted. Great, she'd *need* granny underwear because her butt would be as wide as the truck she'd delivered the baby in if she kept indulging herself. She pushed the half-eaten bag away.

"I'm proud of you for holding your head up in such a difficult situation," Victoria said. "The interview had to be tough."

"It was horrible. Chelsea, I can't believe you went behind my back and hired that man to play Lenny."

"He was wonderful, wasn't he?" Chelsea chirped, ignoring her barb.

Abby sighed in exasperation. "You didn't tell him anything, did you?"

"Of course not. I'm not as ditzy as you think."

"I didn't mean that—"

"I was only trying to help." Chelsea sounded defensive.

"We're both worried about you," Victoria added.

Now she'd hurt her little sister's feelings. "I'm sorry, Chelsea; it's just that this whole ordeal has thrown me into a tizzy."

"Have you heard anything about Lenny?" Chelsea asked.

"No. As far as I know, the police still haven't found any connection between him and Tony Milano," Victoria said. "Although it's just a matter of time."

She didn't have to remind Abby of that. "I know. But I searched all my things and our files, and I didn't find any evidence of the scams."

Victoria made a disgusted sound. "He probably didn't want to leave a paper trail behind for you or the police to discover."

Chelsea broke into the strained silence that followed. "So tell me what you really thought about Harry, Abby. He's pretty hot, isn't he?"

Abby rolled her eyes and checked her hair for split ends. "I didn't notice."

"You didn't notice," Chelsea shrieked. "How could you *not* notice?"

"He certainly seemed to enjoy his part," Victoria commented.

"Yeah, he played it like a pro," Abby admitted.

"You know, he'd never been to the studio before," Chelsea rattled on, oblivious to Abby's turmoil. "What a break for you. Must have been serendipity."

"Yeah, what a break," Abby whispered.

"We'll be booking him for a lot of parts now."

"Probably." Any part that needed a sexy body and a killer kisser.

"Abby, are you okay?" Victoria asked.

Abby twisted the ends of her hair around her fingers. "That's a loaded question. I'm a marriage therapist who just released a hot, sexy book, but I'm so unsexy I can't hold a husband."

"Lenny's sexual preference is not your fault," Chelsea argued. "A friend of mine from the arts center said her first boyfriend dumped her to become a priest."

"But Lenny dumped me for a man."

"It's the millennium," Chelsea said.

"And not your fault," Victoria added in a firm voice. "You're sexy and beautiful and smart."

Abby knew she was feeling sorry for herself and hated it. "I'm sorry. I'll get over it." But a year ago she had thought she'd been in love. How could she, a trained counselor, have been so wrong? How could she have not known her own husband—pseudohusband—liked men instead of women?

"The best way to get over one guy is to find another," Chelsea offered.

Abby shook her head. "Not interested."

"But Harry—"

"Is an actor whom you paid to pretend to be my husband. End of story." She hung up, grateful the day had finally come to an end. And vastly relieved she never had to see Harry Henderson again. She was too vulnerable, and he was too damn appealing.

She grabbed the new journal she'd bought at Wal-Mart earlier as she headed to the bedroom. Maybe keeping a diary would be a good idea. It was a therapeutic technique she had taught her patients so they could purge themselves of their worries in order to sleep. And if anyone needed to be purged from their worries, she did. Abby settled comfortably on her bed and began to scribble.

Rita Herron

Today marked my new start as single doctor who just discovered marriage of last year a fake.

Book doing great. Selling well. TV interview scheduled.

Interview a disaster. Chelsea showed up in banana costume waving actor/husband at me. Sex god with eyes like Russell Crowe and heavenly kiss. Made fool of self. Dropped panties from sleeve into his hands.

Went from stupid to more stupid. Fantasized about complete stranger today.

Do not believe in aliens but if did, would assume they'd invaded my body.

Must be having a mental breakdown. Possibly early menopause.

Should know by now not to trust men. Only women.

Wish I was gay. Life would be so much easier.

As far as Chelsea could tell, the gay dating scene was just as stressful as the heterosexual version. Only the players and sexual inclinations were different.

Chelsea adjusted her pale blue blouse to reveal her tanned shoulder as she climbed onto the velveteen bar stool and ordered a wine spritzer. Not that she wanted to be picked up or hit on by the women, and she certainly didn't expect to be hit on by any of the men, but even in a gay bar, she had to be in vogue.

The first night, she'd barhopped from Uncle Sam's to High Five to Callie's Cove, but no Lenny. Tonight she'd opted to try the trendy Posh-Ten in Little Five Points. The place was packed, techno music wafting from overhead speakers, martinis and cosmopolitans floating in abundance, and soft, muted shades of pinks and grays a backdrop for the animal-print chairs and red pleather futons.

She sipped her spritzer and watched the players make their moves, the meat market slightly off balance with more men than women. Two Hispanic men danced around each other while a female couple played hip-tango to the music. She thumped her foot up and down, ignoring the inquisitive eye of a drag queen as a bodybuilder-type woman wove her way through the crowd. Tall, with a crew cut and leather pants that hugged her butt, she stalked toward Chelsea.

Chelsea squirmed in her seat. The other night, she'd avoided getting hit on by not making eye contact, but this time it didn't work.

"Hey, cutie."

Chelsea nearly spilled her drink.

"What's wrong? First time?"

"Uh, yeah."

"Don't worry, it gets easier." The woman unfolded a wad of bills from a money clip and ordered a scotch. "Can I get you another?"

"No, no, this is fine." God, she sounded like a blithering idiot. *Remember you're an actress. So act.*

The music heated up along with the dance floor.

"You wanna dance?"

"No, I . . . actually I was looking for someone."

The woman twisted her mouth sideways, muscles flexing in her calves as she propped a black-heeled boot on the stool beside her. "You mean you were waiting on someone?"

"No, nothing like that."

"Good." An appreciative gaze shot down to Chelsea's shoes.

Oh, shit. "I mean I'm looking for a guy."

A look of disdain replaced her smile. "You're in *here* looking for a guy?" Her gaze cut across the room. "I think you got the wrong place, baby."

"No, it's not like that. You see, this guy is gay but he was married to my sister." Now she sounded like a total nutcase.

"You're into swinging both ways then?"

The lesbian looked as if she were considering the possibility. Lord help her.

"No. He did, though. At least he pretended to. Oh, hell,

99

he just came out of the . . . the . . ." What did they call it? This woman had her so rattled she couldn't think. "The garage."

The woman chuckled. "You mean he just came out of the closet."

Chelsea snapped her fingers. "Yes, that's it. Thank you." Whew, she would be fine now. "His name was Lenny Gulliver. Maybe you heard of him?"

"Hmm, Gulliver." The lesbian leaned forward and spoke to the bartender, then lowered herself onto the bar stool beside Chelsea. "Yeah, Gulliver used to hang in here occasionally. But Tank there hasn't seen him in about a month."

So she'd reached another dead end. "Well, thanks so much."

Without realizing it, she'd flopped her hand down on top of the other woman's.

The woman curled her fingers around Chelsea's. Releasing a panicked laugh, Chelsea bolted off the seat and ran, wobbling on her heels toward the exit. Next time, she'd better leave her fuck-me shoes behind. They might have been just a tad too much. . . .

Hunter forced his mind off work and Abigail Jensen as he approached his ex-wife's mansion. A knot tightened in his stomach as he surveyed the opulent surroundings, the stately English Tudor, the immaculate gardens full of exotic roses and other flowers he couldn't begin to name, the backyard swimming pool, the silver Mercedes parked in the driveway.

All things he couldn't give his daughter.

Material things didn't matter, he reminded himself. He and Lizzie had fun together. She liked to camp and pal around with him. Just as he had with his own father when he was young.

The rain had dwindled to a drizzle, and the weatherman reported that the storm had bypassed north Georgia. Figuring his ex-wife and her new hubby had gone out on one of their customary romantic evenings, and Lizzie would stay home with the nanny they kept around the clock, he brushed off his wet, wrinkled clothes, climbed from his Explorer, and headed up the winding driveway.

Just as he neared the front, the door sprang open and Lizzie bounded outside clutching her Angelica doll, his ex and her new husband close behind. They were all dressed to the nines, even his darling little daughter.

"Daddy!" Lizzie yelled. "I didn't know you was comin'."

He shrugged and grabbed her as she flew into his arms. "Hey, pumpkin." She felt like an angel. "I thought I'd surprise you."

"It's not your weekend, Hunter," Shelly said curtly.

Hating to expose Lizzie to another confrontation between them, Hunter bit his lip to keep from saying something he would regret. "I know. I was just in the neighborhood—"

She arched a brow and he grimaced. Ok, so he never came to this neighborhood. "I came on a whim." He settled Lizzie back down, brushing her blond braid back in place. "You obviously have plans."

"Mom and Daryl are takin' me and Angelica shoppin'."

"Really?"

"Yeah, and they're gettin' me a mankin."

"A what?"

"A mankin."

"A manicure," Shelly corrected.

Hunter nodded. Lizzie stuck out her fingernails. "I'm getting pretty pink, Daddy."

"Great." Definitely more of a girl's thing than camping.

"And then we're goin' dancin'."

"To the ballet," Daryl said.

"I wanna dance, too." Lizzie twirled around, letting her fluffy yellow dress billow out, and Hunter laughed.

"We need to go." Shelly gave Hunter a pointed stare. "Please call next time. We do have an agreement, Hunter."

" 'Bye, Daddy."

Hunter blew Lizzie a kiss, his chest aching as he watched his daughter climb into the Mercedes between his ex-wife and his ex-shrink. They quickly drove off, leaving him standing in the driveway of their mansion, the ornate Tudor home standing like a fortress that divided him from his child.

Tomorrow's headline about Abby's heroic delivery in the Wal-Mart parking lot mocked him—she might have played the hero today, but she was not a hero to him. She had given Shelly the first brick to lay in building that wall against him. And he could never forgive her for that.

Chapter Eight

The Art of Seduction

Hunter was so agitated when he left his ex-wife's house that he parked his Explorer at his apartment, typed up his article, and faxed it to the office for the morning edition, then threw a duffel bag on the back of his Harley and rode as far as he could make it into north Georgia. His leather jacket's sleeves flapped in the wind, the sound of the motor and the wheels meeting pavement a welcome retreat from the voice in his head: the voice of Shelly telling him it wasn't his weekend to see his daughter. To call first.

The mountain air smelled like fresh rain and cut grass, not like a vixen named Abby who was trying to tempt him away from a story that could help shape his career—a career he needed to advance so he could have more time with his daughter. Lizzie was the only thing that meant a damn to him.

The minute he'd laid eyes on his six-pound baby girl, those little blond ringlets, those chubby toes and stubby little fingers, he had fallen in love. And he'd traded his freedom for her in seconds.

But now Shelly had the nanny. And Lizzie.

And he had no one.

Even worse, he was losing Lizzie.

Which wasn't fair, since Shelly had been the one to want her freedom. She'd claimed she felt suffocated and needed wide-open spaces. Space enough to spread her wings and fly to greener pastures.

A man with more money.

He had been a fool. The one who'd stayed up with his baby at night and fed and rocked her. The one who'd changed diapers when Shelly had turned up her nose at the smell. The one who'd arranged his work at the paper around his daughter's needs.

Yet he'd gotten screwed in the divorce decree and was still getting screwed.

His throat felt thick as the motorcycle spun in the gravel on a hill, and he choked back his emotions. Realizing it was past midnight and there were no camping grounds nearby, he pulled into a deserted wooded area on top of Red Bud Mountain. Exhausted, he sprawled on the ground and stared at the distant stars, wishing his daughter were with him.

Memories of his own childhood echoed with the rustling of the trees. The times he'd camped with his friends to escape his parents' arguments. The strict military stance his father took with him, demanding perfection, offering little affection.

He'd sworn to be different with Lizzie. To try to make things work with Shelly for his daughter's sake. But he'd failed. Then his wife had found the ritzy shrink.

And he'd known he couldn't force Lizzie to live in a house where nightly fights and bickering had replaced the loving atmosphere with tension.

He couldn't sleep, so he pulled out a flashlight and Abby Jensen's book and began to read the chapter "The Art of

Seduction," hoping to find something he could use against her. A tiny seed of guilt sprouted at his plan, but he quickly buried it. Abby had started the wheels of discontent rolling in his wife's head, feelings of dissatisfaction that had ultimately led to his divorce. If she hadn't, he wouldn't be in the position of having to compete for Lizzie in the first place.

Seduction doesn't start when you begin removing your clothes. It starts with that first look. That first whisper of the other person's name. That hint of longing and desire that you see in your partner's eyes.

Take time to play the seduction game and you'll find yourself in sex heaven.

Whether you are new lovers or have been together many times, slowly disrobing can be as erotic as that first touch. Watch the clothes slide seductively over your partner's body, listen to the friction of the garment against her bare neck, her collarbone, her breasts. Feel the fabric slide across her abdomen, rub against her soft inner thigh. Watch the way her breath hitches as she peels her panties down her legs and the cool air brushes her naked skin for the first time. See the chill bumps cascade up her thigh. . . .

Hunter closed his eyes, the images Abby had described flitting through his mind, his sex stirring to life and swelling like an insatiable beast. The woman peeling her panties off, tossing that silver thong at him, was Abby herself. Her breath filtered out in short little hitches as she trailed one finger over her own swollen sex.

Then she stalked toward him, pushed him down on the ground, freed his aching erection, lowered herself on top of him, and whispered all her dirty little secrets.

Hours later, Hunter woke up in a sweat with Abby's thong tangled in his hands. He cursed himself for a fool for still carrying her unmentionables around. But he couldn't ignore the one question that had repeatedly plagued him through the night.

Just why had Abby reacted so hotly to his kiss if she was happily married?

Nightmares of Abby's disenchanted clients strangling her with a pair of granny panties drove her from bed. Even worse, in her dreams, Harry Henderson had watched, waving her thong and telling her she should have stuck with them, that they were too small to fit around her neck.

But they had fit perfectly around his hands. Those big, masculine, strong, dark hands.

Dammit. Harry should have looked apish, like the bigfoot from the movie. Instead, he'd looked sexy and hot and too interested in that thong.

Luckily, Harry Henderson was history. As was her TV career.

She padded to the kitchen for coffee, grabbed the morning paper from her front porch, then stretched out on her sofa for a morning read. Too bad it wasn't Monday, so she could go to work and listen to someone else's problems and forget about her own.

The front-page story highlighted the news about a tanker that had exploded on 285. The expressway would be closed for repairs to the bridge—a nightmare for traffic. Another advantage to the fact that she often worked at home.

The arts section featured her book, with candid shots of her signing, along with an article her publicist had put together for promotional purposes. Rainey had also gathered quotes from readers, raving about how the book had helped their relationships.

She skimmed the rest of the local section, her breath catching when she spotted an article about Tony Milano. Her head pounded as she read.

Police investigating this late-breaking story report that over two hundred fake marriages were performed by a man

named Tony Milano, who posed as a reverend at the Velvet Cloak Inn. Milano offered a special honeymoon package last June that drew lovers from all across the states.
Every effort is being made to protect the victims' privacy
while informing them of their fraudulent nuptials. Even
worse, Milano conned more than half those participants
into investing in a time-share supposedly being built in east-
ern Tennessee.

The police are working to find Milano, recoup the
money lost, and reimburse the victims. Investigators also
suspect that Milano had a partner. Anyone with information regarding Milano, his location, or his alleged partner, please contact the authorities immediately.

Abby rubbed her forehead. Lenny had tried to talk her
into purchasing a time-share there, but she'd refused to buy
without seeing the property. At least she'd used a little
common sense. He had even tried to seduce her into agree-
ing with promises of a second honeymoon at the resort.

Had Lenny known the deal was fake then? If so, why
would he have pressured her to buy? And if the police were
trying to locate all the victims to notify them, were they
already looking for her?

Worse, could Lenny be the partner the police were
searching for?

She turned the page to look for more details on Milano,
when the beginning of article by that insufferable reporter,
Hunter Stone, caught her eye.

HOW KINKY IS DR. JENSEN'S ADVICE?
What secrets does Dr. Abby Jensen hold?
*After being refused yet another interview, I slipped into
the crowd at Dr. Jensen's recent book signing and was
shocked to see her winking at one of the women in line.
Then on TV, Dr. Jensen tossed her underwear at her
husband.*

Rita Herron

Just how liberal is Dr. Jensen? Does she have any real family values or is she simply acting to sell more books?

Abby gaped. She'd been right not to trust the sleazy journalist. She could just imagine how much worse the piece would have been if she'd granted him an interview. Sure, she wanted to sell books so she could help her family financially, but that dirty, rotten rat of a reporter had implied she was a lesbian! Furious, she balled up the page without even reading the rest of the article and tossed it into the trash. If she ever met that man, she would kill him with her bare hands!

She sank back onto the sofa, trembling with anger and disgust. But if Stone found out about her husband's involvement with Milano, he would kill her career. Knowing him, he'd incriminate her as Milano's accomplice on the front page. Good Lord, her worst fear was coming true— she was turning into her mother.

What was she going to do?

Hunter had to take a leak so badly he thought he would explode, but he needed to find a place without poison ivy. Grimacing at the fact that he'd slept ten feet away from a live plant and did not want a rash on his privates, he scoured the wooded area and finally sauntered back to the dirt road. It was the only safe place.

Seconds later, sweet relief surged through him. Resolved to focus on work today, he climbed on his Harley and drove down the mountain. He hated heights, had a phobia of them, but he fought his demons, keeping the bike as far away from the ledge as possible.

Breakfast at a little mountain café gave him time to read the morning paper. He smiled, proud of his article, and wondered what Abby Jensen's reaction to it had been. But his smile died when he noticed Addleton, the ass kisser, had written a piece on the Milano investigation. Apparently the police had discovered hundreds had been married illegally by the fake minister.

Even more had been scammed.

Hmm. The Velvet Cloak Inn was located in north Georgia, not too far from where he'd spent the night. It wouldn't hurt to check it out while he was here. Even if he didn't get to cover the investigation into the fraud cases, he could spark his editor's interest with some personal stories of the couples who'd been swindled into thinking they'd been married. The victims might offer an idea of where Milano was hiding. And if luck was with him, he might even discover Milano's partner. It would be the perfect way for him to showcase his skills and land himself an assignment as a criminal reporter.

He tossed a few bills onto the table to cover his meal and set off to find the Velvet Cloak Inn. The investigation would also help keep his mind off the seductive powers of Abby Jensen.

At least for a few hours.

Abby had to do something to get her life back to normal.

She would start by putting her place in order. First she moved boxes from room to room, sorting them into those she would unpack right away and those she could store for later. Arranging her clothes took the entire morning. Not that she was a clotheshorse, but she dumped everything that reminded her of Lenny. All the designer, have-sex-with-me, colorful shoes, the tiger-striped bra, the red leather pants.

She should have realized he was gay when he'd chosen those outlandish things for her to wear.

In fact, he'd been more excited about their shopping excursions than about their sexual exploits. She'd thought at the time that he simply liked buying her sexy clothes, the kinds of things she'd never buy for herself. Especially the lingerie.

He'd probably wanted to borrow them for his lover.

Or maybe he'd secretly worn the leather and lace behind her back. Come to think of it, several pairs of her expensive panty hose had been missing lately. And that black garter . . .

Disturbed by the extent of his deception and her own gullibility, she shoved every item Lenny had purchased for her into a large plastic bag and carried it out to the trash can beside the house. Next she organized her office, putting all her files about the book away and setting up her computer. Finally she took a break for lunch, then sorted through her kitchen, organizing the cabinets, then reorganizing them when she realized she'd actually alphabetized her canned goods the way Lenny would have. Still running on adrenaline, she scooted the box containing her tea set collection to the corner hutch and carefully unwrapped each set, wiping the delicate china pieces with a cloth before placing them on display.

Collecting the miniature teapots might seem frivolous and impractical, but they represented happy childhood days of tea parties with her sisters and Gran. A time before her father had begun his criminal career and she and her sisters' faces had been plastered all over the local papers. A time when she had been naive, not scarred by derogatory tabloid headlines and the realization that people could be cruel.

She'd wanted to share tea parties with her own child someday. Had dreamed of doing so right here in this cozy little kitchen.

Except her marriage had been a hoax.

Her hand went to her flat belly and she remembered the one false scare she'd had right after she'd married Lenny. She supposed it was a blessing she hadn't been pregnant. How would she have explained to a baby that his father was a liar and a crook?

And how would she ever trust a man again? Or give one her heart?

Tears threatened and she blinked them away, adjusting her glasses and grimacing at the sound of the doorbell.

Praying it was one of her sisters and not a nosy reporter, she checked the front-door peephole before she opened it. Shock bolted through her when she found her uncle Wilbur bouncing up and down on the balls of his feet, his chunky face sweating profusely in the heat.

He raised his fist to knock again and Abby opened the door.

"Uncle Wilbur, this is a surprise."

"I need a favor."

Abby tightened her fingers around the doorknob as he thrust his burly frame through the door and swiped a hand across his freckled bald head. He seemed agitated. "What is it? Is something wrong with Dad?"

"No, he's holding his own." In the pokey.

Abby nodded. "So what is it?"

His breath wheezed out, the sound of an overweight smoker. "The damn cops think the Barely There Club is a front for some kind of mob activity. I need to borrow some money."

Abby frowned. "Money? For what?"

"They canceled my liquor license temporarily." Another loud wheeze. "Without liquor, the business can't make it. I need cash to keep it afloat until I can get the police off my back. At least a few grand."

Abby chewed her bottom lip. Rumors that Uncle Wilbur's business might not be legitimate had circulated through the family for years. All she needed to top off her mounting disaster of a life was to get involved in something illegal. Hunter Stone and the other reporters would love yet another angle to add to their burgeoning gossip vine. . . .

Hunter had been listening to the owner of the Velvet Cloak Inn wail for an hour.

"They've shut us down; I don't know what we're going to do." Edna, a chubby woman in her forties who reminded Hunter of Ethel on the old sitcom *I Love Lucy*, gestured toward the deserted parking lot. More specifically to the police tape on the ground that had once marked the area as a crime scene. "They think we were in cahoots with that preacher."

"You didn't receive any revenue from the weddings or the time-share investments?"

Edna dabbed a tissue at her puffy raccoon eyes. "No, I told"—her words cracked as she broke for breath—"the police . . . all this."

"But you did advertise the place as a honeymoon hot-spot?"

She nodded, looking even more miserable. "That Mr. Milano, he was so nice . . . and he was . . . man of the . . . cloth." She paused and blew her nose so loud it sounded as if a freight train had careened through the room. "And I thought he just wanted to make couples happy." She lapsed into another long-winded wail that pierced Hunter's ears.

"Do you have a list of the people he married?"

Edna nodded miserably. "I gave it to the police along with a list of all the guests."

"Would you mind giving me copies of both lists?"

Edna frowned, sobs racking her beefy body. "I can't do that. It's against the law to release the guests' names."

As if that were the worst of her problems. "Ma'am, I want to write a human-interest piece on the people who were swindled. You know, do something to help them out."

"I don't know."

"Listen, Ethel—I mean Edna—if the tabloids get ahold of this, they'll destroy these folks." He patted her back to calm her. "And you know they'll get their hands on it. Isn't it better if a legitimate reporter for the AJC gets the information first?"

She seemed to stew over the idea. "You'll stir up enough interest that the people swindled might get their money back?"

Hunter nodded. "I'll do my best."

"And you'll make me look good so I don't have to go to jail?"

He nodded again. This woman was an emotional wreck, but he doubted she'd been involved in anything illegal.

Edna twirled a curly strand of hair around one finger, her fake diamonds glittering. "Well, I suppose it would be okay. It's not like we're still open. And the police are gonna talk to the people anyway."

She reached inside the desk, pulled out a file, and handed it to him. "I'm not sure it's complete," Edna said. "But so far, it's the only one I found."

He glanced at the list. Only about thirty names—had there been more? "I appreciate this, Ethel."

"Oh, and Mr. Stone."

"Yes?"

"When you find him, get my money back for me."

"You invested in the time-shares?"

"Yes." Her chin quivered. "And I'd been saving that money for a boob job."

Hunter glanced down at her already generous chest and hightailed it out the door.

Abby couldn't help her uncle. One Jensen in the clinker was enough. "I don't have that kind of money, Uncle Wilbur."

He coughed, his cheeks billowing out. "I've seen how well your book's doing, sugar. You know this family always helps each other when we need it."

She certainly helped *them*. Abby explained that she hadn't started to receive her royalties yet. "So you see, I won't receive most of my money until the royalty checks arrive." Even then, she wouldn't loan it to him unless she knew his business was legitimate.

He dropped into a chair and folded his hands on his knees, wheezing. Fearing he might have a heart attack, she retrieved a glass of water for him, then quickly shoved it into his hand. The telephone trilled behind her, and Abby glanced at the caller ID box. Her publicist.

Good heavens, what now? "Hello?"

"Abby, this is Rainey. Turn on the news. CNN."

Abby's stomach clenched as she surfed the channels. Rainey's voice had sounded odd. Either something was very good or very, very bad.

She paused on CNN, where the picture showed a reporter standing in front of a downtown church. "Today, members of the community have stood up to voice their opinions about Preacher Don McLure's decision to use Dr. Abby Jensen's book *Under the Covers* in his marriage counseling."

Abby gasped as the camera focused on a group of members who shouted and picketed, thrusting homemade signs into the air.

"It's the best thing for our marriage," a woman boomed.

"It's blasphemy," another shouted.

"It showed me how to love my woman," a fortyish man said with a grin.

"Pornography," a heavyset woman yelled.

"As you can see, this book has raised quite a stir," the CNN reporter continued. "Members here are divided, some insisting the book was a godsend, others calling it Satan's work."

"Oh, my God." Abby sank onto the sofa, her stomach in her throat.

"No, this is great," Rainey chirped. "Even bad publicity is good." Her light laughter tinkled over the line. "You'd better get ready, Abby. As of tomorrow, you're going to be more famous than ever. I've had a million calls at home today and I have you booked for a celebrity tour. You're going to hit the *New York Times* list by the end of the week."

"No, Rainey, I can't—"

"Shh, now, don't argue. And bring that charming husband along, too—"

"But Rainey, you know he wasn't"—she lowered her voice at her uncle's watchful eyes—"really Lenny."

"It doesn't matter. You said Lenny's out of the country, and this guy you hired was fabulous. Everyone saw the tape you two did and just loved him."

Hunter barely heard his cell phone jangling over the roar of his motorcycle engine. On the slim chance it might be Lizzie calling to chat or ask to see him, even though it wasn't his weekend to have her, he pulled over to the shoulder of the road and flipped it open.

"Mr. Henderson?"

Thinking the caller had the wrong number, he almost hung up, then remembered his cover.

"Hey, this is Chelsea Jensen," the cheerful voice chirped. "Listen, my sister just called and we need your help again."

He grinned. She'd saved him from inventing a reason to visit the woman. "Really?"

"Yes, Abby's publicist has arranged several TV interviews, and they've requested that her husband come along, so it looks like you have a temporary job if you want it."

Did he? *Hell, yeah.* "You're talking a week or two?"

"Maybe longer. What do you say?"

"I say thank you, Chelsea. You've just made me a happy man." *More than she knew.*

Chelsea laughed. "Oh, and remember, mum's the word. We have to keep this under our hats."

"Right." He struggled not to laugh. "Don't worry, Chelsea. Your secret is safe with me." *Until it hits the newsstand.*

Chapter Nine

Keeping It Up

Abby's doorbell rang again before she could shuffle her uncle Wilbur out the door. Unfortunately she hadn't been able to convince Rainey that she couldn't continue this pretense of marriage. Her uncle had helped himself to the liquor cabinet while she'd phoned Chelsea. Chelsea had been ecstatic about hiring Harry Henderson on a more permanent basis.

How the hell had things spiraled so far out of control so quickly?

Her head was spinning as if someone had punched her number into the speed-dial modem to insanity.

The doorbell dinged again. Abby prayed the cabdriver she'd phoned for her uncle was on the other side, but when she looked through the peephole, her stomach shot to her throat. Her beloved Granny Pearl stood on the doorstep in a pair of Levi's and a handmade T-shirt that read *Red Hot Mama*, her tiny mouth pursed, gray hair escaping her pearl clip, eyes flashing like cat eyes.

If Abby guessed correctly, Granny was as spittin' mad as a rattlesnake.

Suddenly a commotion sprang out, and Abby silently groaned. Her grandmother had obviously brought reinforcements. A dozen blue-haired ladies hobbled up the front walk, all tittering and chattering, waving old-fashioned hankies and hand-painted canes, shaking bony fingers, and whispering in hushed voices.

"Jesus Christ," Uncle Wilbur muttered. "Is there a back door?"

"You don't want to see Gran?" Abby asked.

Uncle Wilbur coughed into his hand. "Nah. I owe her a little money."

"Go out through the kitchen." Abby pointed over her shoulder. "But you're not driving. I called a cab."

Uncle Wilbur waved, tugging at his pants, which had slipped below his bulging belly, and strode to her kitchen. "I'll wait on the curb."

Seconds later, Abby flung open the door and Granny Pearl pushed her way inside, her cohorts leaning on canes, rolling in wheelchairs, and clacking teeth as they filled her den.

"I have a bone to pick with you, child," Granny Pearl said in a no-nonsense voice.

Abby braced herself for a good old-fashioned dressing down, hating the fact that she had disappointed her grandmother. After all, Granny Pearl had been the one stabilizing factor in her young life.

Hunter checked his messages when he returned home, hoping Lizzie might have called, but the answering machine light stared back like a neon sign, not blinking, signaling he had no messages. Shaking off his disappointment, he considered trading his motorcycle for his SUV, but decided the bike would be the perfect cover for an actor. He didn't plan to waste time; he'd visit Abby Jensen at her house and confirm their schedule. And maybe get a sneak peek into her home, her life, and her secrets.

Several minutes later, he parked on the curb down from Abby's small house, once again baffled by the traditional nature of the Williamsburg-style ranch. Leaving his Harley in the shadows of a cluster of maple trees, he crossed the sidewalk, curious at the church van parked in her drive. A quick glance in her front window explained the vehicle. A group of little old ladies were gathered in the front room. Abby Jensen really needed to be more safety conscious and get some damn curtains. Didn't she realize any fool could see everything that was going on in her house through the naked window?

He chewed the inside of his cheek and watched as she adjusted oval wire-rimmed glasses, then peered down at her rapt audience of blue-haired ladies. Each one had a copy of Abby's book in hand or sticking out of her suitcase-sized purse. What was going on? Surely Abby wasn't given sex lessons to these sweet little old ladies.

"I'm sorry, Granny—"

"You should be sorry, Abigail Eunice Jensen."

Abby winced at the use of her middle name. Eunice belonged to her great-grandmother and she should be proud of it, but . . .

Abby's grandmother whipped out a copy of *Under the Covers*, bringing Abby's thoughts to an abrupt halt. "There's not enough in here about seniors and sex. I mean, it's a wonderful book, dear, but women our age need real advice on how to help our men keep it up!"

"That's right," a spirited lady her grandmother had introduced as Doris Day—named after the famous star—seconded the sentiment.

"I tried those scented oils but they don't help," another woman admitted as she leaned on her walker. "Wally gets too danged relaxed and falls asleep on me every time."

Merline, a woman wearing a bright purple housedress,

pushed at her thinning white hair. "And Harold likes to do it in the shower, but I'm afraid he'll fall and break a hip. He had one of those bone-density tests, you know, and it wasn't good."

"Do you have tips on how to pick up a man?" a lady named Sylvia asked. "The pew at church is completely filled with widow women." She gestured toward her wheelchair. "Now my arthritis is so bad and I can't dance much, I just can't compete with some of the younger women on the prowl."

Abby took her grandmother's hand. "You mean you came here for advice?"

"Why, mercy, yes, honey; what did you think we came for?" Granny Pearl's eyes twinkled.

"I . . . I thought you might be upset about the publicity. . . ."

"The only thing I'm upset about," Granny Pearl said with a cheeky grin, "is that I had to wait till the book was on the market to read it." She wagged a gnarled finger at Abby. "Next time I want an advance copy. Family should have some privileges, you know." She turned to her friends. "After all, I taught this girl everything she knows. Well, *almost* everything."

The other women tittered.

"And if you want to do a special chapter for seniors," Gran said, "we'd certainly appreciate it."

The others muttered an amen, gray heads bobbing in unison.

"Gran, does Grandpa know you're here?"

Her granny laughed and flapped a hand over her chest dramatically. "Heavens, no, we told the men it was our bingo night." Granny looped her arm through Abby's. "Now, as much as I love your granddaddy Herbert, after sixty years of being with the same man, things are gettin' . . . well, I hate it admit it, but they're sort of *stale*."

This she did not need to hear.

But she loved her grandmother, and the women were

dead serious, so Abby quickly prepared a round of tea laced with brandy for all of them and offered the women her best advice.

As they filed out two hours later, giggling about stopping by one of the sex-toy shops in Buckhead, she murmured a silent prayer that the women's partners were up to the wild romps the ladies had planned.

And that none of them had to call the ER before their escapades ended.

Thank God her sisters were behaving themselves now; in fact they were the only stable ones in the family.

"I cannot believe I let you convince me to come to this gay bar." Victoria glared at Chelsea as they entered Pete's Prism, a trendy club decorated in the color palette of the rainbow. Loud music assaulted her, along with the scent of cigarette smoke, liquor, and exotic fragrances.

"I told you what happened last time," Chelsea said in a hiss. "Do you want me fending off advances from women bodybuilders and wrestlers?"

"I have a feeling you can handle yourself, sis."

Chelsea glanced at her as she hopped onto a feathery bar stool, her glitter and sequins catching in the flicker of the strobe light, nearly blinding Victoria. "Thank you, Victoria."

Victoria grabbed a napkin, wiped the bar stool, then pulled herself on top, wincing at the squeal of Chelsea's borrowed pleather pants as they shifted to hug her legs while she sat down. Caged dancers moved obscenely, their buffed bodies revealing more skin than Victoria had seen since she'd been on the swim team her freshman year in high school.

"Ladies, what'll you have?" The bartender, a slender guy in his twenties with a goatee, propped his elbows on the bar and grinned as if he knew they were fakes. At least Victoria hoped he knew they were fakes.

"Bottled water," Victoria said.

Chelsea frowned at her as if she were hopeless. "Two cosmopolitans."

"But, Chelsea—"

"We're traveling by taxi. Relax. You might have fun."

Victoria's gaze scanned the wall-to-wall people plastered against one another, gyrating in various contortions as they danced. "I seriously doubt it."

Chelsea handed her the drink and she sipped, begrudgingly admitting it was tasty. Strong but tasty. Chelsea angled her stool to imply that she and Victoria were a couple and Victoria nearly choked. "My boss would die if he saw me here."

Chelsea winked. "You could tell him you're working a case."

"This is not how I work."

"But technically you could be, since you're looking for a criminal."

Victoria sighed. "True."

A handsome black man wearing a purple silk jacket and a sharp black hat inched his way onto the stool beside Chelsea and gave her the eye. "Hey, haven't seen you ladies in here before."

Victoria panicked. "We—"

"We're new," Chelsea said, kicking Victoria on the heel.

"You are some fine specimen, girl." He raked his gaze over Chelsea from head to toe, then slid a card from his jacket pocket. "You ever do any strippin'?"

Victoria coughed into her drink, and her sister glared at her.

"No, but I'm an actress."

The man winked. "Well, well. I should have known." He flagged the bartender and indicated Chelsea's drink. "Make the next round on me."

"That's not necessary," Chelsea said. "But thank you."

He nodded. "You decide you want to dance, check out the Blackhorse Club on Tenth. Tell the manager Horace sent you." He winked. "Pays good, sweetheart. Especially for someone with your talents."

Victoria nudged her, daring the man to challenge her. "We really should go."

The man laughed and wove through the crowd. Chelsea narrowed her eyes at Victoria. "What in the hell is wrong with you?"

"He wanted you to work as a stripper," Victoria said in a hiss. "Or worse. I bet he was a pimp."

"You're overreacting," Chelsea said, blowing it off. "Now, let's remember the reason we came." She tossed a killer smile at the bartender. "Have you seen a man named Lenny Gulliver hanging out in here?"

"Sure." The bartender poured two glasses of Chardonnay while he talked. "Used to come in here all the time. Word is, he and this guy Johnny used to spend a lot of time in the apartment out back. Johnny does the books for the club, so he gets his apartment rent-free."

"Really?" Chelsea sipped her drink. "Does that guy Johnny still live there?"

"Sure. Might be home now, but I doubt it."

Chelsea thanked the man, finished her drink, then leaned over and whispered, "Let's go check it out."

Victoria pushed her drink away. A beefy woman in all black had been eyeing her. "Sure, anything to escape this place."

They paid the bartender and slipped out, then circled around to the rear of the building and found the apartment. The wooden structure looked dark, the curtains shielding the inside. Chelsea reached up and knocked. No one answered, so she knocked again, to no avail. She pointed to the open window. The inside was dark, a musty odor floating out.

Chelsea grinned. "Let's go in and see if we find something that might lead to Lenny."

"Are you crazy? Last I looked, breaking and entering was illegal."

"Where is your sense of adventure?" Chelsea pointed to the opening. "Besides, we're not *breaking* anything."

"Except the law," Victoria muttered as Chelsea crawled headfirst through the window, her bare legs dangling out, her spiked shoes clinking onto the ground. She scooted on her belly, kicking to move forward. "Damn, I'm stuck."

"What?" A siren wailed in the distance.

"I'm stuck. Shove the window open some more."

Victoria whispered, "Just get out and let's go. I hear a siren."

Chelsea squirmed and kicked but couldn't budge herself. "I can't. Push the window up some more."

The sirens wailed louder, coming closer. A bad premonition engulfed Victoria. "God, Chelsea, I think the police are coming here. We have to go."

Chelsea kicked wildly. "Then hurry!"

Victoria reached up to the window and shoved, but just as she did, police cars screeched into the parking lot and several policemen unloaded, a few slipping to the front entrance, a couple inching around back.

"Oh, God." She must have been premenstrual and insane to have listened to Chelsea. "They're raiding the place."

Chelsea dragged herself forward, her butt sticking up in the air as she tried to lunge inside.

"Don't move, ladies. You're under arrest."

Victoria and Chelsea froze as two police officers in uniform strode toward them, their flashlights shining in Victoria's face and highlighting the only visible part of Chelsea, her backside. Victoria closed her eyes, visions of her entire career going down the drain appearing before her.

A clattering noise in the tiny plot serving as Abby's backyard jerked Hunter's attention to the rear of her house. Was an intruder behind her house?

Hunter paused and listened, but the sound faded. Still,

concerned about a prowler, he slowly crept around the hedges flanking the yard and peered over the bushes. A short, bony man wearing a cheap suit was stooped over, plundering through Abby Jensen's garbage. Hunter frowned and studied the man, surprised when his rubber-gloved hands extracted pair after pair of brightly colored thong underwear from a garbage bag. What the hell was Abby doing throwing away all that lingerie?

A black cat hissed at Hunter's feet, suddenly lunging sharp claws into the skin at his ankle. Hunter yelped. The intruder dropped the bag and pivoted, but Hunter lowered his head below the top of the bushes. He clenched his jaw, and with one hand plucked the cat from his jeans leg.

He'd recognize the shifty man anywhere! Mo Jo Brown, a low-rent PI. Last he'd heard, Brown worked for the mob—more specifically for a guy named Eddy Vinelli.

What the hell was he doing pawing through Abby's garbage?

Abby was just waving good-bye to Granny Pearl and the other ladies as they climbed into the church van when a loud clatter rang out from her backyard. Good grief, was that alley cat prowling in her garbage again?

Not wanting the cat to tear open the bag and strew her garbage everywhere, as it had done last week, she hurried to the back door, flipped on the light, and ran outside.

Her heart thudded as she halted on the porch. A beady-eyed little man with a thick, bulbous nose and bushy eyebrows was on his knees pawing through her garbage, several pairs of the thongs Lenny had given her dangling around his arm like charm bracelets.

What kind of pervert was this guy? Some kind of psycho panty thief?

She backed up slowly, hoping to call 911 before the prowler spotted her, but the porch light flickered and he jerked up like a wild animal caught in a pair of headlights. His dark, eerie gaze met hers.

Abby shivered.

A menacing leer curved his mouth, the light from a cigarette glowing like a pinpoint in the dark. She pressed a fist to her mouth to stifle a scream, gasping when Harry Henderson suddenly stepped from the shadows of the live oak tree, yanked the man by his collar, and dragged him out of the yard.

Abby ran inside, grabbed her cell phone, then sprinted to the window to see what was happening.

Hunter towered over Brown as he dragged him through the bushes, temper hardening his voice. "What are you doing snooping around Abby Jensen's garbage?"

Brown's beady eyes narrowed. Hunter recognized the scent of fear and the act of bravado; the man was scared witless. His thin, reedy body shook like a young sapling in the wind.

"None of your business," Brown said in a hiss.

"I'm making it my business—"

"What are you doing here, Stone?" Brown cut his eyes toward Abby's house. "On a story?"

Figuring he had the intimidation factor on his side, Hunter ignored the PI's question. "I asked you why you were pawing through the lady's garbage. Looking for something in particular?"

"Harry?"

Hunter froze, his hand tightening to a choke hold on Brown's collar. Brown's eyebrows rose as if he'd discovered something important.

Abby suddenly appeared around the corner, her cell phone raised like a weapon. "What's going on?" Her gaze shot from Hunter to Brown.

"I found this creep plundering your trash," Hunter said. "I thought he might be trying to break in."

Abby gestured toward Brown to answer. "I'm a private investigator, ma'am. I'd like to ask you some questions."

"I . . ." Abby's voice cracked. "Then you should have

used the door. Now leave before I call the police."

"But—"

"You heard the lady," Hunter said harshly.

Abby frowned, her eyebrows pinching together. "What are *you* doing here, Harry?"

Brown's eyes flared, and Hunter knew the PI'd noticed Abby didn't use his real name. The sleezy PI opened his mouth, ready to give Hunter away, but Hunter shot him a warning look and loosened his grip. He hated to let the damn man go before squeezing some answers from him, but he had to keep his identity a secret.

Brown seized advantage of the moment, yanked his hand free, and ran down the street like a rooster after a hen. Abby backed toward the porch, still wary.

Despising the fact that he'd frightened her, Hunter reached out, but she shook her head. "What are you doing here, Harry?"

He brushed his hands down his shirt to rid himself of the stench of Brown's hands. "Your sister called me about another interview. I dropped by so we could firm up our schedule, but I heard this creep prowling around back. I didn't want him to bother you."

"Where's your car?"

He gestured down the street toward the Harley. "I'm on my bike."

Relief quickly surged through her, evident in the sharp release of a shaky breath. Without thinking about the consequences, he moved to her, took her in his arms, and offered her comfort.

"Thanks, Harry." Her sweet scent bathed his senses, sending a tingle down his spine. "I hate all these people invading my privacy."

She would hate *him*, too.

"You don't have any idea why a PI would be snooping around, do you?"

She stiffened, then shook her head no. He tightened his

arms around her, knowing her fear was real, but that she was also harboring secrets.

Things just got more curious by the minute.

Why would a PI who worked for the mob be interested in Abby Jensen?

Chapter Ten

The Allure of the Forbidden

"Let's go inside," Hunter whispered.

Trying desperately to ignore his body's response to Abby's curves pressed against him, he forced himself to pull away slightly. She nodded and let him guide her back into her foyer, then into the kitchen. Her satiny curly hair tickled his chin, her sweet fragrance made sweat break out on his brow, and the tender way she'd clutched the front of his shirt brought all his protective male instincts to the surface.

He'd read all about the forbidden fruit in her book and realized that he was experiencing the phenomenon every time he touched her. But the want and desire that surged through him was something he couldn't act on.

And didn't want to.

Did he?

Lying to someone to get a story had become second nature, so much that he barely questioned the ethics of it anymore. But he had been raised in the South, and sleeping with a woman for information was out of the question. Especially when he wanted the information to impugn her character.

No, having sex with Abby Jensen was forbidden. Not that she'd offered . . .

"Harry?"

He closed his eyes and grimaced, absentmindedly stroking her hair. The intoxicating scent of her shampoo mingled with her feminine scent, nearly driving him wild. God, he hated that name. Why hadn't he thought of something better in the first place?

"I'm okay." She gently pushed at his arm. "You can let me go now."

He chuckled and slowly released her, missing the warmth of her body against his. "Sorry. Guess I got carried away with how good you feel."

She backed away completely then, her big eyes cautious. "I'm sorry, I didn't mean to be forward. I'm m-married, remember?"

"Yes, I remember." But *happily* married? He didn't think so. She stumbled over the word as if it pained her. And where was her loving groom?

Perhaps he had hired Brown to dig up some dirt on Abby, evidence of betrayal for a divorce settlement? If so, her ruse with him would only add fuel to the flame.

"I guess that pervert out there upset me."

Hunter folded his arms, his gaze tracking her long, slender fingers as she wove them through the tresses of her tangled hair to smooth out the ends. His hands ached to take over the task. "Do you want me to call the police and report him?"

"No." Her reply came too quickly.

"Are you sure? You could arrest him for trespassing. Or harassment."

"Uh . . . no." She averted her eyes, fidgeting with the teacups on the counter, her hands trembling.

"So you can't think of any reason why a PI would be interested in you?"

"No. None at all." Panic momentarily flashed on her face. "I think I'll make some tea to relax me. Would you like some?"

He shook his head, allowing her a brief reprieve. Her jerky movements alarmed him as she filled a kettle with water, set it on the stove, and flicked on the burner. A bag of Reese's peanut butter cups lay open, spilling onto the counter, the only sign of disorder in the room. The last time he'd looked in her house, it had appeared to have been ransacked. Now the place seemed cozy, homey, as if she'd settled in. The pale yellow kitchen had accents of blue in the plates she'd hung on the wall and the placemats on the table. Thick sturdy blue-and-yellow ceramic mugs hung from a wooden dowel, while dainty teapots in various colors occupied a white shelf over the pine table.

Prim little teapots for a not very prim lady.

Who was running scared.

"My grandmother always played tea party with me and my sisters when we were little," she offered, obviously realizing he'd been studying them. A small shrug lifted her shoulders as if the story embarrassed her. "Those memories were the best part of my childhood."

He did not want to know about her sad childhood, or her grandmother, or the reason she collected teapots. Those personal things distracted him, evoked sympathetic feelings that would muddy the waters of his story. Just like the warmth of her body had evoked primal urges that held the same danger.

"Brown said he wanted to talk to you. Do you think he might know something about your husband?"

"What?" Her voice broke.

"You said you weren't sure where he is. I wondered if Brown does."

"I don't know." Abby shrugged and leaned against the counter. "Maybe he wanted to ask about my underwear."

Her attempt at humor failed.

"I doubt it."

She pulled at a loose thread on the blue pot holder. "Then I don't know what he wanted. But I hope he leaves me alone." The newspaper lay on the counter, and she picked it up, crumbled it into a ball, then stuffed it in the trash. "Just like I wish that awful Hunter Stone who keeps writing derogatory things about me would leave me alone."

Hunter gritted his teeth.

"It doesn't matter what I do; if I don't give them some dirt on me, they'll go through my garbage and invent some."

He flinched. Unfortunately, she was right. And judging from the way she was acting, they weren't going to have to invent anything. They would find plenty of real dirt.

Abby mentally chastised herself for her display of emotion.

And for the erotic thoughts she'd let surface while Harry Henderson had held her. Not only had her body thrummed with desire and her heart pounded with excitement, but she had felt safe.

Something she hadn't felt in a long time. Not in the past few days anyway. Not even when she'd been with Lenny.

She couldn't lean on this man, though.

Hadn't she learned she had to fend for herself when her father went to prison?

Besides, this man was an actor, not a friend. He'd come to her now to play her husband only because her real husband—no, the man she'd thought she'd married—had deserted her. And everyone still believed she was happily married.

Therefore, Harry Henderson was a piece of fruit dangling from the forbidden tree.

She couldn't allow her defenses to slip and reveal the truth about the scandalous turmoil in her life. Not just yet. If she even acted interested in him, he'd think she was an adulteress. And if that Hunter Stone got so much as a hint of such a rumor . . . She shuddered at the thought.

She'd devoted a full chapter to the allure of the forbidden fruit, but she'd never experienced the powerful and almost hypnotic draw of it before. Because Abigail Jensen had been the good girl who always played by the rules and minded her manners. The sister and daughter who'd taken care of everyone else.

At least she used to be.

But temptation had never rolled in with dark, mesmerizing eyes, broad shoulders, and a macho attitude, acting like a real-life hero—until now, until Harry.

Still, she had to guard her secrets until Lenny resurfaced. Then she could end the lies. A shiver rippled through her, reminding her of how violated she'd felt when she'd seen that PI snooping through her garbage, her underwear wrapped around his hands.

"Cold?"

She started, then frowned.

"You shivered."

He was watching her, his blue eyes hooded, his powerful presence as unsettling sexually as it had been comforting a few minutes earlier.

"Residual shock waves, I suppose."

"Tell me what I can do to help."

Hold me. Touch me. Make the pain go away.

She closed her eyes and inhaled his musky scent. Leather. Sex. Manly scents that pulled at her womb.

He gently removed her glasses and laid them on the counter. "Tell me so I can help, Abby."

Abby froze as reality intervened. Her book. The PI. Lenny.

Harry.

He was an actor playing a part, and she was a fool falling into his fickle hands.

She opened her eyes and saw the sultry challenge in his. Her stomach knotted. How would a woman ever know the truth about a man who acted for a living? How would she recognize real desire from a one-man show? He probably seduced women all day long and wrote home to his mama about it.

And she had worked too long and hard to earn her reputation to allow herself to be fooled by another man.

Especially one she was paying to pretend to be her husband.

"The only thing you can do for me is to play Lenny." She forced a coolness to her voice that she didn't feel. "And keep silent about the act until he can come home."

Hunter had played cards too many times in his life not to know when he'd lost a hand. He folded gracefully, though heat thrummed through his own body like a brushfire out of control. "All right. I'll do my job." He lowered his hand, brushing her hip and thigh with the barest of touches before he jammed it in his pocket. The fact that she looked all sexy in a pair of white shorts and that slinky tank top didn't help. Her breasts might not be large, but they certainly had felt heavenly against him. "But if you need to talk sometime, I'll be glad to listen."

A slow smile played along the seam of her lips. "I thought I was the therapist."

He willed his body in check, but inhaled and nuzzled his cheek against her hair. "I wasn't offering therapy, sweetheart."

Her smile faded, the tension between them palpable. "Then I can't accept anything."

Regret laced her voice. Had her husband hurt her so badly? "So when do we start?"

The teakettle whistled, and she jumped. "Excuse me?"

"When do we make our next appearance?"

She removed the kettle and set it on the stove.

"I'm still trying to convince my publicist to call off the tour." Her eyes flickered away from him. "If she won't bend, we start this week." She removed a tea bag from the cabinet. No exotic flavor, just Earl Grey. "She and I need to iron out the details of the schedule. I want to make sure I still have time to see a few of my patients. Just give me your number, and I'll fax you the itinerary."

He hesitated, but scribbled his number on a pad. "Is there anything I should know before we go on air?"

She frowned. "What do you mean.?"

"Details on how we met. Our relationship." He studied her. "Things that might come up in an interview."

She arched a brow.

"I wouldn't want to screw up in front of the camera."

She hesitated, her shoulders stiffening as if she might run any second. "I guess you're right."

He noticed a bottle of wine on the counter and gestured toward it. "Maybe we can have a drink while we talk. You seem awfully tense."

"I guess it might relax me." The tea forgotten, she removed two wineglasses from the tray on her counter, and he followed her into the den. *So far, so good.*

By the end of the night, maybe she would reveal the trouble surrounding her husband. And why she didn't want anyone to know he was missing.

Abby played a soft jazz CD in the background, hoping the music would calm her raging nerves and drown out the quaver of her voice as she described the beginning of her relationship with Lenny. The first part, the truth poured out easily, although it hurt to think how he'd deceived her.

"Lenny and I actually met in Chattanooga," she said softly. "I visited the psychiatric hospital there to speak. Afterward, I went sight-seeing at the Chattanooga Choo-choo. . . ." She hesitated and he nodded encouragement.

"It's nice. I've been there."

She smiled, remembering her first encounter with Lenny. "The weather was bad that day. Storm clouds opened up about the time I arrived and I got drenched. But I'd already spoken at the college, so I didn't care. It felt good to be in the mountains and out of the office for a day."

He smiled as if he could relate.

"I was walking along the train when I noticed this man taking pictures of me."

"Really?"

"Yes." Heat crept up her neck. "He told me he had his own photography business, that he entered his work in shows, and suggested I'd make a good subject."

"You didn't think it was a line?"

She laughed. "Actually I did at first. But since we were in a public place and all he suggested was a few poses in front of the train station, I didn't see any harm."

What a fool. She'd been so flattered.

"Did you pose for him later, too?"

Abby's fingers tightened around her glass. She'd never told anyone about her honeymoon. "Why do you ask?"

"He was a photographer, seems natural. Especially since you were married."

Abby didn't intend to discuss her private secrets. "I think you know enough to play the part, Harry."

He sipped his wine, his gaze never leaving her, as if he knew he'd breached the line, but he would continue to push until he severed it. "No, Abby," he said softly. "I don't know anything yet. How long did you date before you married?"

Not long enough. "About three months."

"Where did he propose?"

She envisioned the day in her mind as if it were yesterday, only now she heard the falseness in his words. "He rented a boat on Lake Lanier and we took a midnight ride."

"Romantic guy."

She bit her lip. "Yes, he seemed to be." Only it had all been an act.

"Did we—I mean, did you get married in a church?"

She nodded, pain knifing through her.

"Did your families attend?"

"We sort of eloped." She'd missed her sisters and Granny

135

Pearl that day. But Lenny had been in such a rush they hadn't had time to plan things properly. Now she understood his reasons.

"How about the honeymoon?"

"I'm not telling you the details of my honeymoon, Harry."

"Did you take a cruise? Fly to Europe? Go for a beach getaway?"

She traced a finger around the stem of her glass. "We rented a cottage in the mountains. It was ... very secluded." And a flop of a night. Literally.

Anger warred with mortification. Any normal, sane woman would have recognized they had a problem then. But no, she'd been understanding. She had even tried to smooth over the awkward moment and make him feel better.

"I see." His husky voice wrapped around her again, intense.

"I suppose we made love before the wedding." He chuckled. "I mean you and your husband made love before the wedding."

A soft gasp escaped Abby. "I don't think anyone will ask us that."

"Your book is all about sex. People will expect you to be open and honest."

Honest? No, they really didn't want to hear the truth. "But people won't ask that."

"They *will* ask, Abby. You need to be prepared."

She stood, poured them both another glass of wine, and paced across the room. "That doesn't mean I have to answer them."

"So you want me to ad lib?"

Abby nodded. "Yes, that's fine."

"Great." He set down his drink, closed the distance between them, and brushed a kiss across her cheek. "Then I'll tell them we had the hottest, rawest, wildest sex two people could have.

"Because if *we* did, Abby," he continued in a low voice, causing a thousand delicious sensations to ripple through her as he caressed her cheek with blunt fingers, "that's exactly how it would be."

Chapter Eleven

The Flirting Game

The minute Hunter murmured the sentiment, he regretted it. Abby's eyes flickered with unease, and something else that shook him to the core—desire.

For a brief second, she'd thought about what he'd said and it had turned her on.

Damn, he did not want to be attracted to this woman. And he sure as hell didn't want to get involved with her.

Except to get his story.

Why didn't she put those little glasses back on and throw him out the door?

"You're very seductive, Harry. You have the voice of a lover," Abby said in a measured tone. Her reluctance made him want to reach out and reassure her. Made him want to cross the line he'd drawn for himself. "But let's keep our relationship professional."

Exactly what he wanted. Didn't he? "Sure. I was simply practicing my part."

"Oh." Embarrassment tinged her voice. "I . . . Of course."

Now he felt like a heel.

"It's all right to flirt, Abby. Even if you are married."

"No, it's not." That haunted look returned to her eyes. "I took—take my vows seriously."

He arched a brow, his instincts roaring at her slip of the tongue.

Releasing a troubled sigh, she dropped her head forward and rubbed at her neck, her soft breath filling the darkness. Her hair fell across her face in a seductive curtain. The moonlight from the window outlined the delicate column of her neck, the shadows of fatigue evident in her posture. "I'm really tired. Maybe you should go."

He nodded, his throat tight. "You sure you're okay alone? You're not anxious about that PI coming back?"

Her voice was quiet when she spoke. "Do you think he will?"

"Probably not tonight." Brown wouldn't give up, though. He would show up again; Hunter was sure of it. "I could stay here, if you'd feel better. On your sofa, I mean."

A sharp little laugh escaped her. "No, thanks, Harry. I'm a big girl. I can take care of myself."

Only she didn't know what she was up against: Mo Jo Brown.

And him.

And the other masses of reporters who would dog her once they sensed her marriage had gone awry. It seemed obvious, now that he thought about it. Pictures of her sisters sat on a small sofa table, as well as a photo of an older lady whom he guessed to be her grandmother. But there were no pictures of her husband anywhere. No wedding photo on the wall. No picture of the boat where he'd proposed, or the cottage they'd rented in the mountains for their honeymoon. No young lovers embraced.

His hand brushed his pocket where he kept his wallet and the photo of Lizzie.

She gestured toward the foyer. "I'll fax you the schedule and see you later in the week."

Hunter relented and walked to the door. "Right. Abby, can you tell me one more thing?"

She hesitated, then slowly met his gaze. "What?"

"Why do you hate reporters so much?"

A soft sigh escaped her; then she hugged her arms around her middle as if to protect herself. "It goes back a long way, Harry. Back to when my dad got arrested years ago. I was only a kid. The newspapers and tabloids were filled with humiliating pictures of my whole family."

He tucked a strand of hair behind her ear. "We all have ghosts in our closets."

"And now the reporters and this PI are trying to drag mine out. For the longest time after those photos were printed, Chelsea couldn't sleep. And Victoria . . ." A dark sadness lined her face. "She wouldn't let anyone, including relatives, take her picture, not even at Christmas. She became withdrawn, while Chelsea acted out all the time. Eventually the school counselor stepped in to help."

"I'm sorry, Abby." Hunter's heart clenched. What would he do if someone had hurt his little girl like that?

But it wasn't the reporters' fault, he reasoned. Abby's father's had broken the law and brought the publicity on the family. The reporters had simply been doing their job, reporting the news. . . .

Still, as he said good-bye a heaviness weighed on him. Couldn't they have reported the news without exposing the children to such painful humiliation?

Heat blasted him as he headed to his bike, the dry air nearly suffocating. But he threw on his helmet and headed toward Mo Jo Brown's office. Even though it was Sunday night, he had a feeling the creep would be there. Abby's troubled face floated in his mind. She had focused on her sisters and how much the ordeal had affected them, but she hadn't mentioned her own reaction. Because she'd taken care of them, he realized.

Even though she'd been hurting herself.

* * *

Abby shivered after Harry left, silently chastising herself for being so caught up in listening to his seductive voice that she'd poured out her heart.

She wouldn't let it happen again.

He was an actor playing a part, and he played his role well. End of story.

She'd suffer through a few interviews with him, pay him off, then end this whole charade, and her life would return to normal.

No more playing the flirting game.

It was too dangerous. Her heart hadn't recovered from being broken by Lenny.

She shouldn't have shared the past with him, but . . . well, she was just too tired to hold everything inside. She felt like a kettle on a hot flame, bursting to release some steam.

She made a pot of tea and settled at her desk. Granny Pearl's comments about more advice for seniors needled her, and she decided to address the issue with an article entitled "Sex for Seniors."

She jotted down notes, listing common problems elderly couples experienced, everything from physical and emotional issues to the unique challenges a husband and wife who'd been together for fifty-plus years faced. Granny Pearl and Gramps Herbert came to mind. They had served as Abby's inspiration for wedded bliss since she'd been in diapers.

Unlike her own parents.

Her mom, a free spirit of the seventies, had thrived on fortune-telling and horoscopes, and hadn't believed in the institution of marriage, so she and Abby's father had never officially tied the knot, living together for years in a monogamous relationship. But one day her mother had taken a liking to the pesticide man and decided to experience free love. Frankly, Abby chalked her odd behavior up to too many incense-burning evenings. Her father had discovered the affair and tried to exterminate the man with his own can of bug spray, but her mother and the man had escaped in his roach-shaped van.

She could still hear her dad shouting, "I paid you to kill the bugs in this house, not to act like a rat."

Chelsea had been at the tender age of six and had adored their mother, loved playing in her makeup, and had grown up to be a free spirit like her. Victoria had been twelve at the time and had balked both parents by burying her head in a book and becoming antisocial. Abby had clung to Granny Pearl's Southern values and tried to believe that in the chaos of modern times, couples could survive, even thrive within the sacred bounds of matrimony. All they needed was love.

Yeah, right. And then there was Lenny. . . .

And reality.

Now she had no idea if she was right or wrong about her theories. They certainly hadn't worked with the man she'd joined at the altar.

The telephone jangled and she jumped, realizing she hadn't written a single word of the article. Afraid it might be Hunter Stone—or worse, that slimy PI—she checked the caller ID. Granny Pearl. *Hmm.* She'd barely had time to reach Red Bud Mountain, where she lived.

"Gran, hey, what is it?"

"Honey, I got a question."

She sounded so serious. "Sure, whatever I can do to help."

"Lulu wanted to stop at one of those sex-toy shops in Buckhead before we left town."

Abby groaned.

"I picked up one of those vibrator do-hickeys, but it's not working. Herbert and I have tried everything."

Abby dropped her head against the front of her desk. "Did you put batteries in it?"

"Why, mercy sakes, no!" Her grandmother hooted. "Herbert, get those C batteries out of the drawer."

Abby heard a whir in the background and shook her head.

"Thanks, honey, I gotta go," Gran chirped. "Herbert, I believe we're in business now!"

"Stefan, thank you so much for everything you did tonight." Victoria's skin was still crawling with humiliation from the ordeal at the police station as she opened her apartment door. She just prayed her coworkers at the firm didn't get wind of her interlude with the other side of the law.

"No big deal." Suarez leaned one hand on the doorjamb, his erotic scent sending shards of tension up her body.

But it was a big deal.

She entered the front hall, flicked the overhead light on, and lifted a brow to invite him in. A smile curved his mouth.

"You want to tell me what was going on?"

"Not really." A nervous laugh escaped her.

"Victoria, I don't want to push, but it would be nice if you were honest with me."

"I . . ." Could she break Abby's confidence and trust this man? What if she did and he used it against her sister?

He moved toward her, his tall, lean body invading her space. "You never go out, you refuse me dates, you've shown very little interest"—he paused, then lowered his voice—"and you were in a gay bar; I hate to ask this, but does that mean—"

"You think I'm . . . gay?" Laughter bubbled inside her chest, along with relief. But anger trotted on its heels. "Just because a woman doesn't date a lot or sleep around, it doesn't mean she's a lesbian."

"Then you're not gay?"

"No." Not that she should give him an opening.

Relief softened his eyes. "Thank God, I was worried."

A small laugh floated from her. "Maybe I'm just selective."

"Selective I can handle." He reached out as if to touch her, but Victoria panicked and backed away.

"How about some coffee?"

His dark eyes pierced her. "Coffee would be good."

Man, his voice was seductive.

"So, if you and your sister weren't there to pick up women, why were you in that gay bar?"

She fumbled with a coffee filter. "I wish I could tell you, Stefan, but I have to respect my client's privacy."

He nodded, his look of disappointment evident as he watched her measure out the grounds and water and flip on the coffeemaker. "You mean your sister's?"

Her breath caught. Damn, a telltale sign. She'd coaxed clients not to react, yet she'd forgotten how to play the game.

But she liked this man, and she didn't like lying to him when he'd been nothing but nice to her. "This isn't about Chelsea."

"I was referring to Abby."

Damn. "Why would you ask that?" she said, forcing her tone to be neutral.

"Because I know your sister is married to Lenny Gulliver and you were asking about him in the bar."

"What else do you know about Lenny Gulliver?"

The steady drip of the coffee added to the tension brewing between them. "Not much now, but I can check him out if you'd like."

"You would do that for me?"

He closed the distance between them, then brushed his knuckles gently across her cheek, his dark gaze trapping hers. The whisper of his breath bathed her face, his eyes darkening to black. "I'd do just about anything for you."

Victoria sighed and wet her lips. He watched the movement, then released a low groan of desire, lowered his head, and claimed her with a kiss that rocked her to the core.

* * *

Hunter was wrong. Brown wasn't at his office. He hoped the PI hadn't gone back to Abby's. Frustrated, Hunter drove home, but as he walked up the sidewalk he spotted the bony little man perched on his stoop. He should have guessed the weasel would show up.

"Hello, *Harry*."

Hunter flexed his hands, clasping his fingers together and bending them backward until they cracked. Brown rose, his thin lips forming a frown, and followed Hunter inside his apartment.

Hunter ignored the shadow of the man as he shuffled through the mail on the narrow counter that served as his drop box. Nothing important. Just bills. He noticed the light blinking on his answering machine but resisted the urge to listen to his messages with Brown underfoot.

Without asking, he poured two short glasses of bourbon, handed one to Brown, then turned to face him. Brown's eyes narrowed as if he hadn't expected him to be so cordial.

"So who are you working for and what are you after?" Hunter asked, cutting to the chase.

Brown nearly choked on the bourbon. He coughed, then wiped his mouth with the sleeve of his plaid shirt. Hunter grimaced, remembering the man had had his hands in garbage an hour earlier.

"You talk first. Tell me what kind of story you're doing under cover?"

Hunter shrugged. "Why don't you kiss my ass?"

Brown downed his drink in one swallow, a laugh bubbling out as he removed a pair of Abby Jensen's white lace underwear and wound it around his finger. "No, thanks, I prefer a sweet little tush like the doctor's."

Anger tightened Hunter's jaw. "Somehow I don't think you're her type. And you certainly didn't win any points pawing through her garbage."

"You'd be surprised how much you learn about someone from their trash."

Hunter waited, jiggling his glass and watching the amber

liquid swirl around inside. "So what did you learn?"

"Why do you suppose a sex therapist would throw away brand-new lingerie? Some of those things I found still had the tags on them."

Hunter shrugged. "Maybe they didn't fit."

"The thongs are one-size-fits-all."

"Maybe she stopped wearing underwear at all."

Brown laughed. "We could both fantasize about that."

Hunter refused to go there with this man. "Maybe she put them in a bag for the needy, and they got mixed up with the trash."

Brown shook his head. "You don't believe that any more than I do."

Hunter leaned against his counter and studied the PI. "Then you tell me."

"I think she was mad at the person who gave them to her. So mad that she wanted to get rid of them and everything associated with the person."

Hunter's chest felt tight. He knew where this was going. He just didn't know why Brown would care. "So she and the hubby had a little spat? Why would you be interested?"

"Because the person who hired me to check up on her wants to find Abigail Jensen's husband. Do you know where he is?"

"Nope. I was assigned to do a fluff piece about her and her book, that's all."

Brown twisted his mouth in thought, debating whether to believe him.

"Are you working for Vinelli?"

Brown set his glass down and turned toward the door. "You can't connect me with him."

Hunter saw the truth in his eyes. Brown was working for the mob, but he was too afraid to admit it. "Does this Lenny guy owe your boss some money?"

Brown nodded. "A bundle. Do you know where he is?"

"No." Hunter gave him a warning look. "And I don't

believe Abby Jensen does, although I'm looking into it. Now, you stay away from her."

"Only if you let me know when you find him."

Like hell. "Sure. You keep me posted and I'll do the same."

Anxious about the possibility of more interviews and playing wife to Harry Henderson, Abby jotted down her thoughts in her journal.

Have lowered self to despicable demonic behavior. Paid man to act like husband. Worse, have turned into type of woman always despised—fickle female. Husband been gone less than two weeks and had foolish reaction to actor. No more drinking wine with man. Too dangerous.

Must check self for possible early onset of bipolar disorder.

Bad influence on Granny Pearl, who went to Buckhead sex-toy shop with church friends. Gives new meaning to church friendship circle. Wrote article, "Sex for Seniors." Will send to agent tomorrow.

Must take charge and get life back to normal. Will see patients. Will not flirt with strange actor husband. Will not indulge in corrupting sweet grannies. Will talk Rainey out of needing husband for interview.

Must take control of life. Forget Lenny.

Forget Harry Henderson.

Chapter Twelve

Sex in the Suburbs

The next afternoon, Abby dragged herself back into the office after lunch, grateful for the air-conditioning. The summer heat had been oppressive all day, magnifying her dismal mood. Chelsea and Victoria followed her inside, each of them dropping dozens of packages on the floor of Abby's office. When Abby had found out her itinerary for the week, she'd called her sisters in a panic. They had met for lunch to discuss Abby's situation, and Chelsea, who believed any problem could be solved with a new pair of shoes, had insisted they take advantage of a sale at Shoe Caravan.

Of course, shopping had lifted her spirits, but it had also depleted her wallet.

"I can't believe I just bought three pairs of shoes," Abby muttered. "I don't even need gold pumps. What was I thinking?"

"Heck, I bought thirteen pairs." Chelsea stuck out her feet, her toe ring glittering beneath the fluorescent lights.

"But these flip-flops in all the different colors were too cool to pass up. Now I have a pair to match each of my bikinis."

Victoria rolled her eyes. "Just what every girl needs."

"Well, I couldn't very well go to the pool clashing." Chelsea flicked at her acrylic nail. "Or maybe I could. What do you think, Abby?"

"I think you have a shoe fetish."

"Don't they have a rehab program called Shoes Anonymous we can send her to?" Victoria asked, deadpan.

Abby laughed, but Chelsea shrugged off their good-natured teasing.

"What's wrong, Abby?" Victoria asked, Abby's smile turned to a frown as she thumbed through her messages, overwhelmed with her life.

"I'm losing control, and I hate it." Abby hated the desperation she heard in her own voice.

Victoria propped herself on the edge of the desk. "Have you heard from Lenny?"

"No." Abby thumped her pencil down on her calendar, expecting her two o'clock any second. "Rainey has a week-long schedule all set up. Everything from signings to interviews to cutting the ribbon for a new arts center on Piedmont that plans to specialize in erotic shows for African Americans. It's called Punany."

"Punany?"

"Erotic poetry." Abby hesitated. "It's actually very sensuous—"

"I want to go to a punany show," Chelsea said. "Do you think it's true what they say about African-American men's—"

"Don't say it," Victoria warned.

Chelsea adjusted her toe ring. "I was just curious. Don't you ever think about sex, Victoria? And men and their—"

"Yes, but I'm not obsessed with it the way you are. I want a real relationship."

"I'm not obsessed. I just happen to *like* sex. Maybe if you tried loosening up, wore something besides those boring suits—"

"Girls," Abby cut in. "Do we have to argue about this again? I'm having a crisis here and I need some advice for a change."

"Sorry," Chelsea mumbled, looking properly chastised.

Victoria toyed with a pencil on Abby's desk. "Abby, you have to slow things down with all this publicity. I'm afraid this is going to blow up in your face."

As if she hadn't envisioned the scenario a hundred times. "I know. Rainey promised that after this week, she won't schedule anything else. Do you know I found a PI in my backyard going through my garbage last night?"

"Oh, geesh." Victoria muttered an obscenity. "Do you know his name?"

"Mo Jo Brown."

"You met a real PI?" Chelsea asked.

"He was pawing through my trash."

"Sounds like Brown," Victoria said. "He's a real seedy character."

Chelsea's eyes brightened with interest. "What did he want in your garbage?"

"I have no idea."

Victoria buttoned her suit jacket. "Word is that Brown works for this mob guy. I bet Lenny was playing the books and got into him for some cash."

Abby's feet hit the floor with a thud. "Do you think Brown wants me to pay Lenny's debt?"

"I don't know, but watch out." Victoria straightened. "If he bothers you again, sis, let me know and we'll file a restraining order."

"Thanks, Victoria. I knew I could count on you."

A knock broke into their conversation and her sisters grabbed their packages. Abby hugged them both, then pasted on a smile when her two o'clock walked in. Her patient load had definitely picked up the last few weeks.

Maybe listening to these people's problems would make her forget her own.

At least she had a reprieve from Harry Henderson. Her first interview wasn't scheduled until Wednesday. Plenty of time to convince herself the man was not attractive or sexy, but a menace to her sanity.

Wednesday, Hunter drove toward the state fair, filled with excitement over seeing his daughter and dread over having to ride those godawful rides. When Lizzie had called and told him about the day-camp trip and begged him to come, then cried, saying she wouldn't be able to go on the rides without a parent, he had finally agreed.

How could he not have?

It was one thing he could give her that Daryl couldn't buy—his time.

There was only one small problem: Hunter hated heights. And Lizzie was determined to experience the Dragon and some suicide ride called Drop Dead, Fred. The first ride whipped you around until you were so dizzy you couldn't walk; the second carried you straight up, then dropped you into a pool of water about a hundred feet below. His stomach rolled over simply thinking about the fall. Of course, Lizzie had bragged about how much Angelica enjoyed them, so he couldn't very well decline, not that he was trying to impress a doll, but . . . hell, if Angelica liked the rides, he had to go along or she would make fun of him to Lizzie. Not that Angelica really talked to Lizzie except in her imagination. . . . He just didn't need any additional obstacles between himself and his daughter—even a doll.

He exited the freeway, his mind tracking back over the details of the past two days. He'd busted his butt both Monday and Tuesday, scrambling to keep up with the piddly assignments Ralph gave him, researching several victims who had been swindled by Tony Milano, and looking for information on Abby's husband.

So far he'd learned Lenny Gulliver was a pretty boy. He looked and dressed like a model for a men's fashion magazine, had attended photography school in California, and seemed as squeaky clean as a whistle.

But something smelled fishy.

While none of the records he checked had so much as a blemish, when he'd phoned Gulliver's landlord, the one who ran the apartment complex Gulliver had lived in prior to his marriage, the owner claimed Gulliver had rented an apartment but rarely stayed in it. Gulliver had hosted a few wild parties from time to time, an assortment of what the elderly man had called eclectic types present.

"Lots of swingers, not your run-of-the-mill suburban party," the old man had said.

And he obviously didn't mean swing dancing.

Hmm. Had Abby been part of that swinger crowd?

Before he'd met her, he might have said yes. Then again, she had winked at him when she thought he was a woman.

No, he still didn't think she was a swinger. She was too damn sweet.

Sweet—when had he decided she was anything but manipulative?

Would she slip and give something away at the interview tonight?

"You know, Dr. Jensen," Wynona Crawfish said, "I've seen that *Sex and the City* show and the movie *Bridget Jones,* and I want to be more like those women." Wynona pulled at her threadbare T-shirt. "But Leroy says we live in the suburbs and we're not supposed to do that kinky stuff. He says the missionary position has worked for years and why should an old dog try new tricks?"

Abby winced. She'd heard the same complaint before from men in their late forties and fifties. "Is your relationship working for you, Wynona?" Abby asked gently.

"No." Wynona shuffled on worn tennis shoes. "I'm so

bored sometimes I fall asleep, and he doesn't even realize it."

"That bad, huh?"

"I'm telling you, Doc, I might as well be a sack of flour beneath him. He's so routine I can time him down to the second." She pulled her disheveled hair into a ponytail and tied it with a faded ribbon. "First the left breast. Three squeezes and a tweak. Then the right one. Same thing. Then a kiss on the cheek. A grunt. Next he starts lapping at me like a dog with his tongue." She shook her head in disgust. "I thought I'd get used to him drooling but sometimes he gives me a spit bath, and I have to wipe my face on the pillowcase when he's done."

Abby laced her fingers together, trying to squelch the image.

"Last week I closed my eyes and planned my dinner menu for the week while he finished."

"I'm sorry."

"And I read that section about foreplay." Wynona planted short, stubby hands on her plump hips. "Do you know what Leroy thinks is foreplay?"

Abby was almost afraid to ask.

"He mutes the television after the news and turns to me and grunts."

The man was hopeless.

"All I have to do is grunt yes or no back." She threw her hands in the air. "Most of the time I don't think it matters one way or the other to him."

"Actually men peak sexually at an earlier age than women," Abby explained. "Unfortunately while their drive is dwindling, the female is just becoming comfortable with her sexuality and ready to experiment with more exciting positions."

"I certainly need something more exciting than Leroy." She dropped into the chair and sighed. "I might as well have sex by myself."

Abby calmed Wynona, then helped her outline a plan

to wake Leroy up from his sexual slumber. Feeling marginally better, she reminded herself that the pain of Lenny's desertion would ease every day. Soon the publicity of her book would die down and she could simply do her job as she wanted.

And when she saw Harry Henderson tonight, his sexy swagger wouldn't even faze her.

Round and round and round and round . . .

Hunter gripped the metal brace of the sky buckets, trying desperately to keep his head from being jerked off by the ride. His stomach was already doing backflips.

Beside him, Lizzie screamed. "This is so much fun, Daddy! Angelica loves it, too!"

Hunter forced his aching face into a smile and nodded, wincing when Lizzie let loose a bloodcurdling scream. Her laughter followed, the excitement in her eyes measuring a high point on the Richter scale of fun that equaled his distaste for the torture devices. He hadn't liked the rides as a kid and he hated them thirty times more now.

He couldn't admit the truth to Lizzie, though. Not when she'd hugged him fiercely at the end of each ride, her eyes, shining up at him as though he'd hung the moon.

Round and round and round and round . . .

"Wheeeeeeeeee!" Lizzie threw her hands in the air, not bothering to hold on as the bucket slung her into his side. The other kids' yells pierced his consciousness, the dizzying motion blurring his vision.

He was about to lose his lunch right on his own shoes.

He swallowed and prayed for miracles.

Finally, the sinister metal contraption screeched to a stop. Lizzie jumped out, eyes wide, hair standing on ends, and tugged his hand. "Come on, Daddy! Now let's ride Drop Dead, Fred. Hurry before the line gets too long!"

I'm only doing this because I love you. She dragged him along the line, and finally the attendant snapped a set of ropes around his waist, fastening Lizzie in front of him before he could open his mouth. Within a nanosecond, he was being strung up like a side of beef and dropped like the peach in downtown Atlanta on New Year's Eve, heading straight toward the ground at a record-breaking speed of fifty miles an hour. He tightened his grip on Lizzie, forgot he was a grown man, and screamed. The pool of water rushed toward him like quicksand ready to suck him under.

An hour later, after cotton candy and hot dogs, and a ride on something called the Sky Coaster that had turned him upside down and scared the cotton candy out of him, he dropped Lizzie at his ex-wife's house.

"It was fun, Daddy."

Hunter nodded, fighting nausea. He'd hated every minute of the rides. But he'd loved every minute with his little girl. "I'm glad you enjoyed it, pumpkin." He picked her up and nuzzled her neck. "I'll see you this weekend, okay?"

" 'Kay." She planted a sloppy kiss on his cheek, tucking Angelica under her arm to grab his hand. "Where you going now?"

He hesitated, not knowing how to explain his assignment. "I . . . I'm working on an interview."

"With that sex lady?"

He chewed the inside of his cheek. "What do you know about sex, Lizzie?"

"It's when people kiss yucky with their tongues."

His baby shouldn't know all this stuff. She was too young.

The lights flickered on from the top balcony of the house and Shelly opened the French doors to come out. He did not want a confrontation with her. "I'll see you Friday night." He kissed Lizzie's cheek, then watched her go inside, his heart clenching when the big marble door closed behind her.

His stomach still churning, he drove to the TV station to meet Abby Jensen. He grimaced as he glanced into the rearview mirror and saw his pasty white skin. How was he supposed to play her sexy husband when he felt like hell and looked like he'd been run over by a Mack truck?

Maybe he should skip this interview tonight.

No, Abby Jensen was the person who'd put all those crazy ideas in his ex-wife's head in the first place. She had cost him his marriage and his daughter, and he couldn't forget it.

Lizzie's face flashed into his mind, her powdery baby-doll scent lingering on his clothes. Yes, he had to go through with it.

He would do anything to move up at the paper, so he would have more time to spend with Lizzie and to make her proud of him.

Abby studied the television program's set, impressed with the professional staff of *HotAtlanta*, a new cable show that featured locals, highlighting their talents and achievements. The host, an exotic Asian woman named Kay Lin, had sung praises about Abby's book when she'd arrived and had instantly put Abby at ease with her calm demeanor.

Harry Henderson completely shattered her composure, though, when he strode in, all six-feet-three of pure muscle and male attitude.

On second glance, however, his flirty smile wavered, the color had drained from his face, and his fake dark hair was sticking up like spikes. Worse, his mustache hung askew as if he'd slapped it on at the last minute in a drunken stupor.

Aware cameras were everywhere, Abby rushed to him, grabbed his face, and twisted the mustache upright. He stumbled backward, his shoes squeaking as water seeped from the Italian loafers, leaving footprints on the plush gray carpeting. And a strange odor drifted upward. . . .

"Sorry," he murmured. "Guess I was in a rush."

Abby frowned, ignoring the fact that his Tom Selleck looks lit a fire inside her even when he appeared a little worse for wear.

Kay Lin glanced at the soggy carpet, then at Harry, then

ushered him to the green room, while Abby settled into the love seat for the interview. A few minutes later, Harry wobbled back in, still looking shaken, but his cheeks were rosy with makeup.

Soft trumpet music signaled the introduction of the show; then Kay Lin launched onto the set, hitting the highlights of Abby's book like a pro, summarizing some of the basic communication problems Abby had described and the differences between men's and women's thinking.

"Tell us, Dr. Jensen, if you had to choose one piece of advice from your book, the one you feel is most important, what would it be?"

No need to labor over that question. "I would tell people to listen to their lovers."

Harry squeezed her hand, sending shards of awareness through her as he murmured, "Yes, trust and communication is the key."

Abby tensed, but he toyed with her fingers, pulling them into his lap. His palms felt clammy, the only sign of his nerves.

"That's right," Abby said softly, reminding herself he was simply playing his part. "You can't communicate effectively without trust. Whether you're trying to discuss finances, your future, your dreams, or your children, or if you're making love."

"Do you two plan to have children?"

Abby's heart squeezed. "I adore children. Yes, I'd love to have a family someday."

"Kids are the greatest thing in the world." The sincerity in his voice surprised her; then she remembered he had a daughter. Maybe Harry wasn't so irresponsible after all. What had gone wrong with his marriage . . . ?

"It's obvious you two won't be waiting long," Kay Lin said with a laugh. "Now, Dr. Jensen. You have some exercises in your book that you suggest couples do to improve their relationships. Would you and your husband demonstrate one for us?"

The air jammed in Abby's windpipe. Harry's sideways cocky grin rattled her even more. "Of course we'd love to, wouldn't we, sweetheart?" Harry brushed his lips across her fingers. "We want everyone's marriage to be as perfect as ours."

Chapter Thirteen

Listening to Your Lover

A perfect lie. If the audience only knew . . .

"I suppose we could demonstrate some techniques," Abby murmured, shifting restlessly.

"Great. Before we get started, though, I have a couple more questions. Your book has unleashed some controversy," Kay Lin commented. "Most psychologists say people model their behavior and relationships after their parents' relationships. Would you agree?"

"Sometimes, yes," Abby said. "But not always. A percentage of children recognize their parents' problems and search for a different kind of relationship."

"Is that how you turned into a proponent for the traditional family when your own parents never married?"

A slight intake of breath revealed Abby's nerves, but she quickly masked her emotions. "I suppose so, although as therapist I try to avoid self-analysis."

"Would you indulge us, though, for a moment and speak briefly about your own childhood?"

Obviously uncomfortable, Abby laced her hands on her knees. "It's true my parents never married. My mother is a free spirit, and grew up in the seventies, when love and peace and living together had just become popular, so I guess you could say she was asserting her independence. A woman of the times." Abby laughed. "Or maybe a little ahead of the times."

The audience chuckled, playing into her hand like putty. "And your father?"

"My father adored her, but they ultimately had irreconcilable differences." Traces of pain softened her tone.

"On the other hand, I was very close to my grandparents. They've been together for sixty years, so they provided the inspiration for my beliefs about marriage." She paused. "Also, I think when someone has been deprived of the kind of family he or she wants, that deprivation will motivate him to strive to build a good relationship of his own."

Kay Lin nodded. "And what about you, Mr. Jensen? Did you grow up in a stable family?"

"I had two parents, yes, although they didn't always see eye to eye." He remembered his act just in time to clasp Abby's hands in his and place them over his heart. "But Abby and I plan to have a long and happy life together, don't we, sweetheart?"

His gaze met hers and she nodded, but he recognized deep pain simmering below the surface, and emotions plucked at him.

How could he write a story about this woman and hurt her when she actually seemed sincere about her beliefs? She honestly thought she was helping people. Maybe she did help some individuals.

But she had torn his family apart without even meeting all of them. Shelly had thrown Abby's words in his face time and again in the last weeks of their marriage, pointing out how he failed on any number of counts. His mind drifted back over the time they were together, the differences in them, the fact that Shelly had always complained about him, that she had never been happy.

Had Shelly simply been looking for a way out and used Abby as a scapegoat?

"So what would you say is the most important ingredient in keeping a relationship alive? I know you mentioned listening to your partner; are there others?"

Lenny's deceptive face flashed into Abby's mind. "Honesty. Love. And respect." None of which Lenny had had for her.

"Mr. Jensen, how do you feel about your wife's work?"

Harry cleared his throat, his hand twitching inside hers, but his smile oozed with charisma.

He should land a part in a major film after this charade.

"My wife is a masterpiece with words. She really cares about the people she's helping." He lifted her hand to his mouth and kissed her fingers, his lips lingering seductively. "And of course, I'm glad to offer my help in researching any of the exercises she has in mind."

Kay Lin laughed along with the small audience. "On that note, I think it's time to have our demonstration. Dr. Jensen, are you ready?"

No. "Yes."

"Mr. Jensen?"

"I'm looking forward to it."

Challenge filled his voice, his sultry smile only adding to the quiet tension building between them.

"Okay, Dr. Jensen, it's your show."

Abby inhaled a calming breath and tried to imagine she was in her office, conducting normal therapy, leading a needy couple into one of her relaxation exercises.

"When two people first fall in love, each feels a euphoria at the sound of the other person's voice or when they first walk into a room. Physical reactions prove this," Abby began. "The person's heartbeat accelerates, their palms turn sweaty, breathing becomes unsteady. But later,

161

when the newness wears off, especially after years of marriage, those physical responses fade. We all get distracted by daily life." She paused. "Hectic schedules, the stress of our jobs, children, family issues and problems, there are a million things that can interfere with a person's mental state as well as their sexual drive."

A few people in the audience *amen*ed her comment.

"My program and the exercises in the book encourage people to take time to nurture their relationships. To tune in to their partner's needs, to show more affection. A family should set aside time to discuss problems, so they don't linger and fester and follow the couple into the bedroom."

Abby faced Harry and gestured for him to angle his chair toward hers. "First, I encourage a couple to look into each other's eyes and really see the other person. To listen to the feelings and emotions your partner may express through his body gestures, his movements, the expression on his face."

She demonstrated by gazing into Harry's eyes. Hunger and desire sparkled there, along with other emotions she couldn't read. "I encourage them to focus on the positive things about their spouse, to look for the beauty, the inner qualities that first attracted them to their partner."

"So there's no touching yet?" Harry asked.

The audience laughed.

"Not physically, but there's touching with the heart. With the eyes, with the soul. When you tune in to another person's needs and become more giving, the other person automatically does the same." Abby's soft voice quieted the crowd. "Next, I ask each client to tell their partner the things they admire or like. The things they want. The places that crave the other's touch."

"Show us," Kay Lin suggested.

Abby glanced at the host, then back at Harry. He nodded, his mouth twitching into a smile that twisted mischievously at his broad jaw.

"All right. In the beginning, I ask couples to remain

dressed when they do this. But later on I suggest they remove their clothes and do the same exercise with the lights dimmed. Obviously we can't take our clothes off on TV."

A few people in the audience called out, "Why not?" while others chuckled. Harry Henderson had the nerve to wink. As if on cue, the TV crew dimmed the lighting to a soft glow.

"Sometimes I ask couples to sit in the dark with only a single candle lit." She took the actor's hands, her heart pounding at the electricity that zinged through her. Since she didn't know Harry very well, she focused first on her physical responses to him. "I like the sound of your voice when you say my name in the dark, Har—"

He made eyes at her.

"Lenny. And I appreciate the way you stand by me no matter what I ask of you."

His dark eyebrow arched. "Your eyes hypnotize me, Abby. And your voice reminds me of an old blues song, soft and husky, like a kiss in the night."

Abby swallowed. Wow, he was good. "Your hands feel so strong and warm that just touching them sends desire surging through me. And when I look into your eyes, I see love and strength. I see a man I want to be with."

"Can we touch now?" Harry asked, his voice gruff.

The audience laughed again.

"Not yet," she murmured. "Tell me how you want to touch me."

He coughed, an odd look on his face. "My hands itch to caress you, Abby. To thread themselves in your hair." His fingers tightened around hers. The crowd grew still. "To pull the pins from your hair and let it fall around your shoulders. To sift my hands through those long, wild curls." His eyes became hooded. "To tear that shirt off of you and press my lips to the soft skin at your neck. To suckle your—"

"Well, I believe you have the idea," Abby said, abruptly cutting him off.

She turned to the audience, ignoring the heat rising between her and Harry. Releasing the breath she didn't even realize she'd been holding, she gasped when the front clasp of her bra snapped open. *Drat.* Her breasts spilled over the cups inside her shirt. If she moved the wrong way . . .

She pressed her arms tightly by her sides to keep the underwire pads from slipping into her armpits, and smiled tightly at Harry. Damn, the man had her all shaken up. Her nipples were hard as rocks. And he had only been acting.

Hadn't he?

A few minutes later, Hunter gripped the producer's hand and bade him good-bye, willing his body back to normalcy. He'd made a fool out of himself over Abby Jensen.

Granted, everyone thought he was playing a part, but he'd meant every damn word he'd said.

What the hell was happening to him?

Stress over too much work? Over not being with Lizzie enough?

Being attracted to a sexy woman wasn't a crime, he reminded himself. And although at first he'd thought the woman wasn't his type, now he could see he'd been wrong.

Oh, he'd been dead wrong.

Because Abby Jensen was one sexy lady.

She might not be his type for a long-term relationship, but she had definitely awakened his sex drive—a sex drive that had been sleeping since Shelly had divorced him a year ago. And although he normally was a boob man, her ass looked great and tempting.

Arguments warred in his head. Maybe she *was* his type all the way around. She claimed she wanted marriage and a family. The same things he'd wanted since Lizzie came into his life.

But her methods were unorthodox. She had no right to stir up trouble with her book, making women think they weren't happy with their men. And he wouldn't be suckered in by those haunting angelic eyes or that sultry, seductive voice.

Besides, she claimed honesty was one of the three most important factors in keeping a relationship strong while she was lying to everyone, including him.

And she still had a freaking husband!

He was so lost in turmoil, he didn't realize she'd moved up beside him. They walked together through the backstage, past the other sound rooms, and out into the night. Stars glittered from a moonlit sky, a breeze stirred the surrounding trees, and the whisper of her exotic perfume wafted toward him. He tried to focus on the city lights ahead, the beauty of the Atlanta skyline, the buzz of people and traffic.

She turned to him amidst the hum of it all, a cool, detached look in place.

Obviously she hadn't meant what she'd said about wanting to be with him.

"Thanks, Harry. You did a great job."

"You're not such a bad actress yourself." She winced and he realized his bitterness had rung through.

"I don't like lying like this, Harry." She stood awkwardly, her arms pressed to her sides like a tin soldier.

"Why don't you tell me what's going on, Abby? Maybe I can help."

"I . . . I can't."

He steeled himself against the vulnerable look in her eyes. "I guess it's just a job for both of us then. But you want to continue the charade?" He'd given her the opening. He waited with bated breath, hoping she'd tell him the truth.

Not for the story now, but for him.

She didn't comment, simply gnawed on that bottom lip, and tightened her arms as if she thought he might grab her any second. Damn, it was tempting.

The skin on her bottom lip turned red with her bite marks. He found himself wanting to touch it. To kiss away the pain. To hear her husky voice murmur those words she'd whispered during their exercise. Except this time she would 'mean them.

"I have to keep up pretenses right now," she whispered. "Until I find Lenny."

"Right."

He shifted, his shoes still squeaking with water in the silence.

"What happened earlier, Harry? Were you hungover when you came in?"

"Hungover?" Anger splintered through him. Anger that she wouldn't be honest. That she thought he might be irresponsible enough to show up drunk. Anger at the whole situation.

"No, Abby. For your information, I just came from a harrowing day at the fair with my daughter. I rode the Dragon seven times with her and nearly broke my neck on this ride called Drop Dead, Fred." He shuddered, remembering the feeling of being dropped through the air upside down with nothing but that flimsy rope tied around him. "God, I hate heights, and that one dropped me into a pool of water."

Abby suddenly chuckled, and he realized what he'd just admitted. The fact that she'd driven him to confess his phobia only infuriated him more. And now she was driving the knife deeper into his wounded pride by laughing out loud at him.

"Did you tell your little girl about your acting role?"

Right. Like he'd confess that to a five-year-old. "My daughter is too young to know about your book or sex."

Abby's mouth gaped. "You make me sound like a pervert. I'm not suggesting you read my book to her."

"I didn't mean that, but she's only five."

"Well, granted, that's too young for a full explanation, but insinuating that sex is something dirty isn't healthy either."

"I didn't say it was dirty. I just avoid the subject." He

rubbed a hand over his face, and his mustache came off in his hands.

"Don't you want her to grow up to be a normal, healthy, sexual woman?"

"No. Hell, no." Panic seized him at the thought. "I hope she doesn't find out about sex until she's at least forty."

"That's a tad archaic, Harry."

Archaic? "Look, Dr. Jensen, I don't believe in all this hogwash in your book. And if you want to know about archaic, I'll show you. This is archaic." His temper boiling, he dragged her into his arms, lowered his head and claimed her mouth with his, releasing all the pent-up frustration and fire in his body and his loins into the kiss.

Abby struggled not to succumb to the dangerous passion brewing between her and this actor, but his hands yanked her into the vee of his thighs, his corded muscles bulged against her legs, and her knees buckled. Surrendering was not an option. He was plundering at will.

She had never been kissed like this.

Not by a man who couldn't control his desire for her.

The feeling was drastically unsettling and titillating at the same time. He was like a caveman, barbaric and forceful. His hands cupped her face as he drove his lips over hers and ravaged her mouth with his tongue. The rasp of his labored breath ripped another layer of fight from her, and she clung helplessly to him, her nails digging into the strong muscles of his arms. His hands slowly dropped, brushed across her shoulder blades, stroked her arms, cupped her bottom and pulled her closer—so close his sex hardened and throbbed against her own burning heat. Then his hands were everywhere, stroking and rubbing. His lips traced a path down her neck, nipping and suckling until she moaned and leaned into him. Tortured by his mouth, she could only gasp for breath as his hands found her waist and his fingers danced up to her breasts. Then suddenly he pulled away, a perplexed look on his face. "What the hell?"

Laughter followed.

Abby's cheeks burned as she glanced down and saw the pads of her bra floating up around her shoulders.

Chapter Fourteen

Strange Bedfellows

"Maybe you should just give up on the underwear altogether," Hunter murmured.

Abby closed her eyes for a nanosecond, humiliation scorching her face. When she opened them, he could see her struggling for dignity. "You . . . the clasp came undone. And I was going to go to the rest room to fix it before we left, but the producer didn't give us time."

"Uh-huh." He gestured toward the pads. "You don't really need those, Abby."

Her lips pressed into a tight line. "I have to go. Good night, Mr. Henderson."

She suddenly swung loose from him and headed to her car, stuffing the pads back down into the thin white camisole below her jacket. His hands ached to help her with the task.

He sprinted to follow her, but a rustle in the bushes nearby captured his attention and he halted instead. Anger sparked as quickly as his desire had when he'd touched

Abby. He stalked to the shrubbery, reached in, and yanked out Mo Jo Brown.

"What the hell are you doing?"

"My job," Brown said, brushing leaves from his ill-fitting leisure suit.

Hunter noticed the small camera poking from the PI's pocket and grabbed it. Mo Jo fought like a chicken, spindly arms clawing. "You can't take that; it's personal property."

"Right now it's community property." Hunter flipped the back open, removed the film, and pocketed it. "I told you to leave Abby Jensen alone."

"But her old man owes my boss—"

"Tell him to find her husband then, because Abby Jensen is not paying his debts."

Without another word, he turned and strode away, leaving the weasel scrambling after him. Hunter searched for Abby's car, then laughed when he noticed she was tearing across the parking lot in the vehicle, heading straight toward the PI.

Abby didn't see the skinny man until she'd almost run over him.

Dear God. She threw on her brakes, screeched to a stop, and closed her eyes, praying she wouldn't find blood and guts splattered all over her windshield when she opened them. And that the next time she saw herself on the news she wasn't wearing shackles and chains for murdering a man with her car.

Shaking with adrenaline and worry, she slowly peeked through her eyelids and gasped when she recognized the man—the slimy private investigator who'd been snooping through her garbage.

She should have run over him!

Hands clenched, she opened the car door, counted to ten, and glared at him. "If you come near me again, mister, I'm filing a restraining order."

His bony body shook in his oversize clothes. "I need to talk to you about your husband."

"Leave me alone." Her heart still racing, she climbed into her car and took off the other way. But when she glanced in her mirror, she noticed the man watching her. Harry Henderson stalked toward him. As Harry grew nearer, the nosy man's eyes widened and he turned and ran like a jackrabbit.

Hunter held the steering wheel with a white-knuckled grip. He hated the fear he'd seen in Abby's eyes when that weasel Brown had asked about her husband.

He had to find out the truth about the real Lenny Gulliver.

His cell phone chirped before he could make it home to his computer. "Stone here."

"Hey." Ralph Emerson's voice boomed in his ear. "There's some picketers over at the mall bookstore, stirring up more excitement over that Jensen broad's book. Can you cover it? Addleton's got the freakin' flu."

Probably caught a bug kissing all those asses. "I'll be right there." Hunter wheeled the Explorer in the opposite direction. After all, how could he refuse? The story would be a great lead-in for the bigger one he planned to write.

The beginning of the end for Dr. Jensen.

Just what he'd wanted. He'd finally gotten a break. He should be happy.

Then why did he feel so damn rotten?

"I am finished with men," Abby muttered to herself as she drove toward home. "I finally understand how all these women feel who come in to me and complain." She glanced at herself in the rearview mirror and groaned in horror.

She had never looked worse.

She'd been so angry when she'd left that PI she'd clawed her hands through her hair and torn it from its fancy chignon. Her makeup was smeared from the floodwaters that had opened up, and she had dark circles under her eyes.

Feeling lonely and frustrated and dreading going home to her empty house, she swerved into the mall. She had always been levelheaded and thought things through, but her head had been spinning for days, and she couldn't think at all. A haircut and facial would do her wonders.

She climbed from her car and teetered inside the mall. A commotion at one end trapped her momentarily, until she realized people were picketing outside the bookstore.

The last place she wanted to be.

She didn't know what was going on, but there were too many people there. Someone might recognize her. She went back outside and circled around to a different entrance—one on the opposite side of the mall. An hour later she emerged from one of the local salons with a new look—a few layers to her shoulder-length style, and cleansed pores. If only she had been able to cleanse herself of her problems.

Not yet ready to go home, but still afraid of being recognized—the crowd outside the bookstore had brought back memories of her first stressful signing there—Abby scooted into a nearby hat store. The Braves cap didn't exactly match her outfit, but who cared? Smiling ruefully at the fact that she was about to ruin her new do, Abby pulled the hat low on her forehead. Confident that she was suitably incognito she tried to relax, using her cash to purchase another pair of shoes she didn't need—this time hot-pink sandals.

Now she needed a hot-pink outfit to match. Something that didn't look like the conservative Abigail Jensen. But a big sale sign at the pet store caught her eye, and she wandered over to take a peek. She had always wanted a dog when she was little, but her parents had moved around like gypsies, and most of their apartments had not allowed pets.

She had her own house now.

And she had envisioned a small dog there along with a child.

She no longer had a husband to argue with over the matter either. After all, Lenny had wanted a cat.

Pet stores were generally more expensive, she'd heard, than buying an animal from a breeder, and she could always go to the Humane Society. She should wait. An adorable little white Maltese pawed at the glass window in front of her, big eyes pleading with her for a home, and her heart melted.

She would just go in and look.

The puppy angled its tiny face and whimpered. Nine hundred dollars. *Whew*. A lot of money for a little spit of a dog. She roamed down the aisle and looked at the beagles, an adorable cocker puppy, a pudgy boxer, a yelping yellow Lab. But the white, fluffy-eared Maltese was still clinging to the window, its nose pressed to the glass, tongue hanging out, begging to be held.

The puppy would keep her company now she was alone. It would cuddle and sleep with her at night.

"You want to hold it, ma'am?"

Abby nodded and accepted the wiggling bundle into her arms. The puppy licked at her face, wagged its stubby tail, white hair flopping over its eyes. It seemed so small and vulnerable, lost and lonely and desperately in need of a stable home.

Just like she felt.

Puppies made great friends. Playmates. Bedfellows. He would keep her warm at night. Forget men. She didn't need one.

"I'll take it."

Several minutes later, she stood at the cash register with a host of puppy supplies, waiting on the pimple-faced teenage boy to ring up her purchases. He ran her credit card through the machine. Abby stroked the Maltese's furry head, smiling as it nuzzled her palm.

"I'm sorry, ma'am, but this card won't work."

"What?" Abby frowned and examined her Visa. She'd kept it paid off monthly. "I don't understand."

"I tried it twice." He leaned against the counter with an impatient sigh. "Do you have another form of payment?"

"Well . . ." Abby fumbled in her wallet and dug out her American Express.

He slid it through and shook his head.

Nerves twitched in Abby's stomach. How could it be?

Lenny. The dirty scumbag had maxed out her credit cards. She just knew it.

Why hadn't she thought to check the cards and statements earlier?

Because she was a trusting idiot.

"Let me write you a check." Lenny hadn't had access to her personal account. Thank God she hadn't been that stupid.

"Ma'am, we have to have a credit card number with the check." A small shrug lifted his thin shoulders, making the words *Band Babe* wiggle on his shirt.

Groaning, Abby headed to the ATM, vowing to get a check-card this week, but the boy cleared his throat, his nasal voice halting her. "If you take the dog out of here without paying for it, I'll have to call the cops. It's shoplifting, ma'am."

Shoplifting a dog? Mortified, Abby deposited the puppy back in his arms and ran to the ATM machine. She tugged the Braves cap over her head, praying no one recognized her.

Hunter had been headed toward the bookstore when he had seen Abby dart into the pet store. Curious, he'd paused and glanced in the window. Hiding behind a stack of doggie crates, he had seen her credit cards being rejected. Brown had said that Lenny owed his boss money.

Had he depleted Abby's bank accounts as well?

The pieces of the puzzle slipped into place. Missing husband. Missing money.

Sounded like the man she was protecting was a crook.

Sympathy tugged at him as he watched her finally hand over her cash and take the little white cotton ball in her arms.

Abby Jensen was obviously in trouble.

He glanced at the other end of the mall and saw the picket line in front of the bookstore. And he was getting closer to the truth every day. He had to phone Ralph and ask him for a few more days.

This story was going to be bigger than he'd ever imagined.

Practice what you preach.

The old sentiment rang in Abby's ears the entire way home. Well, it tried to. Actually, the puppy's crying rang in her ears, almost obliterating the nagging voice of distress and despair.

She had been had.

Totally, unequivocally had.

By a man she had trusted and loved—a man with whom she had promised to spend the rest of her life.

She had based her book, her advice, her career, her life on her belief in monogamous relationships. And now she wasn't sure what to think. Maybe Harry, Victoria, Chelsea, and her mother were all right: maybe marriage was an outdated institution, hopeless in today's society.

Tears sprang to her eyes, leaked out, and dripped down to her chin. The puppy rested its front paws on her chest and licked at them, then jumped back down and rubbed its butt up against her leg, yipping and squirming, apparently traumatized by its release from a cage the size of a small television.

Something was wrong with this picture.

The precious creature had been imprisoned and apparently preferred its captivity to the freedom she offered.

Leaning sideways, she reached into a bag of Reese's peanut butter cups, nabbed a handful of the miniature treats, and peeled one open, then popped it into her mouth. The puppy chose that moment to leap from her lap into the bag.

Making a madcap attempt to rescue the candy, she jerked up the bag, but the puppy took it as a sign to play and tore at the plastic with sharp teeth. Valiantly trying to keep her eyes and her car on the road, Abby stuffed the package behind her back, but the dog dove for the treats again.

She yelped.

Her scream frightened the Maltese, and it clambered over the seat, scrambling and slipping. A car swerved in front of her, and she steered sideways to avoid hitting it. Her tires hit the curb. She could see the headlines now: *Lady wrecks car fighting with puppy over bag of candy*.

But hadn't she heard that chocolate was bad for dogs? The sharp turn caught the puppy off guard and practically flew it into the back floorboard. By the time she righted the car, the puppy had lapsed into a pitiful whimper.

"I'm sorry, sweetie," Abby crooned. "But I don't think chocolate is good for dogs. And I can't reach you back there."

The puppy yelped and cried while she raced to her house. When she finally reached her drive, she scooped it up and hugged it to her. "I'm sorry, sugar. That was some ride home, huh?"

A few minutes later, she crawled into bed with the puppy beside her. Tomorrow she would have to give him a name. Tonight she was just satisfied the day had ended.

By the time Hunter reached the bookstore, chaos had broken out. Apparently the bookstore had received a limited number of copies of Abby's book and people were fighting over the dwindling stack. Picketers in front of the store ranged from those protesting the fact that the store had no right to limit the sales to one copy per person to a few who wanted the book banned and sold only in adult bookstores. A small group of crystal-toting New Agers traded barbs with a Bible Belt retreat group who thought the book encouraged adultery.

Even Hunter thought that one was a stretch.

Nowhere in Abby's book had she mentioned sex outside of monogamy. But the religious right pitted against the liberal left served as perfect fodder for his article.

Back at home, he outlined the arguments on both sides, then titled the article with the question plaguing him: "*Under the Covers*—Will It Make or Break Your Marriage?"

Feeling slightly ill at ease about the piece, he reminded himself that he was simply reporting the facts. If he didn't write the article, someone else would. Still, shades of guilt riddled him. Maybe he could write the story *and* help Abby. But he had to know the truth first.

He accessed the Internet and tried to hack his way into the police system to find out all he could on Abby's husband, Lenny Gulliver.

Abby rolled over, her body burning with memories of that hot kiss with Harry Henderson. She had reacted like a naive young virgin, moaning and surrendering to his passion while he had simply been putting on a show for the audience.

Some sex shrink she'd turned out to be.

You are not a sex shrink, Abby Jensen. You're a serious-minded marriage therapist who just happens to be a chump when it comes to men.

Still, she was a liar and a fake.

Two things she'd never thought anyone could truthfully call her.

Her morning brightened when she opened her eyes and found her new best friend licking her cheek. She stroked his furry head, and his stumpy tail flapped wildly. But as she moved to snuggle into him, she felt a wet spot. Puppy training had a long way to go.

Groaning, she climbed from bed, threw on a robe, and

Rita Herron

stumbled to the front door. She had just set the puppy down when she spotted the morning paper on her stoop. Determined to give the dog time to romp and do his business, she slumped down on the steps and thumbed through the paper, her pulse leaping when she discovered another article about her.

Written by that insufferable Hunter Stone.

The story described the commotion at the bookstore that she had staunchly avoided the night before. But she sensed Stone's personal distaste for her book underlying the question in the title and his last sentence.

Do people really benefit from Abby Jensen's advice or is she doling out sex advice just to make a buck?

Old memories rose to haunt her. The articles they'd written about her father's arrest when she was little still stung. And her mother's numerous boyfriends had caused quite a stir. She could still hear the children laughing, the neighbors gossiping, the church members pointing.

Reporting hadn't changed over the years at all. The sleazeballs didn't care about the people they wrote about or the lives they destroyed in their quest for a byline. She had a good mind to confront Hunter Stone and tell him so, too.

She scrunched the newspaper in her fist, wrapped her robe around her, and grabbed the puppy. Maybe she would stop by the AJC on her lunch hour. . . .

Chapter Fifteen

Stoking the Fire

She should have bought the puppy a crate to stay in during the day while she was at work, Abby realized. But she hadn't, so today the little butterball was sleeping in a box beside her desk. She couldn't continue this. He'd cried so much she'd had to hold him during her first session. The couple had been distracted, the puppy had peed on her pants, and she had had to endure the next session with a stain and its accompanying smell. She would pick up a crate today at lunch—right after she visited the AJC and talked to that reporter, Stone.

If she had wanted to be featured in the paper, she would have answered his phone request for an interview. Lord only knew the man had pestered the daylights out of her for days. Only he hadn't called lately. *Hmm*. That was odd. Maybe he'd been out of town. Too bad he hadn't stayed there.

Still, refusing his interview didn't give him free rein to fabricate whatever he wanted about her.

She had one more appointment to get through first; then she would be on her way. She ripped open a few bills that had piled up, her stomach plummeting at the charges racked up on both her Visa and American Express accounts. Hotels, restaurants, gifts, charges were scattered across the southeast.

Except for the airline ticket to Brazil.

Damn Lenny. He had flown the coop with her money and left her to clean up the mess. Was he involved with Tony Milano's fraudulent ways? Should she turn this latest information over to the police?

She phoned Victoria immediately to ask her advice, but her sister was in court, so she left a message. Next she phoned the credit card companies and requested a hold on any more charges until she could figure out how to handle her finances.

Her buzzer sounded. "Yes, Janice?"

"Your eleven o'clock canceled. But there's someone else here to see you."

Good heavens, who now?

"She says she's your mother."

Abby dropped her head forward and sighed. She should have known she would show up sometime. "Tell her to come—"

Before she could finish her sentence, her mother breezed in, bringing the scent of gardenias with her, her long, gauzy skirt billowing around her petite frame. A dozen brightly colored beads clinked as she waved, the tie-dyed sleeves of her blouse flapping merrily. "Hey, honey."

"Mom, this is a surprise."

As usual her mother wasted no time. "I'm so happy your book is doing great. I'm proud of you, sweetheart."

Abby shrugged, praying her sisters hadn't filled her mother in on her debacle of a marriage. She was not up for an "I told you marriage is worthless" lecture. Instead, she directed the conversation to a safer topic. "That ad you did and the free pillowcases really boosted sales."

180

Her mother fluttered ringed fingers through her long, frizzy hair. The one thing Abby had inherited—curls. "I'm glad I could help."

Not that Abby had wanted her help.

"I hate to do this, honey, and I know you're busy, but I need your help."

Support for another venture, Abby supposed. The first one, the candle shop, had lasted six months. "What is it now, Mom?"

"Well, there's the neatest little shop in downtown Chattanooga. I want to turn it into a coffee shop, a place for local musicians and singers and poets to hang out."

Probably not a bad investment, Abby thought. Although she couldn't see her mother baking homemade muffins and cookies for the shop. And she'd hoped her mother had found an outlet for her creativity that might turn into a career at the advertising agency with her latest boyfriend.

"What about the job with Norm, Mom? I thought you enjoyed helping him with that ad for my book."

Her mother wrinkled her dainty nose. "I did, honey, but he was on last month's menu. You know I get bored easily."

A mild understatement if she'd ever heard one. Abby remembered the credit card problem she'd had the day before. "Mom, I'll have to check my finances and get back to you."

Confident Abby would loan her the money, her mother pecked her on the cheek and vanished out the door. Abby grabbed the puppy from the box and headed to the AJC to confront her worst enemy—Hunter Stone. She'd put him in the hotspot for a change and see how he liked it.

"Great job, Stone." Emerson braced his elbows on his desk, wiped Twinkie cream from his shirt, and nodded in approval at the article Hunter had written about Abby.

"Yeah, you really picked that broad apart," Jimmy, one of the copyeditors, added.

Hunter shrugged, a knot in his stomach.

181

"You got anything good on her yet?"

"I'm working on it," Hunter said, grateful to be on his boss's good side for a change.

"Well, let me know as soon as you get it."

Hunter nodded and strode from the office, his instincts humming. His research the night before had definitely proven helpful. He'd discovered a couple of interesting things about Abby's husband. First, he had been thrown out of UCLA for cheating. Next, he had an alias. Last, he had two arrests, which had been swept under the rug.

He wondered if Abby had a clue.

The details were fuzzy about why Gulliver had used an alias, and what the cops had taken him in for. Hunter grabbed a pen and notepad and hurried toward the door. He had a meeting with a cop buddy of his to see if he could find out the scoop on Gulliver. He didn't want to miss it.

Abby tucked the puppy beneath her arm and strode into the downtown offices of the paper, her hair curling and spiraling out of control from the sweltering heat. Air-conditioning immediately sent goose bumps cascading up her arms. *A cold place for a cold group of people*, she thought, reliving the painful memories of childhood. Seeing her father's face plastered all over the paper, his arms and legs bound in thick chains. Having reporters push their microphones into her and her sister's faces, asking them how it felt to have a crook for a daddy. Chelsea's wild antics later, Victoria's harsh reaction.

Granted, Hunter Stone hadn't been so obvious, and some of the other stories about her book hadn't been so flattering, but so far none of them had accused her of actually breaking up marriages to make a buck.

How low could one man go?

The man obviously had a heart of stone to match his last name.

The puppy whimpered and she rubbed its pudgy head.

"Shh, baby, it's okay. This won't take long." Determination filling her, she found out where to locate the dispicable reporter, took the elevator to the fourth floor, and stopped at the receptionist's desk.

"I'm here to see Mr. Stone."

The sleek African-American woman smiled, her slender fingers complete with nail art clicking away at her keyboard. "Is he expecting you?"

"No, but I believe he'll see me."

"Your name?"

"Abigail Jensen."

"Dr. Jensen?"

Abby blushed as the puppy licked her chin. "Yes."

"Shamara Loussard. I just loved your book." The young woman stepped around the circular desk and shook Abby's hand, nearly knocking off a glass paperweight in her haste. "I can't tell you how much my husband and I have enjoyed those exercises."

"Thank you." Abby glanced pointedly at the cubicles visible through the glass doorway. "But I'm afraid everyone doesn't agree with you."

Shamara's cheeks blushed rosy on top of coffee-colored skin. "Well, you know anything good creates controversy." She leaned in as if they were co-conspirators. "A few of the reporters here are really solid and just want to print the facts, but some of them are so hungry to see their bylines, they'd sell their own mother for a story. Sometimes they scratch and fight for the next scoop like nanny roosters hunting feed."

Abby laughed, immediately liking the woman.

"So you're here to knock some sense into Hunter Stone?" Shamara led her through a set of double glass doors, where Abby looked out over a room buzzing with people frantically typing at their computers yelling at one another, and snapping into phones. The hubbub of news, personal stories, and the trading of information filled the room.

"I already e-mailed him and told him what I thought," Shamara said.

Abby hesitated, imagining what Hunter Stone would look like—he was probably short and stout, balding on top with a paunch around his middle, a Danny DeVito look-alike. Except his eyes would be much beadier.

He probably suffered from short man's syndrome and had to make up for his small size by seeking attention in a big way in the paper. Normally she simply felt sorry for people like him, those who stole pleasure at the expense of innocent people.

Retreat and withdraw.

The words silently spoke to her. If she confronted Stone and made a scene, she would only feed the proverbial gossip vine. A distinct memory rose to taunt her—her mother had tried to talk to the press after her father's arrest, but they'd twisted her words until her mother had sounded like a conspirator in his crimes. In fact, if Abby made a scene at the paper, she would be hanging herself out to dry with the dirty linen.

After all, what difference did Hunter Stone's asinine article make anyway? Everyone was entitled to his or her opinion. Half the people in Atlanta probably hadn't even read his comments. Anyone with an ounce of sense read the news and sports pages, then skimmed the others, chuckled over the stories, and used the newsprint to line their birdcages.

As a matter of fact, she would use Hunter Stone's articles to settle her puppy in his new crate. In no uncertain terms, her little friend would tell Hunter Stone exactly what he thought of his journalism.

Hunter had just exited the bathroom when he realized he'd left his cell phone at his desk. Heading back in that direction he came to an abrupt halt when he spotted Abby Jensen talking to the receptionist. *Geez.* What the hell was Abby doing here?

The article.

Of course. She'd read the article, had remembered he'd phoned for an interview, and had come to do what? Tell him off? Offer him an exclusive?

Probably the first.

Her expression hinted at simmering anger. She and Shamara seemed chummy, though. Abby laughed, a soft, musical sound that he'd never heard. Shamara pointed to the cubicle where he had been sitting only minutes ago. Minutes that had spared his undercover stint as her actor husband.

A call too close for comfort.

He ducked behind the awning of the doors and stumbled backward. She and Shamara turned and strode right toward him. Afraid he was about to be caught, he searched for an escape, but the closest hiding spot was the women's rest room. Brenda Davis had just gone in there. He couldn't.

Panicked, he dove beneath Shamara's desk, crawling on his knees, his back bent unmercifully. Seconds later, Abby and Shamara paused on the other side of Shamara's desk. He froze, praying the receptionist didn't decide to sit back down. Not yet.

"Dr. Jensen," Shamara said in a hushed tone. "I have a little question, if you don't mind."

"Sure."

He peeked through the cracks in the metal desk and glimpsed Abby's slender leg stretched out in front of him. His eyes zeroed in on her soft skin. He could almost taste the smooth texture.

"It's about the retreat and withdrawal technique in your book."

"Yes?" A yelp sounded and Abby jiggled the white fluff in her arms. So she'd brought that mop of a dog with her. What did she think it would do—protect her?

"I tried to explain it to Carlos, but he doesn't quite get it." Shamara shocked him by picking up a nearly empty toilet paper tube from her desk. Apparently she'd been out of tissues and had grabbed a roll to help with her allergies. "Would you mind demonstrating?"

Abby's face reddened, but she glanced around, then placed her finger in the center. "It's all about stoking the fire, moving and feeling," she said softly. "We also use the withdraw and retreat technique when we're dating. It's that push-pull: you start to get a little close; then you back off. Call it foreplay for the next stage. People use the same technique with their tongues when they kiss."

"I see," Shamara cooed.

"You may be frantic for fulfillment," Abby continued in a silky whisper, "and sometimes it's okay to go ahead and grab a quickie for release. But it's much more erotic to go fast, then pull back slowly and change your rhythm. It's that game of tease and torture."

"Tease and torture," Shamara mimicked. "Ooh, I like that."

"If he's on top, he can move slowly around in circular motions, then penetrate you deeply and withdraw gradually. If you're on top, move yourself slowly round and round, then lift off of him and impale him deliberately. Close your eyes and feel him deep inside you, penetrating you, filling you until you can't breathe, you're so full of him."

Hunter felt himself grow aroused by her husky voice. Excitement bordering on pain held him a prisoner as erotic sensations built.

Shamara circled the desk and bumped her chair, which sent it rolling over one of his hands. He bit his cheek to keep from screaming in pain and tried to move his finger, but the roller held it hostage.

"I think I've got it." Shamara leaned against the chair, digging the metal feet harder into his fingers. "Thanks, Dr. Jensen. It's all clear in my head now."

Abby tossed the toilet paper tube on the cherry desktop, tucked the dog back under her arm, and hugged Shamara. Her movement hit the chair again and it rolled off him, releasing his hand. He pressed his fist to his mouth to keep from gasping in relief.

"And don't you worry about that Hunter Stone, Dr. Jensen," Shamara said with a laugh. "He doesn't know what he's talking about anyway." She made a *tsk*ing sound. "No wonder he's divorced; the man probably doesn't have a romantic bone in his body."

Hunter snarled silently as humiliation stung him. Shelly had made the same comment.

But it wasn't true—was it?

"I guess you're right," Abby said. "Thanks, Shamara."

"Anytime. I'll be looking for a sequel to your book."

Abby said good-bye, and Hunter watched her shoes disappear from the front of the desk, then heard them clicking on the floor as she hurried to the elevator.

"Excuse me, Mr. Hunter?"

He winced and glanced up at Shamara's curious face peering down at him. On top of his mental and physical injuries, now he had to face the wrath of Shamara.

Chapter Sixteen

The Long-term Lover

"Listen, Bobby," Hunter said. "I'd appreciate anything you can find out about this guy Lenny Gulliver."

Bobby, a rookie cop he'd met when he'd written a story on careers for a special kids' segment, threw back his beer mug and took a hefty swig, studying Hunter. "What's he to you?"

"Nothing, really. Just research for a story."

Bobby cracked a peanut shell with his teeth, sucked out the peanut, and tossed the shell onto the floor. "Something personal?"

Hunter shifted, drumming his fingers on the table. "No. He was married to one of the women I'm investigating for an article."

"Investigating women—sounds like reporting is right up your alley, bud."

Hunter sipped his beer, remembering his hot reaction to Abby's voice when he'd been hiding under the receptionist's desk. *Disgusting.* She certainly hadn't been talking to him or trying to seduce him. She hadn't even known he was there.

"Gulliver's got an alias: Larry Lombardi. Went to UCLA, but he got kicked out. A couple of arrests, but they've been polished over."

Bobby arched a brow. "Is this a criminal story you're working on?"

"Could be tied to one. I think he ran off on his wife and robbed her blind. Not sure what else he's involved in, but I want the scoop. I'll owe you one."

"All right." Bobby swallowed some more beer, then backhanded his mouth to wipe off the foam. "Just remember me if you stumble on something in the alley while you're looking."

This guy probably wanted to make detective. "You know Mo Jo Brown?"

"Hell, everyone knows that creep."

"He's snooping around looking for the man, too. Seems Gulliver owes his boss Eddy Vinelli some money."

Bobby rocked his chair back on two legs. "Well, now you've really got my interest."

Hunter had known the mention of Brown would do it. "Good, I want to find Gulliver before he does."

Bobby glanced around the bar. The happy-hour crowd started to arrive with a riot of noise. A group of ladies who obviously worked out at the gym next door threaded in, dropping workout bags on the floor. A trio from the nail salon followed, flipping their hair and giggling as they ordered martinis. "Deal. Now, here's to bachelor life."

Hunter laughed and toasted, although his heart wasn't in it.

Once upon a time it had been, though. But now . . .

Now his heart lay in being a father to Lizzie.

The clock on the bare wood wall behind the bar struck five, and he tossed a few bills on the scarred wood counter. It was time to turn himself into Harry Henderson for the night—and probe further into Abby's secrets.

* * *

Abby ignored her attraction toward Harry when he arrived. For now, the only man in her life was going to be the four-legged kind. Her dog couldn't deceive her, run off with her money, or cheat on her. And if he was gay, it didn't matter.

She realized she was being cynical, suffering through the stages of anger and rejection that she had counseled so many scorned lovers through, but she couldn't control her reaction or her feelings.

This, too, would pass.

She counseled her clients to let the feelings come, to work through them, then to move on. She simply wasn't ready to move on yet.

"Dr. Jensen, the radio show will be live," the deejay explained. "It's a question-and-answer session. You two have a few minutes to talk until then."

Abby nodded. Great, she had private time with Harry. She could torture herself by looking at a sexy man she couldn't have.

Harry took his place beside her. "Hi, how was your day?"

Abby frowned. He sounded like a husband. "Rotten. My new puppy peed in my bed, this moron reporter named Stone wrote another slanderous article about me in the morning paper, and my credit cards are maxed because someone borrowed them and decided to have fun."

She had no idea why she'd unloaded all that baggage, except that she needed to vent, and Harry Henderson already knew she was lying and was sworn to secrecy, and his husbandly tone had reminded her that she had no husband.

"I'm sorry, Abby."

His quiet apology surprised her. And so did the odd expression on his face. He looked uncomfortable, as if he'd swallowed the proverbial canary and was about to sing.

Heck, she was hallucinating. There was no reason this man would care so much. He was acting, for crying out loud.

"You know, it wouldn't hurt so much," she said, needing to vent some more, "if the article were true. But I have to believe my therapy helps people or I wouldn't continue my work. I can't imagine this Stone guy saying that I actually break up marriages." She hesitated, her breathing quick. "My book, my advice, my therapy, I don't make or break marriages, Harry. Only the people involved can do that."

Harry stared at her long and hard, an intensity in his eyes that she would never have imagined. Maybe she was thinking in clichés, not being fair. He seemed to actually be studying her, looking to see inside her.

She had exposed too much.

Harry opened his mouth to reply, but the deejay waved that they were ready to start. Abby clamped her mouth shut. She'd been ready to spill everything. Why, she didn't know, except that for a moment she'd felt some sort of deep soul connection with Harry.

God, she *was* losing it.

The producer walked toward them.

No time now, Abby thought. Besides, what was she thinking? What did she really know about Harry Henderson except that he was an actor? An actor who was virtually a stranger. He could very well run off and sell her story to the tabloids. That would be even worse than that Neanderthal Stone getting wind of it.

"Ready?" the producer asked.

Abby nodded. No, she wasn't. But she hadn't been ready for any of this other stuff either. She would just have to deal with her problems alone.

"If this goes well, Dr. Jensen," the producer said, "we're hoping to turn this hour into a daily talk show."

"The 'Dear Dr. Abby Hour,'" the deejay said with a wink.

Abby's stomach twisted. She wouldn't do a radio talk show in a million years. The last thing she wanted was to perpetuate an image of herself as the Dr. Abby of the bedroom.

*   *   *

Hunter listened to Abby answer the routine questions, his mind spinning over her earlier comment that nobody could make or break the marriage but the couple themselves.

"Our next caller is a woman from Buckhead," the deejay said in a baritone voice. "You're on, Elaine."

"Hi, Dr. Jensen. First off, I want to thank you for your book. It's so liberating to be able to express myself sexually. I never considered telling my husband what I wanted in bed before I read your book."

"A lot of women, especially Southern ones, grow up being taught that sex is something to hide, to be ashamed of, something that we don't talk about." Abby paused. "We should teach our daughters that sex is a wonderful part of an adult relationship, especially if the two people involved love each other and are responsible."

"Right," Elaine said. "I just feel so much more alive now. And my husband seems to appreciate knowing what turns me on."

Hunter contemplated his relationship with Shelly. Had he listened to her needs when they were married? She certainly hadn't listened to his. Then again, they had been young and their ideals had been so different. Shelly's pregnancy had brought them together, but there were things they should have discussed before they'd said their vows.

"Thank you, Elaine," the deejay said. "Now we have William on the line."

"Since my wife read your book," William said, "all she does is criticize me. 'Do it like this, don't touch me there, you're too rough.'"

"I'm sorry to hear that, sir," Abby said softly. "Can I make a few suggestions?"

"Anything would be better than the way we're going."

"Is your wife there? It might be better if you both listen together."

"I'll get her." He paused, then yelled, "Bernadette, get in here, honey!"

192

Abby grinned. Hunter studied her, thinking that so far tonight he'd agreed with her comments. And she had certainly made him rethink his own failed marriage—and his part in it.

Maybe he'd been blaming the wrong person.

"The key to communication is not to criticize, but to tell the other person gently what you want. Instead of saying, 'You're too rough,' try whispering something like, 'Oh, I like it soft, honey.' When your partner does something right, touches you gently or finds a G-spot, then tell him or her how wonderful it feels." She hesitated. "You can also try doing this outside the bedroom. Start with a simple compliment. Would you like to try one on-air?"

"I reckon," Bernadette said. "William, I sure do like it when you leave your muddy boots in the washroom."

Abby glanced at Hunter, a sparkle of laughter in her eyes. "That's good. Now it's your turn, William."

He cleared his throat, his voice gruff. "Bernadette, honey, your buttermilk biscuits melt in my mouth."

"That's a start," Abby said, her lips twitching. "I have a feeling if you two work at it, things will be all right."

Hunter nodded, her earlier comment still on his mind.

Abby was right. A couple didn't break up because of an argument or two, or even because one of them had read a book or heard a lecture. In fact, now that he thought about it, Shelly had complained about their marriage two months after they'd married, before she'd ever heard Abby's lecture. Hope and promises hadn't fed her blueblood tastes. She'd wanted Tiffany lamps, designer furniture, and a million-dollar house, while all he could afford was a one-room apartment with a leaky faucet and garage-sale furnishings.

Had he blamed Abby for a marriage that failed because he and Shelly hadn't put their hearts in it and worked hard enough? Because they had wanted different things in life and hadn't loved each other enough to compromise?

*   *   *

"What a success," the producer said as soon as they were off the air.

His assistant, a tall woman with German features, pumped her hands in a victory sweep. "We got a record number of listener phone calls. It's looking good for that weekly show."

"What do you say, Dr. Jensen?" the producer asked. "Are you interested?"

"I . . . don't think so. I wouldn't have time with my patient load."

Abby thanked them both and headed out of the station. Harry walked beside her; he'd been quiet during the interview, which had been fine with her—the less touching and flirting the better. In fact, he'd answered only once when a caller had specifically asked about their marriage. He'd chimed in and said they were in heavenly bliss.

She grimaced, hating the lies lining up like dominoes. One mistake could trigger the first one to fall; then they'd all come crashing down around her. Another week and it would be over, she promised herself.

Harry caught her at the door, his hand curling around her arm. "Abby, can we get a drink?"

His invitation surprised her. "Uh . . . I'd better not."

"Come on, just a cup of coffee."

She rubbed her neck where the muscles had knotted. She supposed she could use some caffeine for the drive home. And he did seem unusually quiet, as if something was disturbing him. And she was a counselor. . . . "All right."

A few minutes later, they entered a tiny café, the scents of chocolate brownies, cheesecake, and rich coffee filling the air. They claimed a seat at a small round table in the corner, the bright purple-and-yellow decor cheery compared to Abby's mood.

"I'll have a mocha," Abby said, allowing herself to take a shot of chocolate in her coffee. But no dessert. All those comforting Reese's cups had bulldozed their way straight to her hips.

"Regular coffee, black," Harry said. "Oh, and a piece of that double-fudge layer cake."

It figures. The man didn't have an inch of fat on him, and he could eat chocolate cake till the cows came home. All she had to do was look at it and she could feel her thighs bulging.

They were both quiet until the waitress reappeared with their order. As Hunter picked up his fork to dig in he glanced at her. "You seem upset tonight," he said, surprising her again with his directness.

Abby shrugged and licked at the whipped cream topping her coffee. His gaze followed the movement, until he realized he was staring; then he jerked his eyes back to his cake.

"It's been a stressful few days."

"Wanna talk about it?"

She shook her head. "Thanks anyway, though."

A few heartbeats stretched between them.

"You were quiet, too," Abby commented. "I guess we really didn't need you for the radio interview."

"I was just thinking about what you said," Harry admitted.

"And what was that?"

"That only the couple concerned can make or break their own marriage."

"It's true," Abby said, her voice strong with conviction. "Of course, every situation is different, but both the husband and wife have to want their relationship to work or it won't." Lenny proved that. "All the therapy in the world won't work if the couple doesn't love each other, and if both of them aren't willing to compromise."

He chewed thoughtfully. "I was thinking about my ex-wife and our divorce." A sip of coffee washed down the cake. "At first I blamed her and . . . and her therapist."

"Did you attend counseling together?"

"Oh, yeah."

"That didn't work?"

"She had an affair with our therapist. They're married now."

"I'm sorry." Abby leaned her chin on her hand. "How unethical. And hurtful."

He hesitated, dropping his fork on the plate with a clatter. "Now he gets to play daddy to my daughter."

Bitterness and hurt underlay his words. Instinctively she reached out and laid a hand on his thigh. "I'm so sorry, Harry. I can't imagine what that must be like."

"I'd do anything for my kid." His voice turned rough, filled with emotion.

"That's admirable," Abby said. "Your daughter is very lucky." Her father certainly hadn't felt that way about her.

"Only thing is, this shrink has money, and he and my ex . . . well, they can give Lizzie everything I can't."

"They can never give her a father's love, *your* love," Abby said softly. "Remember that, Harry. There's not enough money or toys or trips in the world to replace that."

She would know.

He squeezed her hand in his, the moment both electrifying and oddly tender, and something changed inside Abby. She was beginning to really like Harry. He was much more complicated—deeper—than she'd ever imagined.

Harry's head came up and he studied her again with that long, steady, intensely unsettling look. That look that reached deep into her soul and ripped apart the protective walls she was trying to erect.

Abby jerked her gaze away, afraid he would see the need and desire in her eyes. She couldn't get involved, even remotely, with another man. Not now. Her pain was too new. Too raw. Too fresh.

But Harry didn't seem to hear her silent battle. He brushed her chin up with the pad of his thumb, lowered his mouth to hers, and kissed her. Not the passionate I-have-to-have-you kind or the earth-shattering I-love-you kind.

The much gentler kind that said, I really like you and I want to get to know you better. The kind that said he wanted more than a one-night stand, that he might become a long-term lover. The kind that was much more intimate and scary.

Chapter Seventeen

The Masterful Massage

Hunter deepened the kiss, sinking his entire body into it as he tasted the sweetness of Abby's mouth. The little hitch in her breath when she'd realized his intention had drummed up more sexual energy inside him than the best issue of the *Sports Illustrated* swimsuit edition. She tasted both innocent and sultry, an odd combination that stirred protective feelings and made his adrenaline pump fast and hard.

Something was happening to him. Changing.

He was growing hard all over. But soft inside.

Losing his objectivity.

Her hands framed his face as his tongue absorbed the honeyed passion of her kiss. He had to pull away or he wouldn't be able to stop. Because he wanted to make every one of her senses come alive. To touch her without clothes, with no barriers between them.

But there were so many lies.

His. Hers.

His chest aching with the effort, he slowly ended the kiss and dropped his forehead against hers, giving them both time to steady their breathing and thoughts.

"Harry, I can't—"

He brought his finger to her lips to silence her. "Shh. I know."

She swallowed, her eyes melting puddles of need and confusion. Their gazes caught and held, his heart thundering, her mixed emotions mirroring his own.

The situation was impossible.

He couldn't allow himself to lose his objectivity like this or he'd never be a successful reporter.

"I have to go," she whispered on a ragged sigh.

"I'll drive you."

"I have my car."

"Then I'll follow you."

She pressed a gentle hand on his chest. "Harry . . ."

He clasped his hand over hers and helped her stand. "I don't have to come in, Abby. I just want to make sure that PI isn't lurking in your bushes again."

His reminder put a fear in her eyes that he didn't like. But she nodded and agreed, and he walked her to her car and said good-night. He wouldn't even get out of his car when they arrived at her house, he told himself. He'd just make sure Mo Jo Brown wasn't there to harass her.

Abby pulled her into her driveway, grateful Harry had followed her home, but her sense of security vanished the minute she spotted her father sitting on her porch.

Granted, she had always been the caretaker of the family, but this was getting ridiculous. First Uncle Wilbur, then her mother. Now her father, who still wore the stamp of prison life on his pale, drawn skin.

She let the engine die, took a deep breath, and exited her car, not surprised that Harry pulled in behind her and climbed out, a frown marring his forehead as his gaze landed on her father. She tried to look at him as a stranger

would—he was a scruffy old man puffing an unfiltered cigarette, blowing smoke circles into the dark sky, his face
pale, age lines framing his mouth.

"My father," Abby said before Harry could ask.

His brows straightened into a line of concern. "Do you
want me to stay?"

"No, he looks rough, but he's harmless." *Except where
your money's concerned. One thing he has in common with
Lenny.*

Boy, she sure could pick the men.

Of course, she hadn't chosen her father, but she still had
to deal with him.

Her father rose from the steps and stared at them, his
frail body and worn clothes a testament to his neediness.
Abby silently willed him to stay put. She had no intention
of introducing the two men and having to explain her situation or her relationship with either man to the other.

"Thanks for seeing me home, Harry. I'll talk to you tomorrow."

He nodded, obviously reluctant to leave, but finally
reached into his pocket and pulled out a small card with
a phone number on it. "Call me if you need anything."

Abby took the card with a small nod, waved good-bye,
and hurried up the steps. "Dad."

"Hey, sugar."

She unlocked the door and gestured for him to enter,
her throat tight. A glance at her answering machine told
her she had several calls to return.

"How're you doing, baby?"

Like he really cared. "Fine. I heard you were paroled."
Abby folded her arms across her chest. "I'm really tired,
Dad. What is it?"

"Can't an old man drop by to see his little girl without
a reason?"

She shrugged. "It's never happened before."

He took a long drag on his cigarette and studied her,
the age lines around his eyes crinkling. How long had it

been since she'd seen or heard from him? Five or six years at least.

"I know I haven't always been there for you, Abby, but I'd like to start over."

She simply folded her arms and waited for the inevitable. "How much do you need to start over this time?"

A sheepish smile tugged at his weathered mouth. She'd ached for that smile so many times when she was growing up, at her graduation from high school, then college. But he hadn't been to any of the major events in her life. "A couple thousand, just till I get back on my feet."

Abby's heart sank. Why did she keep hoping he would change? That one day he would be the parent and she the child?

"I can spare a couple hundred right now, but that's all," Abby said, too tired to deal with him.

"But I thought your book—"

"I don't receive royalties right away, Dad." She jerked open her purse, scribbled a check to him, and held it out. "Here, use this to get cleaned up and to get a place to stay. Maybe I can help more later, but right now I'm strapped myself." *Because the man I thought was my husband maxed out my credit cards and left me with a pile of bills.*

"I am going straight this time." He dragged baggy gray pants up his lean hips. His eyes grew moist, his hands shaking as he reached out and pulled her into a hug. "I swear."

Abby hugged him, sympathy for him surfacing even though she struggled not to allow herself the emotion. Then he loped out the door and our of her life—until the next time.

The puppy yelped from the box in her bedroom, so she hurried to retrieve him, cradling him in her arms while she listened to her messages.

"Abby, honey, this is your uncle. I wondered if you'd had time to reconsider that loan. The big guns are pressing down on me, baby. Please call."

She swiped at a tear and punched the button to hear

the next one. "Abby, it's Mom. I thought I might bring Shank over"—Abby frowned. Who was Shank?—"to meet you. Once you hear his ideas for the coffee shop, I'm sure you'll want to invest." Her mother paused. "We're off to get tattoos now. Talk to you soon."

Next, Granny Pearl. "Abby, honey, the ladies and I were wondering if you'd like to lead a weekend retreat for us. We enjoyed last time so much. Call me."

Rainey's voice piped in next. "Abby, it's Rainey. Listen, the radio show is definitely a go if you're interested. And the tour next week is all confirmed. You and your hubby will have a suite and car wherever you go. I'm so excited. The book is climbing the charts as we speak! I hope you're thinking of a sequel."

Oh, Lord.

She hit the button again and Chelsea's voice rang out. "Hey, sis, it's Chelsea. I was just calling to invite you to a fabulous party. Some single hunks you might like will be there." Chelsea, the incurable romantic. "And, oh, sis, you and Harry sounded great tonight. He's adorable, isn't he?"

Abby rolled her eyes. The puppy whined, lifted its head, and cocked it sideways, as if he thought she was going to desert him again.

"I'm not going anywhere, Butterball."

One more message: "This is Victoria, Abby. You'd better be on your toes. A friend of mine at the police station said someone is asking about Lenny. If the police have any brains at all, it won't take them long to put two and two together." Concern laced her oldest sister's voice. "Call me if you need me."

Abby put the puppy back on the floor and wrapped her arms around herself, feeling as if her whole world were crashing around her. She turned on the TV, half-afraid she would see Lenny and Tony Milano being dragged off in handcuffs. But as she surfed the channels, she heard her name.

A late-night talk show host was making fun of her in his monologue.

How much worse could things get?

She flicked off the TV and picked up her journal, needing to vent.

Most wonderful, sexy kiss by actor. Am afraid I'm falling for him.

Family pulling at me as if I have octopus arms. Press having field day with reputation. Butt of TV jokes. Target of obnoxious reporter.

Another screwed-up day in the life of Abby Jensen.

Tears suddenly erupted like raindrops from a thunderstorm, her body shaking with the intensity of her sobs. The puppy leaped up on the couch next to her and dragged the bag of Reese's cups across the cushions to her, then flopped down in her lap. She let out a wail and the puppy licked at her hand.

Abby sighed, blew her nose on a tissue, wadded it up, and grabbed another. "I don't think those are going to help now." Still, she dove into the bag with one hand.

What difference did it make if her thighs were thirty inches or nineteen? No one was here to see them but Butterball. And he liked her, fat hips and all.

Hunter couldn't say exactly what bothered him about seeing Abby's father on her front porch, but something about the scenario hadn't felt quite right. Before his own father died, he had shared a special father-son rapport with him. Granted, his father'd been military and strict, but he had taken care of Hunter.

He'd always thought fathers and daughters shared a unique bond, too. But Abby's father had obviously let her down.

Weary from the long night, he finished the articles on the two Milano victims he'd interviewed earlier that morning, then faxed them to the paper. One couple who had wed at the Velvet Cloak Inn had been upset over the fraudulent preacher, but they were coping. Since their families had been upset over missing their nuptials, they had decided to have a big wedding and do it right this time. The second couple decided that the fact that they weren't legally married merely saved them from the hassle of a divorce. Ironically Milano had done them a favor. He laughed at the odd way life had of turning things around.

Satisfied with the piece, he dug through the file of names and picked three more people to interview. How many people had Milano swindled who weren't on the list?

Too distracted by the memory of Abby looking lost and small beside her father to pursue the question, he started to punch in her number, but realized she might have caller ID, so he used his cell phone instead. He had it programmed not to show up on caller ID. She answered on the third ring, but a wail punctuated the silence.

The faint sound of an echoing howl followed. Her dog?

"Hel . . . lo?"

"Hey, Abby, it's me. Hu . . . Harry."

"Oh . . ." More wailing in the background. "Hi."

A sniffle followed, twisting Hunter's gut. God, she'd been crying. "Are you okay?"

"Fine." A short pause. "Shh, Butterball, stop that now."

She didn't sound fine. She sounded miserable. "Is your father still there?"

"No, he left a little while ago."

"Abby, what's wrong?"

She didn't answer.

"He didn't hurt you, did he?" If he had, Hunter would kill him.

"No, nothing like that."

"Then tell me what's wrong or I'm coming over there."

"Harry, you're not getting paid to listen to my personal problems."

His jaw tightened. "I'm not asking to be paid. I'm just trying to be your friend."

"Well . . ."

"You do have friends, don't you?"

"Yes. My sisters mostly."

"Now you have me."

Her soft sigh lingered in the air between them. Hunter stretched out on his bed with a beer and relaxed. "Now talk to me, Abby."

As she began to talk, Hunter closed his eyes and listened to her husky voice. And he silently vowed that tomorrow he would change the slant of his story about her.

He no longer wanted revenge or to hurt Abby; he would be satisfied to print the truth. It was about time someone took care of Abby instead of the other way around.

"I'm sorry, Harry," Abby murmured, "I guess I'm just overwhelmed with things. My life seems to have gone crazy lately. I feel completely out of control."

"You like control?"

"I didn't say that. I said I don't like being out of control."

"That's an odd comment for a sex therapist."

"I'm not a sex therapist. I'm a marriage counselor," Abby said in a hiss. "And this isn't about my book or sex."

"Okay, then what is it about?"

The concern in his voice sounded so sincere, Abby felt a new wave of tears rushing to the surface. "First, this book getting so much attention. I never intended that. I only wanted to help people."

"Go on," he said softly.

"I grew up in a very nontraditional family, and I always dreamed that I'd have the perfect marriage and home when I grew up. That as long as I gave it my heart and soul, my life would be just as I planned."

"Yeah," Harry said. "Life sometimes gives you a curveball right when you think you're ready to hit a homer."

"I know I encourage great sexual relations, Harry, but I'm actually pretty private myself."

"Private is good."

His voice wrapped around her, intoxicating in its softness. "And my family. Normally I don't mind taking care of everyone, but right now . . ."

"Now, what?"

"Right now I don't have the energy."

"They should understand that." Was that anger in his voice?

She heard the sound of movement, as if he had stretched out on his bed, and heat stirred within her. Was he getting undressed?

"What are you doing now, Abby?"

"I'm in bed." Although she knew he couldn't see her, a blush heated her cheeks.

"So am I."

Was he naked? Or maybe he was wearing a pair of those minibriefs. Or maybe he was a boxer man? Abby stared at her unpainted toenails beneath her oversize T-shirt. Thank goodness he couldn't see her unsexy attire.

"Maybe someone should take care of you for a while."

Abby glanced at the snoring puppy. "I have Butterball here."

"I was talking about more than a dog." His breath feathered out. "Why don't you lie back and relax?"

"I don't know, Harry."

"Come on, Abby. It's just you and me right now. Friends having a little conversation. Late at night." His whisper was so soothing. "We can talk each other to sleep."

Or something else. Abby shoved the mounds of tissue off the bed with her foot, her misery waning as the lull of his voice washed over her. "All right."

"Pretend I'm lying beside you."

"Okay." She could see his dark eyes studying her, raking over her body.

"You're naked, lying under the cool sheet."

Abby slipped off her T-shirt and crawled beneath the sheets. "I am now."

His breathing rasped out. "I'm pouring massage oil into my hand. Close your eyes and smell the scent of jasmine."

A love scent.

"Now, feel my hands as they slowly stroke your neck. I'm brushing away that gorgeous hair of yours, closing my hands around the indentation of your shoulders. You hunch them when you're tense, don't you, Abby?"

God, his voice was deep. "Yes."

"But I'm rubbing the tension away. Kneading the muscles until you're so relaxed your limbs feel languid. Now stretch your arms above you. I'm crawling over you so I can sit astride you." His voice softened another decibel. "Now I'm reaching my hands up to massage your arms. I start with your palms and move up to your shoulders. Now my hands are moving lower. Rubbing your back, caressing. Now my hands are stroking lower. I can feel your body start to warm beneath me. . . ."

Warm? Her body was on fire.

Harry's handsome face flashed into her mind. There was no way she could get involved with Harry Henderson. She should hang up now. Tell him to stop.

But he did have a wonderful, sultry voice. And he gave a great phone massage.

A little more bedtime conversation wouldn't hurt anything, would it? She just couldn't let it go too far. . . .

Hunter had no idea how it had happened. One minute he and Abby had been simply talking and he had been worried about her, so he'd tried to lull her into relaxing by envisioning a massage. The next minute he had stripped off his clothes, and they were whispering erotic words and massaging each other with mental images that seemed completely real.

He had never indulged in anything so sensual in his life. He might have to try it again—just to make sure he'd done it right the first time, of course. Knowing he had helped her relax had spiked a fever in his body that had only begun to be quenched. He wanted Abby in the flesh.

But that was impossible.

"Abby?"

Her response was so low he could barely discern it.

"Do you think you can sleep now?"

"Hmm. Definitely."

"Well, good night. Call me if you wake up in the night and want to talk, okay?"

"Thanks. I will, Harry."

He hesitated, wishing he could say more. That he could be honest with her. Then again, she was lying to him. She was still married. He cleared his throat. "I'll see you tomorrow."

"Good night, Harry."

He winced at the name.

"Oh, and Harry?"

He slunk down lower in the bed. In spite of the fact that so many lies stood between them, his body still thrummed from the sultry sound of her voice. "Yeah?"

"Thanks for being such a good friend."

His hand tightened around the phone. The sound of the click on the other end of the line jarred him almost as much as her thank you. Sure, she was deceiving him, and refused to tell him the truth about her husband.

But he'd gone into the deception knowing something was fishy. She had no idea he wasn't who he claimed to be. That he wasn't her friend at all. That he was the obnoxious Hunter Stone, the reporter who'd slandered her in his articles. The man she most despised.

Sweat beaded on his body as reality intervened. Abby Jensen was going to hate him when she discovered the truth about him.

And he couldn't blame her.

Chapter Eighteen

The Tease

The next day Hunter tried to shake off the unsettling feeling that he might be falling for Abby Jensen, a married woman. He'd written up his articles for the day and driven to his ex's house to pick up his daughter for his weekend with her, his mind on overload. Lizzie was in the bathroom, and he was pacing the floor, trying to figure out how to get out of the interview scheduled for today, or explain the charade to his daughter without making himself look like a low-down, sneaky, conniving liar.

Which he was beginning to think described him pretty damn well.

"Daddy, is this a caterpillar?"

He pivoted in the hallway and silently groaned. Lizzie had found his fake mustache and hair along with the flowery dress he'd worn that day at the book signing. "Daddy, you been playing dress-up with my clothes?"

Hunter grimaced. "Lizzie, come here; let me explain something to you."

Lizzie's big eyes widened as she followed him to the den and climbed onto his lap. She wiggled the mustache in her hand. Angelica lay beside her, watching. "Look, it crawls like an inchworm."

Hunter grinned, lifted the strip of hair from her fingers, and placed it over his lip. "It's a mustache. See?"

Her blond eyebrows crinkled together. "You look furry, Daddy."

Hunter chuckled. "I know. Listen, I've told you about my job. How sometimes I have to pretend to be someone else to get information from people."

She bobbed her head up and down, blond pigtails flopping.

"Well, this is one of Daddy's props. I use it as a disguise when I play this guy Harry. And tonight you'll get to see me in action." If he couldn't get out of it.

She clapped her hands together. "Oh, boy, can I playact, too?"

Hunter nodded. "As a matter of fact, you can. You can keep my act a secret. Dr. Abby thinks my name is Harry."

Lizzie giggled and pulled at the mustache.

"And when I go on TV with Dr. Abby, I pretend to be Lenny, her husband. So, you have to play along."

Good Lord, What was he doing? He clasped her hands in his and pressed them to his chest. "Do you think you can remember that? When we meet Abby, I'm Harry the actor. And when I go on TV with her, I'm her husband Lenny."

She scrunched her lips in thought. "Dr. Abby thinks you're an actor?"

Hunter nodded. "Yes, honey, she's paying me to act like her husband."

"Why, Daddy?"

Good question. "Because her real husband couldn't come tonight."

"Oh." She wiggled in his lap.

"Understand, pumpkin?"

Her head bobbed up and down again. "Do actors get paid big money?"

He shrugged. "Some of them."

She released his hand and held out her small one, palm up. "Then pay up."

Hunter stared at her hand, realized he'd been conned by a five-year-old, and wondered at his own sanity.

He handed her a dollar anyway. Then she held out Angelica's hand for her payment, too. He groaned and forked it over.

Abby had been so busy all day she'd barely had time to think about Harry and the night before.

Well, almost.

One of her clients had confessed that her marriage was in trouble, that her husband's cell phone had become a permanent appendage, so Abby had suggested the wife shake him up by phoning him on his mobile and giving him a mental massage.

Harry's titillating voice the night before boomeranged in her mind. This flirting game had to stop. She absolutely could not get in the habit of indulging herself in such crazy, risqué behavior with strangers. Especially when she was supposed to be married to someone else.

How pathetic was she?

She needed distance between herself and Harry. It shouldn't be too hard tonight; after all, he had phoned to say he was bringing his daughter along. As much as she loved children, a child underfoot would undoubtedly throw cold water on the hot flame of passion. Most of her clients insisted children were the best form of birth control available. More effective than condoms any day.

The doorbell dinged, Butterball yelped, and Abby scooped up the puppy and hurried to answer the door. Tonight she would be safe with Harry.

And tonight there wouldn't be any late-night phone

calls. When Harry left, she didn't intend for him to take her heart with him.

"Hi, Abby." Hunter squeezed his daughter's hand as she ducked behind his leg, a sudden shyness attacking her. He prayed she wouldn't give him away.

"Hey. Come on in." Abby gestured toward the foyer with a flick of her head. Her hands were busy petting the mop in her arms. And she didn't quite make eye contact, as if she was embarrassed about their intimate phone massage the night before. "You look nice and rested," he said, unable to keep from mentioning it.

A blush slid onto her cheeks. Just as quickly, her eyes flashed him a warning. "I slept very well. Thank you."

Lizzie's head reappeared at his hip when she noticed the puppy, and he stepped inside, dragging her with him. "This is my daughter, Lizzie."

Abby grinned and stooped down to Lizzie's level. "Hi, Lizzie. It's nice to meet you."

"Nice to meets you, too," Lizzie mumbled. She pushed Angelica in front of her. "This is my friend, Angelica."

"Hi, Angelica. I'm glad to finally meet you."

Lizzie giggled. "You're that sex lady, aren't you?"

Abby blushed again. "Not really, honey. You can call me Ms. Abby."

"Daddy says you're a doctor?"

"That's right."

"Are you gonna give me a shot?"

Hunter caught Abby's startled gaze and shrugged, enthralled with Abby's tenderness toward his daughter. "Honey, Dr. Abby isn't that kind of a doctor."

"What kind of doctor is she?"

"I listen to people's problems and try to help them," Abby explained softly.

Lizzie quirked her head in thought, her ponytail bobbing. "So if me and Angelica gots a problem we can come and tell you?"

Abby searched Hunter's face for an answer and he nodded. Better she explain than him.

"Sure, honey. You can call me anytime, night or day, to talk. Do you have a problem?"

"Nope, just wondering."

The puppy squirmed, raised its head, and perked up its ears, bright eyes shining beneath the fluff of hair. Lizzie giggled. "That your puppy?"

Abby nodded. "You want to pet him?"

Lizzie inched toward her, finally releasing his leg. "What's his name?" Lizzie looked up at him and winked. "He looks like a Harry, Daddy, don't he?"

Hunter's heart pounded. "Well, yes, sort of."

"That's a great name," Abby said softly. "But I've been calling him Butterball."

Lizzie giggled. " 'Cause he eats butter?"

Abby laughed. "I have a feeling he would eat anything. He's already chewed up my tennis shoes."

"You could call him Sneakers."

Abby laughed again. The puppy squirmed, and Lizzie stroked its head with a tentative hand.

"Come on in and you can hold him," Abby said.

Abby led them to the den. Several oversize throw pillows lay on the floor in front of the fireplace, and a chew toy in the shape of a tennis shoe had been tossed in the middle. The room looked lived-in, much cozier than his own dreary apartment.

He wondered what her bedroom looked like. If she had a brass bed or a four-poster one. If she had simple cotton sheets or satin. If she'd made up the bed since the night before . . .

Lizzie dropped to her knees, laid Angelica beside her, then took the teeny puppy in her arms and nuzzled it.

"Daddy, can we get a doggie like this?"

Hunter frowned. "He's not a real dog; he's a mutant throwback."

Lizzie wrinkled her nose. "A what?"

213

"Are you insulting my dog?" Abby asked.

Hunter shrugged. "No, but I want a man's dog. He's a sissy dog."

"He's beautiful," Abby argued. "I saw a whole pageant of them on TV—"

So had he. He'd had to cover the pageant for an article. Had Abby seen him there?

Surely not or she would have mentioned it by now.

"I seen it, too, Daddy, and I loves him," Lizzie whined. "I wants one, too. I could dress him up in my baby-doll clothes."

Hunter squelched the urge to groan.

"We'll get a real dog for you, honey," Hunter said.

"One like this?"

"Tell you what, sugar." He knelt and tweaked her ponytail. "We'll see what animals they have tomorrow at the Humane Society, and you can pick a dog. Okay?"

" 'Kay." She rocked the puppy in her arms as if it were a baby, then leaned over and whispered. "I loves you, Butterballs. And Daddy says I'm getting one just like you tomorrow."

Abby chuckled. "What should we tell the producer about Lizzie?"

"I'll tell them she's my niece."

"Are you okay with that, Lizzie?" Abby frowned, as if it bothered her to encourage the little girl to lie.

Lizzie revealed the space where a tooth would have been as she smiled. "Yep, Angelica and I are actors like daddy." She pulled out a dollar bill from her pocket. "See, I got big bucks for tonight. And Daddy paid Angelica, too."

Abby's skeptical look made Hunter feel about two feet tall. Some role model he was for his daughter.

If his ex found out he was paying Lizzie to lie, she'd probably banish him from seeing her.

The interview went off without a hitch. Abby shook the deejay's hand, grateful one of the staff had taken Lizzie on a tour of the radio station so she couldn't hear the adult topics they'd discussed.

Wiping a hand across her forehead, she sighed, realizing she'd been more than discombobulated by the way Harry had doted on her, too. She'd never had a man be so attentive and affectionate and downright blatantly sexual in the looks he cast her way.

He was teasing, flirtatious, and more macho than any man had a right to be.

During the show, they'd discussed everything from the woman who teased but never followed through to the foreplay that could make a marriage a minefield for orgasms. Through every word, every comment, Harry had watched her intently—playing the ultimate tease himself.

He pressed a protective hand to her lower back and guided her outside, his daughter's hand clasped firmly in his other one. The fading sun painted the sky with purples and oranges, the heat dropping off to a bearable eighty-five. But just as they opened the door to exit, a reporter and a cameraman accosted them.

"We're from the AJC; will you give us an interview, Dr. Jensen?" The rail-thin man pushed square glasses up his nose. "We heard the show and want you to comment."

The camera flashed, and Harry pushed Lizzie and Abby behind him. He tried to grab the camera, but the cameraman shoved him away. "Leave Dr. Jensen alone. You're not from the AJC. You're from that tabloid, the *Inquisitor*."

Abby grimaced. Was he right?

The camera flashed again. Abby tried to shield Lizzie from the photos and hide her own face as well. "Daddy," Lizzie cried.

"Get out of here," Harry shouted. "Before I call the cops for harassment."

"It's a free country," the reporter yelled. The cameraman, a young guy who'd barely escaped adolescence and still harbored the pockmarks of pimples to prove it, ran toward a van.

Harry hurriedly ushered his daughter and Abby into the car, dove inside, and started the engine. Traffic was thick as he veered onto the busy street. Abby buckled her seat belt. "Thanks, Harry. I appreciate your taking up for me."

"No problem. That guy's bad news."

Abby tried to forget about the awkward encounter with the tabloid, but Harry's comment nagged at her subconscious.

"Harry?"

His jaw was clenched so tightly she could practically hear his teeth grinding. Lizzie had curled up and fallen asleep in the backseat. "What?"

"How did you know that reporter wasn't from the AJC?"

Harry's eyes flickered with something like guilt for a brief second, but his big shoulders lifted and fell. "I'm an actor, Abby. The tabloids are always after us."

Abby nodded and chuckled softly. "Right. Of course. I don't know what I was thinking."

Hunter knew exactly what she was thinking. After all, how many unknown actors were hounded by the tabloids? Luckily, Abby seemed willing to let the matter drop. He silently called himself all kinds of names, *idiot* at the top of the list, for almost blowing his cover. And he'd hated for Lizzie to see him fighting. The outrageous stories the *Inquisitor* had printed lately flashed into his mind.

What if that picture got printed and his ex saw it and . . . ?

No, he couldn't panic. He'd call the tabloid and see if he could convince the editor to hold it. Whether or not he could convince them was the big question.

When they reached Abby's house, he searched the parameters for Mo Jo Brown, but the area seemed secure. He started to get out.

"No, don't leave Lizzie in here alone," Abby whispered. "I'll be fine."

He struggled over what to do, but finally agreed. Besides,

Abby was a big girl, and he was falling for her, and he had to slow down.

She would hate him when she found out he had tricked her.

"Think you'll be able to sleep tonight?" he asked, unable to resist the question as unbidden memories of the night before rushed to him.

Abby brushed a strand of that curly hair from her forehead and opened the car door. "Yes. I'm pretty tired." She hesitated, then placed a gentle kiss on his cheek. "Thanks for being so gallant tonight and defending my honor."

He swallowed, unable to reply, but his heart climbed to his throat as she sauntered up the drive. Abby had been nothing but kind to his daughter, sincere in her answers in the interview and . . . nice to him.

God, he felt like such a jerk.

Lizzie stirred as Abby slipped inside and closed the door, so he backed out the drive and headed home. A few minutes later he pulled into his apartment complex and carried Lizzie inside, the scent of baby-powder and shampoo engulfing him. She was so small and trusting, he wanted to protect her forever.

As he'd wanted to protect Abby today.

She snuggled into the extra bed, hugging Angelica to her chest. "Get puppy tomorrow, Daddy?"

He kissed her pug nose and tucked the comforter over her. "Yes, pumpkin. I promise."

"Just like Butterball."

"We'll see." For several minutes he stood and watched her sleep, his heart aching. He wanted to be with her always.

Then he headed to his room, talking with his conscience along the way. He wanted to write a positive story about Abby, to exonerate himself when she discovered the truth and to portray her the way he was beginning to see her, as a caring and sincere woman. But how could he do that and impress his boss at the same time?

*   *   *

Abby crawled into bed with Butterball, laughing when he snuggled against her arm and fell sound asleep. The night had gone much smoother than she'd expected. Harry had been fabulous, both on the set and off. His little girl was a doll, too.

You could tell a lot about a man's character from the way he interacted with his children. And Harry was a wonderful father. Perhaps his acting wasn't earning big bucks, but love was definitely more important than money. And his daughter obviously adored him. Just the fact that she wanted to be an actor like her daddy proved that.

Feeling marginally better about things, she lay back with her journal to record the events of the day.

Radio show went great. Harry is super actor and stand-up guy.

Good father to precious daughter. Accosted by tabloid reporter outside radio station. Harry saved day. Like knight in shining armor.

She paused, then continued to write.

Afraid am falling for this guy. Know it's crazy, but he's decent and honest and a nice guy. Not lying cheat like Lenny. Or despicable, like reporter Hunter Stone.

Must tell him truth about Lenny soon . . .

Hunter was counting the cracks on the ceiling of his bedroom, debating whether to get a broom and knock the spiderwebs from the left corner, when the phone trilled. He rolled his head sideways and simply stared at the offensive machine for several seconds, wondering if Abby had decided to call and give him a phone massage tonight.

Just the thought stirred his sex and sent heat rushing through his body. "Yes?"

"Stone, it's Bobby Falcon."

"Yeah?" He sat up, instantly alert. "Did you find something on Gulliver?"

The cop whistled. "Did I? This guy's a piece of work."

Hunter rubbed a hand over his face. "Okay, give it to me."

"He got kicked out of UCLA for seducing a teacher. He's been married twice, confiscated both women's savings and checking accounts, and ran a credit card scam in Vegas, where he worked at a hotel as a photographer for newlyweds."

He was right: Gulliver had conned Abby out of her money and had now deserted her. The perfect headline flashed into his mind: *Dr. Abby Jensen, proponent of marriage and happily-ever-after, jilted by professional con artist.*

He balled his hands into fists. Could he print that about Abby?

Chapter Nineteen

Friendly Foreplay

" 'What women want' is the topic of the TV show you'll do Monday," Rainey explained. "And Tuesday's topic will focus on what men want."

"I'd rather cancel the whole thing," Abby said. "Last night I was almost accosted by a reporter. If it hadn't been for Harry jumping in front of the camera—"

"That guy is turning into hero material," Rainey commented with a dramatic sigh. "And the picture in the paper this morning looks great."

"What picture?"

"Um . . ." Abby heard the telltale sound of Rainey's pencil tapping, a dead giveaway that she was nervous. "You didn't see it yet, huh?"

"No. What paper is it in?"

"The *Inquisitor*."

"Oh, dear heavens." Abby dropped her head into her hands. "Why would you be excited about that, Rainey?"

"Like I told you, any publicity is good. It creates a buzz,

and people buy the book just to see what the hoopla is about."

"I don't want them to buy the book just because I'm in a little article in a tabloid."

"Well, actually it's not a little article, Abby." The pencil tapped faster. "You're the feature. You and Harry are on the front page."

Abby cringed. "Okay, I'll bite. What is the headline?"

Rainey chuckled. " 'Sex Doctor and Hubby Have Secret Baby.' "

Hunter tossed a five-dollar bill on the checkout counter at the local QT to pay for Lizzie's doughnut and chocolate milk, frowning when the teenage girl behind the counter squinted blue-eye-shadowed eyes at him. He didn't need the hassle of some kid staring at him; he already had a headache from trying to convince the senior editor at The *Inquisitor* to scratch the piece on him and Abby. He hoped he'd finally gotten through to the man.

The other cashier, a plump middle-aged woman with a bandanna around her head, whispered in Spanish to the manager behind them. Other customers milled around, purchasing snacks and paying for gas.

"What?" Hunter asked, rubbing a hand over his jaw. "Do I have toilet paper stuck on my chin?"

The young girl giggled, and pointed to the spread of magazines to the side. Hunter gasped when he saw his face plastered on the front—well, Lenny's mustached face plastered on the front right beside Abby. And Lizzie . . . So much for convincing the tabloids to hold the story. In the photo, Hunter was poised as if he might attack the cameraman, Abby stood behind him, clutching at his arm, and Lizzie was hiding behind his legs, Angelica dangling from her hands. They looked as though they had been caught doing something illicit. Then his gaze fell on the headline and his stomach plummeted. *Sex Doctor and Hubby Have Secret Baby.* In the first paragraph the reporter questioned the little girl's parentage: "Is the doctor hiding her child because she is illegitimate? Does the little girl belong to her husband or does Abby Jensen have a ghost lover in her past?"

Good Lord, what crap!

"Daddy, look! Me and Angelica are in the paper!" Lizzie squealed.

Hunter grabbed the stack of papers and flung them on the counter. "I'll buy them all."

The checkout team exchanged confused looks, but the girl accepted his Visa with a grin.

Lizzie pulled at his sleeve. "Daddy, I've never been in the paper afore."

Hunter silently counted to ten. "I know."

"I gotta show Mommy!"

Panic slid down his spine. "No, honey . . ."

The checkout girl pushed his card back toward him with three-inch silver nails and cut him a sharp stare, then grinned at Lizzie. "You look cute, sweetie."

Lizzie clutched one of the papers to her chest. "I'm keepin' it for my scrapbook."

"Let's go get that puppy now," Hunter said. "We just have to make a couple of stops first." *More than two hundred*, Hunter thought, as he mentally mapped out every grocery and convenience store that might sell the tabloid. He had to buy as many as possible. When Shelly saw the piece, he'd have some major explaining to do.

And Abby . . . What would she think when she saw the story?

Abby tried desperately to block out the image of the tabloid photo and the article as she jotted notes for two upcoming shows, but her gaze kept straying to the picture. How dare that reporter suggest she was hiding a child from the public?

A nonhusband yes, but not a child.

She shook her head, her words swimming before her.

What women wanted, what men wanted—what did she know anymore?

Except that she desperately wanted her life to return to normal.

The doorbell dinged and she nearly spilled her coffee on her papers. She swiped at the hot liquid with a napkin before it completely ruined her work, and walked to the door, expecting her sister. Chelsea had volunteered to watch the puppy while Abby completed the upcoming weeklong tour.

Butterball raced beside her, nipping at her feet, and she scooped him up, hugging him to her chest as she opened the door. But her stomach clenched at the sight of the police car in her drive and the officers on the stoop. A tall woman with German features stood stoically beside a broad-shouldered Latino.

"Dr. Jensen?" the woman said in a crisp, no-nonsense voice.

"Yes."

"We're detectives Barringer and Suarez from the APD. Can we come in?"

"What's this about?" She spotted the tabloid in the female officer's hand and winced, wondering why the police would be interested in the sleazy newspaper.

The Latino man, Suarez, inched inside, his presence almost as domineering as his thick voice. "We have some questions about your husband, Lenny Gulliver."

"Daddy, why are you mad about the picture?" Lizzie asked.

He hadn't realized he'd been so obvious. "I don't like that paper," he explained. "They print bizarre things about people. They don't care if what they write is correct or not." His temper rose at the idea of their slandering Abby.

Yet hadn't he done the same thing?

But he hadn't fabricated a story. "In fact, if they can't get a story, they'll make one up."

"You mean they lie?"

His jaw tightened. "Oh, yeah."

"But we lied when we was acting."

Out of the mouths of babes. "That's different." Although how, he couldn't explain. "We're not trying to hurt anyone."

"So it's okay to lie if you don't hurts someone?"

He ran a hand over his face. "No, I didn't mean that. But radio is different from real life." Surely she should understand that.

She scrunched her nose in thought as he wove through the outskirts of the city to the Humane Society. So far he'd confiscated as many tabloid copies as possible; his backseat was piled high. But Lizzie had gotten impatient to go puppy picking, so he'd had to calm down and stop his psychotic rampage.

"There, Daddy, I see the doggie sign."

Hunter pulled into the parking lot, irritated with himself for justifying his actions to his daughter when he had lied to Abby at first to hurt her. As a responsible parent, he should be teaching Lizzie not to lie under any circumstances. Even if he had rationalized his behavior as part of his job. Was he really any better than that tabloid creep?

Feeling surly, he frowned at the run-down condition of the building. What kind of place was this for animals? A few minutes later, they strolled the walkway between the tall cages, searching for the right pet. Dobermans, German shepherds, several mixed kinds of terriers and Labs, a small, yellow, floppy-eared mutt that resembled a beagle, a part Dachshund.

"That's a wiener dog," Lizzie said.

Hunter smiled and reached through the rungs of the case to pet the mutt, but it nipped at him. "Definitely not that guy."

"Daddy, I don't see any Butterballs."

Exactly. He hadn't expected to find a white mop-dog here. They had only real dogs, a man's kind of animal. The thought of bathing that white fluff ball after a roll in the mud made him shudder. "I know, honey, but these doggies are here because they're homeless. They need someone to love them and take them in."

"But Butterball doggies needs a home, too. I seen 'em at the pet store."

"I know that, sweetie. But look, there's some cute small dogs here. And if they don't find homes . . ." He hesitated, realizing Lizzie's ears might be too sensitive for the truth.

"What, Daddy?"

"Honey, pick out a couple to play with and let's see what we think then."

Lizzie twisted her small mouth, but finally nodded. Seconds later she'd climbed inside a fenced-off area on the lawn and was rolling on the grass, playing with three different dogs: a dark brown mutt that reminded him of a bulldog, a spotted puppy with cropped ears and a limp, and a short, stout animal that resembled a cross between a beagle and a basset hound.

His cell phone jangled and he grabbed it, keeping his eye on her and the animals at the same time.

"Stone," his boss snapped, "what the hell is your picture doing in the *Inquisitor*? I thought you were getting a story on Abby Jensen, not trying to make headlines for yourself in another publication."

Abby's hands shook as she led the officers to her kitchen. Had they connected Milano to Lenny? Did they suspect Lenny was his accomplice? Worse, did they think she had had a part in the scam? "Would you like some coffee?"

"No, ma'am," the woman officer named Barringer said. "This is business, not a social call."

"Thanks, that would be great." The Latino smiled, earning a glare from the female gestapo cop.

The male detective studied her kitchen with an inquisitive eye, a smile lining his mouth at her teapots.

"My grandmother turned me on to collecting them," Abby explained, as she handed him an oversize mug.

"I was close to my grandmother, too," Suarez said. "She still lives in—"

"Can we get on with this?" Barringer asked, cutting Suarez off. "We're not here to get a signed copy of her book, Stefan, or to play, so put the boy back in his pocket."

Abby stiffened at the woman's crude suggestion, and Suarez's smile vanished, his dark eyes flashing with temper. "There's no need to be rude, Barringer. We're here to ask questions, not harass her." He winked at Abby. "Besides, I happen to know Dr. Jensen's sister, Victoria."

"You do?" Relief spilled through Abby. Maybe they weren't going to arrest her.

Barringer glared at Suarez, then spread the tabloid photo on the table. "Ma'am, where is your husband? We'd like to speak to him."

Oh. They thought Harry was her husband. "He's . . . he's not here."

"When will he be back?"

"I . . . I really don't know." Abby sank into the wooden chair, eyeing them both warily.

"Can you tell us where he is, Dr. Jensen?" Barringer took the chair beside her. "Will he be at your next interview?"

Abby hesitated, her pulse racing. She couldn't lie to the police. "Yes. No. Actually that man in the photo . . ." She paused, gauging their reaction. "He's not my husband."

A dark eyebrow rose above Suarez's inky eyes. "He's not?"

"No, he's a double."

Barringer patted her side as if she were ready to handcuff Abby any second. "An actor."

"Why would you hire an actor to play your husband?" Suarez asked.

"Because Lenny's not around."

Barringer made a clucking sound with her teeth, waving her hands jerkily. "Just spit it all out, Dr. Jensen. We need the truth, and we can do it here or down at the station."

She did not want to have to go to the police station. "Why are you looking for Lenny?"

"We believe he may be involved in a scam with a man named Tony Milano." Suarez sipped his coffee, his voice steady. "You and Mr. Gulliver were married by Mr. Milano?"

Abby knotted her hands in her lap, inhaled, then nodded. "Maybe you'd better sit down. This may take a while." The officers joined her at the table and she related the entire story, praying they would believe her. Relief to have the truth finally out in the open, at least on some level, filled her.

"Don't feel so bad." Suarez patted her shoulder in an effort to console her. "This isn't the first time Gulliver has conned a woman."

"What?"

Sympathy for her was evident in the detective's handsome face. "He was married twice before and stole money from both wives." Suarez shrugged. "We never would have caught the connection if some reporter hadn't started snooping around asking questions about him."

"A reporter?"

"Yeah, some guy named Stone."

Abby balled her hands into fists. Hunter Stone, the man who had already tainted her reputation in the paper, had now turned the police on her tail. Even worse, now he had the rope to hang her; he was on to Lenny.

Hunter settled the black mutt with the pudgy face and crooked tail into Lizzie's lap. They had finally decided on the cross between the beagle and the basset hound, but Lizzie still didn't seem convinced they'd made a good choice. "He's not a Butterballs." The mutt stuck its butt in her face, and aimed its head at the window.

"But he's friendly, and he needs us."

"He don't got much hair."

"Then he won't shed all over the furniture."

Lizzie patted his stout back. "He gots a smashed-in face."

"That just makes him more lovable."

"Can we takes him by to see Butterball?"

Hunter cranked the engine and veered from the parking lot. "I guess so. Let's see if Abby's home."

The dog dropped down on his belly, spread out all fours, and began to snore. Lizzie folded her arms cross her chest, gave him another skeptical look, and sighed. Hunter just hadn't been able to bring himself to buy a sissy dog. After all, a man's dog should reflect something about his personality.

Another sound rippled through the air, and Lizzie squealed. "Eww, Daddy, he farted."

Well, maybe not *everything* about a man's character. Hunter rolled down his window. "He's a guy dog," he said, as if that explained everything.

Lizzie pinched her nose and scooted the dog off her lap, her fingers extended as if she'd just touched a sack of garbage. The puppy crawled between Hunter and Lizzie and stuck his nose into Hunter's crotch. Hunter squirmed and pushed the dog from his sniffing venture. The puppy collapsed between them with a sigh and let another one rip.

Lizzie giggled. "Gross!"

The dog responded with a loud snore.

A car horn blared and Hunter jerked his mind back to the road. Bright sunshine nearly blinded him as he wove along the azalea-lined drive to Abby's house. Flowers decorated the suburban neighborhood like brightly colored balloons, dotting the lawns with a homeness missing from his apartment complex.

He needed to buy a house, even if it was a small one, so when Lizzie came to visit, she felt more at home. Where the dog could have a place to run and roam. But how he could finance it?

"Daddy, why's the police at Dr. Abby's?"

He spotted the squad car and grimaced. *Good question.*

Had something happened to Abby, or were they here about her husband?

"Will you let us know if you hear from him?" Barringer asked as Abby escorted the officer to the door.

"Yes." Humiliation stung her face at the woman's suspicious glare. It was bad enough that she'd had to admit that her husband had left her and charged up her credit cards, but to admit she'd paid someone else to pretend to be him had stolen her last ounce of dignity.

The policewoman had grilled her like an FBI interrogator, certain Abby had been involved in the resort scam. Apparently Lenny's name had been tied to a joint account with Tony Milano, so they'd figured out the connection.

"Take care, Dr. Jensen," Suarez said in a sympathetic tone. "Oh—" he leaned forward—"and tell Victoria hi for me."

"I will, and thanks." As the police walked down the driveway she sighed in relief, but her stomach hit the floor when Harry's Explorer coasted by her house. Obviously having spotted the police, he rolled down the street as if he didn't know whether to stop or flee. He probably didn't want anything to do with her troubles.

The sun baked her as she watched the police pull away. Harry returned within seconds, climbed out, and strode toward her, his daughter holding Angelica and dragging some ugly mutt behind her, her big floppy T-shirt and pink sandals flapping.

"Come on, Snarts," Lizzie cajoled. "We gots to go see Butterballs."

Harry's dark gaze met hers. "I hope you don't mind that we stopped by."

The mangy mutt stopped to sniff and trample the flower bed Abby had diligently planted by the mailbox. Harry reached out and brushed her cheek with his knuckles. "Is everything all right, Abby?"

No, she wanted to scream. *Nothing is right. First the tabloid, then the police.*

But his concern touched her, and Lizzie and her dog bounded toward them, so she bit back a harsh retort. "Everything's fine."

His expression made his disbelief evident, but she ignored it. Instead, she dropped down to a squatting position to speak to Lizzie. "Hey, sweetie." She slowly reached out so the animal could sniff her hand. "Who's your new friend?"

"He's my dog," Lizzie said with a huff, as if Abby wouldn't recognize him as such. "They didn't got no Butterballs. And Daddy said we should give this guy a home 'cause he's homely."

"Homeless," Harry corrected gently.

"He says he's a real man's dog."

Abby lifted a brow and stared at Harry, watching him squirm.

"He says dogs 'sposed to detect what a man's like." As if on cue, the dog flopped down on his fat stomach and whined.

"I said a dog is supposed to *reflect* what a man's like," Harry said tightly.

"So are you going to flop down on your belly and whine?" Abby asked.

Lizzie giggled. "Yeah, Daddy, do it."

Harry's direct gaze promised retribution to Abby later. "I don't think so."

Abby stroked the dog's nearly hairless back. "What's his name?"

"Snarts."

"Why did you call him that?"

" 'Cause he snores and—"

"Lizzie, I don't think Ms. Abby wants to know."

Lizzie blew a gust of air, sending her bangs fluttering. "Can he play with Butterballs?"

Abby nodded and gestured for them to follow her,

but the dog bounded off and ran through the house. Suddenly the sound of crashing glass rent the air. Lizzie raced after the dog, Hunter and Abby on her heels. When Abby found them in the kitchen, Lizzie was staring wide-eyed at one of Abby's teapots on the floor.

"He broked it," Lizzie cried, horror-struck.

"It's okay, Lizzie," Abby said, hating the fear in the little girl's eyes.

Hunter consoled Lizzie, searching Abby's face. They knelt at the same time to clean up the glass before Lizzie cut herself. "We'll replace it," he said. Snarts disappeared under the table, his head ducked, his paw over his head.

"No, it's all right. The teapot wasn't expensive."

"I'm sorry," Lizzie cried again. "Don't hates me and Snarts, Ms. Abby."

"Her mother is pretty particular about her fancy things," Hunter explained in a low voice.

Abby's breath caught in her chest. She dropped the glass in the trash, then brushed Lizzie's bangs back and hugged her. "Honey, don't worry. I don't hate you or your doggie. It's just broken glass. I can buy another teapot."

Hunter gestured toward the collection on the shelf. "They must be special to you."

"Yes, but they're not expensive." Abby grabbed a tissue to dry Lizzie's eyes. "I collect them because my grandmother and I played tea party when I was small."

Lizzie's eyes widened. "Can we play tea party sometimes?"

"Sure."

"Right now, put Snarts out and let him walk, though," Hunter advised.

Lizzie plucked out a pair of sunglasses and settled them on the bridge of her nose. Abby frowned. Bright orange sunglasses with rhinestones. Wasn't that cross-dresser wearing a pair just like those at the bookstore? "Where did you get those, Lizzie?"

"I don't 'member," Lizzie said. "But aren't they cool?"

231

"They're a dime a dozen at the QT," Hunter said. "Now take Snarts outside, Lizzie."

Lizzie bounded out, and Abby grabbed the tabloid and used it as a dustpan.

His gaze fell to the headline. "You saw the paper?"

Abby hesitated, then scooped the glass on top. "Yes."

"I'm sorry, Abby." He placed a hand over hers. "I don't like the ugly things that tabloid guy implied."

Abby shrugged. "Neither do I. And I'm sorry they involved you and Lizzie."

His expression looked pained for a second.

"I'd really like to forget about it," Abby said.

"Yeah, I know what you mean. Most people don't pay any attention to the junk the tabloids print anyway." They finished cleaning up the glass, then stood in awkward silence.

"So what are you and Lizzie up to today?"

"We planned to grab a picnic and take it to the park." His eyes searched her face. "Would you like to go?"

Abby hesitated, then smiled. "Sure, that sounds great." Finally, something normal to do for a day. Maybe a picnic would distract him from wondering why the police had been at her door.

"Daddy, did you gets the condoms?" Lizzie asked.

Hunter nearly tripped over a tree root on the way to the picnic site. He'd barely had time to recover from panic over the sunglasses, and now this.

Abby halted, clutching the blanket to her chest. "The what, Harry?"

"The condoms. You know, the ketchup, the mustard," Lizzie said.

"You mean the condiments," Hunter clarified. "And yes, I got them."

Lizzie plopped down on the ground, Indian-style. "Mom gots other condoms. Not like mustard and ketchup. They looks like balloons."

Hunter and Abby exchanged raised brows. "Did she show these to you?" Hunter tried not to react as he helped Abby spread the blanket, yet his heart danced in his chest.

"No, I founded 'em and filled 'em with water." Lizzie tossed a stone into the creek and watched it splash. "But Mommy gots mad and said little girls aren't s'posed to play with them."

One thing he and Shelly agreed on. "Mom's right about that," Hunter said, catching the gleam in Abby's eyes. "Did she tell you what they were for?"

Lizzie tossed the stone and watched it ping off the tree. "No. She said we'd talks about it when I gets bigger."

A good plan, Hunter decided. He was grateful when the dogs dove toward the food and so did he and Abby, ending the discussion.

Two hours later Hunter stretched out on the blanket, exhausted from romping with Lizzie on the playground and coaching Snarts to get some exercise. It had been an incredible afternoon. Abby had been adorable, totally at ease goofing around with the dogs and Lizzie.

He'd had to reel his mind in from wandering down the wrong path. From thinking about what life with Abby and Lizzie and another child might be like. Snarts collapsed on the ground beside them, living up to his name as he sawed logs. Abby's puppy lay curled into a ball at her feet like a dainty lady waiting on a pedicure.

Abby plucked a strawberry from the container and popped it into her mouth. Lizzie lay on her stomach watching a caterpillar forage through the grass near the sandbox a few feet away.

"Abby, thanks for not yelling at Lizzie and the dog about the teapot." He snatched a strawberry for himself. "I'd like to buy you one to replace it."

"Harry, Lizzie's feelings are more important to me than some glass object. What kind of a person do you think I am?"

Harry studied her, his first impression totally dispelled. "I think you're pretty special."

"Thanks, Harry," Abby said softly. "This has been the nicest day I've had in a long time."

Hunter folded his hands behind his head and leaned back against the trunk of an oak tree, enjoying the shade. And the scenery. And the silky, satiny voice that belonged to Abby. "So the famous sex therapist doesn't mind a touch of normal life?"

"Normal life would be a welcome change." Her mouth closed around the strawberry, the red juice spilling down her lips. He swore silently, wishing he could lick off the juice and taste the sweetness of her mouth.

"Why were the cops at your house earlier?"

Abby hesitated, then picked at the fruit bowl. "They're looking for Lenny."

"I thought he was in Brazil."

"I don't know where he is," she admitted quietly.

"You want to tell me what he did to you, Abby?"

A canyon of silence yawned between them. She looked so vulnerable and lost and troubled, he couldn't resist covering her hand with his. "I'd like to help if I can." And this time he meant it.

"Thanks, Harry." Abby laced her fingers with his. "But I can't."

He scooted closer and brushed her hair back with his fingers. "I really do want to help, Abby."

She met his gaze then, her eyes filled with sadness. "I appreciate that. After Lenny, and then that awful Hunter Stone, and now that tabloid guy who trashed me in the papers, I didn't think there were any decent men left."

She raised a hand and placed it on his jaw. "Thank God every man isn't like that. It's nice to be with someone who's honest."

Oh, God. If she only knew.

"Someone I can be myself with, someone who's not trying to get something from me. Someone I can talk to." She curled her feet beneath her, squeezed his hand, and brushed a gentle kiss on his cheek.

He swallowed.

"I know exactly what I want to say when I do Monday's interview."

"What's the topic?" he asked, emotion thickening his voice.

"What women want." The fading sunlight dappled rays of gold and red across her face. He ached to wipe the sadness from her eyes with a night of lovemaking. To erase all her problems. To wipe his own slate clean so she would never know his deception.

He would make it up to her when he wrote the final piece.

"What do women want?" he finally asked.

She traced a short fingernail up his shirt, making his nipple tighten. "They want love and romance and passion. They want friendly foreplay."

"Friendly foreplay?"

"Yes, being friends is important in maintaining a long-term relationship." Abby sighed and pressed her hand against his heart.

"Hmm, I never thought about it like that. What else do women want, Abby?"

She snuggled into his arms. "They want a nice man like you, Harry. Someone romantic."

Shelly hadn't thought so. But he could be romantic; Abby seemed to bring out that side in him. "What else?"

Her voice grew soft. "They want someone they can trust."

Chapter Twenty

What Women Want

"What do men want, Harry?"

He caught her hand and dropped his head forward, an odd, almost pained look on his face, as if he was struggling with his answer.

"Harry, did I say something wrong?"

He closed his eyes and shook his head, then kissed her fingers, one by one. The simple gesture was so erotic that Abby wanted to throw herself at him right there in the middle of the park.

Shadows from the trees surrounded them, creating a private haven that evoked images of long, lusty afternoons lying in his arms, naked and affectionate, loving each other all day until the moon finally found its way into the sky.

But his daughter and their dogs lay a few feet away, a staunch reminder of reality.

"You're not going to answer me," Abby finally said, when he remained silent.

"Ahh, Abby," Harry finally murmured. "It's a tough

question. A lot of men want sex, just fast, hard sex. Then others . . ."

"Others what?"

"Others want the same things women want."

"What about you, Harry?" She was flirting with fire, but she didn't care. The day had been incredibly romantic, and he hadn't even tried to make it that way, which made him even more appealing. He was so damn sweet and protective and such a good father. "What do you want?"

"I . . ." He suddenly slid his hand beneath the back of her neck, lifted her hair, and pulled her toward him. "I want you, Abby."

Uttering a low growl full of desire mixed with frustration, he closed his mouth over hers and kissed her. Abby melted in his arms and clung to him, wishing the moment could last forever—but knowing their destiny together was probably doomed.

"Daddy, why you kissin' Dr. Abby?"

She and Harry jerked apart, both stunned and shaken. Harry mumbled something about Abby having a boo-boo; then he quickly gathered the picnic supplies and led the way to the car. Abby scooped up Butterball to follow, and Lizzie struggled to drag Snarts out of his deep slumber.

Hunter flipped the radio to a soft-rock station while he drove Lizzie home, smiling at her sleeping form curled against his lap. The mutt lay sprawled at her feet, its tail twitching occasionally, the only sign of life the dog emitted, other than that occasional ripple of a snore.

What a dud of a dog.

He forced his gaze back to the road, but his mind wandered to Abby and their conversation. Guilt had attacked him like the plague when she'd said she trusted him.

But if she trusted him so much, why hadn't she confided the complete truth about her husband? And the reason the police were looking for Lenny?

Had his conversation with his cop buddy, Falcon, pointed the police in Abby's direction?

Another reason to feel guilty, he thought, wiping perspiration off his forehead.

The turn to his ex's mansion came just as automatically as the feeling of trepidation that engulfed him. A world of money and snobbery he'd never feel comfortable in surrounded his daughter's home. Why hadn't he seen what his wife really wanted when they were married?

Because they hadn't listened to each other, he realized, remembering Abby's book and advice. They'd each been traveling their own road, oblivious to the other's needs or wants. When they'd tried to ride together they'd actually collided, their cars a tangle of anger and differences. Finally, one day they'd reached a crossroads and parted.

But Lizzie was stuck in the middle.

She was all that mattered now.

Except for Abby, a little voice whispered.

The streetlights of Buckhead glittered like Christmas decorations around the mansion as he parked in the drive. Lizzie rubbed her eyes and peered at him while Snarts planted a paw over one eye and moaned, peeking out of the other as if to ask why he really had to move from his comfort zone.

Hunter hopped out, came around to Lizzie's side, and opened the door, then lifted her in his arms. To his surprise, the massive front door of the house burst open and out sauntered his ex-wife, jewels sparkling, her silk pantsuit shining like polished glass. The fury in her eyes stopped him cold.

"We have to talk, Hunter."

Lizzie squirmed and woke up. "Daddy, can I takes Snarts with me?"

He'd planned to keep the dog at home, but he was going to be out of town all week. "You have to ask Mommy."

His gaze pleaded with Shelly, but she took one look at the mutt, who chose that moment to scratch his ear as if he were a flea-infested mongrel, lifted her nose in disdain, and shrieked a *no* that he knew was final.

"Please," Lizzie begged. "He's homeless, Mommy."

"There is no way that sorry excuse for an animal is coming into my house." Shelly jabbed a finger toward the dog. "He'd probably urinate on the Persian rugs and chew up my Chippendale furniture."

Lizzie's lower lip trembled. "I know he don't look good, Mommy, but Daddy says he needs us."

"What that dog needs is to be put out of his misery."

Lizzie burst into tears and buried her head on his shoulder. "Don't get rid of Snarts, Daddy; please don't let her get rid of him."

Anger flashed through Hunter like heat lightning. "Mommy's not going to do anything to hurt Snarts, sweetheart. I promise." He aimed a worried look at the dog, but Snarts had crawled onto the floor to hide. Maybe the dog had some sense after all.

"We have to talk," Shelly said. "Lizzie, go on inside."

Lizzie wiped at the tears streaming down her face and Hunter's gut clenched. "It's okay, baby. I promise I'll take good care of Snarts for you. You can play with him next time you visit."

"But he'll forgets me."

"Lizzie—"

"Shelly, give us a minute." Hunter barely controlled his anger. He brushed Lizzie's hair down. "He won't forget you; he loves you just like I do. I may not get to see you every day, Lizzie-bug, but I think about you every minute. I know Snarts will, too." He lowered her enough to pet Snarts good-night, then kissed her and watched her run inside, clutching Angelica as if she were her only friend.

Shelly stared at him with fury in her eyes. Because of the dog?

"Listen, Shelly, every kid needs a pet."

"And does every child need to be in the tabloids, Hunter?" She whacked him in the chest with the photograph, then launched into a tirade about his being a horrible father.

Hunter closed the SUV door so they wouldn't disturb Snarts, then waited silently until she'd vented her anger. Finally he sneaked a word in and explained about the article.

"I don't care about your crummy job, Hunter. But Lizzie looks like she's been rolling in the mud, she probably has ticks from that mongrel, and I know your apartment is unsanitary—"

"Unsanitary?"

"And if you expose my daughter—"

"*Our* daughter," he said through gritted teeth.

"If you expose our daughter to more tabloids or dangerous situations—"

"She wasn't in any danger."

"How do I know you aren't taking her along when you investigate criminals?"

Rage built inside him. "Because I wouldn't do that."

"But you let them hint that she was your illegitimate daughter. For God's sake, my parents saw this and have already called, hysterical."

He'd never liked her parents anyway. "Listen, I'm sorry, Shelly; it was a mistake."

"No, trusting you with Lizzie was a mistake."

"What?" The air in his lungs squeezed. "You can't mean that, Shelly."

She jabbed him in the arm. "I do. I'm warning you, Hunter, if you do anything like this again, I'll sue you for full custody and you'll never see Lizzie again."

Victoria pounded on the door to Stefan Suarez's apartment, furious and hurt. She had just spoken with Abby and learned he had questioned her about Lenny.

The door swung open, surprise lighting Stefan's handsome face. "Victoria, how nice—"

"Nice?" Victoria pushed past his bare chest, ignoring her

body's response to the sight of him half-naked. Damn the man; she had almost fallen for his charismatic manner. She whirled around, shooting daggers at him with her eyes. "I can't believe I ever trusted you."

"What?" He rubbed a hand over his jaw, the bristle of late-evening beard even darker in the shadows of his dimly lit apartment. "I don't know what's upset you, but let's talk—"

"No, I'll talk; you listen." She averted her gaze from the dark hair tapering down his washboard stomach to his low-slung jeans. "How dare you make out to be my friend, rescue me and Chelsea like some knight in shining armor, kiss me till my toes curl, then go behind my back and interrogate my sister as if she were a criminal."

He folded muscular arms across his belly and simply watched her as she vented, his calm expression only fueling her temper more.

"I never want to see you again."

He raised a brow, a spark of temper flashing in his nearly black eyes. "Are you finished?"

She recognized the barely checked anger in his voice and glanced at the door. Maybe she shouldn't have come.

"Don't even think about running until you hear me out." With a backward kick of his foot, he slammed the door behind him and glared at her, stalking toward her with the intensity of a lion after its prey. "First of all, I did not play nice to you to get you to reveal information about your sister. I played nice to you because I like you and want to be with you." He held up his fingers, using them to tick off his points. "And second, when I questioned your sister, I was simply doing my job. I'm a detective, Victoria. I told you I would do almost anything for you, but I won't compromise my job."

"So you admit—"

He silenced her with a slash of his hand. "No, I never used you. The precinct is investigating the Tony Milano scams; you've heard of them?"

Victoria gulped. "Yes."

"We found a bank account that connects the two men. That's the reason we went to talk to your sister."

So he was a man of conviction—she had to admire him for that. "Oh."

He stood within inches of her, the heat of his body and temper flaming her desire. "I do think your sister was an innocent victim of Gulliver's, but if she has information regarding his business with Milano—"

"She doesn't."

He raised a thick, dark brow. "You're sure?"

"We talked about it when the news about Milano first hit. She searched Lenny's belongings, but she couldn't find anything incriminating or we would have turned it over to the police."

His slight look of distrust rankled her. Even hurt.

"I wouldn't lie to the police, Stefan. Abby wouldn't either." She lowered her voice. "We just didn't want Abby's involvement plastered in the news. They haven't exactly been kind to us over the years."

"I can understand that."

"And Abby deserves better. She's sincere and works hard. She's always helping people, and God knows she was the calm one when we were growing up and my dad . . ." She hesitated, appalled at how much she was about to reveal.

"I know about your father," he said in a low voice. "And your mom."

Embarrassment heated her face. "I'd better go."

He caught her arm. "No, I don't care about your parents, Victoria." The sincerity in his husky words touched her. His voice turned low, intimate. "You have to believe that I would never hurt you. That I only want to help."

"I . . . I guess I'm just used to taking care of everything on my own." She had to glance away from the deep, knowing look in his eyes. How could this man see inside her, read her so well?

He tipped her chin up with his thumb and angled her face so she had to look at him. Had to face the volatile chemistry between them. "Just tell me one thing."

"What?"

"Did my kiss really make your toes curl, Victoria?"

A heady sensation flitted through her. Damn, why had she admitted that about his kiss?

His cocky, satisfied grin told her he already knew the answer.

Oh, hell. "Yes."

He swept big hands down her face, then onto her shoulders, and skimmed them to her waist. Then he pulled her to him, his whisper featherlight against her ear. "Then just think what making love will be like."

She tensed. "You scare me, Stefan. I don't want to think about making love with you."

"Then don't think, my sweetness." He kissed the soft shell of her ear. "Just feel."

For once in her life, Victoria took a chance. She reached up and spread her hands on his bare chest, released a shaky breath, then pulled his mouth to hers and let Suarez take it from there. She desperately wanted to understand the hoopla about all this "under the covers" talk.

And Stefan was just the man to help her do it.

Abby curled up with Butterball and pulled out her journal.

Day started off with bang. Cops showed up. Thought they might arrest me. Wanted to know where Lenny is. Wish I knew. Will strangle the man when see him.

Harry came by later with Lizzie and pathetic excuse he calls man's dog. Men really are from Mars. Loves his little girl, though. Sweet nature makes up for idiot brain in picking mutt.

What does this woman want?

An honest man who isn't running from the law. Maybe someone like Harry.

She lay back on the pillows and sighed. Exhaustion weighed her down, and she closed her eyes, finally allowing herself the freedom to imagine her life the way she wanted it to be. A life spending her days working, her weekends with her children, and her nights making love to Harry.

No, not Harry. She couldn't be in love, not so soon after being hurt by Lenny.

She meant a man *like* Harry.

Hunter woke with the mutt dead-asleep on his face, his mind screaming with anxiety. First he'd dreamed that his ex had confronted Abby about the tabloid picture, then spilled the beans about his undercover job. When Abby discovered the truth, she was so mad, she joined forces with Shelly. The judge had ruled him an unsuitable father and had given Lizzie to Shelly permanently, denying him visitation rights.

He rolled to his side and pushed Snarts off of him, frowning as the dog cut one loose. He jackknifed up. His chest hurt, his insides ached, every part of him throbbed with tension.

He could not lose Lizzie.

No, he had to finish this job, and earn that promotion so he could have more time off to spend with Lizzie. That way he'd never have to take her along on an assignment again. But would he be able to keep that promise if he became a criminal investigative reporter?

He stared at the bare walls, at his grungy apartment, worry rolling through him.

He had two hours before he met Abby for their week-long trip. A week with Abby that could be heaven if not for the hellish situation he'd gotten himself into. He crawled from bed, walked the dog, then showered and dressed.

A half hour later, he'd called all the vets and found that the only place that could take Snarts on such short notice was a pet resort and spa that would cost him an arm and a leg. Knowing he'd exhausted his choices, he dragged the dog from his Explorer, cursing when Snarts sprawled onto the grass and refused to budge. The stubborn animal weighed a ton when he dropped down like a rock. Finally Hunter picked him up, grunting as his back almost gave way, and hauled him inside Precious Pets.

A cheery young redhead wearing a pink, heart-shaped smock checked off items on a clipboard as she questioned him. "Would you like to have him groomed while he's here?"

"Yeah, sure." A bath certainly couldn't hurt him. Get rid of those ticks and fleas Shelly was certain he had.

"How about dental work?"

"Is it necessary?"

"Unless you want your dog's teeth to fall out."

Then he couldn't chew his furniture. Still, that didn't seem fair. "Go ahead."

"How about his nails?"

Hunter frowned. "Clip 'em, I guess."

The girl smacked a wad of gum. "What about playtime?"

"Excuse me?"

"Do you want to schedule playtime with the other animals?" She flashed her braces at him. "We try to make the animals more social. If he has trouble—"

Hunter glanced at the snoring animal. "I don't think he needs it." Hunter didn't wait for more questions. He rolled his eyes and walked out the door, figuring the next thing they would have wanted to know was whether he needed a psychiatric exam. The dog didn't, but after he'd paid two hundred and fifty dollars for a week's stay, he certainly did.

Abby feasted on Harry's good looks as they readied for the Monday show. They had flown to New York for two days; then they were on to California, making a brief stop in San Francisco before heading to LA. When they returned to Atlanta, they would end the tour with a spot on the *Good Day, Atlanta* show. Then Rainey had promised the charade would end as well. Of course, so would her relationship with Harry.

But she would enjoy the next five days with him. Muscles rippled and bulged beneath the crisp blue shirt, the aroma of his cologne wafted around her like an aphrodisiac, and his blue eyes devoured her hungrily.

She was certain his devoted look was planned for the camera.

But she could fantasize otherwise.

Of course, an analyst might say she was riding a slippery slope, that her ego needed a boost after the fallout from Lenny.

"Let's talk about what women want," Monica, the anchorwoman of *Battle of the Sexes*, a slim, yuppie-looking, brassy blonde, said.

"That's a tough question, because every woman is an individual, so each woman has her own dreams, desires, secret fantasies."

"Give us some examples, Dr. Jensen."

Abby crossed her leg, aware Harry watched the movement, his breath hitching. Was he acting for the camera now? "Most women I work with want love, respect, and friendship from a partner."

Monica flitted her hand at Harry. "I suppose you two have that."

Harry gave her a sultry look. "We have it all, Monica."

Abby smiled, willing him not to pour it on too thick. He'd been doting on her ever since they'd arrived, touching and caressing her as though he'd never be able to get enough of her. His affection was almost unbelievable; no man was that devoted.

"And women want emotions, love, romance," Abby explained. "All the old romantic clichés too, like flowers, candy. Some of them want to be wined and dined, while others prefer a wild ride on a Harley."

"We do have romantic dinner plans ourselves later," Harry interjected. "And then I'll take her on the Harley."

The audience laughed, falling right into the palm of Harry's hand.

"Varying the routine is important in keeping the romance alive, too," Abby said, attempting to stay on track, although now images of her and Harry on that Harley tortured her. Her legs straddling his, her arms around his hard middle, breathing in his manly scent with the wind in their faces.

"Many women complain about being taken for granted," she continued. "Their husbands or boyfriends take them to the same restaurants, the same movie theaters within a five-mile radius. Granted, they have legitimate reasons for staying close to home, but people can sink into a rut if they're not careful."

"I've been there," Monica agreed.

Several women in the audience clapped.

"Women want a man to be honest," Abby continued, barely able to drag her gaze from Harry. "To be loving and to take care of her. To encourage her to be herself and to pursue her dreams."

"What are the most common types of fantasies you hear about?"

"Many are romantic in nature. Making love on a moonlit beach. In the back of a horse and carriage. In various rooms of the house. Playing with food and spreading it on a lover. Having sex in the back of a limo with champagne and chocolate." Abby threaded her fingers together in her lap, maintaining a straight face. "Then some people entertain more daring fantasies."

"Such as?"

"Many women fantasize about having sex with a stranger. Some with multiple partners." She hesitated, her body heating up at the blatant raw look of sexuality in Harry's eyes. "Some fantasize about voyeurism—performing in front of the camera."

Harry's breathing grew shallow, his eyes smoky.

"Although many women might not want to engage in

group sex in real life, fantasies are a safe way to play out those darkest, wildest urges."

"Any other common ones?" the host asked.

"Of course, some women fantasize about having sex with another woman."

"The lesbian-lover fantasy."

"Exactly. Actually," Abby said with a grin, "men often fantasize about watching their partner with another woman."

A bead of sweat burst out on Harry's forehead. Abby frowned as he wiped it away.

"Another common fantasy is relinquishing control. Women either dream of being dominated or of dominating their man."

"And how about you, Dr. Jensen? Tell us one of your fantasies."

"I . . ." Abby froze, uncomfortable sharing her fantasies on TV. Finally she improvised. She pulled Harry's tie, making him lean toward her. "That's actually easy. I fantasize about kissing my husband on television."

Laughter rippled through the audience. The heat of the moment swept her away, along with the burning look of lust in Harry's eyes. If he could act for the camera, so could she.

She jerked him to her and laid a lip lock on him. Only she wasn't acting.

Hunter had been hard and hurting all night.

Ever since Abby had walked onto that television show and talked about fantasies in that husky, low voice of hers—a voice that dripped with sultry undertones, arousing his darkest fantasies and unleashing beastly needs within him. And that kiss onstage . . .

How was he going to spend five more days with her and not have her?

She's married, he told himself. *Even if her husband has*

temporarily run off, you don't know if he'll return one day. If they'll reconcile.

The silent lecture did nothing to alleviate the burning ache in his body, though.

They finished their candlelight dinner and strolled through the city, finally giving in to exhaustion and returning to their exquisite room at the Plaza. Unfortunately, since the show had made the arrangements, they shared a suite with one bed and a plush sofa. Beautiful cherry wood furniture and fabrics in dark, rich tones gave the room an elegant ambiance, and the marble tubs and crystal wineglasses waiting with complimentary champagne set the stage for intimacy.

"Thanks for helping me out, Harry," Abby said quietly.

He laced his fingers through hers. "You're worth it, Abby."

She turned to him then, a dozen different emotions in her eyes. Her perfume intoxicated him. The kiss they'd shared earlier still lay emblazoned on his lips like a fever. And now here they were in this romantic haven, all alone.

He poured them both a glass of champagne and toasted the success of her show. "Tell me one of your real fantasies," he whispered softly when she'd settled on the purple velvet sofa beside him.

Abby smiled and played with his fingers, rubbing the ends. "I'd be with a man who wanted me more than anything else," she whispered. "It wouldn't matter where we were, although sometimes I dream we're making love on the side of a mountain, in the bare grass, dandelions and wildflowers dotting the ground around us, the wind blowing cool air on our naked skin." She hesitated and lowered her head as if she'd said too much.

He lifted her chin with his fingers. "Go on."

She licked her lips, her tongue peeking out to torture him, then slipping back inside her mouth where he wanted to be. "We'd make love all night, teasing and loving each other with kisses, and then we'd stare at the stars and he'd take me to the moon again right before it disappeared in the early hours of dawn."

Her voice had faded to a soft whisper, a sound that sent blood racing through his body and caught him on fire. He couldn't fight his urges anymore. Rational thought fled as he pulled her into his arms.

Her mouth found his in a hungry frenzy, tasting of champagne and desire; his hands dragged her to him, lifting her body on top of him so she straddled him. She rocked forward on his aching erection and he groaned, plunging his tongue into her mouth and finally tasting the sweet heaven he knew he would find.

Their tongues mated, danced, sang a song of hunger that only they could hear. With a low growl, he found the buttons of her blouse and slid them open, then tore at her bra with his teeth, watching in awe as her glorious small breasts spilled from the lacy cups and beaded with delight in the dim light of the room.

Chapter Twenty-one

What Men Want

Abby's body tingled with erotic sensations, her heart pounding with excitement. Harry cupped her breast in his hands and stroked her bare skin, then lowered his head to lift a pert nipple to his mouth.

A sudden shriek broke into their hushed cries of pleasure.

Abby froze, pressing herself to Harry. An apologetic female voice filled the room.

"Oh, excuse me, folks." Out of the corner of her eye, Abby spotted the maid, a young Hispanic woman in her twenties, her eyes bulging.

Harry jerked Abby's blouse together, wrapped his arms around her, and pulled her close, peering over her head.

"I ... I'm so sorry. I came to turn down your bedding." The maid backed away, her gaze still pinned on them. "I knocked but no one answered."

Because they'd been so involved they hadn't heard her ...

The woman turned and fled, slamming the door behind her. Abby moaned in mortification and gathered her composure. Dear heavens, what had she been doing?

The next day Hunter dressed for the noon interview, his body a raging mass of unsatisfied need, all because of one sexy marriage therapist. After the maid had fled, so had Abby. She'd refused to talk about the incident, so he'd left her alone and gone to the gym to work off his agitation. Then he'd slept on that damn purple sofa alone with her not more than a few feet away. Only he hadn't slept because the scent of her perfume had lingered on the sofa along with the scent of their desire.

The only thing that had stopped him from joining her in bed and pushing the subject was the fact that she was still married.

Well, and the lies.

And his guilt over deceiving her and writing those articles.

Shelly's threats still haunted him; he had to figure out a way to salvage this job and his relationship with Abby, and get Shelly off his back about this custody issue.

What men want.

Abby studied her notes, praying she didn't make a fool of herself onstage. She had no idea what men wanted anymore.

If she had to speak from her own experience, she'd say they wanted to screw you, steal your money and pride, then leave you to pick up the sorry pieces.

Not exactly what her audience expected to hear. And ironically, although Lenny had screwed her money-wise, he hadn't wanted to screw her in bed.

Squelching the bitterness didn't come easily, but she checked off the day on her calendar. In four days, this whole ridiculous charade would be over.

Her life would return to normal.

The police, hopefully, would find Lenny.

And Harry would move on to another acting gig. And probably to another woman.

Disappointment tightened her throat, but she swallowed it. He was only acting.

Only they hadn't been on camera the night before.

No performance. Just her throwing herself at Harry. What man would refuse?

And that, she thought, was the answer to her question. Men wanted exactly what she'd offered Harry.

Sex without ties or emotions or commitments.

As Hunter and Abby settled into the limo, he curved his arm around her and pressed her close. "Did you sleep well last night?" he murmured, although, judging from the dark shadows beneath her eyes, he suspected she hadn't.

Her nervous gaze flitted to him. "Uh, yes. How about you?"

"Actually I didn't," he admitted. "I kept fantasizing about you."

"Harry." Her voice softened, and she closed her eyes as if she could block him out and stop this crazy wanting. "That was a mistake. Like you said, we got carried away—"

"It wasn't a mistake, Abby," he said gently. "And I wasn't acting."

"Harry, please don't." She fidgeted, pulling at her black satiny skirt.

He placed his hands over hers to still them. "I can't help it, Abby. The more I'm with you, the more I want to be with you." He traced a finger over her cheek, his heart racing. "We could play out that fantasy in the limo."

"I . . . I can't do a one-night stand. That's just not me."

He brushed a kiss over her hair, inhaling the sweet scent of strawberries. "I'm not asking for a one-night stand."

She clutched his hand, squeezing his fingers. "Look, you're an actor, and you're just starting your career." Her voice quavered. "And I can't do a relationship right now.

Not with . . . with everything in my life the way it is."

Not with her husband still missing. He understood and knew she was right. But it didn't stop him from wanting her. And somehow he had to convince her that all men weren't like her bastard husband.

Abby paced the green room, her mind racing. The crew hadn't been too fussy: the makeup artist had covered the dark circles under her eyes and fluffed her hair, the sound guy had attached the mike to her clothes—after reassuring her it wasn't turned on yet—and then they had left her to prepare mentally for the show. But all she could think about was Harry. Why had Harry been so sweet in the limo? Was he serious about wanting a relationship with her?

If so, should she pursue it?

She certainly liked Harry a lot. She admired the way he handled and loved his daughter. Although his taste in dogs was atrocious, he did have good intentions in buying his daughter a pet. And he must have a kind heart to take in a creature like Snarts. He was sexy and strong, too, and he'd defended her with those pond-scum reporters. And his touch did feel heavenly. His lovemaking would probably send her over the top in seconds.

No. A relationship would never work. Once his acting career took off, he'd move to LA or be traveling and . . . once this whole mess with Lenny was resolved, she'd return to her practice.

"Abby?"

She halted in front of the makeup chair. "Is it time?"

"No, we have a few minutes." Harry shifted on the balls of his feet. "Can I talk to you for a second before we go onstage?"

Abby nodded and he led her to a partitioned area filled with extra camera equipment. A canopy of curtains obliterated the harsh overhead lights and cocooned them in a cloak of darkness.

Harry's masculine scent filled the small space, making her dizzy.

"I want you to know I meant what I said in the limo on the way over."

"What—you want to play out a fantasy by making love in the limo?"

"No." He chuckled and moved closer to her, his knee brushing her thigh in the small space. "Well, yeah, I wouldn't mind doing that, too." He cupped her face with his hands. His breath bathed her face as he whispered in the dark, "I want us to really get to know each other."

Abby's heart slammed against her ribs. "Harry—"

"No, listen, I know you've been hurt before, and so have I, but we have a strong connection. I can feel it when you look at me, when I hear your soft, sultry voice, when I touch you."

His voice played along her nerve endings, winding them into taut strings of desire.

"I want you, Abby."

Did he have to sound so sincere?

He threaded his fingers through her hair and drew her face so close to him, she saw the pulse at the base of his throat beating, felt the whisper of his breath as he lowered his mouth to hers.

"I'm falling for you, Abby."

The softly spoken words severed her cords of resistance, and she melted into his arms again, the heat from the night before that had simmered between them erupting into flames.

His mouth tasted, feasted on, devoured her. She gave him the same, playing with his tongue in a teasing game of passion that surpassed her own fantasies. His hands covered her breasts, stroking and teasing through her silk blouse until she tossed the jacket aside and silently willed him to undress her. His gaze took in her sleek camisole, and he lowered his mouth to taste her, suckling her through the flimsy undergarment. Then he pushed that up, opened her bra, and filled his hands with her breasts, sucking and pulling her nipples until liquid heat pooled in Abby's womb.

"Oh, God, Harry." She moaned and tossed her head back, giving in to wild abandon as he slid his hand up her skirt and found her moist essence. With a low growl, he lifted the skirt to her waist, then pushed her panties aside and feathered his fingers over her sex tenderly. She sank her hands into his hair, flung her head back, and moaned.

"Harry, we have to stop—"

"Not now, baby. You feel like heaven."

Which was exactly where he took her.

"Oh, Harry, don't stop!" She clutched at his arms, her legs buckled, and she almost fell backward, but grabbed a lighting pole to steady herself. He drove her wild with his fingers, playing with the fire inside her, igniting it to a burning flame that threatened to consume her. Screeching his name, she rocked sideways and the pole rocked with her, back and forth, back and forth, until Hunter plunged his finger inside her. The shock of the intimacy jerked her body into a wanton frenzy, and she dropped the pole. A loud crash reverberated through the tiny space, but a thousand sensations burst within her, and she couldn't catch the pole or stop the echo of metal boomeranging throughout the backstage area. Just as the height of pleasure reached a crescendo, applause broke out from the set up front.

Too late, she realized the host of the show was calling her name.

Hunter heard the announcer calling Abby's name and groaned. What the hell had come over him?

"Oh, my God!" Abby hurriedly tried to fasten her clothes, her hands shaking. Her normally pale complexion had metamorphosed into a bright crimson, her hair was tousled, and his beard stubble had left red scrapes on her face.

He smoothed down her skirt while she fumbled with her bra. But her hands were trembling so much, she couldn't work the clasp, so he took over the task. She closed her eyes, her breathing still labored, mortification mingling with panic. Maybe she should call and get Chelsea to do a sanity spell on her.

"It'll be all right," Hunter whispered in a soothing voice. "Just relax. Take a deep breath."

The one she released sounded shaky and torn from her lungs. "I can't believe I forgot where we were and that people were waiting, and—Oh, heavens—"

"Shh." He handed her her jacket, brushed at a makeup smear gently, and kissed her forehead. "You're going to be dynamite. In fact, you *were* dynamite."

Her face brightened more. "What if they know what we were doing?"

"Don't be silly; how could anyone know?"

As soon as Abby and Hunter neared the stage, Abby caught a grin from two of the cameramen. The lady from the green room raced over, fluffed her hair, and reapplied lipstick, then brushed powder across her cheeks, all the while humming, "How Sweet It Is to Be Loved by You."

Abby's stomach curled.

They knew. She had no idea how, but she had a gut instinct that the backstage hands had heard them. Probably when she'd dropped that pole and it had crashed.

"Ladies and gentlemen, welcome to our new late-night talk show, *Male Talk*. Here's Dr. Jensen to talk about what men want." The crowd roared, and the announcer waited several seconds while they settled, then added with a wink, "although I think Dr. Jensen and her newlywed husband just demonstrated to us what men want."

Abby's eyes widened as the handsome African-American man pointed to her microphone. *Oh, God, oh, God,* she silently cried. Harry must have accidentally tripped her microphone on. She swung her gaze to the audience. The snickers and grins told her they had definitely overheard the escapade behind the curtain.

Including her orgasm.

She was never, ever, going to be able to show her face in public again.

What if Granny Pearl saw this episode? No, surely Granny wouldn't be watching a late-night men's show.

Harry suddenly squeezed her hand. "That's right, Chuck. Abby decided to act out a little scene offstage to introduce the subject for today's show. She wanted everyone to realize how hot it can be to slip away and make love on the spur of the moment." His fingers squeezed hers almost painfully, as if he were coaching her to play along. "Right, darling?"

Abby nodded like a marionette. "Right. What do men want?" She licked her lips, but her heart was beating so fast she thought it might explode. "They want sex anywhere, everywhere, and any time of the day."

The crowed applauded again, several men in the audience pumping their arms in a signal of masculine agreement. Harry and the host confirmed the male's exuberance, launching the show into an entirely different direction than Abby had expected. Suddenly Abby wasn't talking about men wanting to screw a woman without emotions or commitment, but rather how many ways and places a man could take a woman to be his lover. Finally the host decided to poll the audience, which consisted mostly of men.

"But why did she keep yelling, 'Harry'?" an elderly man asked. "Was she fantasizing about someone else?"

"She likes my hairy chest." Harry patted his chest for emphasis and the crowd laughed.

"My fantasy—fast and hard and whenever the mood strikes," one man said.

"Mine," a middle-aged man in a business suit said, "is to take her under the boardroom table with all my partners watching."

"I'd like to video her doing a striptease for me," a young college coed stated.

A bearded man in jeans and a flannel shirt stood up. "Two women at once."

"I want my woman to go down on me more," a black man said, flexing his muscles when the other men agreed.

Abby nodded and mentally took notes; then a dark-haired man in the back row caught her attention. "I want my woman to take control, put me in handcuffs."

"I just want to please my wife," Harry said. "Giving her pleasure is a turn-on to me."

But Abby didn't respond because she couldn't drag her gaze from the man in the back row. He was wearing a Dodgers baseball cap, a black jacket, a cream colored polo shirt, and khakis.

And he looked exactly like her real husband, or rather, the man she thought she had married—Lenny Gulliver.

Chapter Twenty-two

Ménage à trois

Hunter had no idea what had upset Abby, but during the last five minutes of the show, her porcelain complexion had turned completely ashen. She had stared out into the blinding sea of lights and the enthusiastic crowd, and fixated on one point. And she'd never completely regained her composure.

Or had she fixated on one person? A man?

Jealousy snaked inside him like a slithering, poisonous reptile.

He had no right to be jealous of Abby.

Regardless, now that the show had ended, he had to force himself to focus on the host as he jabbered on and on about women, his own fantasies, and how his partner had misunderstood when he'd asked her to play sex games. How did Abby tolerate listening to people whine about their problems all day? She must be a saint.

He shifted, shoved his hands into his pockets, and reminded himself he was an actor, so he had to act interested—when he really wanted nothing more than to drag Abby outside and force her to tell him what had upset her.

But she'd disappeared offstage, and it was killing him not knowing where she'd gone.

"You're so lucky, man, to have a woman who will give in to your whims," one of the stagehands said. "Tell me the darkest fantasy you and your wife have acted out."

What was this guy, some kind of pervert? Did he think their entire marriage consisted of nothing but wild sex?

Hunter froze as the realization that he'd been thinking of his and Abby's marriage as real hit him. "A gentleman never tells," he said quietly, looking the man in the eye. "And besides, if I told you, it wouldn't be a private fantasy anymore. That's what makes fantasies exciting, isn't it? The secrecy?"

He didn't bother to wait for a reply. He grinned and hurried backstage to find Abby.

"I can't believe you're actually here." Abby stared in shock at her former husband, or the man she'd thought had been her husband, as he ducked into an unoccupied room in the back of the studio.

"You look great, Abby. I loved the show." Lenny rubbed his finger along his upper lip where his mustache used to be. The clean-shaven lip wasn't the only thing about him that had changed. He'd died his hair strawberry blond, wore green contact lenses, and must be wearing lifts in his shoes, because he was at least two inches taller than she remembered.

But his smile still radiated false charm, smooth as honey and twice as sweet.

And now, behind the charm, she saw the con man, the evil that he'd disguised so well. Why hadn't she seen it before?

Because she wore rose-tinted glasses. She was trusting and caring; she always looked for the good in people, not the bad. She had to wake up and not be so naive. . . .

Folding her arms across her chest, she ignored the fresh wave of pain assaulting her. "What do you want, Lenny?"

"What? No kiss for your old husband?"

She glared at him. "We're not married, remember? So technically you aren't my husband or anything else." *Except a living nightmare.*

Lenny's shifty eyes traveled over her body from head to toe. "I heard you doing the actor guy before the show."

She wanted to kill herself.

"I have to say I'm surprised, Ab. I didn't know you had it in you."

"To have sex with another man, or to get over you so quickly?"

He made a clicking sound with his teeth. "Both. And that guy . . . you really think he looks like me?"

"No, he's much more handsome."

That wiped the smug smile off his face.

"You changed your appearance."

His finger rubbed his bare lip again. "Yeah, well, that had to be done."

"So the police wouldn't find you." Abby sighed, her irritation mounting. "Aren't you afraid they'll look for you here, Lenny? Are you sure they're not watching me, waiting for you to contact me?"

He shrugged, drawing the black sport coat up his narrow waist. "I figure if you'd ratted on me, I'd have seen it in the papers. Instead, I've been reading how well your book's doing."

A bad premonition engulfed Abby.

"I bet you're pulling in a nice hunk of change."

The feeling grew stronger. "Is that why you're here? You expect me to give you money? Didn't you steal enough from me and those people you and Tony Milano scammed?"

"A guy can always use more cash," Lenny said. "Or I could walk out there and introduce myself to the host of the show. I'm sure he wouldn't mind doing a follow-up episode with your real husband."

Except we're not married. Abby's temper flared. "And risk getting caught? I doubt you'll do that, Lenny."

Lenny threw his head back and laughed—a dirty laugh that crawled up Abby's spine like spiders in the dark. "Oh, Abby, you underestimate me."

The spiders picked at the back of her neck.

"I don't plan to expose myself." He held up an envelope and pulled out a photograph. "But I have a feeling everyone would be interested in these."

Abby legs wobbled as she realized what he held in his hand: the nude photos he'd taken of her on their honeymoon.

Hunter scoured the entire back area of the studio, the green room, and the curtained area where he and Abby had enjoyed their little romp earlier, but couldn't find Abby.

"Have you seen Dr. Jensen?" he asked the makeup artist.

"No. Maybe she's playing hide-and-seek with you."

Hunter mentally groaned and strode back down the hall to check the vacant studio rooms; then he saw Abby emerge from the back, a stricken look on her face. The overhead light caught her expression as she pivoted to say good-bye to the man she'd obviously been hiding out with, and he saw fury etched on her face as well as shock.

Relief that she hadn't been kidnapped by some maniac ballooned in his chest.

The man bent to kiss her cheek, and Abby stepped backward, her gaze lethal.

What the hell was going on?

Was the man a cop looking for her husband? Another tabloid reporter or PI?

No, a cop or reporter or PI wouldn't try to kiss her. Could it possibly be her husband? Had the real Lenny Gulliver resurfaced? And if so, what did he want?

Realizing Abby wouldn't appreciate his spying on her, he ducked back down the hall and into the green room to wait for her. The clicking of her shoes told him when she approached. A few seconds later she entered, her arms tight by her sides, her expression blank.

"I need to do some errands this afternoon," she said in a barely controlled voice. "You take the limo and I'll grab a cab."

He moved forward, worry pressing like a brick on his chest. "I'll go with you."

"No."

Hunter recognized the finality of her answer in her tone, and her panic-stricken look alarmed him. "What's wrong, Abby?"

He tried to take her hands in his, but she squared her shoulders and pulled away. "Nothing. I just have some things to do. And I need to do them alone."

He didn't like it one damn bit, but he nodded. "All right. I'll take the cab."

She barely spared him a glance as she headed toward the exit. "Just keep the receipt and we'll reimburse you when you're paid at the end of the week."

And just like that, she'd demoted him from the man who'd given her a behind-the-scenes orgasm to the hired help. Because she was going to meet her real husband?

While the driver circled the interstate, Abby vented her fury on her fingernails, nearly ripping them to the quick. Unfortunately now she was getting carsick.

She'd thought Lenny couldn't get any lower on the food chain, but he had slunk down to the lowest form of life. A rat. No, a mole. No, a boll weevil.

Hell, she didn't technically know what the lowest form of life was, but she had a new name for it.

Lenny Gulliver.

The rat fink wanted money for the pictures. Money to keep his silence, to keep them from the tabloids and the television shows and her family. And the Internet.

That had been the clincher.

She didn't much care what her father thought, and her mother would probably just laugh about the pictures, but Granny Pearl . . . granted, her grandmother was a modern granny, but seeing erotic photos of her granddaughter plastered all over the tabloids and Internet might even push her limits. And what about her clients? And her sisters? Chelsea would weather it all right, but Victoria would be humiliated in front of her coworkers. She'd already worked hard enough to overcome the stigma of their father; she didn't deserve any more strife.

Harry's concerned face flashed into her mind, and she fisted her hands. What would Harry think? He was a father, for heaven's sake. And God forbid his little girl saw the pictures.

She buried her head in her hands. What was she going to do?

She hit the button and rolled down her window, inhaling the fresh air, although heat seared her face. Not knowing what to do, she phoned Victoria.

"Steedleman, Warscheiner, and Boles," the receptionist chirped. "How can I help you?"

"May I speak to Victoria Jensen?"

"I don't think she's taking calls right now. She's in a meeting."

Damn. "Tell her it's her sister, Abby, that it's an emergency."

"Well," the woman said in a nasally voice, "all right."

Seconds later her sister's voice echoed over the line. "Abby, what's wrong? Are you hurt? Is it Chelsea?"

"No, no, I'm sorry, it's nothing like that."

"Then what is it? I'm in the middle of a meeting—"

"It's Lenny. He's here."

"What?"

Tears flooded Abby's eyes. "I'm sorry, I'll call—"

"No, wait." Victoria's voice softened. "Just give me a

minute, okay? I have to give my client some good news. Now don't hang up."

"I won't." In spite of her strong resolve, Abby felt the emotional strain wear on her, and the tears began to fall. Her hands jerked around the phone.

A minute later, Victoria returned.

Abby had tried to collect herself. "I'm glad someone got good news."

"Yes, I told you I had a father who was being denied his rights."

"That man Marcus, the one who called me for counseling recommendations?"

"Yes, well, his ex is in jail for contempt of court and he finally got to see his kids." She paused. "Now, where is that cockroach, Gulliver?"

"He's . . . here."

"Tell me where you are, Abby."

"In New York, the TV station." She sniffed, feeling miserable. "He showed up in the audience."

"That asshole's got some nerve," Victoria said angrily. "You should sic the police on him."

"I know. I'm going to tell them he's back in the States, but there's something I have to do first."

"I hope it involves maiming certain body parts."

A laugh escaped between her sobs. "Victoria, he has these pictures of me. Nude pictures he took on our honeymoon. I don't know why I let him—"

"You don't have to explain or justify letting a man you thought was your husband photograph you, Abby," Victoria said softly. "I'm not as big a prude as you think."

Abby exhaled, trying to control her tears. "But he's going to give them to the tabloids. And Gran and Chelsea, and Harry and Lizzie—"

"Who's Lizzie?"

"Harry's little girl." An ache clutched at her chest. "She's only five and I don't want her to think I'm a hussy."

Victoria chuckled. "You're not a hussy, sis. But why is she so important?"

"Because she's Harry's little girl."

"Isn't Harry that actor who's playing Lenny?"

"Uh-huh."

"Oh, mercy," Victoria said. "Are you involved with him?"

Victoria obviously hadn't seen the interview yet. "That's not important. Can you go with me to withdraw the money to buy the pictures from Lenny? I could use some moral support."

"You're not actually going to pay him, are you?"

Mortification swept over Abby at the alternative. "I have to. But just as soon as I get my hands on the negatives, I'll turn him over to the cops."

"Just let me know when you're ready, sis. I have a friend; he'll help us."

"Suarez, that cute Latino guy?"

"Yes," Victoria said, her voice carrying an odd ring to it.

"Is there something going on between you two?"

Her sister's silence said it all. Thank God one of the Jensen sisters had a decent romance on the horizon.

She hung up, her mind a jumbled mess. To hell with the charade and the book. She had let Lenny screw her once.

She didn't intend to let him do it again.

Hunter realized Abby needed time alone, but he couldn't ignore the situation. The redheaded man who had upset Abby sat in a rental car outside the station, so he stripped off his mustache and fake hair and followed him to a local bar. The Flamingo Club had been decorated for its namesake with pink flamingo birds painted on the walls, island greenery motifs decorating the tables, and hot-pink strobe lights flickering around the room in a dizzying motion. Heavy perfumes and colognes mingled with the scents of sweat, cigarette smoke, and liquor.

The place was a living sea of colors, nationalities, and ages sporting a dance floor that showcased strippers, both male and female. And a small group of patrons dressed oddly, as if they might be gender-confused. He wove his way through the smoky den, careful to keep his distance, and ordered a beer. The man stopped at a booth in the corner, embraced a dark-haired man, then scooted in beside him. A tall woman with *executive* written all over her followed him into the curve of the booth.

Hunter's eyebrows rose. The redheaded man obviously wasn't a cop. And he didn't carry himself like any reporters Hunter knew, that was, unless he wrote for the society column, or the gay-liberation section.

The three looked awfully chummy. Had they met for a ménage à trois? And if so, how were they connected to Abby?

Former patients? Reporters?

He remembered her talk about women fantasizing about group sex. Surely Abby wasn't into a threesome? Or could she have been in the past?

Heads bowed and bodies huddled together as the trio whispered back and forth and sipped frozen drinks. He meandered through the crowd to reach a spot where he could unobtrusively listen to their hushed conversation.

"So you were married to Abby Jensen?" he heard the woman say in a thick Southern accent.

"That's right. I'm the real Lenny Gulliver. That guy onstage with her is just playing the part."

Hunter fisted his hands by his side. So this was the man who'd hurt Abby.

Only the man failed to confess to his friends that he'd run out on her.

The music piped up a notch, drowning out their voices, and Hunter swore. Just what was the man up to? And what had he said to Abby to upset her so badly? Surely she wasn't still in love with this man, was she?

The three moved to the dance floor together and began

gyrating in a triangle of arms and legs and erotic movements. He had seen enough.

He only had more questions. Maybe it was time he confronted Abby.

He grabbed a taxi back to the hotel, his mind humming with questions, his heart humming with fear and hope. The elevator took forever, and he sucked in a deep breath as he approached the suite. His heart pounding double time, he raised his fist and knocked on the door.

Maybe if he offered her a comforting ear, she would open up and talk to him. Then all their secrets could be revealed and they could start over and really get to know each other.

"He did what? He's where?" Chelsea leaned forward in the mirror and plucked her eyebrows, one ear glued to the phone.

"Lenny showed up in New York and tried to blackmail Abby," Victoria said on the other end of the line.

"Oh, my God, I can't believe this is happening."

"I know. I hope the police catch him and he rots in jail."

"Is Abby going to pay him for the pictures?"

"Yes, just to get them back. Then she's turning him in."

"Good. What can I do?"

"Nothing except be there for Abby. She's going to need our support when all of this comes out."

Chelsea agreed and hung up, but studied her face in the mirror. She had to do more than offer her support. Not only had Abby always been there for her; she'd loaned her money over the years and never once asked for payment. And after that little episode with the police, Victoria really saw her as a screwup.

Abby would probably be broke after paying Lenny off. It was time for Chelsea to pay her sister back. Only, after buying those gold lamé pants she was strapped for cash. She took the card that the man had given her at Pete's Prism from her purse. She had called once to check it out and discovered she could make a bundle if she worked just one night. They were always looking for fill-in dancers. And she was an actress; she would have to do nude scenes sooner or later. She might as well practice.

She shuffled through her costumes, grabbed a stack of clothing, and stuffed it into her bag. Then, before she could lose her nerve, she drove to the Blackhorse Club. A few minutes later, Enrique, the manager, had set her up for a show; she'd go on after the Angel of Darkness, a sultry, dark-haired vixen dressed in silver. In one of the dressing rooms she had found a fabulous Lady Godiva outfit and shimmied into it. It was much better than any of the outfits she had brought. The long wig reached to midcalf—perfect. When she stripped, if she draped the hair in all the right places, it would hide most of her private parts and still tease the crowd.

Nerves fluttered in her stomach as she listened to the calls and whistles of the packed bar as they reacted to the Angel. She peeked through the curtain and watched the exotic dancer tear off her angel wings and hurl them into the crowd. Men cheered and tossed money at her left and right. The lights dimmed, the dark room filled with the scent of cigarette smoke, liquor, and a hazy sensuality. The Angel climbed the pole, flung her head back, and dropped her silver string top, big breasts bouncing. The men roared their approval and threw more bills at her. She strutted across the stage and stripped to a thong, and the crowd went wild. A puff of smoke enveloped her, then faded to reveal her standing with her arms held out in supplication.

Chelsea chewed her lip, wondering how she could follow such an act. Her stomach spasmed as the music died and the announcer introduced her show. Dressed in a gold ensemble with the wig of blond hair brushing her butt, she strutted onstage and began to gyrate to the music. Her years of dance lessons saved her. The song, "I Want to Be Loved by You," blared out of the speakers, and she wrapped herself around the pole dramatically, then flung her head back and let her hair touch the floor. She was just about to drop her top when a loud voice rent the air, overpowering the music.

"How dare you try to steal my act!"

Before Chelsea realized what had happened, an Amazon woman with implants the size of cantaloupes and fingernails as sharp and long as Ginsu knives attacked her. Chelsea jumped back and tried to run, but the woman reared her arm back, grabbed Chelsea's wig, and flung it into the crowd. The men applauded, believing the catfight was part of the show. Chelsea saw the woman bear her teeth, though, and she knew the Amazon was out for blood. She turned to run, but the woman balled her hand into a fist, reached back, and punched her in the eye. Chelsea screamed and fell backward, then saw black stars swirling amidst the pink strobe lights just before Enrique jumped onstage and dragged her off.

Chapter Twenty-three

Real Sex, Take One

Abby had to end it with Harry. She could not continue flirting with one man while another still haunted her like a dog-eared demon. Taking care of Lenny and those evil pictures would be the first step. Calling the police would be the second.

Then the public would have to learn the truth.

What if Harry discovered her sordid story before she could tell him?

You're worrying about nothing, she reminded herself. *Harry is a hired actor playing a part.* And he was a talented actor—so good he'd convinced her he actually cared about her.

Didn't all actors seduce their costars? A different woman with every part they played? A knock sounded at the door and she jumped, pulling her silk robe around herself like a coveted shield. Instantly her insides quaked as she imagined Lenny lurking on the other side, more nude photographs of her in his hands. On the heels of that image,

Abby imagined a red-horned reporter named Stone ready to snatch them from his hands.

Gathering her courage, her knees knocking, she crept to the door. "Who is it?"

"It's me, Harry." His voice sounded oddly gruff. "Can I come in, Abby?"

The interlude behind the curtain burned fresh in her brain, sending a wave of embarrassment and renewed tingling through her. Still, the memory of Lenny's leering lingered like a bad odor clinging to her. "It's late, and I'm tired. Can't we talk tomorrow?"

"It's only nine o'clock, Abby." He paused, his breath gushing out loudly. "Please. I need to see you."

The hand that reached for the doorknob was amazingly steady considering the rapid beating of her heart. She slowly opened the door, his magnificent size immediately overpowering her. His shoulders looked even broader tonight, his eyes darker, his expression more sensual and seductive.

Maybe he just seemed larger than life to her because she knew the power of the pleasure he'd given her, and the fact that he'd asked nothing in return. She didn't realize they made men like that anymore. Ones who enjoyed pleasing a woman yet had no ulterior motives.

His unselfish loving made him ten times as sexy and a hundred times harder to deny.

As he stared at her, his hungry eyes raked over the contours of her body encased in nothing but silk, and she imagined dropping to her knees, unleashing his sex, and giving him the same incredible pleasure he had given her earlier. Her nipples hardened and strained against the fabric of her thin gown, her body quivering from the image of him gloriously naked in front of her. He would be impressive. . . .

"Abby, if you don't stop looking at me like that, we're going to do a whole lot more than talk."

His voice woke up her brain. *Thank God.* "I'm sorry. I . . . wasn't—"

"The hell you weren't." He pushed his way inside the room, his long steps purposeful and determined, but he stopped at the sofa in the suite, poured himself a scotch from the bar, and turned to her, his gaze penetrating. "Not that I'm complaining, but we do have to talk first."

She swallowed, his refusal to deny the obvious chemistry between them as titillating as if he'd touched her with his fingers.

"You know we're going to make love, Abby. It's just a matter of time."

She opened her mouth to object, but he stopped her. "It's going to be the best sex you've ever had." His voice was thick with heat. "And it's not going to happen just once either."

Her pulse clamored. He stalked toward her until his face was mere inches away from hers, his erotic masculine scent suffusing her with images of lusty nights, his body on top of hers, pumping and grinding, filling her with his love.

So this was the reason women liked to be dominated. She finally understood.

"What . . . what did you want to talk about?"

He caressed her cheek with one thumb, the rough texture singing along her nerves. "The man who upset you at the studio."

He couldn't have spoiled the mood any faster had he told her *he* was gay.

She backed up, poured herself a glass of Chablis, and sank onto the sofa, weary. She wanted desperately to deny Lenny had upset her, but Harry'd obviously seen her reaction. He had come to know her pretty well. He was very observant. She supposed watching and listening to people closely was a necessary skill for an actor.

"What did he say to you, Abby?"

She clenched her fingers in her lap. "He's my problem, Harry, not yours."

He was beside her in a flash, his jaw tight. "What if I told you your problems were mine?"

How could that possibly be? He didn't even know her problems. She stared into the wine, swirling it in her glass, wishing the pale liquid held answers. "But they're not, Harry."

"Maybe they are, more than you know."

His softly spoken words clawed at her self-control. "No, Harry, you're just an actor and we're playing roles—"

"We're more than that, Abby, and you know it."

Did she? Silence stretched between them, full of questions and hope and the kind of sexual tension Abby had only written about in her book.

"I want you, Abby." He took her glass from her and set it on the table alongside his, then gripped her arms and forced her to face him. "And I think you want me, too."

She gazed into his eyes, the fire of desire burning like a brightly lit flame. It flickered and grew, just as the embers of her own hunger for him surged within her.

"I do, Harry, but—"

"Right now there are no buts. Just trust me, Abby; *talk* to me."

His husky whisper shattered the last remnants of reason. She suddenly ached to trust him, to have someone strong to lean on. To touch him and make him burn in her hands and mouth the way he had done to her.

He must have sensed her surrender.

Releasing a soft groan, he dragged her closer, traced a finger over her lips, then met her mouth with his, his tongue plunging inside to taste her. Abby sank into his arms, the power of his assault so tender, yet so passionate that breathing no longer mattered. She clutched at his shirt, stroking his jaw and angling her face to take him deeper into her mouth. He tasted like scotch and man, a combination that intoxicated her.

Warmth spread through her like honey, and she tore at his shirt, sending buttons flying. Her hands swept over his chest, stroking and soaking up the heat from his torso, the coarse, dark hairs on his chest caressing her hands like a lover themselves. His hands played along her back and spine as his lips left hers to lave her neck, the sensitive shell of her ear, then lower until he parted her robe and his hands and mouth trailed inside, loving her through the silky nightgown.

She wanted more. She wanted nothing between them but sweat and bare skin.

A low, guttural groan escaped his throat, and he suckled her until she thought she would come apart from the exquisite torture.

"Oh, God, Harry."

He suddenly stopped, laid his head on her breast, then looked up at her. "Abby, I want you so badly." But instead of taking her, he stood and tore himself away, facing the wall. "But we can't. Not . . . I can't take you knowing you're still married."

Abby closed her eyes, the pain of his withdrawal almost as overpowering as his lovemaking. She had to trust him with at least part of the truth. Her voice was barely an audible whisper when she spoke: "I . . . I'm not married, Harry."

He swung around, his shocked gaze searching her face for the truth.

Her chin quivered as she licked her lips. "It's true. I . . ." How could she tell him the humiliating truth; that she had never been married to Lenny, that she'd been a victim of his and Tony Milano's scheme? She couldn't, not with her gown torn open, her body exposed, her breathing ragged with desire for him. He would think she was the worst kind of fool. "We're divorced."

He took a minute to process that statement. "It's final?"

She closed her eyes, the part truth, part lie lodging like dry toast in her throat. "Yes. It . . . it just happened when the book hit the stands, but my publicist had put together this tour and I couldn't get out of it."

Confusion clouded his face for a moment, followed by turmoil, as if he couldn't quite decide what to do with that information. "Are you still in love with him, Abby?"

"No." A shudder rippled through her. "Heavens, no."

As if her admission released him from the moral clause he'd clung to, a slow smile spread over his face. His lips parted as he came toward her, a flush of renewed desire and determination in his hungry gaze.

And Abby knew that he intended to follow through with his promise, that she was about to experience the best sex of her life.

For one brief moment, Hunter hesitated. His journalistic voice screamed at him that he had a great story in the palm of his hand.

But his emotions argued that he had a great woman in the other.

He had a choice.

But one look into Abby's eyes and the idea of choosing the article faded like storm clouds overcome by the brilliance of the sun. Steam sizzled between them, heating his body as he folded her in his arms. She melted like hot chocolate, deliciously rich and wicked in taste.

He tried to remember the advice he'd read in her book about slow seduction and titillating touches, but his hands had a mind of their own, and his body refused to acknowledge *slow*. All he knew was this fierce need to possess her that consumed him.

He stripped off her nightgown, pausing a second to drink in the glory of her naked body. She was all textures and angles, her hips flaring in enticing curves that made his hands ache to hold her. Her breasts were small but perfect, supple and irresistible. The dark, rosy peaks begged for his mouth, her flat stomach beckoned for his touch, and the soft triangle surrounding her femininity whispered for his hands.

Giving him a look as sultry and sinful as an exotic

dancer, she slowly feathered her slender fingers down the outline of her body, stroking her inner thighs, then shuddering. Her gaze said, *Take me; I'm yours.*

Unable to resist a second longer, he ran his hands down her arms, then cupped the weight of her luscious breasts in his hands. "You are so beautiful, Abby."

"I want to touch you, too," Abby whispered.

He smiled and flared his arms out by his side, his body jerking when she licked her lips and stepped forward. Her bare breasts swayed as she reached for the edges of his shirt. Slowly she bared his chest while he stood silent, gazing down at the tangled curls spiraling around the curve of her shoulders.

She dragged the shirt down his arms, her gaze raking over his hair-dusted chest and tracking down his stomach as she dropped the garment to the floor. His muscles bulged and jumped at the heat in her eyes; then she reached for his belt, and a dark, hungry look crossed her face as she leaned forward. She licked his nipple, then lowered one hand to cup his sex, and he thought he would explode from the pleasure.

A low, throaty moan escaped him as he grabbed her hand and brought it to his bare stomach, smiling at the disappointment that flitted into her eyes. "All in good time, sweetheart."

"I want to see you," she whispered raggedly. "I've tried to imagine what you'd look like."

The sound of her heady admission nearly drove him over the edge. Feeling his control slipping with each inch his sex grew, he shucked his jeans and underwear and stood before her, letting her look her fill.

Her vibrant eyes turned darker as she took in his size. "Let me taste you," she whispered.

He shook his head. "Later." With another low growl, he swung her into his arms and carried her to the bedroom. She groaned as he pushed her onto the bed, then sighed with sweet surrender when he clasped her hands above her head and began to feast on her. She tasted like sin and sex and woman, a heady delicacy that he knew he would never forget.

One he would like to dine on every night.

The thought shook him to the core, but he didn't stop. He plundered her mouth with his tongue, licked his way down her neck, circling the entire globe of her breasts before he completed his journey by teasing her nipples. One at a time, he loved and pulled and twisted them with his teeth until she writhed beneath him, struggling to free her hands.

But he couldn't let her touch him yet. No, not yet.

So he pushed her hands harder into the bed, driving her wild as he nudged her legs apart with his knee. His sex bulged and jutted toward her, straining for the heaven she offered, yet he denied himself and simply stroked the insides of her thighs with his shaft, rising above her to stare into her eyes. To see the dark hunger and passion flaring there for him.

Her wild, abandoned look warned him she teetered on the brink of release, but he didn't want to end the sweet torture. Not yet. He straddled her instead, pinning her with his weight, letting his bulging shaft lie at the tip of her opening, taunting her unmercifully with tiny strokes as he kissed her again. She arched and begged, bucking her hips up toward him and parting her legs wider.

"Please . . . I want you."

Empowered by her admission, he lowered his head and began the same torture on her breasts again, licking and suckling her until her moans of pleasure echoed off the walls. Her body quaked beneath him as he finally pushed his sex into her. She squeezed his hands and groaned, the insides of her body clutching at him, quivering with the intensity of her orgasm. Finally he released her wrists, cupped her face in his hands, and kissed her again as he began to pump wildly inside her.

She clawed at his buttocks, her movements savage as

Rita Herron

she met him thrust for thrust and cried out in ecstasy. He jerked her legs around his waist and rode her like the primitive beast that lived inside him, filling her, then retreating, then thrusting farther until he couldn't stand the torment. She was his woman, now and always. His release came swift and hard, and he buried his head in her breasts and sank his whole heart into riding the crest with her.

Still quivering with the aftermath of their lovemaking, Abby cuddled into Hunter's embrace, the scent of his sweat and sex clinging to her skin. "That was incredible."

He curled his arm around her and pulled her into the vee of his thighs, their legs tangling. "It was more than incredible."

Abby rubbed a finger over the nub of his nipple, smiling when he shivered. "You are going to pay for not letting me touch you, though."

A chuckle rumbled from deep with him. "I have a feeling this is one payback I'm going to enjoy."

Abby laughed and nuzzled her face into his chest.

His voice rumbled out: "Abby, are you into threesomes?"

She froze, pushing away slightly to look into his eyes. "No, why do you ask?"

"Just thinking about the fantasies you mentioned."

She narrowed her eyes. "Is that one of your fantasies, Harry? A ménage à trois?"

"It's okay in the movies." He threaded her hair around his hand, then rolled her over on top of him. "But in real life, I don't like sharing my women."

"Women?"

"Woman," he corrected.

"So is this when you start beating on your chest and bellowing like Tarzan?"

He laughed, then cupped her bottom with his hands. "No, this is when we start real sex, take two."

Abby arched a brow.

"You didn't think that was going to be the end of it, did you?"

Abby traced a finger over a tiny scar at the top of his forehead. "Oh, no. I hope not." Dropping her head forward, she crawled down his body, letting her hair tickle his chest and legs as she licked at his thighs. "I told you I was going to pay you back for torturing me."

Then she finally got to touch him, just the way she wanted. And this time he was the one begging for mercy.

Victoria glanced at Suarez, who had phoned her after Chelsea had phoned him, then peered down at Chelsea's swollen eye. Her stomach convulsed. "Dear God in heaven, what happened?"

Chelsea wobbled toward her, her hands clinging to her head as if it might fall off and roll across the floor if she let go. "I . . . was attacked."

"By whom?" Victoria glared at the manager of the Blackhorse Club as she sank into one of the chair's in his office. What had Chelsea being doing in a place like this?

"Some Amazon. She, um . . ."

"Spit it out, Chelsea."

"She thought I was stealing her act."

"Which was?"

Chelsea's voice was barely a whisper. "Lady Godiva."

Victoria closed her eyes to gain control, then opened them, not sure whether she was more angry or frightened. Stefan moved toward her and laid a comforting hand on her shoulder. Odd how reassuring his touch felt. "And were you?"

"I . . . I didn't know it was her act." Chlesea's voice broke then, a pitiful cry escaping. "I only wanted to make some extra money to help Abby." She tried to stand, but swayed and flopped back down, the tattered gold outfit billowing around her.

"This is unbelievable," Victoria muttered.

"Do you want to press charges?" Enrique asked, looking nervous.

"No," Chelsea said in a squeak.

"Yes," Victoria said at the same time.

Suarez knelt and handed Chelsea a tissue. "You shouldn't let her get away with this, Chelsea. You were a victim."

Silence stretched between them all.

"I just want to go home and forget tonight ever happened," Chelsea said in a small voice.

Victoria and Stefan exchanged worried looks; then Victoria stood. "We'll let you know, Mr . . . Enrique."

Stefan offered one hand to Chelsea while Victoria wrapped a supportive arm around her waist.

"Just call me if you want to work again, Chelsea," Enrique said. "You have real potential."

Victoria frowned and held her shoulders high as the three of them walked through the crowded area to her car. "You are not stripping again," she said as she helped Chelsea into the car.

"I know. Thanks for coming, Victoria." She gave her a pleading look. "I'm sorry I got knocked out." A nervous laugh escaped her. "But at least I didn't get knocked up."

Victoria shook her head. Then she couldn't help but laugh. "You know, Chelsea, you might get into messes, but at least you have a sense of humor. Abby's going to need one, too, to get through her own troubles."

Stefan slid a hand to Victoria's neck. "Will you call me if you need me?"

Victoria turned to him and kissed him thoroughly, smiling when she pulled away and saw Chelsea's shocked expression. "Let me take Chelsea home and put some ice on her eye; then you can come over."

On the Friday flight back to Atlanta, Hunter studied Abby. One more interview and their week of playing husband and wife would end. Abby had fallen asleep on his shoulder, her eyelids fluttering gently as they coasted through the sky. The last three days had passed in a blur of simmering sensuality, sinful sex, and interviews. Hunter had never been so sated in his life.

Or so nervous.

He was walking a tightrope with Abby, and any minute the truth about his identity might shake the foundation beneath him and he would crash to the ground. He only prayed that when that happened, that she could forgive him.

Only Abby hadn't mentioned the future.

Not that they'd talked a lot.

They'd been too busy giving each other pleasure.

But when they'd come up for air twice, he'd heard her on the phone with her sister Victoria, the lawyer, speaking in a hushed, urgent voice. Something was seriously wrong.

He only wished she would confide in him so he could help her.

Odd, since he'd started out wanting to hurt her.

Abby stirred and opened her eyes, her hand still curled on his chest. His heart instantly picked up its beat, his body alive and thrumming with tension.

"I'm going to the rest room," she whispered. With a sly wink, she reached down and cupped his sex, then stood and moved down the aisle. He glanced down, his mouth growing dry when he saw that she'd laid her panties in his lap.

Hunter instantly lurched from his seat, his body hard as he watched her hips sway. He stole glances around them to make sure they weren't being watched, then slipped inside the small bathroom with her. She came at him with such fervor that he feared he might lose it before he could get inside her. "I've never done anything this impulsive and wild in my life."

He cupped her buttocks in his hands. "Me, neither."

She reached for his pants, unzipped them, and freed his already throbbing sex from its prison, stroking him hungrily as he pushed up her shirt and found her heaving breasts. His mouth suckled her until she whimpered and climbed on top of him.

"I have to have you," she whispered in a passion-glazed voice.

The cramped quarters made it awkward, and she bumped her head as she wrapped her body around him. But the bump was forgotten as she impaled herself upon him. He caught her moan of pleasure with his mouth. They rode together, pumping and grinding, clinging to each other as the tension mounted and spiraled through them. And just as the plane began to descend and the captain ordered everyone to buckle back up for landing, they climbed to heaven and soared there together.

Abby hated for the week to end. The past few days with Harry had been incredible, full of the most erotic love-making of her life. And sprinkled in with their lust, she also sensed some tender emotions that were fighting to rise above the mound of distrust.

But as they neared her home, reality nagged at her. What if Lenny was waiting?

Harry stroked a finger along her thigh, and she squeezed his hand. She wanted to tell Harry everything. But she had trusted Lenny enough to marry him and she had misjudged him terribly. What if Harry considered their weeklong romance simply a fling? She was the proponent of marriage and romance and love—he'd never marched to that tune.

The limo ate at the miles, the tension between her and Harry thick as they pulled into her driveway. The impatiens and marigolds she'd planted mocked her from the flower bed, reminding her of lost dreams and the life she'd imagined when she'd moved in the house, of her life before all this craziness.

Harry had seemed unusually quiet the entire ride home. They had one final appearance on *Good Day, Atlanta* Monday morning; then he would be free to go.

Would she see him again after their final appearance?

*   *   *

What was Abby thinking?

She'd been quiet and anxious the entire ride home.

He'd hoped their incredible week of lovemaking would have destroyed some of the walls she'd built around herself enough for her to confide in him. He'd given her a dozen chances, but each time she had retreated into a shell of silence. As they neared home and the acting gig came to a close, his anxiety mounted.

The driver parked in front of her house and Hunter helped Abby out with her bag. He itched to ask her to let him stay the night, but he had to leave the choice of an invitation up to her.

"I . . . Thanks for a great week," Abby said in a quiet voice once she'd unlocked the door and stepped inside.

He started to reach out and stroke her cheek, but she backed away slightly. "I . . . It's late, Harry. It's been wonderful, but maybe we should get some rest before the final show on Monday."

"Right." Was she already cutting him off? Writing him out of her life the way he would cut an awkward sentence or a misused adverb?

"I'll see you Monday morning."

"I'll call you Sunday night."

She nodded and started to close the door, but Hunter couldn't let the week end on this strained note. He grabbed her, pulled her into his arms, and kissed her once more, putting his tongue and his whole heart into the moment. And when he walked back to the car, he carried a small amount of satisfaction in knowing that she had looked just as confused and passion-stricken as he felt.

At least she would have something to think about until Sunday.

A half hour later, the driver dropped him at his apartment. The place looked even more dismal than ever. Inside, it would be quiet. No Abby. No Lizzie.

Not even that irritating doll, Angelica.

285

But a FedEx envelope sat propped on his stoop. He gathered it and hurried inside, dropped his garment bag, and tore it open. His heart thundered in his chest as he read the notice. Apparently Shelly had seen the TV interview in New York when the audience had overheard them panting and heaving in the curtained area. *Dear God. No.*

His ex-wife was suing him for full custody of Lizzie.

Chapter Twenty-four

Mutiple Orgasms

Abby had never had as many orgasms as she had with Harry.

Which made it even harder to be alone.

The doorbell rang and Chelsea bounded in, Abby's heart lurching when Butterball wiggled and squirmed to get to her. "Hey, buddy. Did you like staying with Aunt Chelsea?" She scooped him into her arms, laughing at the colorful bow Chelsea had clipped to his hair.

"He looks like a girl," Abby said.

"You don't think it'll confuse him sexually, do you?"

Abby laughed. "I doubt it." Then she noticed Chelsea's black eye and her smile faded. "What happened to you?"

Chelsea hesitated, touching her puffy eye. "Oh, a little accident with another actress. We were practicing a pretend fight for this scene, but the girl missed the air and hit me by mistake."

"Oh." Abby peered at her sister. Something about the

story sounded odd, but she couldn't quite put her finger on what it was.

Chelsea dropped the pizza on the counter and popped open a soda. "I saw the interviews with you and Harry. Pretty hot stuff."

"He's a good actor," Abby said, afraid her feelings about the man would show through.

Chelsea laughed. "That behind-the-scenes sex was not acting, sis, and there's no way you'll convince me it was."

Abby snuggled her face into Butterball, trying to hide her blush.

"All right, tell all, sis." Chelsea rubbed her hands together excitedly. "And this had better be good. I dumped my baggage of a boyfriend last week and the gay bars just don't cut it for me, so right now I'm living vicariously through you."

Chelsea had gone through another boyfriend? Had a black eye. Had been cavorting in gay bars. Abby wondered what was happening to her; she'd been so wrapped up in herself, she didn't even know what was going on with her sister.

Misery was too tame a word to describe Hunter's feelings. He tried all night to get in touch with Shelly and Lizzie, but no one was home. Finally the housekeeper answered the phone Saturday morning and informed him the Jeffries's had gone out of town until Tuesday.

Lizzie was *not* a Jeffries. And she never would be.

His chest ached from worry, his head hurt from exhaustion, and his eyes throbbed from trying to hold back tears. He had to change Shelly's mind. He'd spoken with a lawyer and she'd agreed to set up a meeting with a mediator, but nothing could be done until Shelly returned.

It was ironic that the very story he'd thought might help him climb the ladder at the paper and give him more time with his daughter might now cost him her company forever.

Meanwhile, what was he going to do about the article? His boss had left a message that he expected the story in the next week, but Hunter couldn't think straight. The words that flowed through his mind were not for the public.

They were for Abby, private thoughts about his feelings for her. . . .

Words he might make public someday, but not in the newspaper.

He couldn't stop thinking about her. He wanted her again. And again and again. But not just in his bed—in his life. Forever. With him and Lizzie.

Frustrated and lonely and so damn worried he felt as though he might have a nervous breakdown, he fed Snarts, then grabbed his sunglasses, climbed on his Harley, and took off. Maybe a ride in the mountains would clear his head, help him focus on the slant for his article—or that would save his position at the paper and his relationship with Abby. *Yeah, right.* Like Chicken Little, the answers to all his problems would probably fall out of the sky and hit him in the helmet.

Abby had tried to pry information from Chelsea about her gay-bar comment before she'd left, but Chelsea had flitted from one topic to another and had never quite answered her, except to say she'd had an adventure. Abby had a sneaking suspicion Chelsea might have gone looking for Lenny, but Chelsea had sidetracked her with questions about Harry. As if she didn't have enough of her own.

All night she'd tried to make some sense out of her feelings for him. She'd hoped distance would make him look duller, less desirable. Instead she ached for his hands and his lips and his body.

Irritated with herself and the mess she'd gotten herself into with this publicity stunt, she almost bumped into Victoria outside the bank. Her sister'd promised to meet her for moral support. Chelsea had wanted to come, too, but an audition as a broccoli pod superseded.

Victoria clutched a double latte in her hands, her black business outfit professional, but she'd forgone her usual chignon to let her hair lie loose around her shoulders. *Hmm, maybe this guy Suarez is the reason.*

She, on the other hand, had been so depressed she'd dressed in baggy jeans and a denim shirt, dreading the morning's trip to the bank.

"Are you sure you want to do this?" Victoria asked. "We could have Lenny charged with blackmail."

"And leave those photos floating around out there?" Abby shuddered. "No way. I'll press charges *after* the pictures are back in my hands."

"You don't think he's dangerous, do you?"

Abby gnawed on her stub of a nail. "No, he's too much of a wienie to hurt me. Humiliation and robbery are more his style."

Victoria heaved an angry sigh. "I hope I get my hands on him when we're through."

As they stepped into the First Union Bank, Abby's pulse clamored. Her temper boiling, she slid the savings withdrawal slip up to the cashier.

Victoria gave her a sympathetic look. Thank goodness she'd tagged along for moral support.

"You want to withdraw ten thousand dollars?" the teller asked.

Abby nodded. Why didn't the lady just shout it out?

"I need to see some ID, please. And you'll have to fill out these forms." She shoved some papers toward Abby.

Abby winced, opened her purse, and pulled out her driver's license.

The elderly woman smacked a wad of gum as she plucked the license from Abby's fingers. Her beehive hairdo barely wavered as she angled her head and studied Abby, trying to decide if Abby's face matched the photo.

"I'm having a bad-hair day," Abby said, willing her to hurry.

"I'll say." Her eyes suddenly widened. "You that Dr. Jensen on the TV?"

Abby nodded tightly. Victoria moved closer to try to shield her from curious onlookers.

"You look better on TV." The woman handed her back the picture, then began to fill out the forms.

When she finished, Abby slipped the money into her tote bag, old bank-robbery movies replaying in her mind. Huddling together like two spies in a cheap thriller, the two of them slunk away, trying not to look conspicuous as Abby clutched the bag to her side in a death grip.

"Don't look now, but I think we're being followed," Victoria whispered.

Abby's heart pounded. Good grief, she was going to be robbed. Then she couldn't pay Lenny.

Victoria caught her elbow, sandwiching her closer as they slowly moved toward the door. Abby caught the reflection of a skinny guy in the glass, wearing a yellow-and-green-plaid coat and bowling shoes.

He wasn't a bank robber.

It was Mo Jo Brown, that perverted panty-thief detective who'd followed her once before and nearly scared the bejesus out of her. Where was her hero Harry when she needed him?

The mountain breeze blew the scents of freshly cut grass and honeysuckle toward Hunter, the wind a welcome distraction from the stifling heat, but even the scenery and beautiful weather couldn't brighten his mood.

His phobia of heights kicked in, and he steered the bike as far from the ledge as possible, avoiding looking at the vast expanse of canyon below. The last time he'd ridden up here, he'd been planning the article, planning to use Abby to further his career. He'd been thinking about the one girl in the world who meant something to him: Lizzie.

Now Abby meant something to him, too. But he might lose them both.

The Velvet Cloak Inn peeked through the sea of greenery, and he decided to stop in and see if the owner had opened the place back up. He still had dozens of couples to interview for more articles. Maybe he could talk his boss into dropping the piece on Abby and focusing on the Milano victims. A long shot, but it might work—after all, the publicity on Abby should die down soon.

Steering onto the graveled road that led to the facility, he coached the bike uphill, then parked on the leveled-off area in front of the inn. A few other cars sat at various angles, and the sign on the door read *Open*. Tall elms and maples hugged the property. Weeping willows dotted the front, giant azaleas flanking a wide porch filled with rocking chairs for guests to enjoy the magnificent view of the valley.

He removed his helmet and strode up the steps, not surprised to find the same woman he'd spoken with before at the front desk, but this time instead of bawling her eyes out, she smiled brightly. A dozen yellow daisies filled a vase on the oak countertop, the red velvet carpet that covered the steps exemplifying the inviting atmosphere of the place. The lobby had undergone a face-lift, all signs advertising the chapel missing.

"Can I help you, sir? Do you need a room?"

He shook his head. "Edna, it's me, Hunter Stone from the *AJC*. I spoke with you a while back about the Milano mess."

Her smile wilted. "Oh, yes, I remember you." She leaned over the counter and spoke in a whisper, "We're trying to get past that now. Although I think some people have driven up here out of curiosity. I think your pieces on the victims really helped."

He dug his hands into the pockets of his faded jeans. "I have a lot more people to interview. You haven't heard anything more from Milano, have you?"

"No." Her eyes flickered around like a nervous hen's. "But I did find a backup disk with a bunch more names of folks who had been married by Milano." She paused to pick at a cuticle. "Do you know what?"

"What?" He'd learned a long time ago to be patient, that some people told stories in their own good time.

"That sex therapist lady that's been on TV; why, she was one of them."

Hunter felt as if the wind had been knocked out of him.

He'd known all along that Abby had secrets. That she was lying to him. But he'd never imagined she'd actually been married by Milano.

"And you know what else?"

He swallowed, dread filling him.

"I heard someone say they think her husband, well"— she gave him a conspiratorial wink—"the man she *thought* she married, he was in cahoots with Tony Milano. Won't the shit hit the fan when all that gets out!"

Damn straight it will. "So Lenny Gulliver was involved with Milano? He might have been a party to Milano's entire scam?"

Edna scrunched her mouth and bobbed her head up and down as if she'd won the big jackpot.

Hunter gripped the wooden counter, the last pieces of the puzzle falling into place with an audible click. What if Abby had known about Lenny and his involvement with Milano? Could she possibly have been in on the deal?

She had told a lot of lies. What if she'd been covering up for Lenny? Was that the reason the police had been at her house?

Did they suspect that Abby was an accomplice? Had Lenny returned to reconcile with her and give her her cut—was that what that little meeting backstage had been about? Or had he come to steal more money from her?

Sunday afternoon, Abby's breath hitched at the sound of the jangling phone. She'd half hoped—no, she'd wanted— Harry to call all weekend. To tell her they didn't need distance, that he didn't care if she'd lied to him about her husband, that he didn't want to go to LA to be an actor, that he wanted to stay in Atlanta and make a life with her.

Not that she couldn't move to LA, but the Hollywood life didn't appeal to her.

And she had to admit, after her last fiasco of a marriage, her ego couldn't survive the competition of the women who would play opposite Harry. Pathetic, but she realized most actors had to play nude scenes at some point in their careers. Granted, she was liberated and modern, but the idea of women touching and gawking at Harry's body just didn't sit right.

Plus, she wanted a family,—the whole nine yards, as old-fashioned as it might seem. The kids, the minivan, the PTA. The phone rang again and she grabbed it. "Hello?"

"Hey, baby, it's me."

The scoundrel. Anger replaced every emotion in her body. "What do you want, Lenny?"

"Did you get the money?"

"Yes."

"Good." His cocky tone irritated her even more. "I'll meet you after the show tomorrow."

The phone clicked, signifying the end of the conversation, and Abby slammed down the receiver, barely stifling a scream. She couldn't let Lenny get away with this.

She had to call that Detective Suarez and his partner, the Nazi, Barringer, and tell them to meet her at the show so they could arrest Lenny. Maybe if she explained her situation to Suarez, he'd understand and let her confiscate the pictures first.

The doorbell rang, and she nearly jumped out of her skin. What if it was Lenny? No, he wanted to meet her in public, banking on the fact that she wouldn't make a scene in front of a crowd. Must have been a tactic all crooks learned in Criminal Behavior 101. Figuring it was Victoria or Chelsea, she hurried to the door, ready to vent her hatred for Lenny, but Harry stood on her doorstep instead.

Handsome and sexy as ever.

An odd expression tightened his face, though. She couldn't quite put her finger on the difference in his mood, but his blue eyes were troubled, almost scrutinizing.

She was just too frustrated with Lenny to analyze the situation or what might be bothering him, though. Without waiting to ask why he'd come, she fell into his arms and kissed him. "I missed you, Harry."

He tore his mouth from hers and leaned his forehead against hers, his breath ragged. "Did you really, Abby?"

She cupped his face and looked into his eyes. She wasn't sure what was wrong, but she instinctively knew something had happened to upset him. And although she couldn't tell him the truth about everything, she could be honest about her feelings.

"Yes, Harry, I did. I . . . I think I'm falling in love with you."

Hunter trembled inside, his body a mass of hurt and anger and confusion. Still, he couldn't deny himself the sweet pleasure of holding Abby in his arms for a few more minutes, especially when she'd just made that heartfelt declaration of love.

Could he believe her?

Had she told the police the truth? Had she known what Lenny and Milano had been up to?

He didn't want to believe she had . . .

The entire way to her house, his temper had thundered at the realization that she might have been using him, that he'd almost given up the story, his career, that he might have lost Lizzie because he'd gotten involved with her, because he'd fallen for her.

It was disgusting, but even wondering about Abby's intentions didn't diminish the physical need to hold her that was pulsing through his veins. He walked her backward inside her house, not bothering to hide his intent as he reached for her T-shirt. He tore it over her head and stared at her blatantly, letting his gaze speak for itself.

"If you don't want me, tell me to stop now." His voice was so gruff, it was almost lost in the whir of the ceiling fan spinning above.

But she said nothing. She simply dropped her shorts to the floor and offered herself to him. Shadows from the window played along her skin, the moon highlighting her creamy skin. He accepted her invitation, his chest heaving with his fierce need.

There was no show of romance or flowery words or slow, titillating touches. He ripped off his clothes and pushed her to the floor, his hands hungrily seeking the thrill and comfort of her body, touching, teasing, drawing her into the web of desire he had been caught in ever since he had first kissed her. She arched and begged for him, spreading herself open in wild abandon, and he rolled her to her stomach, stretched his body over hers, and drove inside her, pushing her legs apart and thrusting inside her until she cried out and waves of pleasure rocked through her. He raised her arms above her head and rode her until she lay still, a supple whimper of spent need below him, and he could do nothing but collapse on top of her.

He took her again and again that night, the orgasms quaking through Abby more intensely and suddenly than any she'd ever experienced. At times he was tender, erotic, whispering all the naughty things he wanted to do to her, the places he wanted to touch her, the ways he wanted to possess her. And then he was savage and starved and full of raw passion, a beast crying out his need. And she always answered.

She always would.

Multiple orgasms—Harry had invented the term. Passionate positions—he invented a few of those as well.

Abby curled into his arms in the early hours of the morning, knowing she was in love. And knowing that today she would end this farce with her book and say goodbye to Lenny forever.

Then she could move on with her life.

She only hoped Harry would be a part of it.

"Harry?" She traced his jaw with her finger, studying him as he slowly opened his eyes.

"What?"

He sounded sweet and sexy and half-asleep. "What was bothering you when you came over last night?"

He lay so still she wondered if she'd made a mistake by probing. Finally he threw an arm over his face and cleared his throat. "When I got home Friday night . . ." He paused to clear his throat again, and Abby's chest squeezed at the emotions thickening his voice. "My ex-wife served me papers."

"What kind of papers?"

"She's suing for full custody of Lizzie."

Abby's throat closed. She reached for Harry to comfort him, but he jackknifed up and off the bed before she could. "I'm so sorry. Is there anything I can do?"

He stopped and met her gaze, his blue eyes pools of anguish. This time she recognized the anger and hurt. His body was such a powerful masterwork of muscle and sinewy strength and masculine sexuality, yet his heart had a tender side and right now it was bleeding for his child.

She had never loved anyone the way she did this man.

Desperate for him to know that she was there for him, that she would testify on his behalf, she crossed the space to him. He was so stiff at first she wasn't sure he would accept her comfort.

"Harry." She pressed her hands to his jaw. "I'm here for you. I want you to know that. I love you. Just tell me what you need and I'll do it."

He waited a painful heartbeat before he replied. "You can tell me the truth."

"I am." She struggled for control. "I told you I love you, and I meant it."

"Your husband—"

"Is past history. I swear."

He kissed her again, this time with such tenderness that tears filled her eyes.

And she had the oddest feeling as he dressed that she'd caused part of the anger and pain she'd seen in his eyes. She just didn't understand what she had done to hurt him.

Daylight dawned with an overcast sky, perfect for Hunter's mood. Turmoil tightened every muscle in his body as he and Abby entered the Atlanta TV station for their final interview. Had Abby told him the truth? Did she love him?

He wanted to believe her feelings for him were real, but how could he be sure?

If she had lied, both offstage and onstage, about her marriage to Lenny, could she be lying to him? Had he totally misread her? Could she have been involved with Milano's scam? Was she going to take that jerk Lenny back into her life? Into her bed?

He clenched his teeth, seeing red. Had he lost his mind? Taken a chance on losing his career, giving up a great story *and* his daughter for a woman who might be using him? For someone who might not even care for him?

Hell, he'd wanted to declare his love, but he hadn't been able to, not with secrets and lies still between them like a brick wall that he might not be able to scale afterward.

As soon as they arrived, the crew whisked them into the green room. Minutes later, they both stood outside the set, listening to last-minute preparations. An audience seating area sat to the right, where he noticed Abby's sisters, along with several other guests.

Abby turned to him and clenched his hands. "We have to talk after the show, Harry."

He nodded, knowing the day of reckoning had arrived. "Yes, we do."

She frowned, reached up and kissed him, then adjusted his mustache. It would be the last time he paraded as Lenny Gulliver. One thing he didn't understand—if the police had made the connection from Milano to Gulliver, why hadn't they already shown up to arrest him? And they hadn't arrested Abby, so they must believe her innocent . . .

"We're ready," the director announced.

"My knees are knocking." Abby clung to his hand as they walked onstage and settled into the set's love seat.

The host, an attractive African-American woman, Deborah Long, introduced the two of them.

Suddenly a voice shot out from the audience. "That man is an impostor. He's not Abby Jensen's husband."

Abby gasped and Hunter squinted through the blinding lights to see who had spoken.

"Excuse me." Ms. Long stood. Her gaze swung to Abby, then Hunter. "Is this true?"

"Er . . ." Hunter began.

Abby gaped at him.

Security started toward the woman, but the host held up a warning hand.

"I'm Trina Thomas from the *National Wonderer*." the woman said. "And that man is a reporter from the *AJC*."

Abby's sharp gasp echoed across the stage.

"His name is Hunter Stone."

Chapter Twenty-five

The Awkward Morning After

Shock waves trickled through Abby at an alarming speed.

This couldn't be happening.

The host's gaze swung to Abby, then Harry. "Is this true?"

"Uh, yes," Hunter said in a gravelly voice that knocked the wind from Abby. "But I can explain."

The pain that knifed through her was so intense she had to be visibly bleeding. She gaped at Harry, certain he'd instigated some kind of joke, but guilt riddled his face as clear and plain as the horror that was stealing through her, sucking the oxygen from her lungs.

"Abby, I can explain," Harry—no, Hunter—said in a low voice. "Just bear with me. Please."

Bear with him!

Good heavens, she had bared her body and her soul and heart to him.

She had told him she loved him.

And he was Hunter Stone—the man who had written

the dreadful articles about her in the paper. The extent of his deceit slammed into her like a sledgehammer. He had not only written about her and hounded her for an interview, when she had refused it he had invaded her personal life, seduced her with his charm and false concern, taken her to bed, and—even worse—made her fall in love with him. He had even used his child to help pull his scam. Nausea rose in her throat, nearly choking her.

To think she had imagined him her hero, rescuing her from the other nosy reporters, from that ghastly PI, when all along he had simply been keeping her to himself so he could get an exclusive. Why hadn't she seen through his act? For heaven's sake, he'd used that ridiculous name, Harry Henderson. Suspicion snaked through her as a flashback of those sunglasses shot through her mind, and she glanced at his hands.

The manly hands that had held her. The ones that had seemed too large for the cross-dresser in line at the book signing. The orange sunglasses Lizzie had worn that seemed so familiar . . .

She staggered backward. "You dressed like a woman to spy on me?"

Hunter reached out to console her, but she shook her head vehemently.

"Would someone like to explain what's going on here?" Deborah Long's voice broke into her pain-glazed subconscious. Hunter opened his mouth to respond, but Abby suddenly stood. *Damn him.* If anyone was going to tell her story, it would be her.

She was tired of being victimized, of hiding behind an act, of deceiving the people she cared about—her patients. Victoria and Chelsea both stood as if to rescue her, but she shook her head.

There were no heroes left in the world. If she wanted rescuing, she had to rescue herself.

"I'd like to say something," Abby said to Deborah.

Out of the corner of her eye, she saw Harry—Hunter—

watching her every expression, but she steeled herself against her emotions, tucking them away until she could deal with them and have a full-blown meltdown later. In private.

Where she would probably hide for the rest of her life.

"Certainly, Dr. Jensen," Ms. Long said.

Abby faced the camera, inhaled a calming breath, and was surprised at how easily her confession came.

"It's true, this man is not really my husband," she said, her voice strong although her legs pinged back and forth like broken violin strings. "As I told the police"—Suarez gestured to her from the back while Barringer moved to cover the door—"I'm not sure where Lenny is at the moment," Abby finished. Although she suspected the weasel was somewhere in the crowd, slinking in a dark corner, waiting on his money.

Abby continued, her voice growing stronger. "A few weeks ago, the same day my book debuted, I received a Dear John letter from the man I thought was my husband. But it turned out that we hadn't been legally married at all. I was a victim of the Milano scam."

More gasps and oohs and ahhs filtered through the room, along with a few pitying looks. The host filled the audience in on the details of the scam, having recently interviewed a number of the victims on her show.

Abby tightened her hands by her side. "I've been a marriage counselor for several years, and I've heard people talk about the hurt and anger and shock they experience when a spouse indulges in an affair. I've listened to stories about depression and the sense of failure when a marriage ends. But I never understood those feelings the way I do now that I've experienced them myself."

She paused, sensing she had the crowd's full attention.

"I was in shock when I received the letter from Lenny. When my publicist called and wanted me to do this tour with my book, I didn't know what to do. I was afraid people wouldn't take me seriously if they thought I didn't have the perfect marriage myself." The crowd was so quiet she could hear her own breath quavering into the microphone. "I know now that was wrong. But at the time I felt humiliated and embarrassed. Despite my situation, deceiving the public was not right, but because I was in such a vulnerable emotional state, I allowed myself to get swept up in a publicity stunt." She gestured toward Hunter without looking at him. "I let this man pretend to be my husband onstage.

"Unfortunately, I was conned again. I didn't realize the man I hired was the reporter who had been hounding me for a story." She turned to the female reporter from the *National Wonderer*. "Mr. Stone has his exclusive." She did look at him then, all the pain and anger she felt churning inside her. "He's certainly earned it."

He could have his story now. He had already taken her heart and broken it.

She clutched her hands together, barely holding on to her emotions. "I do hope that whether you buy my book or not—whether you decide it's worth it or not after this publicity stunt—that if you're in a relationship you'll take the advice offered in *Under the Covers* the way it was meant, to help open the doors of communication. And please remember that honesty is the best way to maintain a long-term relationship. Secrets and lies will only destroy you."

Abby turned and shook Ms. Long's hand. "Thanks for letting me be here today."

Then she turned and walked offstage, shoulders squared, head high. Surprisingly, the audience burst into applause, but she was too relieved to care.

Her sisters greeted her. "Are you okay?" Chelsea asked. "I can't believe that actor was a rat."

"I'm so sorry," Victoria said, hugging her.

Abby embraced them both, searching the area for Lenny. She gripped Victoria's arms. "I'm going to hunt for Lenny."

"We'll go look, too." Her sisters scattered in opposite

directions while Abby ducked backstage and worked her way through the vacant studio rooms. She hoped Detective Suarez had already caught him.

Near the back entrance, she froze in shock. Lenny was trying to sneak out the back door, but Hunter Stone snatched him and dragged him into a holding room.

She grabbed a folding chair for support. Apparently Hunter was going to get a quote. *Damn him.* He would probably also get the pictures to add to the story he had under wraps.

The panty-pervert PI darted into the room behind the two men. Had he been working with Hunter all along?

Hunter had never felt lower in his entire life.

He ached to go after Abby, but he'd spotted Lenny Gulliver lurking behind the scenes and he had to catch him. He couldn't let the jerk get away after the way he'd hurt Abby. Maybe turning him over to the police would be the first step in proving to Abby that he really cared about her.

The pain in her eyes when she had discovered his deception had been excruciating. He didn't know if she *could* forgive him, even if he wrote the most complimentary story about her imaginable, but he had to try.

His heart pounded like a runaway freight train as he pushed Gulliver against the wall. Mo Jo Brown slunk in behind him, arms crossed, waiting his turn.

Hunter adopted an intimidating stance. "Okay, Gulliver, the game is up."

"Not yet." A cynical sneer lifted the corners of the redhaired man's mouth. "I have something I think you'll be interested in seeing."

He doubted it, but he'd play along. "What is it?"

Gulliver removed a manila envelope from a briefcase and offered it to him. Hunter took the bait, his instincts telling him he wasn't going to like the contents of the envelope. Slowly he peeled open the top and reached inside. His hand contacted slick photo paper, and he pulled out several photos of Abby.

Nude shots of her in erotic poses.

"Got those on my honeymoon," Gulliver bragged.

Brown inched forward to sneak a look, but Hunter shoved the pictures back into the envelope, not bothering to examine them, his fury mounting. Dammit, he didn't want Brown or anyone else to see them. "Does Abby know about these?"

Gulliver laughed, a smarmy sound that sickened Hunter.

"Yeah, she was supposed to bring me some cash today for them, but that tabloid chick ruined the show." His smile faded. "Now I figure you might pay more. Some Internet sites would get a kick out of these."

Gulliver had been blackmailing Abby. No wonder she hadn't told him everything.

Fury boiled through him. He crumpled the photos in his fist. He was going to kill the man with his bare hands.

"What the hell are you doing?" Gulliver asked.

Hunter grabbed him by the throat, making sure his first punch connected with the man's nose. "That one's for Abby." Bones crunched, a mild sense of satisfaction filling Hunter at Gulliver's babylike yelp.

"Let me go!"

"And this one's for me." He had just pulled his arm back to hit him a second time when Mo Jo Brown stepped forward.

"Let me have him, Stone."

"What for?"

"I know someone who's looking for him. And when this guy gets done, his face won't be the only thing smashed."

The mob. So Hunter had been right. Vinelli would take care of him. *Tempting . . .*

But two officers raced in, saving Hunter from having to choose between his conscience and his need for vengeance. "Thanks for nabbing him, guys, but this is a police matter now."

"What?" Gulliver whined.

"Yes, Dr. Jensen phoned us yesterday, Gulliver." The male Latino reached for his handcuffs. "You're busted, you scum."

Brown sputtered an argument, but Hunter tossed Gulliver toward the cops like the sack of garbage he was. Then he stuffed the envelope of photos under his arm and strode from the room, determined to talk to Abby.

Her love life was over, her career was over, her life as she knew it was over.

Over.

Blinded by tears, her body racked with sobs, Abby hailed a taxi home, well aware the cabby thought she was a lunatic.

It was a far nicer word than the one most Atlanta residents would be calling her once they witnessed her debacle. If she ever wrote another book, she'd title it, *Most Embarrassing Moments*. She could fill the pages with her own experiences.

The cabdriver dropped her in front of her house, and she tossed him some cash, then ran up the steps. Inside, Butterball was sleeping, so she locked the door, turned on the message machine, then intended to throw herself on her bed and cry until she passed out. She hoped she'd be so exhausted she'd crawl under the covers and sleep for a month. Or at least as long as it took for most of the gossip to die down.

But the sheets where she and Hunter had lain this morning, where they had made love—no, when they'd had sex—still lay rumpled on the floor.

He had trashed her in the paper. Lied to her. Used her. And done it all for a lousy story! He'd probably earned a promotion or a big raise out of her humiliation.

Hatred, mixed with anger and hurt, mushroomed inside her. She ripped off the sheets, grabbed a pair of scissors and shredded them, then shoved them into a garbage bag. Next went her comforter. Then the pillow that reeked of his scent. Feathers flew everywhere, dotting the floor with white, but a stretch of solid black peeked from her bed like a scorpion. Hunter's boxers.

She grabbed them and ripped them with her bare hands until they were nothing but strands of broken thread. Feeling marginally better, she brushed at the tears streaming down her face, picked up her journal, and let it all out.

Hate men. Lenny Gulliver is pond scum. Hunter Stone is cockroach pond scum.

Career in jeopardy.

May move to mountains. Become recluse. Take up cross-stitch or basket weaving. Maybe pottery . . .

Hunter barely escaped the wrath of Abby's sisters. Chelsea and Victoria chased him to his car.

"You freakin' creep . . ." Chelsea broke into a litany of vulgar names and threw her clunky shoes at him. They hit him in the butt and bounced off.

Victoria jabbed a finger at him. "You print anything to disparage her and I'll bury you with a lawsuit you'll never be able to crawl out from under."

His backside and ears burning, Hunter jumped in his Explorer and drove like a maniac toward Abby's house.

Talk about the awkward morning after—this had been the awkward morning after from hell.

Figuring his boss would hear about the fiasco and want the scoop, Hunter phoned him and related the story.

"Great work in catching Milano's accomplice and getting the dirt on the sex therapist," Emerson bellowed.

Yeah, he was thrilled about it.

"Listen, if you want that criminal investigative-reporting position, it's yours."

Hunter told him he'd call him back, then hung up, a bittersweetness assaulting him. He'd finally achieved his career goals, but he'd lost everything in his life that mattered.

No, he hadn't lost Lizzie yet. But if he took the job . . .

The fifteen-mile ride turned into a nightmare while he struggled with his thoughts. He blasted his horn at the early morning traffic, cursed a woman putting on her mascara in front of him, shot the bird at a man on his cell phone who wove into his lane, and banged the steering wheel with his fist when a fender bender up ahead brought traffic to a grinding halt.

Desperate, he swerved over into the HOV lane, checking his mirror to make sure a cop wasn't watching, then sped past the line of stopped cars, but suddenly a siren burst through the agonizing silence in the car and blue lights swirled behind him.

Muttering an obscenity, he kept driving until he could find a shoulder to pull off, onto then parked and tapped his foot impatiently. Hunter read his name tag; Officer Suarez.

The cop adjusted his Ray-Bans and stared down at Hunter condescendingly. "You realize you were in the HOV lane?"

"Yes." He'd be an idiot if he didn't.

"And you know there's a hefty fine if you're driving in it illegally."

"Yes." Who cared about money when his whole future was at stake?

"You do know that the HOV lane is limited to cars with two or more people."

"Yes. I'm not a moron." Everyone in Atlanta knew that.

The cop's eyebrows climbed his face. Attaching a glare to his intimidating stance, he leaned his hands on his knees and peered into the car. Hunter recognized him as one of the cops who'd arrested Lenny. "I don't see a second person in there."

"Look, Officer," Hunter said. "There's not a second person in here. I'm just in a hurry because I need to see this woman—"

"You're driving in the HOV lane because you're going to see a lady?"

"She's not just a woman; she's Abby Jensen."

"Don't you think you've hurt that woman enough?"

Jesus, of course he would take Abby's side. "I want to make things right—"

"You tricked her to get that story about her. And you invaded her privacy."

"Well, yes, but that's my job." He wasn't going to declare his love for Abby to this cop. "Listen, if you're going to give me a ticket, go ahead, so I can move on. I have to talk to her."

"Going to harass her again."

"I'm not harassing her."

"Victoria Jensen is a friend of mine."

Oh, dear God.

"I think you'd better step out of the car, mister."

"But you can't arrest me."

"Resisting arrest?"

"No."

"Then step out of the car."

Hunter opened the door, fuming. "Really, Officer, what will it take to just settle this?"

"That sounds like a bribe."

"No, but if it would work . . ."

"It would not."

"Well, you can't blame a guy for trying."

The cop slapped a pair of handcuffs around his wrist.

"Hey, what are you doing?"

"Attempted bribery is against the law." Officer Suarez pushed him toward the squad car. "And like you said earlier, Mr. Stone. I'm just doing my job."

Abby knew Chelsea and Victoria would come to her aid, and they had. Armed with enough Reese's peanut butter cups to feed an army, martini ingredients, and Kleenex, they had trashed Hunter Stone so badly that if he'd been psychic, his ears wouldn't have been burning—they would have rotted off.

The fact that Hunter had not called or shown up to at least try to simulate an apology cemented the fact that he was lower than the lowest form of life. Which Abby still didn't know the name of, but she didn't need to. Regardless of what it was, the name Hunter Stone fell below it in the feeding chain.

Of course, he and Lenny were vying for the lowest of the low.

Not that she wanted Hunter to call or that she would believe him if he did try to make an apology, or that she would even listen to one.

"But he could have at least tried to apologize," she muttered.

"This is all my fault for hiring him," Chelsea said miserably.

"No, it's not. He fooled me," Abby said.

"I'm going to concoct a spell so his thing falls off," Chelsea said, slurping her martini. "That'll teach him to screw a good woman."

"I'd like to see him rot in jail," Victoria added, showing an uncharacteristic bit of emotion. Abby didn't understand the grin that followed, but she chalked it up to the drinks.

"I never want to see him or hear his voice or his name again." Abby kicked at the newspaper. "And I'm canceling my subscription to the paper tomorrow."

"You want us to crash here tonight?" Victoria asked.

"Yeah, we can have a pajama party," Chelsea offered.

Abby hugged her sisters. "No, I'll be okay. But thanks." Abby turned to Victoria. "I appreciate Detective Suarez's help."

"He's pretty cool," Victoria admitted.

"Yeah, he saved our butts that night at the gay bar—"

Chelsea stopped midsentence as if she'd revealed too much. Victoria kicked her.

Abby tapped her foot on the floor. "What are you talking about?"

Chelsea shrugged. "Look, Victoria, it's over now and no harm done, so—"

"We were only trying to help," Victoria added.

"Help? How?" Abby asked.

Chelsea explained about their adventure, of course embellishing the story with all the details about the dinginess and stench of the inside of the holding cell. Then Victoria filled her in on the scene at the strip club.

"Boy, that hooker sure packed a punch." Chelsea rubbed at her still-black eye.

"I can't believe you two," Abby said. "You did all that for me?"

Victoria hung an arm around Abby. "We'd do anything for you, sis."

"Okay, but no more gay bars or fights or stripping."

Chelsea laughed. "All right with me. I just wanted to help, Abby, so you and Victoria wouldn't think I'm such a screwup."

Victoria tucked her hand in Chelsea's arm. "You're not a screwup, Chelsea. We love you just the way you are."

Chelsea blushed and sniffled.

"I think we're all pretty lucky to have each other." Abby fought the tears but they spilled over anyway. "Come here. I love you guys so much." The three of them gathered in a group hug, vowing the bond of sisterhood would always keep them together.

Hunter tossed and turned on the prison floor, unable to believe this was happening. The stench of urine and sweat and other body odors he didn't even want to think about filled the dingy cell, the absence of cots or chairs forcing all the inhabitants to lie on the floor like animals. He was convinced that at least two of the prisoners were murderers, one of the others a rapist. A hulking three-hundred-pounder with a Mohawk winked at him and he shuddered.

When he saw his lawyer, he was going to wring his neck for being unattainable when Hunter needed most to attain him.

He folded his arms behind his head and stared at the toilet in the middle of the cell, then at the big Bubba with the bald head and tribal tattoos covering his hairy arms. He had to piss like a crazed bovine, but he'd be damned if he'd whip out his dick and give this thug any ideas. The man looked at him and leered and Hunter forced his gaze to the ceiling. He'd count the cracks and read the obscenities etched on the dirty texture until morning. There was no way he would close his eyes inside this hellhole. No telling what some of these beefy hoodlums might do to him.

By morning, his lawyer had damned well better get him out of here.

Then he had to talk to Shelly about Lizzie and get her to forget this stupid custody hearing. He'd settle into a nice, quiet job, and buy a little house somewhere so Lizzie could have her own room. Hell, he'd give Angelica her own room if he had to in order to get Lizzie to stay over.

And somehow, once he accomplished all that, he would achieve the impossible and convince Abby to forgive him. To give him another chance.

He had to make her see that he really loved her.

Chapter Twenty-six

Sexless and Single

Abby rolled over and ducked under the covers at the sound of the telephone, but the message machine kicked on and Rainey's excited voice piped up.

Excited? Hadn't she heard about the disastrous *Good Day, Atlanta* show?

"Abby, this is Rainey. You won't believe it; a number of news broadcasts aired clips of your interview from the *Good Day Atlanta* show, and you were wonderful! Everyone who hadn't already bought a book ran out yesterday and bought one—*Under the Covers* hit the *New York Times* bestseller list!"

Abby groaned. *Unbelievable.*

"We have to get that sequel under contract. Why don't you call the next one *Between the Sheets*? Well, I'm off to celebrate. Call me."

No sooner had the machine clicked off than the doorbell dinged. She dragged the quilt higher, praying whoever it was would leave. She just wanted to be alone.

The bell dinged again, ding, ding, ding. Whoever it was certainly was insistent. Probably Chelsea or Victoria checking in on her.

The phone rang and the machine clicked on again. "Abby, this is your mother. I saw you yesterday and I'm so sorry about that reporter. But look at the bright side: I heard your book made the *New York Times* bestseller list." A pause followed. "About that loan . . ."

A car horn blasted from the driveway and Abby punched the covers. Who in the world?

Pushing her tousled hair from her eyes, she loped to the front door in her T-shirt and boxers, then peered outside. If this was her father or Uncle Wilbur wanting money, she was going to scream.

Maybe Hunter . . .

No, she didn't want to see that creep.

She looked through the peephole but didn't see anyone. The doorbell dinged again, however, followed by the blast of a car horn. Abby scanned her porch one more time. Finally she glanced down and spotted her visitor.

Lizzie, clutching Angelica, wearing an oversize Harry Potter T-shirt, pink shorts, and sandals, her hair tousled, her eyes puffy and red, stood at her front door.

She reached for the doorbell again, Snarts wobbling in her little arms, a taxi sitting in the drive—the source of the horn. Was Hunter here? Had he put his little girl up to ringing the bell?

Anger hit her, but she searched the front lawn and cab and didn't see anyone but an irritated-looking driver. Worry immediately slammed into her. What was Lizzie doing here alone?

"Dr. Abby, please be home!" Lizzie wailed.

A sob punctuated the air as she opened the door. "Lizzie, honey, what is it? Did you take that taxi all by yourself?"

The driver saw her and waved, then sped off. Lizzie collapsed against her legs, the dog flopping onto Abby's feet with a whack, Angelica banging her knees. "Yeah, I gots the number off the 'frigerator. Me and Angelica and Nanny takes the taxi all the times." She backhanded a tear that dribbled out. "I gots to talk to you."

"Well, of course, honey." Abby knelt and ushered her and Snarts inside. "Let's give the puppy some water, and we'll put him in the backyard with Butterball."

Lizzie sniffed and nodded, clutching Abby's leg with one arm and Angelica with the other as she walked inside. Snarts trudged behind them at a snail's pace, tail wagging, sniffing everything in sight. Finally Abby ushered him outside, where he and Butterball faced the water bowl at a standoff. The dogs would have to work out their problems; she needed to tend to Lizzie.

Abby took the patio chair, then lifted the weepy little girl into her lap. "Now, tell me why you're here by yourself. Does your mama know you came here?"

Lizzie shook her head, her crooked blond ponytail swinging, more tears flooding her cheeks. "No, and you can't tells her."

She had to, Abby thought, but she'd get to the bottom of the situation first. "Suppose you tell me what's going on."

"You saided people comes to you if they gots problems."

"Yes, that's right."

She threw up her hands. "Well, I gots Jolly Green Giant problems."

She hugged the little girl to her. "What's wrong, honey?"

Her lower lip trembled. "My mama don't wants my daddy to see me no more."

Ahh, so that part of Hunter's story had been true. "Why not?"

"She saided his job is dangerous, and that he has sex on TV."

Abby flinched. "Have you talked to your daddy yet?"

"No, he ain't home."

He was probably at the paper writing his prizewinning article about her. Renewed resentment swelled inside her.

315

"Sweetie, I think your mother is probably just trying to be cautious because she loves you. I'm sure your father and mother will work things out."

"No," Lizzie wailed, her little body trembling with sobs. "She don't want to fool with Daddy; I heard her."

Abby's chest tightened.

"What else did she say?"

"She saided it's easier this way, on account of Daddy don't like schools with boards and they wants to send me away."

Abby frowned. Something was lost in the translation. "Schools with boards?"

"Yeah, where the kids live without their mommies and daddies. Like a jail."

"You mean boarding schools?"

Lizzie nodded, rubbing at her nose with her sleeve. Abby handed her a tissue. "And she saided that Snarts can't go either. And I wants him with me, even though he's homely, but he won't likes jail either. And neither will Angelica."

Tears stung Abby's eyes but she blinked them away. This problem wasn't hers, but she couldn't ignore it either and watch Lizzie get lost in the shuffle of bickering parents. She'd seen it happen to kids too many times and had heard Victoria bemoan the issue. "Don't worry, Lizzie. I'll talk to your mommy and daddy for you."

Lizzie cuddled into her arms, her little eyes droopy as if she'd exhausted herself. "I know Snarts ain't as cute as Butterballs, Dr. Abby, but he kinda grows on you. And his farts don't stink no more since Daddy gots him real dog food."

"I want to sue them for false arrest," Hunter snapped at his lawyer as he signed his release papers. "I did not try to bribe that cop."

"Be quiet," Duncan Bailey hissed. "At least contain yourself until you're officially out of here."

Hunter clenched his teeth, exhaustion and anger and worry all colliding inside him. Having to be locked up when he needed to be making amends with Abby and saving his daughter from being taken away from him had been the cruelest form of punishment he could have imagined.

Well, it could have been worse had Bubba decided to act on his obvious attraction to Hunter. Geez, the stench of the place clung to him like a dead animal.

He shuddered, snatching his cell phone as Duncan collected his personal effects from a manila envelope. Praying Abby might have phoned him, or Lizzie might have called, he instantly checked his messages. A frantic one from Shelly, telling him to call her, immediately made his blood run cold.

Had something happened to Lizzie?

Duncan was walking briskly and Hunter followed, ignoring the stares pointed in his direction as they stepped into the morning sunlight. He was too busy punching Shelly's number and worrying to care if he had coffee or food or sleep or a shower, all the mundane things that he had dwelled on the past twelve hours.

"Shelly, what's going on?"

"It's Lizzie." Shelly's normally snotty tone evaporated. "She's missing, Hunter. Is she there with you?"

Here with him? He shook himself, grateful she didn't know he'd been in jail.

"What the hell do you mean, she's missing?" He stopped in the parking lot, his breath coming to a painful halt. Duncan must have realized something was seriously wrong because he stopped, too, his gray brows knitted.

"I mean she's not here. I . . . I found a note."

"What kind of note?" Hunter closed his eyes on a prayer.

"She said . . ." Shelly's voice broke, "she said good-bye."

"Good-bye." *Oh, God.* She'd run away. "You're sure she's alone?"

"Yes. I thought maybe she went to your house."

His stomach plummeted as he looked back at the jail.

317

"I wasn't home." He couldn't very well tell her about his stint in jail, or she'd use it as ammunition against him.

"How long has she been gone?" Please, not overnight.

"Her bed's been slept in, so she must have gotten up early and left."

And where the hell was Shelly and the damned precious nanny? He gnawed the inside of his cheek to keep from lashing out. "So she's on foot?" *Hitchhikers, truckers, rapists . . .* Panic sucked the air from his lungs.

"Actually I think she took a taxi, the same one she and the nanny take—"

His phone beeped, signifying he had another call. "Hang on, Shelly. I've got another call."

"You're leaving me hanging to talk business, or is it that woman—"

"For God's sake, Shelly, it might be Lizzie."

Silence; then she sputtered, "All right, get the damned phone."

He clicked over, shocked to hear Abby's voice. "Hunter—"

"Listen, Abby, I really want to talk to you, but not now."

"Wait—"

"I can't." His voice was choked. He clicked back over to Shelly. "Look, I'll be there as soon as I can and we'll figure out what to do."

Abby slammed down the phone in a fit of rage. How dare he hang up on her when she was trying to help. Did he even know his daughter was missing? Or had his feelings for Lizzie been a lie, too?

She had a good mind to let him stew. Torturing Hunter would be nice revenge for her, but she couldn't let Lizzie suffer another minute. The little girl nuzzled up to Snarts and Abby's heart broke. No, she needed to resolve this situation for the little girl's sake.

Determined to get through to Hunter, she dialed his cell phone again. He answered on the third ring.

"Hunter, don't hang up this time."

"I can't talk, Abby. I want to, really, I love you and I'm sorry for the way things went down, but—"

"This isn't about us, Hunter."

"Then, I . . ." His words trailed off. "God, Abby, Lizzie's missing. She might be hurt or worse; if something's happened to her . . ."

Abby cleared her throat. "Hunter, listen to me. That's why I'm calling. Lizzie's all right. She's here with me."

"What? How did you get her?"

"I didn't *get* her," Abby said in a tight voice. "She took a taxi and showed up at my place about a half hour ago."

"But why would she come there and not to me?"

"She did go to your house, but you weren't there."

He let that sentence linger. Pride kept him from revealing his whereabouts.

The same kind of pride that had forced Abby to keep her secrets from him.

"She brought Snarts here with her. She's upset and she knows I'm a counselor."

"My daughter is five and needs a counselor?"

"Yes, apparently she does, because she has imbeciles for parents!"

That shut him up. "I'll be right over."

"No."

"What?" His voice grew stronger. "Listen, Abby, I know you hate me, but you can't keep me from my little girl."

"I'm not trying to do that." Abby recognized hysteria in his tone. "But she came here because she's upset." Abby hesitated. "I don't want to get into it over the phone. Can we meet?"

"Yes, of course, whatever you say."

Did he really trust her to take care of his daughter?

"I want you and your ex-wife to meet me, Hunter. This situation involves both of you. Can you get her to come?"

"Yes, sure. She was just on the phone with me."

That was a good sign. "All right. Meet me at my office

319

at eleven. If you both agree to it, I'll act as your mediator."

Hunter's shaky breath rattled over the line. "Thanks, Abby. I—"

"I'm not doing this for you, Hunter. I'm doing it for Lizzie."

Hunter dragged Lizzie into his arms, nearly suffocating her with his hugs and kisses. He even kissed Angelica. "Lizzie, honey, I love you; you scared the daylights out of me."

She clung to his neck. "I loves you, too, Daddy. And I don't want to go to jail."

Jail? Did she think just because he'd been in jail she would have to go? He claimed the love seat in the corner of Abby's office and brushed Lizzie's tousled hair back from her cherub face. "Darling, no one's going to jail."

He caught Abby's eye as she introduced herself to Shelly. "Please sit down." She gestured toward the armchair near the love seat.

"Lizzie, sweetie, why don't you sit here in this chair." Lizzie scooted away from Hunter and settled into a maroon chair facing both him and Shelly. The subtle meaning of the arrangement sank in, and Hunter realized this was Lizzie's show.

Heart pounding, he folded his hands and glanced at Abby, hoping for some personal connection, but she showed none. In fact, she avoided looking directly at him at all.

"What's this about?" Shelly asked, her back instantly up.

"It's about Lizzie," Abby said in a calm voice. "Not you, Mr. Stone, or you, Mrs. Jeffries, or your feelings for one another. It's about *not* putting your daughter in the middle of your problems or using her as a battling tool."

Shelly gasped.

Hunter clenched his jaw. "I'm not doing that."

Abby held up a hand. "I'd like for you both to listen to Lizzie."

Lizzie's legs dangled back and forth, kicking the chair,

her fingers winding one of Aneglica's braids around and around.

"It's okay," Abby coached. "Just tell them what's on your mind, honey."

Lizzie glanced first at Shelly, then at Hunter, then nodded, her eyes wary. "Me and Angelica wants to still see Daddy."

Shelly opened her mouth to argue, but Abby silenced her with a stern look.

"And we wants to keep Snarts. And we don't wants to go to jail."

Hunter shook his head in confusion. How did she know where he had been?

"Why do you think you're going to jail?" Abby asked quietly.

" 'Cause Mommy saided she's sending me to school with boards."

Shelly frowned, and Abby spoke up. "She's talking about a boarding school, right?"

Guilt suffused Shelly's face. "Yes."

"You aren't sending Lizzie to boarding school!" Hunter shouted.

Abby glared at Hunter. "Calm down, Mr. Stone."

"But—"

"I said, please keep your voice calm."

Lizzie crinkled her nose, a sign she was near tears, so Hunter ran a hand over his face and sat back, chewing over this latest bombshell.

"I . . . I didn't know you heard Daryl and I talking," Shelly explained.

"I don't wanna go." Tears flooded Lizzie's eyes and dribbled down her cheek, plopping onto Angelica's head.

"You don't have to," Hunter assured her calmly. He turned to Shelly, pleading. "What's this about anyway?"

"Daryl and I are taking a three-month trip to Europe in the fall and, well, it just seemed the best idea. The school is well equipped to take care of Lizzie—"

"So am I," Hunter said, furious.

"Really?" Shelly's eyes blazed. "I can't trust you with Lizzie. You got her picture in the tabloids. For all I know you're chasing criminals, and you'd be dragging her along. And you had sex on TV with her!" Shelly pointed to Abby. "What kind of father is that?"

"What kind of mother—"

Lizzie burst into tears, dove into Abby's arms, and buried her head, sobs racking her chest.

Hunter and Shelly both froze, Hunter's heart breaking. He gaped at his daughter in despair, knowing he might lose her. His anger at Shelly didn't matter. He had to do whatever it took to make peace and keep Lizzie in his life.

Even if it meant forgetting about the criminal investigative work.

"Listen, Shelly," he said quietly. "We'll work this out. I admit I've done some things I'm not proud of lately." He glanced at Abby but she avoided his look. "And I haven't been a great role model for Lizzie. But I'm going to change all that."

Shelly seemed to waver, her gaze flitting back to Lizzie, emotions warring in her eyes.

Hunter cleared his throat, his voice strong. "I'll change jobs. I'll do the sports section or something else, so I don't have to expose Lizzie to any more undercover assignments or tabloids or anything dangerous, I promise." Heck, he'd cover dog pageants all day long if he had to in order to keep his daughter.

Abby slowly met his gaze, a smile of approval softening the hardness in her gaze.

Lizzie stopped wailing long enough to look at her mother, tears streaming.

"All right," Shelly agreed quietly. "Then Lizzie and that mangy mutt can stay with you while we're away."

"And you'll drop the custody suit?"

Shelly nodded.

"And we gets to keep Snarts?" Lizzie asked.

"Yes, honey," Hunter said. "We keep Snarts. The most important thing in the world is your happiness."

Lizzie leaped up and ran toward both of them, and they all embraced. Finally Lizzie popped her head up, red eyes questioning. "Daddy, does this mean we can go back and ride Drop Dead, Fred? 'Cause Angelica says she really wants to ride it again."

Hunter ruffled her hair. "Don't push your luck, kiddo. I still have night sweats from the last time."

Abby stood in the waiting area to her office, her heart clenching at the touching family scene unfolding in the other room. At least she'd learned one thing—Hunter Stone definitely loved his daughter. He was willing to change his job for her; that said a lot. She'd seen the utter fear and devastation on his face at the sight of Lizzie's tears, and heard the fear and sorrow when he thought she was missing.

Darn it, she was not going to go soft on the man again. He had hurt her. Even worse, he'd taken advantage of her at a time in her life when she'd been the most vulnerable.

The sound of footsteps approaching alerted her to the fact that the three of them were leaving the office. Shelly looked shaken but relieved; Lizzie had a parent's hand clutched in each of her own.

"Thank you, Dr. Jensen," Shelly said. "I was really worried about Lizzie."

"No problem." Abby ruffled Lizzie's hair. *Poor Lizzie*. Just like most kids, she simply wanted security, wanted her parents to get along. Just as she and her sisters had wanted when they were little. "I just want her to be happy."

Shelly nodded, hugging her daughter to her side, oblivious to the tension between Abby and Hunter.

"We gots to come get Snarts," Lizzie said to her dad. "He's playing with Butterballs."

"We'll stop by now, if that's okay with Abby."

Abby steeled herself against him and nodded. "I'll meet

you there." Hunter and Shelly said good-bye, and Abby fled to her car, needing to escape the suffocating closeness of being near Hunter. Of remembering how heavenly it felt to be in his arms. Of the pain of his betrayal.

A few minutes later, Hunter and Lizzie pulled into the driveway behind her. Lizzie ran around to the backyard, where they had left the puppies, while Hunter followed Abby inside.

"Abby, can we talk?"

"There's nothing to talk about, Har . . . Hunter."

He flinched but she forced herself not to care.

"I really do care about you, Abby—"

"Care?" She whirled on him. "The only thing you care about is your story."

"Abby, wait, that's not true; I love you—"

"You cared so much you didn't even bother to call."

"I wanted to but I was detained."

"Another story, I'm sure. Who were you chasing this time?"

"It wasn't like that, dammit. . . . I got arrested. I spent the freakin' night in jail because I was in the HOV lane—"

"They don't put people in jail for driving in the HOV lane."

"I know." He rubbed a hand through his hair, spiking it. "But the policeman said I tried to bribe him—"

"Oh, please." Abby crossed her arms. "No more lies or stories, Hunter. Just take Lizzie and your dog and go. I may have been naive and trusting once, looking at life through rose-colored glasses, but no more."

Lizzie dragged the mutt in and Hunter started to say something else, but Abby cut him off with a lethal glare. He bit his tongue, refusing to argue in front of Lizzie and upset her again.

" 'Bye, sweetheart," Abby whispered. "You take care of Snarts, okay?"

" 'Kay, and I'll bring him back to play with Butterballs."

Abby smiled tightly, her gaze meeting Hunter's over Lizzie's shoulder. They both knew that was not going to happen. Then she hugged Lizzie and Angelica for what she knew would be the very last time.

Chapter Twenty-seven

Rekindling the Romantic Flame

"Is Dr. Abby mad at you?"

A mild understatement. Try hate. "What makes you think she's mad?" Hunter steered the car toward his apartment.

" 'Cause she didn't smile and hugs you like 'afore. And her face gots all red and her eyes pointy when she looked at you."

Very observant. "Well, honey, she's mad because I wrote some articles about her that weren't really . . . nice."

"You was mean to Dr. Abby?"

"I . . . I wrote them before I knew her." Her glare scorched him. "Which goes to show you that you shouldn't talk about people before you really get to know them."

"Can't you say you're sorry?"

"I already did." A truck pulled in front of him and Hunter resisted the urge to swear. "But she's still mad."

"Why?"

"Because I didn't tell her truth about who I was."

Lizzie hugged Snarts in her lap while Angelica sat

strapped in beside her. "But you said it was okay to lie when you was acting."

She wouldn't let up. "I know, but I was wrong." Finding out a parent made mistakes wouldn't traumatize Lizzie forever, would it? "Lying and keeping secrets from people you love usually hurts them." He placed his hand over hers and patted it. "So if something's bothering you, honey, you can always come to me. You don't have to keep secrets or lie to me if there's a problem."

She tipped her head sideways, her tiny nose scrunched. "So you won't lie no more?"

"No, I won't lie no more. I mean anymore."

"Does that mean I have to tell Snarts he's ugly?" She covered the dog's ears with her hands so he couldn't hear. " 'Cause he kinda is but I loves him anyway. And I don't wanna hurt his feelings."

Boy, that was a tough one. Hunter coasted onto the freeway, the afternoon sun nearly blinding him as he crept through the thick traffic. "No, you don't need to tell him he's ugly. And you're correct: it's not right to hurt someone's feelings."

She scrunched her nose again, looking more confused than ever. "Then I have to tell him he's pretty?"

"You could just tell him he's beautiful because you love him." The way Abby had gotten more beautiful the better he'd gotten to know her. "Or you could not mention his looks; just tell him you love him."

Lizzie took her hands away from Snarts's ears. "You hear that, buddy? I loves you."

The dog merely grunted.

"I loves you, too, Daddy. And I loves Mommy. And I loves Dr. Abby."

"So do I," Hunter admitted.

"You wants to kiss her again, huh?"

Hunter sighed wistfully. "That would be nice."

Lizzie kicked her feet against the seat. "Then you gots to get her back."

Hunter mentally groaned and cut across the lane to the exit for his apartment. "Got any ideas?"

Lizzie thumped her legs up and down, then leaned over to consult Angelica, whispering back and forth. "Well," she said finally, "Mama likes Daryl 'cause he gives her flowers. And he takes her places." She hesitated. "And he readed her rhymes."

"Rhymes?" Hunter frowned. "Oh, you mean poetry?" So Daryl was romantic.

Once Abby had said he was, but he had let her down. If he had the chance to start over, he would make sure he did things differently.

He'd be romantic, even if it killed him.

The next four days passed for Abby in a blur of misery. She waded through the hours at work, seeing patients, and was relieved that her clients had been understanding. In fact, they had been more supportive than she could ever have imagined. So at least she still had her job.

But by the time Friday came, exhaustion pulled at her. Thoughts of Hunter were also wearing on her nerves.

Every day she had received some kind of romantic gesture, as if he thought mushy cards and flowers and Godiva chocolates could soften her.

Good thing he hadn't sent Reese's cups.

She unwrapped a truffle anyway, reminding herself not to grow too accustomed to the expensive candy, since she couldn't afford it money-wise or calorie-wise, on a regular basis. The doorbell rang, and she peered outside warily, not surprised to find another gift on the stoop. Mixed emotions flooded her when she looked up and saw Hunter's Explorer coasting down the road away from the house. Wondering what he had sent this time, she opened the box and laughed.

A double pack of granny-panty underwear and five bags of Reese's cups. She opened the card. *I love you, Abby. Hope these fit.*

She struggled over the anger and bittersweet memories. Didn't Hunter realize a reconciliation could never work? The trust was gone; too many hurt feelings lay between them.

Flopping back on the sofa, she noticed her message light blinking like a neon sign; she punched the button and listened.

Uncle Wilbur still wanted money for his business.

Her mother had changed her mind about the coffeehouse and now wanted money for a make-your-own-stuffed-animal shop.

Her father needed money for clothes so he could job-hunt.

The last message was from Hunter.

She closed her eyes as his gruff voice reverberated over the line. "Abby, please, just meet me for a drink. I really want to make things up to you." A pause. "I know I hurt you, but I really do love you. Just give me a chance. Give *us* a chance."

Yeah, right, a chance to add more details to his article. The police had phoned to tell her they'd arrested Lenny, and he'd claimed he'd given the pictures to Hunter. Every day she'd searched the paper, expecting to see the article about her. And every time she'd gone to the grocery store, she'd expected to see herself naked in some compromising positions on the front of the tabloids or on some porn Internet site.

It was just a matter of time.

She shut off the machine, fighting another onslaught of tears. She couldn't speak to him yet, but she could talk to her family. Any therapist would conclude that she'd enabled her family to be dependent on her. She had constantly backed her mother's whims, hoping one day she'd find something she enjoyed; then she'd settle down and be a real mother to all three girls, the kind of mother the girls had needed growing up. But that was never going to happen. Abby had to accept her mother the way she was and love her anyway.

But the time had come for all her needy relatives to fly the coop; her role as caretaker was finished.

Her uncle sputtered with disbelief when she broke the news.

"I'm sorry, Uncle Wilbur, but I have to take care of myself for a while." She hung up and phoned her mother before he could reply.

"But honey, this shop will draw tourists like crazy," her mother argued.

And she'd be crazy to keep supporting her mother's ventures. "I'm sorry, Mom, but you and Dad are grown now. It's time you took care of yourselves. The Bank of Abby is closed."

Her father had left the number for a boardinghouse, so she simply left a message.

No sooner had she hung up than the doorbell rang. Surely the three of them couldn't have driven over so quickly.

Praying it wasn't Hunter, she checked the peephole and spotted her sisters and Granny Pearl on her doorstep. Did they need something now?

She felt as drained as a dish rag.

Still, she invited them in. "Listen, you guys, if you need something—"

"Mercy no," Granny Pearl said. "Honey-child, I know you're always taking care of everyone else, but this time we're here to take care of you. I feel like this is partly my fault anyway."

"Your fault?"

Gran clacked her teeth. "Why, yes, I always wondered if that Gulliver guy didn't butter his bread on the other side, but I just hated to say anything. You can't be sure these days."

Oh, now she felt better. Her eighty-year-old grandmother had suspected Lenny was gay, and she hadn't had a clue.

"Here. This is from all of us." Chelsea handed her an envelope, and Abby eyed the strips of hairless flesh on Chelsea's arm.

"I'm auditioning for a commercial advertising this home-made wax kit," Chelsea explained. "They really do work, but *ouch*."

Abby winced and vetoed the idea of buying one for herself.

"We thought you might like a little R-and-R by yourself," Granny Pearl said as Abby opened the envelope. "We all chipped in."

Abby glanced at Chelsea. "You didn't earn the money stripping again, did you?"

"Stripping?" Granny Pearl asked.

"It's a long story, Gran. I'll tell you later." Chelsea blushed. "And no, I returned some shoes. Who needs genuine imported snakeskin boots anyway?"

Everyone laughed and Abby stared at the envelope. It would be nice to get away from her problems. The phone. The bed she had slept in with Hunter.

"Have you talked to him yet?" Victoria asked, as if she'd read Abby's mind.

"No, and I don't want to. He'd probably make up another excuse the way he did about that HOV lane."

Victoria winced. "He didn't exactly make that up."

"What do you mean?"

Victoria shrugged. "I sort of asked my friend for a favor—"

"Suarez?"

Victoria nodded sheepishly.

"You didn't!" Chelsea exclaimed.

"I wish I could have seen him in jail," Abby said.

Granny Pearl hooked her arm through Abby's. "Come on; we'll help you pack." She handed Abby a bag. "Here's a little something I picked up at that gift shop with Lulu.

You might need it if there aren't any hunky eligible men where you're going." She leaned in for a conspiratorial whisper. "And by the way, hon, the batteries are already included. I bought two sets, just in case. . . ."

"Hunter, where in the hell is that piece on the Jensen woman?"

Hunter held the phone away from his ear at his boss's loud bellow. "It'll be there for the Sunday edition."

"Good. It's taken you long enough."

"That's because I want it to be right." The very reason he hadn't written it. He knew his boss expected him to write in the same vein as his original pieces, but he couldn't bring himself to slander Abby.

He flexed his fingers, his mind searching for the perfect angle. His conversation with Lizzie echoed in his head. The fuzzy outline of an article began to emerge, the headline clear: *You Can't Judge a Book by Its Cover: Who Is the Real Dr. Abby Jensen?*

Two hours later, he printed the piece and skimmed it, smiling to himself as he stood and stretched. He had to show it to Abby before he turned it in.

Lizzie strolled in barefoot, a bow taped to Snarts's head. "Now he really is pretty, Daddy."

Hunter laughed. "Come on, kiddo; let's take a ride."

"Can Snarts come?"

Hunter glanced at the sorry excuse for a dog with the makeshift bow. "Sure." He could use all the help he could get. Maybe Snarts could play on Abby's tender side.

He grabbed the envelope with the photos of Abby inside, along with his keys, and they headed to the door. Maybe after Abby read the article, he could drop Lizzie at her spend-the-night party; then he could convince Abby to have dinner with him.

His body hummed with desire. And maybe later they would wind up back in each other's arms, where they belonged.

*   *   *

Twenty minutes later, Abby's sister Chelsea opened the door, took one look at him, and yelled for her sister Victoria.

Victoria met him with an icy gaze identical to Chelsea's. "What do you want?"

Lizzie peeked from behind his leg. "We comes to see Dr. Abby."

Chelsea and Victoria's expressions both softened at the sight of Lizzie and the sorry excuse for a dog. "Hey, honey. Abby's not here right now."

"What?"

Chelsea seemed to take pleasure in his misery. "She left for the airport a few minutes ago, Mr. Stone. I'm afraid you just missed her."

Abby couldn't believe she was doing something so spontaneous as taking off without planning ahead. But apparently her sisters had thought of everything. They'd booked her a ticket to a resort in the Smoky Mountains, a secluded place where she could finally be alone. She could certainly afford to take a few days off of work. Rainey had been pushing her to start the sequel to *Under the Covers*, but Abby wasn't sure there would be a second book. She didn't know if she wanted to endure more public scrutiny. More important, could she stand behind the values and therapeutic techniques she usually advocated?

The taxi swerved to a stop in front of the airline check-in and she hopped out, tipping the cabby generously before rushing inside the airport.

Three whole days of nothing but relaxation, resort activities, and fun. No phone. No reporters. No work. No family calling with their problems.

And best of all, no Hunter Stone.

Hunter's chest constricted. "Where did she go?"

"On vacation," Victoria said, refusing to give any more information.

An elderly woman with sparkling green eyes and permanent laugh lines hobbled toward them. Her face lit up when she saw Lizzie and the dog.

"Hello there, honey. What a nice dog."

"His name is Snarts."

"What an unusual name."

"It's 'cause he snores and he farts."

The woman popped her hand over her mouth and giggled. "How clever."

"He wants to play with Butterballs."

The dog suddenly shot in, surprising them all, and Lizzie chased him. Butterball yelped and the trio raced around the house, circling through the den and kitchen and back again. Hunter moved inside and shut the door, then tried to catch Snarts. He had never seen the dog run before, but apparently he liked the game, because he slipped past Hunter and galloped down the hall. Lizzie followed, yelling at both of them to come back.

"Can you tell me where Abby is? I have to see her." Hunter hated the helplessness in his voice.

"Gran, this is Hunter Stone."

Both sisters folded their arms and simply stared at him. The grandmother tapped a clunky shoe impatiently.

"I know you're all mad, but I want to make everything up to Abby." He extended the article as a peace offering. "Read this. I think you'll see how much I care."

The girls traded questioning looks, then turned to the elderly woman. "I don't know if we should trust him," Victoria said.

Lizzie ran back in, squaring her chin. "My daddy's not a bad man."

Chelsea knelt at eye level with Lizzie. "Honey, we didn't say he was." Although her glare toward Hunter spoke volumes.

"He just lied 'cause he wanted me, and Mama was pitching a fit for custody."

"Lizzie, you don't need to defend me," Hunter said, his neck burning with embarrassment.

Lizzie silenced him with a look. "But Angelica says we do. She says you're the best daddy in the world and Dr. Abby should forgives you."

Victoria tucked a strand of Lizzie's ponytail back into the pink rubber band. "What do you mean, honey?"

Lizzie planted small fists on her hips, bunching up her floppy T-shirt. "See, Daddy thoughts getting a good story would help him not work so much and have more time with me on account of my mama wanted to send me away to a school with boards."

"It's a long story," Hunter added when both of Abby's sisters traded skeptical looks.

"But Dr. Abby fixed everything so I don't have to go away," Lizzie finished.

"Yes, well, Dr. Abby is a good fixer, isn't she?" Gran said.

Victoria patted Lizzie's back. "Yeah, it's time someone fixed things for her."

"I'm trying to do that," Hunter said.

"Yeah, 'cause Daddy knows he was wrong, wrong, wrong—"

Hunter felt his face heat. "That's enough, Lizzie."

Abby's grandmother scrutinized Hunter over her bifocals, then motioned to Chelsea and Victoria to gather close. "Let's talk, girls." She swung a gnarled finger at Hunter. "But you have to wait outside." With a *tsk*ing sound, she pushed him into the backyard, all the way against Butterball's small doghouse, then slammed the door.

Hunter stared down at the doghouse and winced; they'd obviously put him in his place. Even Snarts had gotten to stay inside. The sweltering temperature was suffocating, and his mouth went dry. The damned insufferable women hadn't even given him water. They would have been kinder to the animals.

Perspiration rolled down his face, the blazing sun like a ball of fire. If the Jensen women didn't hurry up, he was going to pass out from heat exhaustion. He eyed the dog-house with envy. If the damn thing was a little bit bigger, he'd crawl inside. He wiped at the sweat on his forehead and rolled up his sleeves, shuffling his feet impatiently. Suddenly the door banged open, and Snarts and Butterball raced out. Granny Pearl motioned for him to come in.

"Are you sincere with all this?" Granny Pearl asked, waving the article like a white flag.

"Yes."

"No more tricks or lies?" Victoria asked.

"No. Never."

"You're not acting now?" Chelsea hitched out a hip. " 'Cause you were pretty good, at least for a beginner. And I do feel responsible, since I hired you."

"I'm not acting. I am in love with Abby and I want to make everything right."

"So," Granny Pearl said, her mouth pursed, "what are your intentions?"

Hunter smiled slowly. "I'd like to marry her, if she'll have me."

Granny Pearl and the sisters shared skeptical looks back and forth for another minute before Gran finally nodded and handed him a printed itinerary. "All right, son, she's on this flight. But you'll have to hurry."

He started toward the door and remembered Lizzie. There was no way he'd make it in time if he waited to take her to the party. "My little girl—I have to take her to a party."

"We can drop her," Chelsea offered.

Lizzie ran in and Hunter explained. "Would that be okay with you, Lizzie?"

"You're going to get Dr. Abby?"

"Yes."

"Can Snarts play with Butterballs till you get back?"

"Yes." Although the mongrel had already collapsed under a shady tree as if his work were done.

Granny Pearl pointed to the tea sets on the shelf. "We'll

have a tea party with her until it's time to take her to her friend's house."

"Goody!" Lizzie squealed, clapping Angelica's hands together with her own.

Hunter nodded and hugged Lizzie. "Your mom is picking you up from the party in the morning."

"Okay. Go get Dr. Abby, Daddy," Lizzie whispered. "Me and Angelica likes her."

Hunter ran to the car and sped away, turning onto I-85, but then cursed at the heavy traffic. He'd never make it.

His palms sweating, he glanced at the HOV lane and salivated. . . .

Chapter Twenty-eight

The Ass Man

The wind whistled behind Abby as she rushed into the Atlanta airport, the overcast sky and rumbling dark clouds signifying that a storm was brewing behind her. She hesitated as she walked in, the back of her neck prickling.

Had someone called her name?

No, it must be the wind. She'd already said good-bye to her family, and Hunter . . . well, he wouldn't be coming. Sure, he'd sent flowers and gifts and made other romantic gestures, and he'd phoned a dozen or more times, but he was probably looking for more food for his story. By now he should have gotten the message that she didn't want to talk to him again.

Ever.

It wasn't as though he would come chasing her to the airport or to Tennessee. Not that she wanted him to . . .

Refusing to wallow in her self-pity, she went through security, then took the tram to the C terminal. The plane was already boarding when she arrived, so she wheeled her bag on and found her seat, settling next to a wiry man with legs so long they pushed against the seat in front of him. She climbed over him to reach her window seat, prayed she didn't have to go to the bathroom during the flight, then pulled out her bag of Reese's cups and indulged herself. Her butt was probably spreading, but who cared?

A heavyset woman plunked down in front of her, and threw her seat back so she was practically lying in Abby's lap. The flight attendant roamed the aisles, checking for seat belts, and motioned for the woman to raise her seat.

"I can't," the woman said, struggling with the lever.

The attendant tried to help. "Oh, dear, it's broken."

Abby grimaced and searched the plane for any vacancies, but the cabin was filled to capacity. Minutes later, the plane sailed through the sky. Abby stared out the window, kissing Atlanta good-bye for a few days so she could get her head on straight.

And forget about Hunter Stone.

Thunderclouds covered the sun and cast a grayness over the sky, the gloomy weather mirroring Hunter's mood. He vetoed the idea of the HOV lane, his aggravation mushrooming when the temperature gauge in his Explorer's engine suddenly shot up. If he kept driving, he'd blow up his engine. But he didn't have time to stop.

He had to catch Abby.

Cursing his bad luck, he flipped off the air-conditioning and turned on the heater, hoping to draw the heat from the engine. Keeping one eye on the temperature gauge, the other on the car in front of him, he maneuvered through traffic. The idea seemed to work temporarily and the gauge dropped, but it was a million degrees in the car and he was sweating like a pig, so he rolled down the windows.

"Just don't let it rain," he muttered.

Two miles down the highway, though, the sky opened up and spilled water like a dam had burst. Rain slashed the window and pelted his elbow and arm, so he had to roll his window up slightly. Sweat drenched his clothes as the heat blasted him. Even the roses on the seat beside him began to wilt. He briefly wondered if it had been worth the time to stop and pick them up. Yes, he decided, flowers definitely couldn't hurt in his quest to win Abby back.

Thunder rumbled and crackled, lightning zigzagging across the nearly black sky. He switched on his radio. "Severe thunderstorm warnings are in effect until seven P.M. tonight. Stay tuned for more details as the weather bureau delivers them."

Great. Just great.

On the other hand, maybe it was good. Maybe Abby's flight would be delayed and he would catch her before she boarded.

The traffic slowed to a crawl, the sound of metal crunching and tires squealing echoing over the storm. He grimaced and tried to change lanes, but just as he did, his car died. The Previa behind him braked and barely missed him, then the driver laid on his horn.

Hunter wiped sweat from his brow and tried to start the engine again, but the motor screeched, sputtered, then gave way to silence. He stomped on the gas pedal and cranked the key in the ignition again and again, but he knew it was useless. Meanwhile, a symphony of horns blasted the air. Hunter cursed, snagged his cell phone, called for a tow truck, then grabbed the wilting roses and slogged the last mile to the airport.

Rain assaulted him as he dodged cars and forged ahead. A MARTA bus screeched to a stop inches from his knees as he ran across the airport entrance. Another mile past the economy and hourly parking, another half mile to Delta ticketing. Lightning flashed, almost catching a lamppost, and Hunter quickened his pace, panting and squinting through the downpour. Finally he jogged inside, where a long line of soccer players stood ready to check in. He ran toward security and the terminals, wove through a Japanese group searching for the international terminal, and checked the overhead screen.

He was too late.

Abby's plane had already gone.

Abby woke up as the plane screeched to a halt. Her legs were cramped from being pinned between the broken seat and the man next to her, her neck ached from her sleeping position, and her heart ached from missing Hunter.

She had just had the most erotic—and incredibly romantic—dream. Hunter had been chasing her across the country, but they kept missing each other. When he'd finally caught her, he'd made love with her until dawn, then whispered that he didn't care if her boobs were too small, that he was an ass man himself.

Disgusted with her foolish fantasies, she shook her sleep-numbed legs and tried to stand as the passengers began to deplane. She had to erase Hunter from her mind like a bad computer virus. He didn't love her. He had used her and lied to her . . . nothing he'd said to her had been real.

Confusing thoughts held a debate in her head.

She remembered his tortured voice when he'd thought Lizzie was missing, and his stricken face when he'd thought he might lose her to his wife. Maybe he had spoken the truth about his feelings for his daughter.

But for her?

No . . .

He sent gifts and cards and apologies all week, a little voice inside her head whispered.

Still, it isn't enough, the other voice argued.

"Ma'am, aren't you getting off?"

Abby jerked her head up at the sound of the flight attendant's question, and realized she'd been holding up the line. She instantly hurried forward and retrieved her carry-on bag.

Maybe she would try out some of the activities at the resort. Something challenging and unusual that she'd never ventured to do before. Something exciting that would get her adrenaline pumping . . . something that didn't involve a man.

After sleeping in the airport, Hunter finally caught an early morning flight. The next few hours were almost as harrowing as the trip to the airport had been. And during his stay overnight he could have sworn that when he'd woken up, a punk kid with orange hair had been standing over him. The plane landed in Chattanooga with a jolt. He shuffled as quickly as possible down the aisle, wove through the crowded terminal, hailed a taxi, then jumped in, still carrying the wilted roses.

Two hours later, after a harrying ride, he stood at the hotel desk, pleading with the manager to tell him where to find Abby. "I'm sorry, sir, but we can't give out room numbers."

"At least phone her room for me."

"Certainly." He realized he looked a tad weather-beaten, but the man frowned at him as if he were some psycho stalker after Abby.

Hunter tapped his hand on the counter as he waited, but the phone rang and rang.

He balled his hand into a fist. Maybe she had simply taken a walk. He'd get a room, sit down in the lobby, and wait for her. He glanced at his clothes and frowned. Or maybe he'd get a shower first. Surely this resort had a clothing store, or at least a gift shop where he could pick up an extra outfit. At least some clean underwear.

"Let me have a room, please."

The clerk shook his head. "Sorry, sir, but we're all booked."

Hunter leaned over the counter, his jaw tight. "I think you can probably find one room here somewhere."

The man's reedy voice grated out, "Sorry, but we have the Shriners' convention here. There is no space."

Okay, dammit, he'd sleep on the floor, then get a return

flight to Atlanta. But he had to apologize first. "How about a store?"

The manager pointed a finger down a long hallway. Hunter found the gift shop, frowning at the clothes emblazoned with deer antlers and coyotes. He finally chose a modest T-shirt imprinted with the words *The Great Smoky Mountains* then added a stash of underwear and a pair of running shorts to the pile along with some toiletries.

"Eighty-five dollars and four cents," a perky teenage brunette said.

He reached into his pocket and pulled out his wallet. His heart roared in his ears.

His credit cards and cash were missing.

A flashback of the morning scene hit him: the young punk standing over him at the airport when he'd awakened had robbed him! Furious, he reached in his pocket for his cell phone and realized it was missing, too.

"Sir, eighty-five dollars—"

"I know." Hunter shook his head. "Could I pay you later?"

"Do you have a room number to bill it to?"

"No."

"Sorry, mister." The girl snatched the items and pointed to the door.

Abby boarded the Cessna with the other four guests who'd decided to take the plunge through the open skies, adrenaline racing through her. She'd taken a skydiving lesson this morning and had decided a real adventure like this was the only way to take her mind off Hunter.

The clear blue sky stretched in front of them, the mountains rising and filling the distance with vast greenery. She checked her backpack and supplies. The adventurers would be dropped at a clearing near a legendary waterfall, camp overnight, then hike their way back down the mountain. She hoped the physical activity would start the process of purging Hunter from her system.

* * *

An attractive blonde in a shocking pink dress, a woman whom he once would have pegged as his type, but who now didn't even stir his libido, had been staring at Hunter with a combination of distrust and pity while he'd whiled away the morning moping in the lobby, trying to convince someone to tell him where Abby might have gone.

Finally, her pity won over her distrust.

"Listen, Mr. . . ." She hesitated, a look of recognition crossing her face. "Are you Hunter Stone?"

"That's correct."

"You're the reporter who wrote all those articles about Dr. Jensen. That one today was so sweet."

Hunter hadn't known his boss had run it. For the first time in years, he'd actually gone through a morning without reading the paper or checking to see his byline.

Some things were just more important. Like finding the woman he loved and convincing her he wasn't the total snake she thought him to be.

Her green eyes shimmered with approval. "It sounds like you have a thing for the doctor yourself."

Aha. Why hadn't he thought of using the honest approach?

Because he'd grown accustomed to telling lies.

"I do," he admitted. "And I came all the way up here to tell her that I love her." He indicated the pitiful roses and her smile faded slightly. "It's a long story," he said, giving her the short version of a night from hell.

She tapped long pink nails on the sleek cherry-wood finish. "I'm not supposed to do this, but in this case . . ." She paused and gestured toward the flowers. "I'll make an exception. Dr. Jensen booked a flight—"

"She's left already?"

"No," the young woman said. "She's taken our special skydiving excursion."

Hunter's stomach plummeted down to his feet. "Skydiving?"

"Yes, sir, it's a wonderfully exhilarating experience."

"I know. I did it in the service." And it had scared the crap out of him. "When . . . when will she be back?"

"Oh, not until tomorrow."

Hunter groaned.

"We have another plane leaving in a few minutes. If you're interested you could meet up with her on the ground."

Hunter's legs trembled like broken guitar strings. He loved Abby desperately. He missed everything about her; the sweet way she'd taken care of his daughter, her intelligence, the way she defended marriage, the way she loved that little mop of a dog, her long, curly hair, that porcelain skin, her husky voice, the way she tucked her bottom into the curve of his body when she slept. . . .

Yes, he had to admit it, he missed her butt. He was no longer a boob man, but an ass man, as long as that ass belonged to Abby. And right now he wanted to hold it in his hands so badly he was shaking.

Or maybe he was shaking at the thought of diving out of a plane again.

He'd come too damn far to wait another day to see her. Besides, the way his luck was running, he'd wind up missing her again.

But could he really face his fear of heights and jump out of a plane for her?

Chapter Twenty-nine

Fulfilling the Fantasy

Abby recited the details of operating the parachute in her mind as the time for the group to make their jump approached. Sunshine glittered off the mountain peaks, casting the trees in a golden glow. Puffy white clouds floated along like cotton candy, the hum of the plane mingling with the wind.

The two men dove first, the next skydiver a middle-aged woman who squealed and squawked as she stepped up to the doorway's edge. With a hoot of excitement, she yelled, "Geronimo," and jumped. Abby's heart raced as she watched the others freefall, then pull the ripcord to open their parachutes.

"Are you ready, Dr. Jensen?"

A moment of apprehension attacked her, but her reasons for the jump flooded her, so she nodded, took a deep breath, and made the dive.

The air swept her into its current, and she thought she heard the guide shout, "Bombs away," as he jumped after her. Then Abby lifted her arms and floated down, reveling in the wind beating her face and the freedom of flying. And as she soared toward the lush green grass, she remembered the fantasy she had told Hunter about—the one about making love on the side of a mountain.

That fantasy would probably never come true—because her heart belonged to Hunter.

And he was out of her life forever.

After two horrible relationships, how could she even think of another?

Hunter glanced out the plane, the wind rushing through the opening, pulling and sucking at him as if it would jerk him out any second.

His stomach was tied in as many knots as a rope he'd once used for practicing his Boy Scout loops. He'd never unraveled those knots; would his stomach come untangled once his feet hit the ground?

Provided he made it that far and didn't have a heart attack in midair.

The plane soared close to the mountain, the engine sputtered, and the plane jerked. Cool air surged inside the cabin, the whistle of the wind screaming, and he wrapped his fingers around the metal handhold in a death grip. The instructor eyed him skeptically as he reminded Hunter of the basics.

"We can go out together if you want, sir."

Hunter stared at the scrawny twenty-year-old and grimaced. So the young man was a daredevil. Hunter couldn't help it that he had an irrational fear of heights. "No, I'm fine. I've done this before." *And lived*, he reminded himself. He couldn't very well act like a wienie in front of this kid. But nausea rose to his throat, almost choking him.

He'd charged this excursion to the paper, he reminded himself. And he'd promised his boss a story out of it, his first for the sports section, another reason he had to go through with the jump.

He hugged the window and looked out, his legs trembling as the scenery whizzed by in a blur. Taking a calming breath, he willed his head to stop spinning and his heart rate to return to normal. But his pulse was hammering away, the blood roaring in his ears, battling against the loud sound of the plane's engine.

"We're almost there," the guide said, pointing to a clearing. "The other group just landed."

Hunter nodded, his gaze glued to the daunting distance between himself and the ground. It was a long way down.

"Okay, are you ready?"

Hell, no.

"You're kind of green, mister. You don't have to do this if you're too nervous."

He glared at the young boy and thought of Abby. He couldn't back out now.

Praying he didn't freeze and forget how to operate the parachute, then end up splattered in pieces all over the mountainside, he stepped to the edge, closed his eyes, and jumped. He would prove to Abby he loved her.

Either that or he'd die trying.

"Oh, my heavens," Winnie, the middle-aged woman with Abby's group, cried. "We've got company."

"That guy needs to pull his cord." The guide shaded his eyes with his hand as he stared at the sky.

Abby studied the man's features. Something about him seemed familiar, but he was falling so fast she couldn't see his face.

"Pull the cord!" the guide yelled.

"Do it now," Winnie shouted.

"He's going to crash," somebody else exclaimed.

They all screamed at once for him to pull, but the wind grabbed their voices and tossed them away. The man threw out his arms and rocked from side to side, throwing his body off balance, and the wind swept him toward the forest.

"Pull!" everyone shouted again.

Abby held her breath. Finally he stiffened and released his parachute. It jerked him up slightly; then he floated downward, but his delay in pulling the cord had caused him to veer so far off course, he was sailing straight toward a grove of trees.

Abby's group ran toward the woods, all yelling for him to hang on.

A man's yell echoed in the wind. The parachute caught on a tree and he dangled like a rag doll, arms and legs flapping wildly while the excess material floated down on top of him. He jerked and pulled and pushed, trying to clear his head from the leaves and the billowing parachute. Several seconds later, his head bobbed out.

Abby's mouth gaped open in shock. "Hunter?"

He jerked his legs and arms, trying to untangle himself. "Abby, I had to see you."

"Hang on," the guide shouted. "We'll get help."

Hunter kicked and swung his body toward a lower branch, but missed and dangled back, legs flailing wildly. He tried it again, the sound of the tree limb breaking rending the air.

"Don't move," the guide shouted. He motioned to the group, and they ran for assistance.

"Hunter, what are you doing here?" Abby shouted. She'd fantasized about having the man on his knees, but hanging from a tree? "I thought you were afraid of heights."

"I am!" The parachute slipped, the branch vibrated and cracked, and Hunter's body swayed with it. "But I love you, and I'm more afraid of losing you than I am of heights."

Abby's heart constricted.

"I tried to catch you in Atlanta. I went to your house, but your sisters and grandmother said you'd gone." The branch lowered another notch. "And I tried to make it to the airport but my car broke down and it was storming—"

"Hunter, stop moving!" Abby shouted. The tree branch groaned again.

"Then the flights were canceled because of the weather, and I had to stay the night at the airport on a bench and my wallet got stolen—"

"Oh, my gosh," Abby whispered.

The tree popped again.

"And when I arrived, there weren't any vacant rooms, and you'd already left to come here."

He had jumped out of a plane for her.

The branch cracked in another place, wood splintered and rained downward, and he slipped a few more feet. Winnie screamed. Abby pressed her hand over her mouth to keep from doing the same. Hunter stared up at the yards of parachute and the tree, then at the ground, the color draining from his face.

"I mean it, Abby. I love you, and don't you dare stop looking at the world through rose-colored glasses. The world needs more people like you, and if I live"—his voice shook in the wind; she could hear his fear—"I'll spend the rest of my life making up for all the stupid lies and those dumb articles about you."

Abby yelped. "Hunter—"

The limb cracked completely in two and gave way. Hunter yelled as he careened toward the ground.

As Hunter flew through the air, his life flashed in front of him. The headlines would read: *Idiot Man Afraid of Heights Dies by Falling out of Tree while Proposing*. He could see the photo of his body flat on the dirt, the roving grizzlies nibbling at him like bear meat. Or if he did survive the fall, his lungs and throat would start bleeding from altitude sickness. Or worse, he might smash his skull and end up brain-dead or paralyzed.

He just wished he could hear Abby say she loved him one time before he died.

Determined to fight for his life, he gripped the parachute

ropes and tried to bend his knees, remembering the tips the guide had offered so he wouldn't break a leg in the landing. But the tips were meant for a parachute soaring in, not for a man attached to half a tree traveling straight down at full speed. Wind stung his face and nausea rolled through him, but he had to tell Abby one more time that he loved her before he died.

"I love you. Marry me!" The wind caught his words, the echo bouncing off the mountain and repeating itself. *Love you, marry me . . . love you, marry me . . . love you, marry me . . .*

Then his body collided with the ground, his head hit a rock, and blackness swirled in front of his eyes. One moment of heaven flashed in front of him in the form of Abby's face before his vision faded. Abby lifted his head in her lap and brushed his hair back so tenderly, tears pricked his eyes.

Or maybe it was blood trickling over his face.

"Did you mean it, Hunter?"

"Yes, marry me, Abby. . . ."

Abby pressed her lips to his and whispered yes just before he passed into darkness.

Later that night, Abby and Hunter lay curled together on a blanket under the stars, the moon gleaming like candlelight across the valley below. He had sprinkled the wilted, crushed flower petals all around her in the shape of a heart.

"I was trying to be romantic, Abby. I wanted to make love to you on a bed of rose petals."

"You are romantic, Hunter. You jumped out of a plane for me." Abby stroked the bandage on Hunter's head. "Are you sure you're all right? We can still get them to airlift you out of here."

Hunter shot her a crazed look. "No, no, I'm fine. But I think I'm finished with flying for a while."

Abby chuckled, her laughter dying when Hunter reached

up and pulled at her shirt, slowly unbuttoning the top button. "I'm sorry I lied to you, Abby."

Abby bit down on her lip, emotions clogging her throat. "I told a few of my own."

"But I understand your reasons now." He quirked his head sideways. "I have something for you."

She arched a delicate brow, her breath hitching when he handed her the article.

"Hunter, it doesn't matter—"

"Yes, it does." He pressed his finger to her lips. "Read it."

She nodded, unfolded the paper, and read the beginning of the article.

You can't judge a book by its cover. I learned that lesson when I went undercover to get the dirt on Dr. Jensen. Instead of a scandalous author with loose morals, interested only in self-promotion, I found a woman with strong values and a lot of love in her heart—a woman who possesses all the best characteristics of a traditional American wife and mother, while maintaining her identity as a modern sexual woman. In short, Abby Jensen has it all.

Abby blinked back tears. "It's beautiful."

"That's how I feel about you, Abby." He handed her an envelope—the pictures Lenny had taken.

"I didn't look at them," he said, reading the question in her eyes.

Her other eyebrow rose.

"Well, maybe a glance." He chuckled. "But we're burning them, baby, 'cause the only pictures of you naked that I want around will be ones I take."

A smile tugged at Abby's mouth. "Oh, so are you into kinky sex?"

He shrugged. "I'm into pleasing you."

"I like the sound of that." Abby laughed. "Maybe that should be the title of my sequel."

"Only if I get to help you research it."

Abby slid her leg between his, rubbing the hard muscles of his calf with her foot. "Or I could write one on unusual proposals. I think you parachuting from a plane and proposing while dangling from a tree would make a catchy opening."

Hunter traced his finger over the sensitive skin behind her ear. "That sounds like blackmail."

"Well, maybe if you promise to get naked, I'll keep it out of print."

Hunter laughed. "The price a man has to pay."

She kissed his forehead. "We might be able to work out a trade-off if you really don't like the terms."

"I love you, Abby. Don't you know by now I'd do anything for you?"

"Anything?"

"Anything."

She quirked her head sideways. "Okay, there is this one fantasy I have. . . ."

He opened the rest of the buttons on her blouse, then cupped her breasts in his hands. "I promise to make all your fantasies come true, Doc."

Abby pulled at his shirt; then she slid her finger down his chest, cupped his already hard sex, then unzipped his jeans. "Are you sure you're up to this with your injuries?"

Hunter licked the tip of her nipple, moved his hand to the back of her neck, then pulled her forward. "Oh, yeah. But we might have to stay under the covers a lot when we get back, so I can recuperate and get this pillow-talk thing right."

"I think we can manage that," Abby whispered.

With a growl of delight, he rolled her over, stripped her clothes, and slid his hands to her rear. "You know I'm an ass man, right?"

Abby giggled. Now she *knew* he loved her, that he was her soul mate for life.

Then she whispered her fantasy and he fulfilled it. He

made love to her in the tall grass, with wildflowers dotting the mountainside, the moon spilling its golden light across her supple body, and nothing but the wind to hear her cry his name in ecstasy.

And this time when she cried out, the echo of her saying his real name instead of Harry boomeranged across the mountain.

Marry Me, Maddie
Rita Herron

Maddie Summers is tired of waiting. To force her fiancé into making a decision, she takes him on a talk show and gives him a choice: Marry me, or move on. The line he gives makes her realize it is time to star in her own life. But stealing the show will require a script change worthy of a Tony. Her supporting cast is composed of two loving but overprotective brothers, her blue-blood ex-boyfriend, and her brothers' best friend: sexy bad-boy Chase Holloway—the only one who seems to recognize that a certain knock-kneed kid sister has grown up to be a knockout lady. And Chase doesn't seem to know how to bow out, even when the competition for her hand heats up. Instead, he promises to perform a song and dance, even ad-lib if necessary to demonstrate he is her true leading man.

___52433-3 $5.50 US/$6.50 CAN

Dorchester Publishing Co., Inc.
P.O. Box 6640
Wayne, PA 19087-8640

Baby, Oh Baby!

ROBIN WELLS

The hunk who appears on Annie's doorstep is a looker. The tall attorney's aura is clouded, and she can see that he's been suffering for some time. But all that is going to change, because a new—no, two new people are going to come into his life.

Jake Chastaine knows how things are supposed to be, and that doesn't include fertility clinic mixups or having fathered a child with a woman he'd never met. And looking at the vivid redhead who's the mother, Jake realizes he's missed out on something spectacular. Everyone knows how things are supposed to be—first comes love, then comes marriage, then the baby in the baby carriage. Maybe this time, things are going to happen a little differently.

The Misconception

Darlene Gardner

Evolutionary scientist Marietta Dalrymple views romantic love—like the myth of the monogamous male—as a fairy tale. Men are only good for procreation. And she has found the ideal candidate to satisfy her strongest biological urge—motherhood. On paper Jax Jackson has all the necessary advantages, including a high IQ and a successful career. In person his body drives her to reconsider the term animal magnetism. But in the aftermath of their passion, Jax claims there has been a mix-up; he is not the sperm supplier with whom she contracted, but an aspiring family man. The erudite professor is stupefied. Until she recognizes that she has found the wrong donor, but the right man for her heart.

ROBIN WELLS
OOH, LA LA!

Kate Matthews is the pre-eminent expert on New Orleans's red-light district. It makes sense that she'd be the historical consultant for the new picture being shot on location there. So why is its director being so difficult? His last flick flopped, and he is counting on this one to resurrect his career. Maybe it is because he is so handsome. He's probably used to getting women to do as he wishes. And now he wants her to loosen up. But Kate knows that accuracy is crucial to the story Zack Jackson is filming—and finding love in the Big Easy is anything but. No, there will be no lights, no cameras and certainly no action until he proves her wrong. Then it'll be a blockbuster of a show.